CONSTABLE
OUTREACH 35

A Fiction Thriller Based in 1985 **JAY CADMUS**

CONSTABLE OUTREACH 35

A

CENTRAL-AMERICAN THRILLER

BASED IN 1985

*

JAY CADMUS

Thebes Publishing

Printed in the United States of America

First Printing, 2018

Print ISBN: 978-1-54392-454-1

eBook ISBN: 978-1-54392-455-8

Thebes Publishing, dba

Houston, TX 77058

www.Thinkwerk.com

thebes@thinkwerk.com

outreach35@thinkwerk.com

jaycadmus@thinkwerk.com

Limited Printing

First Edition

Tegucigalpa, Honduras

Toncontin International Airport (TGU)

Latitude: 14.0342 North

Longitude: 87.1301 West

Central Standard Time (GMT -6)

US Agency Outstation – Constable Outreach

Monday – 23 September 1985

The planes came from US military bone yards. The Arizona and California deserts housed older airplanes in rows. When a need surfaced, government agencies had a selection to choose from. Here at Toncontin Airport some modified planes met mission specific operations. Ongoing ops dictated every action taken. Older military equipment is modified to meet the needs of today. The gathering of equipment in certain areas was always a point of interest – and, discussion.

The hangar was large. Its doors closed. They only opened to hide the arriving or departing planes. A temporary home to a Fairchild C-123K Provider. A Sikorsky H-34 and Bell UH-1Y Venom. And, on loan - a Super King Air 200B, battlefield reconnaissance plane. Others would come and go. From time to time, a modified Skyraider would arrive for a day or two. The need dictated what equipment would find its way into this area of operation.

Constable Outreach operated from the second floor. The exposed cat walk led to three offices. Operations was first at top of the stairs. Communications tied to ops by an inner door. Equipment blocked the outer door entry. The next door opened to the station supervisor. Maintenance office hidden in the tool crib on the hangar floor.

Lester Russell climbed the stairs to operations. He had been on station thirty days. Years earlier, he boxed in welterweight class. His physical frame proportional to height. He passed Tony Mercado. They stopped midway to chat.

"Morning, man."

"Hey, brother."

"How's the mod coming on the extraction system?"

"Good. Should be done today."

"I see the commercial cookie sheets arrived."

Tony said, "I think they want to drop on Friday," and continued down the stairs.

"Doesn't give us much time. Better get my ass in gear."

Lester watched Tony disappear as he mulled over what he needed to do. He scanned the hangar floor, to find a spot between the airplanes. A spot near the outside wall would be perfect. The pallet build-up for airdrop required an undisturbed space.

Lester continued to Ops….

…When a teenager, Lester Russell boxed Golden Gloves with the Police Athletic Club. He attended qualifying matches. Hopeful, he ranked for the big prize. Welterweight Golden Gloves Champion.

In 1964, he was finishing his senior year in high school. The same year his father deserted his family. After a tournament, he returned home having suffered a punishing loss. On the walk home, he met a neighborhood bully. An older teen. Egging Lester into a confrontation. A street fight started. The older kid sustained severe injuries from the beating Lester doled out.

Lester had directed the pain of his tournament loss and many years of parental abuse at the older boy. All his anger focused onto winning this fight. The older boy was unconscious in the hospital.

Arrested. Jailed for aggravated assault. He stood before a county judge. His trainer and other police officers testified on his behalf. The judge's verdict, either enlist in the military or go to jail. Probation until he finished school. Boot Camp or Jail, his choice thereafter. If he enlisted, the future take-away would be "No Criminal Record." That record would be sealed and expunged. When he had completed an honorable four-year term of military service, in any one of them.

Recruiters clamored for an opportunity to present their offers. Lester's file noted with Golden Glove training and experience. Most recent coming in second State Wide in the Golden Gloves Tourney." One heck of an asterisk on his pre-induction file. He breezed through the physical. Test scores for job qualification were moderate-to-high. He was trainable. His psyche evaluation, borderline due to "anger issues."

The selection of enlistment contracts was his choice. The most interesting offer came from the Air Force. He would learn rigging. For aerial delivery support as a parachute rigger. In his off hours, he would train for the inter-service boxing tournament. Held yearly.

His mother signed the enlistment papers with him. He was seventeen.

Selected by Air Force on a four-year enlistment. He liked what he did. Years of service went by.

His personnel file grew with completion of many specialist schools attended.

Ten years would pass....

Combat ground troops left Vietnam in 1973. The airlift continued in support of the South Vietnamese. In 1974, he was flying as a C-123 Loadmaster. He gained the interest of two agencies. Building covert aviation services.

Lester entered the Ops Office.

Not every agency outstation had its own aviation unit. Presidential Executive Orders opened the door for upsizing this station. Agency administrators determined it would include aviation participation. In support of the insurgent forces crossing the border into Nicaragua. For every extended operation by contra-revolutionaries, aerial delivery support had to be provided. Support of aviation participation included a station mechanic.

Antonio De Garza Mercado opened the maintenance shop. To maintain these birds for flying.

Tony was born in Aguadilla, Puerto Rico. Remembered stories his parents told. Stories about the B-52s that flew out of Ramey Air Base. And, in the mid-50's an occasional visit from President Dwight D. Eisenhower. Columbine III, a Super Constellation would fly him in. Bringing the President and golfing partners. For a two-day round of golf and conversation.

When he graduated from high school, his interest surfaced in enlisting in the Air Force. An uncorrectable, slight medical condition prevented him from enlistment. He made his way to San Juan. Trained to become an airframe and power-plant mechanic. Being able to work on heavy jets, he traveled to Chicago to work for United Airlines.

He met his mentor on an afternoon in 1982. Evenings discussing possibilities, introduced him to the government side of aviation maintenance. A matter of months later, Southern Air hired him. He flew as a crew chief on L-100s through various South American Airports. He and Lester met in Charleston, SC. Going different directions on agency planes.

Tapped to be the maintenance chief at Tegutch Outstation, when it opened. He answered to Tony, among friends and associates. A good choice for this outstation. Others within the region would call him for advice on moving a plane, point-to-point.

Once during his assignment to Toncontin, Tony flew into Montevideo, Uruguay. The embassy arranged a twin-engine small plane, to fly him North to Artigas. On the border with Brazil. He repaired the ailing agency plane.

It was not on an official flight. Not supposed to be there. The agency plane had followed flight paths of black marketers. Flying out of Southern Brazil. As far as the locals knew, the folks on board were small businessman. Seeking to take part in the lucrative black market, supplying Northern Uruguay.

Other than an occasional chopper trip, he made Tegutch his home with this team. For most of the last year.

Lester Enters Ops

"Morning, everybody." Heads lifted from the desks which they occupied. As quickly as heads rose, they returned to the work at their hands.

US had a significant military presence in Honduras. Exercises between the host nation and military units reported as training activity. The purpose for which was something else. A reason to be in the region. Eyes looking forward to the eventual overthrow of the Sandinista government of Nicaragua.

The previous Nicaraguan dictator Somoza, had been ousted by the leftist Sandinista party. The overthrow influenced and established through an insurgency.

Aided by the Cuban government. Backed by the USSR. In the past, Fidel Castro displayed a great deal of resilience and push back to United States. He was an active rebel rouser before 1960.

After the Cuban Missile Crisis, Fidel Castro expanded his activities.

In the Caribbean, Central and South America. Toppling the Nicaraguan dictator of Anastasio Somoza Debayle. One coordinated through efforts between local Marxists, Cuba and the Soviet Union.

Roberto Suazo Cordova, M.D. became president of Honduras. He had won the Honduran general election in 1981. He promised to carry out an ambitious program of economic and social development. Tackling the Honduran Country recession. He counted on a massive infusion of financial aid from the United States. This Honduran President had hoped that U.S. money would turn around the Honduran economy.

It was a country of importance for the United States. Its interests in Central America dictated the prevention of another state falling to Marxists. Aid came in the form of U.S. military money. Other agencies participated with specially selected programs. This to support the need for the intelligence officers in the embassy.

International relations with the United States provided a foothold to build a peace. Allow for stability and economic development. Yet, there was opposition to the buildup of American presence.

With the good promised by President Cordova, came the admitting to the mistakes of their past. Political strife that ended in assassinations. Death squads that kept communities in line. Those in power before him had perpetrated many human rights abuses.

Argentinian military officers had worked alongside - and in an exchange with Honduran military counterparts. The Argentine Army, too had been accused of human rights violations. Some of the Argentine officers remained active in Honduras.

That was only part of what gave Honduras a black eye. Under the government of Polycarpo Paz Garcia, their association with Peruvian and Argentinian military. The spawning of the notorious Battalion 3-16. Brigadier General Gustavo Alvarez Martinez commanded this secret intelligence corps. Operating as a cell within the Honduran Army. It gained international attention in 1982.

Constable Outreach was a temporary answer to a much larger agenda.

Toncontin – Outreach Hangar

Latitude: 14.0342 North

Longitude: 87.1301 West

Central Standard Time (GMT -6)

23 September 1985

Sun was rising. The Super King Air taxied to the ramp. Stopping in front of Constable Outreach hangar.

"How was the flight?" Tony asked.

"Nothing out of the normal, droning through the night." The smiling Jack Thompson, a six-foot, thin framed pilot. Graduate of Embry Riddle. Always had a pleasant approach and delivery in conversation.

"Anything I should know?"

"Log book is clean. Normal entries." Jack walked into the hangar. Passing the Sikorsky on his left and the Provider on his right. He strode the full length of the hangar floor to the catwalk.

Tony prepared the plane for towing into the hangar.

"Jack, can I see you in my office?" Tom McKay asked.

"Be right up."

The King Air electronics officer stripped the recordings, photos and data from on-board equipment. At their host base the files were collected to an encoded file in a heavy metal case. Making the electronics equipment ready for the next sortie. On the ground, he removed the case from the plane. Carried it to operations. It would be given to the agency communications folks during debrief. Analysts in Virginia would have access to the transmitted files within one hour.

"Discovered something we hadn't seen before." The electronics officer commented. "Look at this." Pointing out a finding to the communications technician.

"Is that an airfield?"

"Looks like it. A single lane road, off the highway. Disappears below the forest canopy. On the same azimuth, it reappears in an open area. A road wide enough for a C-130." He commented, then added, "Electronics should give the topography. And, sounding."

Jack arrived outside Tom's office. The electronics officer joined him. Recordings and data had been passed. They both stood on the catwalk. Tom asked them to enter.

"Morning guys," Tom started.

"Interesting night. Though quiet. A lot more activity towards the coast. Pinpointed the LRRPS and The Contra Team. Some body heat East of them. Could be smugglers. No other recognizable activity." Electronics officer reported.

"Appreciate what you guys are doing for us," Tom replied.

"You got an op starting soon?" Jack questioned.

"Yes. An airdrop using the Provider. It's our first attempt. We're going to see how it goes." Tom paused. "I'd like to tighten your surveillance parameters. It's in the same general area. For your flight tonight, we'll give you specific coordinates for your flight plan. The night before our drop, we'll look again."

"Sounds good." Jack said. Electronics officer and co-pilot both nodded. "See you tomorrow."

The King Air crew left his office. Their falling feet heard making way down the metal stairs to the hangar floor.

The crew could relax, once outside of any surveillance area. Away from the plane. In a hotel where recharging by relaxation and rest was found. One nice thing about foreign hotels, one could order a beer at eight o'clock in the morning. Without raised eyebrows or a look of disapproval. After a couple beers, each could head toward their respective rooms.

Lester was leaving the ops. He reviewed the check-points on airdrop pallet building. Most important were three points. Cargo secured to the pallet. Nothing overhanging that would prevent smooth exit across the ramp. The rigger had to visualize the pallets, as they were extracted from the plane.

He looked towards the hangar doors. Over the hangar floor he could see the Huey, Sikorsky and the Fairchild Provider. The C-123 came from the Davis-Monthan boneyard.

USAF Tail Number 55-4505 (N20166) had now been designated Constable Outreach 35. Outreach 35, the shortened call sign.

The Outreach Crew had flown her on a test flight last Friday. It was a slow meandering dance above the Honduran countryside. It allowed the pilots

9

and Tony, to determine what she could do. This airplane used effectively in Vietnam. It was a Ranch Hand bird. Later it provided spray operations in the United States.

The mix of new and old surface skin told a story of war wounds. The high over-fuselage wing held two Pratt and Whitney radial engines. It handled well with the throttles pushed all the way forward. Stops prevented over-revving the engine. In banking, was capable of high G twists and turns. The Provider allowed for seven pallet positions. A slick floor for hand loaded cargo. It could carry up to 61 troops or 50 litter patients.

Stripped for a specific application, it passed for the intended use.

Lester's task was to build airdrop pallets. Then fly on the bird. To coordinate the drop from the loadmaster position. Two activities he had performed many times in Southeast Asia on the C-123. His designation, "cargo handler." But, it didn't tell the whole story. Stories of experience and ingrained knowledge.

While stationed at Rickenbacker Air Base, he worked in the aerial delivery shop. Spent months in the lower desert of Arizona and the Mojave, North of Edwards Air Force Base. His special operations experience with other aircraft added color to his resume. Flying aboard two configurations of the C-47 "Gooney Bird." One used in cargo movement and low-level paratroop drops. One a sister to Spooky and Puff – raining fire from the sky. And, on CV-2 Caribous used for short field insertions and extractions.

He went to the floor next to Tony's tool shed. Between the shed and outside wall, he cleared an area. That section would insure space to throw the nets. It would also allow turning space for the forklift to maneuver. Items left undisturbed when out of sight. Overnight.

The three-pallet build-up began.

Used and unserviceable civilian pallets would provide the base for each gathered load. They were light. Disposable. Easily modified to add strength. Loading them into the cargo bay of the Provider could be done by forklift. These pallets would make a one-way trip from Tegutch to the drop zone.

The ULDs, called cookie sheets were stacked ten high. Lighter than military pallets, they could be moved by one person. Lifting one corner, he slid each one into its buildup position. He surveyed the cargo. Grouped and interlocked to make the lowest profile. Even weight spread across the flat surface.

Lester was building a three-pallet train. The last pallet loaded in the plane would have a drogue chute mounted to start the sequential offload. The first pallet had to be slightly higher and heavier in the rear to ease the extraction. The other two would be lighter.

Lester worked judiciously. In and around the delivered cargo, he selected items that would weigh down the four corners. Providing a box within which other items would fit. The center of each pallet filled with smaller and looser items. Double netting and security strapping needed. But, that would come after the load had been built. Combat supplies. For the soldier on the ground.

The initial cargo placement took approximately 3 hours.

Tony appeared from the tool shed, walking Lester's way. "Want to do some lunch?"

"Sure," Lester replied.

"How's the build-up going?"

"Like putting a 3D jigsaw puzzle together. Had to review the TO. Refresh my memory."

"The support blocks are about ready. When we get back from lunch, I'll show you what the modification looks like."

"Good. Where do you want to go for lunch?"

While the two stood in decision mode, Tom McKay approached.

"I'm on my way to the Embassy." Tom paused. "How do we look for Friday?"

"On time. On target." Lester replied. "I'll update you in the morning."

"Good." Touching Tony's shoulder, asked "How's my favorite mechanic?"

"Doing great boss." Tony watched him walk away, turning to Lester.

"How about La Plata? It's right around the corner from the gate. We can eat. Be back in an hour."

The two walked toward the side hangar entrance. They noticed the heat difference once outside the door. It was a short walk to the security gate. Sounds of landing and departing planes serenaded their walk. Heavy jets landed from Panama City, Bogotá and Caracas. As hyphens, between big jet landings were smaller private and Honduran military trainers.

The airplane sounds reverberated between the two walls of adjacent hangers. Once through the gate, the sound lessened. Street sounds of cars and motorbikes played a welcome symphony. The humid air filled with the smell of burned oil and gasoline. It hung there most of the day. But, at night the cooler mountain air would wash it away. The night air filled with the smell of sweet hibiscus.

The Café de La Plata filled with early mid-day diners. Tony selected a table near the front window, off to the side near the alley. Seat selection giving them four routes of escape. The sun was almost directly overhead. A café umbrella shaded their table.

A waiter arrived. "Buenas," he nodded. "Cervesa?" He asked, handing them a one-page menu.

Tony began to speak in Spanish. "No, gracias. Agua embotellada. Dos, por favor."

"¿Algo de comer?" The waiter asked.

"Nos dan un minuto. Mientras nos fijamos en el menú."

Lester's grasp of Spanish was not as good. His reasoning, 'As an American, the locals had to think of you as a tourist. Not a want-to-be native. And definitely, not a long-time local operator for the United States government.'

Nicaraguan Forest

Latitude: 13.90079 North

Longitude: 86.15321 West

Central Standard Time (GMT -6)

Monday Afternoon – 23 September

A long-range reconnaissance patrol moved quietly. Not a word spoken. Hand signals for communication. No twig broken. The only movement, the air around each soldier. They would steal into an area, by foot. And, they would exit without detection.

The mission was reconnaissance only. They were to have no contact with man, beast or local militia. Moving at about 3 km per day, the sun would rise and fall as they skirted village and farm. Shunning any contact with locals which would sound an alarm.

Should they happen upon targeted individuals, they would observe. They were there to mark location by coordinates. Number of persons counted in the local party. Types of weapons. Dialects of Spanish spoken. All without being seen or heard.

The unit was small. Their purpose was in the collection and reporting of raw information. Having reported what they saw, would steal back across the Honduran border. Support would provide extraction. A Sikorsky H-34, with Honduran Air Force markings would arrive. They'd be flown back to a military base in Danli.

On this six-day mission, they encountered one group. The dialects were mixed. Some Guatemalan, Honduran and Nicaraguan. The nuances between each dialect were finite. Yet to the trained linguist in the patrol, he was able to parse which rebel tied to which country. He wasn't always right. But with a 90% success ratio at linguistic school, no one doubted him.

The weapons specialist collected information on combatant weaponry. Could call the make of most world weapons. Especially, European and Soviet Bloc manufacturers. The supposed date of manufacture. His talent was displayed during some games among fellow Special Forces person-nel. He'd be blindfolded, given a weapon. Then he'd be asked to identify its make and model.

Unlike the linguist, his success ratio in this game was about 60 percent. There was always somebody trying to fool him. And, he occasionally lost money wagered.

A radio operator was the extension of team leader. Supplying informa-tion by code in their most stealth position. Communicating with opera-tions at Tegutch Outstation. Outreach Radio plotting their movement.

LRRP Commander would report twice daily. Most of what his team got was redundant. And, boring. Today was a high point in recent reporting.

This report was of a small Sandinista group. Totaling ten men: two Guatemalan, four Nicaraguans and four Hondurans.

Some of the weapons were crude or modified. Not identifiable. Seven were from World War II, Russian and Eastern Bloc countries. Weapons man counted two AKs, three Czech Mausers, a Tokarev SVT-40 and a Simonova AVS-36. Nothing new. The others made from parts. Reconfigured into crude weaponry.

This party had no heavy weapons. No machine guns or rocket propelled grenade launchers. A "light infantry" rebel unit.

From what the observers could see, there wasn't much ammunition carried. The observing force leader surmised that extra ammo was wrapped and tucked in pockets.

Among all the weapons seen, each required a varied cartridge size. A sophisticated armorer would have to collect and ship the right round for each gun seen. Someone would deduce they were supplied from Russian or Cuban armories. Worldwide, 7.62mm cartridges were in abundance. One question, the age of their rounds.

'A firefight would be a pushover,' thought the stealth unit leader. 'A better way to neutralize them would to take them out one-by-one as they moved through the forest. Quietly. Slower yes, but without one round being fired.'

The purpose for the observed patrol being at this location was not determinable. 'Were they clearing the area for drug mules? Preparing an incursion into Honduras? Or, reconnoitering for other unknown purposes?'

LRRPs were not in this business of analyzing collected information. They were only there to collect it. Their reports were sent to analysts. Combined with other gathered observance, that information presented a larger view.

'There had to be a serious supply chain. That meant there was an operating base near. Following them might lead to the location of the supply operation. Their staging point for their movements.'

A young man approached. His movement through the forest telegraphed his arrival. Heard long before seen. Breaking the silence. All in their encampment were alerted. Readying their weapons. The city-raised boy approached their site. He was unaware that this collection of weapons trained on the noise he produced.

The LRRP Team watched the rebel group point their rifles on the approaching sound. Ten weapons were pointed at the trail he walked. To the average ear, the sound he generated was of a large animal rustling. Digging for a vegetarian delicacy. Or, the chasing of prey by predator.

Some weapons clicked from safe position to ready. The bolted weapons had rounds in their chambers. No one heard a bolt unlock and slide, to chamber a round.

Without a concern, the boy of 18 walked into camp center. The leader of the rebel group recognized the young man, ordering his men to stand down.

"Hola." The leader greeted.

"Buenas," the young man replied.

Removing his backpack, he continued the conversation in Spanish. "I brought some home-cooked food."

"How is The Senora?"

"She sends her greetings. And this envelope." he said. Pulling the envelope from his backpack. Handing it to the patrol leader. Going back in concentration to unpack the food his mother sent. The smell of home-cooked food permeated the camp ground. Smiles and light banter came from the mouths of this mixed ethnic team.

"It will have to be heated."

"These men can eat it like it is. We are trained for combat," their stated. "This is not a college dorm." His sharp words spoken like a father admonishing his son.

He was seasoned. One could see that his hardened face and hands spoke to the man of dirt he once was. His demeanor one of strength. Yet, appearing weary from the battles he had fought in the past.

'*Was he a farmer who had taken up a fight?*' The LRRP leader questioned. '*Never returning to the dirt he tilled. Had the fight taken him away from growing food for his family? To places where his good intentions were needed? Did he miss the family life, he left behind? Or, was he a trained guerrilla? A pro? Could he fight with his hands?*'

LRRP commander's thoughts were broken. The young man spoke.

"My mother sends her best."

"Tell your mother, I am honored that she thinks of me." From that exchange, the young man went about distributing the unheated food.

The camp became quiet as the men enjoyed the home-cooking. The sun had four more hours of exposure remaining. Arriving unannounced was a gift. Both foreign patrols would have to move from this site into heavier vegetation for the night. Their exposure here was an invitation to joint discovery.

"Señor Perez, gracias," one of the fighters offered. Others in this group nodded in approval of the salutation.

The young man nodded and smiled. "My father would be proud. My mother will help in any way she can."

The seasoned leader handed the young student papers. A bundle tied by a bit of string. "These are the sites in Honduras which can be compromised. Tell her to pass them…"

He stopped in midsentence. The site became quiet. All the fighters were watching, listening for the next intruder. Looking over his shoulder, he touched a finger to his lips. He did not move. Waiting for that sound to come again.

The young man developed a puzzled look. His brow furrowed. His lips pursed. He was not sure of his surroundings. A pause only broken by distant sounds. No one moved.

Slowly, these men reached out for their weapons. They attempted to do it silently. But in a forest, man is the foreigner. The sound he makes is different. Distinguishable from the silent groaning of forest growth. The ease and uncontained growth of the forests goes on quietly, every minute. Every hour. Every day. When man invades this quiet cathedral, his unfamiliar sounds change the paradigm. Difference a bit to note.

The young man broke the silence. "What do you hear?"

The rebel leader moved to the young man. Putting his arm around the young man's neck, he tugged slightly. In a whisper he said, "I can teach you things that your father did not."

In the brush, the LRRP leader closed his eyes. The bodies were frozen among the vegetation. Minds becoming one with the forest in which they lay. Observing for this length of time could only expose their position. But they could not move. Movement would be worse than making their adversary discover them. Errant fire from an untrained soldier has caused many a death. The death of friendlies. Sometimes your own, more so than the enemies you are pitted against.

'Quiet. Breath. Settle. Relax.' The silent mantra of this stealth soldier. 'Make yourself one with the landscape. Quiet....' He repeated.

Sensing his surroundings. Each member could feel the others in his team going through their own individual mantras. Teams were one in spirit. Moved as one. Lived and died as one. Again, they were one with the forest. Alive!

Seconds passed. Seconds became a minute. The sound heard by the seasoned rebel leader did not repeat. Not duplicated. Sounds of the forest returned to dominance. Quite rustling of leaves in the tree tops whispered. The forest in its friendliness, returned the wisp of its control. The rebels, returned to vigilance learned from this encounter. Without a word, the rebels finished their meal. They repaired the site to give back, to the forest that owned it.

"Tell your mother, I will come see her."

"We will look forward to your next visit. Thank you. Viva Las Sandinistas." The young man said, grabbing the hand of the leader.

"Gracias." The leader pulled him close. Their clenched hands touched shoulder to shoulder. The respect for the young man's father, was now being given the son.

Tegucigalpa, Honduras

Latitude: 14.0723 North

Longitude: 87.1921 West

Central Standard Time (GMT -6)

23 September 1985

A registered letter arrived at the U. S. Embassy for Tom McKay. It was from an analyst, friend passing information across the system. He came to retrieve it from the embassy mail room. There was time for him to make a stop. Before the mail room closed.

The sign on the wall read U. S. Military Attaché. The name plate had removed some months earlier. His friend Fred Matthews hadn't taken the time to have his placed.

Tom steals a moment, but cannot stay. The chat would be short.

"Hope I'm not interrupting." Tom prefaced his entry.

"Just preparing for my next round. How are you doing?"

"Moving along with our project."

Fred Matthews shuffled papers. Appearing to search for something specific. "The Honduran government wants your hangar operation shut down." He said without looking up.

"Where did that come from?" Tom asked.

"They've always been a little sensitive about exposing their connection to the agency." Fred Matthews replied. Now looking at Tom.

Fred would be one of the first to know. A Military Attaché in the U. S. Embassy. He was privileged to morning security documents that circulated through the building,

"How can we operate and support our guys in the field?"

"Seems President Cordova wants more tourism. He referred to us as, 'those of our kind.' Tegutch airport is too small for upscale military ops."

"If the Sandinista mentality spreads into Southern Honduras, there won't be any tourism."

"You're right. But, he has a point. One runway locked amid the barrio. Slums, hills and commercial real estate prevent it from expanding."

"I can see that."

Fred looked up toward his door. A female motioned for his attention. "The heads upstairs are working on that now."

He stood and walked toward the female. "Just a minute." They spoke in whispers. He closed the door. "Look, I have to go. Thanks for sticking your head in. We'll have to talk later."

This brief conversation meant that the agency would be planning a move. For now, he could be with his own thoughts. He exited the Attaché's Office.

It would be Tom's worst position. *'Beginning something that gets stopped by politics. Nothing ended well when politicians got into agency business. Careers ended. Persons displaced without notice. Teams split. Some died.'*

Pressure for the move came from a detailed report. Supplied to the Congressional Intelligence Committee. The last closed-door hearing sent word back to the agency. They wanted it moved. It fell right into the mixed political leanings in Honduras.

After Vietnam, minds turned a simple counter-revolutionary operation into full blown war. *'One thing led to another.'*

Escalation by parties in a squabble always led to more military involvement. More attacks. More troops. More press coverage.

The Domino Theory was not in anyone's list of favorite explanations. They would not be words used in any Congressional Hearing. Some members of the committee weren't imagining a small, insignificant station that housed airplanes. What they saw was a similar build to the previous Asian failure. A build-up of force in a territory, 1800 miles from Washington, DC. In the same hemisphere.

There were American soldiers on the ground in Nicaragua. A combined force of secret operators kept eyes and ears open for intelligence. Contras engaged opposing forces.

A probing force of Contra-Revolutionaries was operating across the Honduran border. A US Army Special Forces trainer led them. But to most in the group, he was just another mercenary.

They now moved between the Towns of Ocotal and Jalapa. Their mission was to find and probe defenses. They were prepared to fight and die.

A team of Long Range Reconnaissance Personnel also moved in that area. Military LRRP teams roamed the northern edge of Nicaragua. In search of operating Sandinista cells. Their mission was to observe and report. Not seen or heard. Only once had they crossed paths with the Contras. The latter was unaware of their presence.

Background

But, the Sandinista locals got stronger with training from the Cuban advisers. The whole area had fallen into a proxy fight. Based on ideological input from the Soviet and American governments.

When US military souls operated in hostile territory. They deserved more than a passing thought. Their protection came in oversight. Supply was required to maintain the mission. Knowledge that, *someone had their six*' provided mental comfort. They deserved the utmost gratitude for placing their lives in untenable, yet necessary situations.

Still in the Cold War in 1975, the United States faced many external concerns. American combat troops left Vietnam while the NVA continued their push. Then there was the embarrassment of Saigon falling to the North Vietnamese. The USS Mayaguez seizure by the Cambodians in international waters. Operation Baby Lift was one bright spot. Then, one C-5 crashed killing 138 on board.

In the states, the Weather Underground bombed the main office of the State Department. The Watergate Trial. Then came the Rockefeller Commission Report on CIA abuses. A wild bunch in California, sent one of their own in an attempted assassination of President Ford.

Tom McKay was present during the embassy evacuation in Saigon. He had transferred to the agency that year. He had come from Army Intelligence. Four tours in Vietnam. He had moved between Ft. Belvoir, Ft. Meade and MACV Headquarters in Saigon.

He didn't consider himself a young man. Depending on the activity, he could hold his own. Steeped in his work, his family saw him with less frequency. This new front threatened U. S. Southern border. He felt compelled to volunteer for the Central American Desk.

The letter he came to retrieve might give him new insight on his career projection. He wanted back in Washington, DC. At home with his family.

Tegucigalpa operation opened in late 1984. Tom had been there from its start. Since last year, they had built it from a listening station to one with aviation support. They named it Constable Outreach. As the unit size grew, they twice had moved until obtaining the hangar at Toncontin Airport.

He had never been visited by his counterparts in Honduran intelligence. This produced an uneasy feeling in the pit of his stomach. The acceptance of Constable Offices had changed, based on Honduran Presidential appeals.

Battalion 3-16

Long before he got here, there was folkloric, documented reports of torture. Intelligence Battalion 3-16 named in most of them. According to the reports he read, there were some of those folks still lingering in the military. Danli Military Barracks headquartered the intelligence unit.

Host Country Economics

Honduras was now experiencing economic woes. The U. S. Presidential office thoughts were in assisting Honduras. The country's finances, needed a boost. Expecting that the politicians would turn a blind eye to agency operations. Those activities against the Sandinista-controlled Nicaraguan government.

Constable Outreach Operations

This was a busy end to the month for Constable Outreach. A LRRP Team would be finishing their six-day intelligence gathering mission. The Contra strike force had crossed the border on their third day of defense probing. McKay's team had been planning a maiden C-123 airdrop. Missions to supply the Contras. Present and future. The mission would drop supplies North and West of Jalapa. Call sign Constable Outreach 35.

Changes created by political concerns kept everything in a state of flux.

Once a week, Tom McKay would go to the Embassy. There, he would sit in conference with his local counterpart, Fred Matthews. As many as twenty-five others in the region were connected through an electronic feed. Some in listen-only mode. An overview of White House desires would be made. Analysts would brief those in attendance. Significant, up-to-the-moment information would be passed from the outstations. Suggestions for operational improvement collected.

Fluidity dictated operational execution. One could expect momentary change. Change was inevitable. Swift acceptance was a must.

Tom McKay marched to orders from the Agency Director. Somewhere in there, an office in the White House would have their say. Agency operators had to take an order. Dissecting its parts. Following the path which best exemplified the use of a situation. Molding orders to the best possible outcome.

Tom and the Agency were a good fit. It required the intelligent application of ordered goal accomplishment. Molding the application to daily changing scenes. Using assets in an efficient manner. And, being invisible.

Tom felt called to this work. Having a proud family heritage.

From what Tom McKay had been told as a child, his family came from a long line of Scottish warriors. Clan MacKay supported Robert the Bruce. During Scottish fight for independence in the 14th century. In the transition from then to now, the name was shortened to McKay.

The family immigrated to the United States before it was a declared union. They participated in the Armies of Independence. His great-great-grandfather fought and died in the Civil War. Great-grandfather fought in the trenches of World War I. Grandfather in World War II. Father in Korea. And, he in Vietnam. It was a long prideful history for men of the McKay Family. A painful, sorrow-filled litany for the women married to any McKay.

Now, he wasn't on the front line. He managed insurgent movement from his office at this airport. The hangar could accommodate many planes. There was always room for one more. The floor looked like an airplane jigsaw. Puzzled together by shapes made of planes and choppers. A savvy mechanic ensured their safe placement.

Tom turned his thoughts to the airdrop on Friday. Aerial delivery for his probing force. More important than what might happen in the future. He had been reminded as a young man, *"The future takes care of itself."*

Stealth Watch

Latitude: 13.895578 North

Longitude: 86.150333 West

Central Standard Time (GMT -6)

Monday - Tuesday

23 & 24 September 1985

From the encounter on Monday afternoon, the LRRP team leader had to decide who he would follow. The young man. Or, the local band, led by the seasoned experienced fighter. The embrace by the two spoke of familiarity. The young man had moved East out of the camp. The local patrol going West.

'Going away from and in opposite directions of one another. Wanting to follow both might prove in being two sides of the same coin. They met at the edge, seen by this reconnaissance patrol.' The American thought.

The long-range patrol leader made a quick decision. Acting upon it would take time to fulfill.

'The young man would not expect following. He would leave a trail. LRRP point would be able to pick up that trail, the boy left behind. The nature of stealth is that no one suspects you are there. You are. Yet, you are not.'

The team kept distance between them. They had moved East on Monday afternoon. Out of purpose, their trained senses dictated every movement. The choice on who they would follow, at the discretion of their leader.

That afternoon they followed the unaware teenage boy.

In a cleared area, cattle grazed. Dotting the field. It opened South and West. A structure sat on the South end. In the dying light of dusk, no human could be detected. Team leader selected this spot for a night stay. Rearguard was sent back on the path. To check for any signs of their movement.

The cat-like placement of his steps, returned him to last man in formation. Taking one knee facing West. Rearguard waited for the team to close the distance between them. Radio operator selected a spot for all to gather. Silence was maintained. Discussion of the following day plan done without spoken word. On an erasable board. A palate on which words were written. Using an unscented marking pen. Hand signing between members replaced the use of their tongues.

LRRP team slept arm-to-arm, backs touching. Radio hidden in the hole between them. Before the sun would lighten the Eastern sky. Each man would take a two-hour watch. Night watch monitored radio communications. The ear wig passed. Vigilance did not stop at sundown.

Each man listened with expressed intent. No one at watch would sound the alarm. Any night without a firefight, was a good night.

As the last soldier on night-watch stirred, others came awake. One by one, the team members would eat. They would ensure drinking of water for hydration.

One noted to being low on water. The group could last days without food. Yet, their days numbered without water.

Morning light filtered through the forest canopy. As the forest floor lightened, it was time to position for observation.

Cows moved in the open area. One cow broke silence, welcoming the day. The pasture held a small herd – separated by distance between them. Cool dew of morning dripped from the trees. Dew droplets hit the forest floor, sounding like splashes on a glass plate. Jungle fatigues were wet from the night air. Steam rising from their heated bodies. Men and cow alike. Body heat would dry a soldier's outer coverings.

Op plan of the day was to move close to the farmhouse. It would be the second human intelligence item, reported on this mission. It was time to move. Linking the young man to what they had seen.

'Wishing so doesn't make it happen. There was a risk of exposure observing this close to the farm house. Viewing the activity around this farm might produce an exclamation point to this mission.' The LRRP commander thought. *'The caution was not to expect what one might find. You reported what was found or seen. Verifiable by other eyes. Reportable activity for the analysts to read. Included in the volumes collected from many sources.'*

Point in the team changed out at least once a day. All team members, excepting the medic would serve in that forward position. Each team member was cross-trained. But, none as highly trained as the Team Doc.

They skirted the East edge of the pasture. Bringing them closer to the farmhouse. A third of the morning getting to a position for observation.

Sun transited the Southern hemisphere and had moved overhead. Each hour, the team would stop. Coordinates taken and plotted. Moving in jungle or forest, the next goal may only be 25 meters. Sometimes less. Sight distances calculated to each new objective.

Getting to the chosen point. Team leader signaled to stop.

Reaching their plotted watch location, they could see the farmhouse.

Sent one fresh soul to reconnoiter. Moving South, to a position facing the farm house.

No activity seen. Only sounds of a two-cycle engine heard.

This team stayed well inside the forest, at the clearing edge.

The two-cycle mountain bike, heard all morning was now seen. The sound of cows blurting, came from the West side of the pasture.

When the scout returned, he briefed the LRRP commander.

'Two people, one male, one female, South side of farmhouse. Friendly conversation. One automobile parked to the West of structure. One in front. Two-cycle, two-wheeler – helmetless rider - male gender. Australian sheepdog roaming. Unable visual – North side. No road in from North or West.'

They would have to get closer to see if the young man they sought was at the house.

LRRP patrol moved to the Southeastern side of the farmhouse. A better point of observance. They moved two meters through the forest. It would take a half-hour to cover that distance.

While moving, they heard an automobile start. Watching it drive away, the motorbike approached the house. It stopped in front. The engine turned off and rider dismounted. There was no good visual on the rider.

Reaching their point to observe, each man took up his respective position. Some facing out, away from the house. LRRP leader positioned to view the front of the house.

Voices, though unintelligible heard in conversation. Then became quiet once more. As quiet fell on the soldier's ear, only sound of gentle wind. Wind meandered through the tree tops. An occasional bird was calling. Some flew from branch to branch. In the distance, cows continued their sounds. LRRPs were in their element. A world without the interruption of a human voice.

A sheepdog lay silent on the porch of this ranch house. From the front, it looked more like a scene from a Western movie. Ranch houses seen in the 1950s. An overhang covered the porch. Posts from ground level supported its roof. Two steps lead from ground level to the porch floor. The front door of the farmhouse set dead center of the building. Small windows, spaced on each side. But in this part of Nicaragua, it considered a palace.

A dirt road split the trees to the left. It ended in a gravel area in front of the house. A rider-less motorbike appeared as a red flag on the gravel. Human activity was not heard. They would wait to see the young man they had followed.

Each soldier held his own thoughts.

'By the grace of God, I was born in America...'

'I will be faithful to the trust placed in me...'

'I will never forget, I am an American soldier....'

One team member, watched the farmhouse. Tapped the commander. He passed the binoculars. The front door of the farmhouse was opening. A young man stepped out, followed by a woman in her thirties.

'That's him!' The commander said to himself. *'Watched him pass documents to the seasoned soldier.'*

Soldier to his right confirmed the sighting.

The knowledge they gained would be valuable. How it fit, he could not know. But his job here, was to observe and report.

The dog had been resting quietly on the porch, until the two humans reappeared. Tail wagging, the dog sought attention from the young man. Dog danced around the woman, while the two humans conversed. The conversation could not be heard. Yet, the body language displayed one of love and understanding. The young man gave the woman a hug. The exchange from her, a love-pat to the boy's cheek.

'Were they, mother and son? Or, some other relation?' Questioned the leader.

The woman went back in the house. The young man moved around the dog. He was paying attention now. Picking up an object, he threw it out on the gravel. When the dog reached the object, he stopped. Looking away from the thrown object.

Alerting, his ears stiffened. Head turning in effort to pick up sound or sight. Listening, he looked down the road. Then looked toward the positions held by the LRRP team. Another vehicle approached.

The dog barked, then looked at the young man. Faced down the road. Then back at the tree line. Repeating that movement three times.

On the road, a vehicle broke through the tree line. Approaching the house.

Constable Outreach Hangar

Latitude: 14.0342 N

Longitude: 87.1301 W

Central Standard Time (GMT -6)

23 & 24 September 1985

Lester entered the tool shed, looking for Tony.

"Tony, you in here?"

"Back here."

Talking about the upcoming airdrop between the two would be normal. But, Lester had developed other concerns.

"You got a couple minutes?" Lester asked.

"I was in the middle of signing log entries. But for my friend, I always have time. What's up?"

"I don't know how to approach this subject. Without sounding like a scared kid."

Tony finished adding an entry. Looking up with puzzlement on his face.

"I've been having night sweats. Waking to the sounds of my own screams. Not being able to get back to sleep immediately. Some nights, I get up. Walk around. Take a shot of Beam."

"How can I help?"

"Most of the dreams are the same. Vietnam. Hot LZs. The aircraft not being able to takeoff. Staying in the dirt. Wheels bogging down. Taking fire. Hearing the words of my mom. Until I wake in a sweat."

"Post-Traumatic Stress?"

"Never diagnosed with it. But, the images seem real. See the faces of pilots I flew with. My mom's voice clear as day. Like I'm talking to you now."

"What do you hear her saying?"

Lester pulled a chair to face Tony across the desk. "She keeps repeating: F in fear is false."

"False?"

"Yeah, when we were kids. Afraid about something. She'd sit on the bed listening to my fear of the day. I was kind of screwed up as a kid. After I told my story, she made me say what I feared. We'd talk it out. Then she would finish by repeating the letters of fear. F is for false. E is for events. A is for appearing. R is for real."

"Never thought of the word that way."

"Just being able to verbalize it helps. Worried. I see myself making the same mistakes over and over, again. Love my job! But, I'm thinking more about the consequences." He paused, "You know I won't quit. Past couple of days, building pallets reminded me of U-Tapao. Nha Trang. Combat offloads on LZs in Nam."

"What brought those thoughts back?"

"Guess the pallet build. Coming drop. No air-cover. Unknown factors on the drop zone." Shaking his head. Not knowing the cause.

"How does your mother fit in."

Lester thought. Slowly mulled the question. Just shook his head. "Don't know."

"A drop without air-cover would concern me." Tony paused. "But, I haven't done what you have."

"Intel doesn't report weapons that could bring down a plane. Flying low-level always presents the possibility of taking light weapons fire. Not enough to bring it out of the sky. But, the possibility of taking fire from a prepared force. That's concerning!"

"None of the King Air reports have shown troops. I mean concentrated build-up. Most likely, the local militia haven't advanced enough to be carrying heavy weapons."

"I know. Just needed to verbalize. Talk it out. Put some of those thoughts out."

"What about your mom?" Tony returned to that part of the puzzling dream combination.

"There were things she said, that always stuck with me."

"Like?"

"Keep moving. Don't look back. We'll be OK." He paused, "the fear acronym."

Tony thought about the significance of each set of words. How they affected Lester.

"You know I'm always here." He said, more to fill the silence. "What would Yoda say?"

"Yoda?" Lester questioned. The question jarring him from the rabbit hole his mind was sliding into. "Oh, you mean the Star Wars Yoda."

"I don't have one of his quotes that fit. But, imagine. What would Yoda say?"

"Fear not? Fear creates its own? Look at fear dead in the eye?"

"Well, sort of. Think if you answer that question, you might overcome the night sweats."

"Yup. Just don't want anyone to see this side of me. Questions might arise."

"It'll be just between us. You'll handle it. Like you always have. Otherwise, you wouldn't be here."

Lester thought about the confidence Tony had in him. "I'll let you get back to your paperwork."

"Well, thank you. This is the least favorite of my activities."

Tony continued, putting his eyes back on the page. Searching for his last entry in the log book. Lester left the tool shed.

Rancho Perez

'This dog was intelligent. But, he probably barks at the movement of lizards,' the LRRP Commander thought.

Eyes watched the young man. As he watched a vehicle approach. Coming to 100 feet from the porch, it stopped. Two figures exited.

"Hola, Señor." The Spanish-speaking driver said. Dressed in the uniform of the Cuban Defense Force.

"Hello."

"I came to visit Señora Perez, Senior Jaime." Major Sanchez said.

The other man was much taller. He, unlike the driver was wearing a suit jacket. In this heat, it was unusual. But it gave him the aura of being official. He was Russian. Both he and the driver approached the house.

The ranch house front door opened. The woman reappeared. Her young man stood away.

"Señora." Maj. Sanchez greeted.

Turning toward the younger, she said "Go into the house, son. Now!" He followed her stern instruction. She moved these men farther from front of her home. "Talk quietly, I don't want my son to hear. It is good to see you, Major Sanchez. How can I help you?" She knew him. But, not the tall one.

The Cuban Major spoke, "Col. Alexandr Dutrov." Nodding toward his partner.

Colonel Dutrov gestured. "My respects. We have come to alert you of increased Contra activity around Jalapa."

Stepping closer to the men, she asked quietly, "And, why should this be a concern of mine?"

"You are Señora Perez. The widow of Miguel Valesquez."

"Yes, why does that matter?"

"We came out of respect for you and your late husband. Hoping that we could be of some assistance."

Only a short time before, she discussed the same subject with the Mayor of Jalapa. Though she had training as a guerrilla, she never saw herself in that role. She loved a man who was a guerrilla fighter. They bore a son, who now was behind the screened door.

These three adults knew of her husband's many successes. He was a revered Guerrilla Commander. And she, his wife and lover. But, that was yesterday. It had been two years since her husband's death.

"This was a courtesy call," the Russian spoke. "We have established a Cuban garrison in the training facility. The Mayor of Jalapa urged us to bring you this news. If you have a need of assistance, please contact Major Sanchez. It was a pleasure to meet you."

"Thank you," she replied. "I will be talking with the major soon."

"Good day Señora," Major said, as bowed slightly to show her his form of respect.

Both men got into the car and drove off. The son came from behind the screen, where he had tried to listen.

"Who was that mama?" Son asked.

"Major Sanchez, you know. The other man, Col. Dutrov."

"Anything wrong?"

"There are soldiers operating nearby."

"Contras? Americans? How does he know?"

The son had interest. His desire was in protecting her. He was now a man of the house. He would fight – if he knew how. He was not brought up in guerilla camps. That military styled existence. His mother had seen to that. She didn't want her only son to die in battle.

"And, what do you know of Americans?"

"The talk is around town. My friends hear their parents talk."

After his birth, they stayed far from the fighting her husband experienced. The father missed the better parts on his son's early years. Occasional visits, allowed the father connection with them both. Their conjugal visits were short. He loved his wife. Shielded his son. Yet, addicted to the thrill of battle. But, wanted his son to be President of Nicaragua.

Juanita Perez wanted her son to graduate from an American College. Now that he was eighteen, she would send him to family in the United States. A family that publicly shunned her existence. They had been visited by the FBI. But, would take the boy

She, known among the Nicaraguan politicians. Well known by Cuban officials. Soviet and United States intelligence offices, also knew of her. Her husband Miguel Valesquez had put her on the radar. Presence here in Jalapa put her on the map. She dropped the name Valesquez to attain anonymity.

Friends – who fought at the side of her husband - were involved in the Sandinista fight. They respected her desires.

Not much was known about her 18-year-old son. He attended a private school in Managua. His friends had fathers who also fought against the counter- revolutionaries. Others in his school, would stay away from that group. They were told by their parents to be cordial, but not friendly. In Central America, political change came quickly. Without warning.

"One never knew which way the wind would blow. Today the Sandinista. Tomorrow we may return to another dictatorship." Group thought, rarely expressed.

This was a politically changing atmosphere. It was hard to know which life was best. Always in a state of change and flux. The best way to survive, was to go about your business. Shun all discussions of politics. Only address the political scene when asked. And, always take the temperature of the room before making comment.

They sheltered their children. Yet their children still became part of the discussion.

There were the haves and have-nots. The street children were not as lucky. Through the Sandinista government, they saw a way to increase their lot. Many became soldiers in the fight against the Contras. Professional muscle to protect the wishes of their leaders. Some having crossed over from gangs. Where the drug trade was protected. And, through which drugs were offered to any buyer. The melding of nationalism and organized crime. Those soldiers did not come from private schools. What they learned came from the streets. For them, existence was war.

LRRPs and The Dog

Latitude: 13.8955 N

Longitude: 86.1503 W

Central Standard Time (GMT -6)

24 September 1985

Dog began to bark again. Facing Southeast, he alerted. Pointing. Running toward the tree line. The dog stopped and looked back. Entering the woods, the dog disappeared behind the wall of greenery.

The woman watched the dog. Un-phased, she reentered the house. The boy looked toward where the dog was standing, before he disappeared. Then began to walk around the motorbike. They weren't concerned about the dog running into the woods.

Straddling the motorbike, the youngster stroked the motor crank. The engine fired. Stood the bike and pushed the kick-stand. Revved the engine twice. Released the clutch and rode down the long driveway. He returned a minute later.

It was normal that the dog followed him. When he rode back toward the house, the young man did not see his dog. He shut down the motorbike. Called for the dog - repeating the call twice more. His dog did not appear.

The last time he saw the animal was when it entered the wood line. Recalling the spot of entry, he moved toward it. Calling twice more, he listened. There was no movement in the brush. He entered the woods. As he moved deeper, the vegetation became heavier. He called again.

Scanning the forest floor, he saw his dog. The dog's body lay limp. Moving closer, he saw blood at dog's throat. He knelt. Touching the lifeless body. Lifted his eyes to gaze forward. Then looked over his shoulder.

His last exhale came with a hand covering his mouth. An arm wrapped around his throat. He tried struggling. With the strangle hold applied to his neck, blood flow stopped reaching his brain. He fell limp, like the dog.

LRRP protocol was broken. A dog had alerted on their scent. He had to be neutralized. And now, the young man was being held by a member of their team.

Two mistakes that need not have happened.

Killing the boy was an initial option. It was a thought. One soldier's conscience would stand in the way of taking his life. The boy was not a soldier. A boy caught amid a clandestine war. The American couldn't take his life.

Another option had thought hours before. Capture. It was one of many from which the LRRP commander had to choose. Taken, to be released far from his ranch. Returned to their Honduran compound for interrogation. Subjecting the young man to pain and suffering. Far removed from any scrape he received by dumping his bike. Risking the boy's death at the hands of Honduran Interrogators. None of the options were favorable.

'Not good. But, we can't stay here. Waiting for someone else to find us.'

LRRP team leader ordered the men to move. With expedience. Returning to as near a stealth operation before the capture. He would think during this movement away from the ranch. This team was not to be caught. They were gone.

Juanita came out on the porch. Seeing the motorbike, she called for her son. The late afternoon sun was high in the Western sky. She called – again and again. It was not like him to stray so far without telling her.

'I could go looking for him. Which way would I go? Where would I look? Too much ground to cover.'

The earlier visit by Maj. Sanchez had placed doubting fear in her mind.

Running in the house. She telephoned her friend, the Mayor of Jalapa. He gathered some men from the local reserves. They sped toward her farm in an aging pick-up.

The Mayor's Rapid Defense Force

The local Sandinista Reserve Force is commanded by the Mayor of Jalapa. They are the initial action team for any emergency. The force established much like their fire department. Volunteers. Juanita Perez heard the pick-up coming toward the house.

"It is not like him." Juanita told the Mayor.

"We will find him." He replied.

"The dog is also gone."

"Be calm, Señora. All will be well."

An hour passed. The dead Sheepdog found. But, no sign of the boy. One of the local militia carried the limp dog back to the front porch.

The sun was disappearing behind the treetops to the West. Limited light began to hamper their search. With flashlights, the locals continued. One by one, a man would appear behind a beam of light at woods edge.

"What has happened to my Jaime?" Juanita muttered. A mother's protection had failed. "Oh, my God. Help him reappear."

The Mayor attempted consolation. "We will find him."

With all the responding reserve force out of the woods, they reported "No young man was found." The 18-year-old had disappeared.

"Lo siento, Señora." One man said, offering his comfort. The responding force had done their best.

"Contras. Bastardos," Juanita shouted. "Y mi hijo?"

The lead militia-man shook his head. Mayor's volunteers could do no more.

The aging pick-up cranked to start. One by one, the militia members bid the Señora their heartfelt words of comfort. The Mayor was the last to take her hand. He motioned one of the men to get out of the truck bed.

"Tomas will stay tonight. Give him something to keep the chill off his body." He said, indicating that this man would guard the Ranch House. "We will be back in the morning."

The mayor entered the passenger side. The engine idled. Lights were on and five bodies sat in its bed. The truck drove away into the evening air. Down the long access road. Juanita heard the truck for a moment or two. Then it was gone

"Thank you for staying, Tomas."

He would be of no comfort to her bruised heart.

Wednesday – Thursday

It would be a two-day hump across the Nubarrones mountain range into Honduras. With situation reports and coordinates sent twice daily. The site at Tegucigalpa would track LRRP movement. The Super King Air last reported their location. Inside the Nicaraguan border on Tuesday night. They were putting as much distance between them and Jalapa - as fast as possible.

This team knew how to move. With swift precision. Now, silence was a secondary concern. With capture of the young Nicaraguan, their pace slowed. It required half-carrying and half-prodding. The barrel of a weapon used like a cattle prod. Their movement less quiet. Sound carried. Disturbing the natural habitat. Birds and other mammals were sounding their location.

On their forced march across the mountains, they came across two campsites. Reporting them gave both agencies two new sets of coordinates for drug movement. Drug mules made their way into Honduras on that trail. Trafficking between Costa Rica and the Honduran border was never questioned. It was permitted. And, protected.

They reached a clearing large enough for extraction. Sixteen kilos from the Nicaraguan Town of Jalapa. They stopped moving. The perimeter was set. They waited for the Sikorsky H-34. Radio silence was not as much of a concern on this side of the mountain.

The Honduran Air Force had been salted with various airframes after Vietnam. The HAF pilots were flying Bell UH-1B and the UH-1H "Huey" Iroquois, since the mid-70s.

Now, the Sandinista government presented more of a problem. The agency searched for and withdrew more equipment from the desert. Older planes from an undefined source. Pilots worked across language barriers as they trained Hondurans. And, flew the older planes.

The H-34 was one of those called back into service during this Contra War. It had been out of the US military inventory since 1973.

It flew from Danli, Honduras. The military headquarters of Intelligence Battalion 3-16. A compound secreted on the western edge of town.

What went on behind the gates of this compound was for military and agency eyes only. Only a few military uniforms were seen through the fence. The comings and goings of choppers spoke to the continual training for the Honduran Air Force. The American faces added spice for those who speculated and wondered.

"Team Two, HAF-28, come in." An accented voice called for the LRRP Team. Words heavy with Spanish enunciation.

"HAF-28, we have you in sight."

The bulbous nose of the H-34 protruded forward of the high mounted cockpit. It's landing gear was of rubber tires. Long struts supported the wheels that seemed to come from under each pilot's seat. The top of its tail boom sloped to the tail rotor. The ground clearance more than the Iroquois. Piston power seemed antiquated in this new age of turbine powered helicopters.

It would lift this six-man team and their captive. On the thirty-five-kilometer flight to their base.

Low Spanish styled barracks stood across the parade field from Battalion 3-16 Headquarters. A two-story agency building seen on the North end. It was a small black site that the agency and Hondurans operated. In conjunction, yet not a secret. In the Town of Danli, Honduras.

Toncontin - Outreach Operations

Latitude: 14.0342 N

Longitude: 87.1301 W

Central Standard Time (GMT -6)

Thursday – Late Morning

26 September 1985

Jake entered Tom McKay's office. "You have to see this." Handing him the printed message.

As the document held for him to grasp, Tom asked "Where are we on the flight?"

"This may have bearing." The paper, full in the Tom's hand. The message confirmed two separate subjects.

One paragraph discussed Constable Outreach shut down.

The second, reported a break in stealth protocol. The agency's eyes and ears for this operation, had captured a boy. LRRPs had walked him out of Nicaraguan territory. Arrival at Danli Agency Site that day.

"Get me all the raw reports for that LRRP team." Tom ordered. "This will create problems. We have to get ahead of it."

Jake left. Tom fell deep in thought. Anticipating the questions such a breach would generate.

The phone rang on Tom McKay's desk. As it rang the second time, he picked up.

"Tom McKay."

"Daddy? Is that you?"

Surprised, he replied "Hi sweetie. Good to hear your voice."

"Mom needs you. Can you come home?"

"You're not in school today?"

"No." Rebecca said, faking a cough. "I'm sick."

He searched for something to immediately say. He couldn't refuse his daughter. Not a request, nor a phone call. Yet, he tried to think of some easy way to say, "not now."

"I think I can make some arrangement. What's going on?" He suspected it was over the arrest of his son. The Family McKay had been three-person household. With an occasional visit from the father. It happens to all service personnel. Whether military, State Department or in the agency. The job took you away.

Once assigned to an area of operation, station managers fulfilled the requirements. A move into the country of operation, if possible. Household set up good enough to supply your basic needs. Sometimes living out of a backpack or suitcase. In a hotel, if you were fortunate. It was the work that was important. The work itself was consuming. It sucked the life out of anybody participating in agency operations. The outstation controlled your life.

It was the thing that caused difficulty in committed relationships. Long separations created distance between the joined souls. Jumping thoughts crossed from the left to the right side on Tom's brain. A hop-scotch. Ping pong. Bad mitten.

'*Was it the distance? Was it the fact that the agency was a woman? Competing for the affection of the man? Or, was it the simple act of moving away? Traveling for the agency mistress? Which was it that caused divorces?*

A spike in divorce rates related to wartime activities. The thrill that someone gets from being part of something greater than self. It kept many soldiers choosing it over their commitment to spouse.

"I'll work it out, honey. Might be able to get out of here in a day or two."

"Please, daddy," pleading, with the turned-up question in her voice.

"I will," he said. "I'll call you tomorrow and let you know what I was able to work out. And, no more skipping school!"

She had been caught. But, admitted nothing. "Bye daddy. I love you."

It was moments like this that ripped at an area just below his solar plexus. The great gaping hole that could be filled with nothing. But the immediate touch of a loved one.

As he hung up the phone, he stood. In emotional tension. Unexplained pain. Staring at the floor. Until jolted from his thoughts. The hole filled with current agency business.

Not focusing, Tom sensed a body walk through the opening door.

"You alright, Sir?" Jake asked

"Yeah, just got a call from my daughter." Settling his focus on the man standing before him.

"Yes Sir, I know. Put it through because she said it was an emergency." He paused, assessing Tom's demeanor. "Here are the docs you requested."

"Just some family business." He began to collect his jangled edges. Feelings of inadequacy were temporary. Put aside. He hadn't heard the second statement. "Where are my reports?"

"That's why I'm here." Jake said, handing Tom a multi-page merged report. A look of concern overtook Jake's facial expression. The boss was always focused. But, not at this moment.

Taking the document from Jake he said, "these things get bigger every day. A lot of background material. Must give someone a job rewriting the facts. I should be able to sift through it. Find what I want. A short briefing."

Jake chuckled, with a twinge of nervousness. "You should have to sit in radio room. I hear way, too many words that don't need saying." Thinking of something to add. "I'm married to that electronic mass. But, one good thing. She says I'm a good listener."

The attempt at humor did not phase Tom. He replied, "Thanks, Jake." Tom settled in, turning his attention to the twenty-page report.

It was the operational control that motivated Tom McKay. He had been in differing situations in Vietnam, Germany and in Washington. The agency always provided an interesting workplace.

There were many things that he would've done different. Had it been him at the helm. Most of how one sees the big picture, comes from their background. Experience. Knowledge that they've developed.

Once in Germany, he took part in a prisoner swap. It involved a loose-fitting document. A memorandum between them and the Russians. The dealings were civilized. Almost friendly.

His contact was a Russian spy operating in Berlin. Their meeting place, a beer garden near Checkpoint Charlie. The discussion between the two opposite agency contacts was like talking with your brother. If they hadn't been on opposing sides, Tom would have invited him to a Sunday barbecue.

Once the prisoner swap was complete, the memorandum destroyed. To the world, the incident never happened. Things went back to normal. His short-term friendship ended.

What was bothering him was his family situation back in Arlington. His son, Robert got arrested for possession of pot. Son and a friend were driving home from a party and got stopped for speeding. Walking up on the automobile, the officer smelled the odor of marijuana. Once the kids were removed and placed in a squad car, the officer searched the vehicle. Less than 1 ounce of marijuana found on the passenger side.

He could not have prevented the nighttime arrest. Control of the situation left his purview with him being in Honduras. There were things he knew he could control. Having the drug talk with your kids, didn't prevent them from experimenting. He didn't control other parents. Or, their children. The atmosphere in which children were found was much less under parental control. More in the control of others. Besides dealing with hormones, most children felt that they were more adult than child.

Stuff like this bothered Tom. Because he was not at home when it happened. His daughter was showing her rebellious side. Causing Mom fits. Discussions over the phone never settled the situation.

'What they needed was his presence.' Tom thought.

His wife had told him many times, *'Raising these kids is only half done right. While you're gone, a part is missing. I am only half of the core equation.'*

But, he needed this last posting. It was the end of his fulfilled requirements. In being considered for management at agency headquarters.

His spouse was a strong woman from Boston. From Irish heritage. Sally just sucked things up. Moved from day to day, without thinking about the steps she would have to take. She just moved ahead. That was her mentality. One foot in front of the other. Doing what as required for family.

A military approach. *'Which she wouldn't admit....'*

He was always thinking ahead – sometimes three and four steps ahead. Working scenarios in his mind, he could almost pinpoint the outcome of any situation. He got more of that from his study of human nature. Tom's discipline was in International Relations. That's what it said on his award of Master's Degree.

'That degree from Georgetown University, which was not helping my wife raise our children.'

If he had applied, his work ethic to raising his children. This marijuana situation might not have come to this embarrassing end.

'If you'd spent more time at home," he thought. *'My influence might have made the difference.'*

He had wanted a family. From the time, he graduated high school. He met his wife in college. While they dated, talked about family. Planned for their future after graduation.

The military had injected itself into the middle of their plans. In his last year of deferment, he obtained a notice to appear before his draft board. After the discussion with his girlfriend, they postponed their wedding. He went for his pre-induction physical. Passed. One-A. Waited for his draft notice to appear.

That was 30 years ago. There was basic training. During which, every recruit tested for their abilities. Their natural bend toward career desire. His tests came back in the 90th percentile. His military IQ score was 134. That put him in line for officer candidate school. Which he accepted.

All through the training, he found parts of himself that led back to the MacKay warrior in him. His parents discussed, the history of Clan MacKay. During many dinner conversations.

He displayed an early interest in war craft. Playing war games and acting out James Bond scenarios as an adolescent. That part lay dormant in his mind, as a student. His interest resurfaced as a young Officer Candidate. It helped him score high on the weekly tests.

It was at the end of that schooling. He discovered that he would not become a Combat Engineer Lieutenant. He was assigned to Army Intelligence

Command. There would be another three months of training. Following with Vietnamese language school.

This abrupt left turn caught his girlfriend by surprise. And, distress. She wanted him to do something else. Her desire was not to be. The love that had developed between them, now had third party influence. Injected by national security needs. He would go to a country far from the shores of Massachusetts. The Domino Theory had nothing to do with a lazy Saturday morning on the quad. Where the game dominoes was played.

All around them were voices building against the war. Yet, Tom moved forward. This was something much bigger than himself.

He did not want their earlier discussions to be for nothing. Tom was an inductee. He would do his duty. And he would return home, discharged from the Army.

But this was 1985. Marriage. Two children. A career in intelligence.

"How could I be so stupid?" Tom asked himself, relating to thoughts of his family. *'Is this what they talk about? Being conflicted? Concerned about my son smoking marijuana? Could I have seen the signs?'*

Reasoning with himself over that reaction. *"How was this so different? Now that the one smoking was just like me."* He had smoked marijuana in college.

Honduran – Nicaraguan Border

Latitude: 13.9756 North

Longitude: 86.2513 West

Central Standard Time (GMT -6)

26 September 1985

Earlier in the week, a Contra-Revolutionary team inserted fifteen klicks West of Jalapa. Crossing the Honduran border, into the Sandinista homeland. Their mission to probe defenses. Make their presence known. Fight where necessary.

A Special Forces tactics leader operated with the team. Fluent in Spanish and dressed as one of the Contras, he blended well. In the event he was captured, he might be able to continue the ruse.

Daily, LRRP reports fed them information. And, a collection of other data through agency operations. The latest report, a small Sandinista team was heading West. Toward them. There was a lot of real estate between. The two opposing forces could miss one another.

Unlike their LRRP counterparts, they did not operate in silence. They could move quicker. Making more noise. Any habitual uses could point to their location. Use of cigarettes, talking, food smell or clanging equipment would give away their position. Yet, they smoked. Talked. Made fires for their dinner. Making less effort in concealing their presence.

They could have been a drug-band returning from a delivery.

On this outing, they would be resupplied. An aerial delivery, demonstrating agency capabilities. A covert mission for the aircrew. Contra Team Four moved South to the designated drop zone. Toward DZ Alpha.

They were fierce fighters. Some had seen action in Grenada. El Salvador and Guatemala. Once having the tastes of war, an individual finds normal life dull. A soldier is always seeking to replicate the high of combat. The adrenaline flowing in his blood, heightens every sense of awareness. Without that rush, some cannot exist.

Expectation begets anticipation. No team wants to walk into an ambush. No team wants to come upon a battle by surprise. Soldier on point becomes more vigilant. Rearguard turns and scans with more intensity. They were talking less. Tonight, they would eat without cooking their meal. The sun would transit the sky. Would follow with a full moon.

Thursday – Noon

The H – 34 Sikorsky set down in the middle of Danli compound. Fifty-nine kilometers from Tegucigalpa. Buildings stretched on either side of the parade field that had become a landing zone. LRRP commander was the first out. Standing near the landing gear wheel, he motioned for his men to bring out their captive.

The eighteen-year-old captive blindfolded. An olive drab neckerchief covered his eyes. His hands tied in front of him. His trousers had a rip in one knee, from a fall he took crossing a rock bedded stream. The scab on his knee was a day old. Two days prior, he was riding a motorbike at Rancho Perez. Now, 119 kilometers by auto from Japala.

Pulling him from under the rotating blades of the H - 34, one soldier finally spoke. "This is your new home." The hand pulling the rope around his wrists released.

Another hand grabbed at the same spot with force and tugged.

"I am your master." The rough voice said, tugging down, left and right Erratic movement to confuse. Questions developing in the captor's mind. "You and I will get to know each other well!"

The prisoner did not speak out of fear. He had no idea why brought to this place. Or, where on the map it located.

'Wherever here was, it was a long walk from home. It didn't smell like home. Smelled of burning trash. I don't hear my mother's voice. The voices of men, speaking English and Spanish. This wasn't home!' Thought running the course through prisoner's brain.

The new master controlled his blindfolded moves. Pulled at him so fast, that his normal gait became a stumbling and awkward looking dance. The dance continued. When disoriented, the master spun him 180° to a stop. Against a wall. The force shocked the breath from his lungs. His back slid down the wall. His buttocks reached a wooden seat.

"Now, don't you go nowhere." The voice said mimicking a Southern American accent.

Prisoner could hear a conversation going on 5 feet from him. They talked low and even laughed at what was said. Time dragged, sitting on this bench. With no visual input, he concentrated on what he could hear, feel and smell. His wrists were sore from the rope used to tie them. The knee relaxed to a throbbing counterpoint to his heart beat. The smell of cooking made him hungry.

Minutes seemed like hours. The smell of beans cooking lifted past his nose. The young abductee realized what his stomach was trying to tell him.

'You are hungry. You never went this long without eating. The last thing that crossed your lips was water. How long ago was that?'

Footsteps crunched through the dirt and gravel. They came closer. There was a presence in the body standing over him.

'Was it the Master? Or, was it someone else?'

"I am Jorge. Usted apprendera a respentarme!" The voice demanded.

Grabbing his tied wrists, he pulled hard. The prisoner jettisoned from the seating position into the air. Falling on his knees. He felt pain from the cut knee. The hand pulled harder, dragging the young man across the dirt and gravel.

"Stand up! Stand up now!" Jorge barked. "I am not dragging you all the way! Stand up, I said!"

The eighteen-year-old struggled to his feet. Immediately he felt the forceful tug forward. He knew not North from South. He was up. But, would be down in the time to come.

Interrogation

His captors worked through a series of interrogations. He was one of many. More than one and less than ten. He heard muffled footsteps. Moving in the hall next to the space he now occupied. Heard just forward of where he sat on the floor. Feet in labor. Dragging something. Or someone, down the hall. Activity moving left and right.

He knew he was on the other side of something solid. With his eyes still covered by the neckerchief, his orientation was limited. He concentrated on what he could hear.

Footsteps stopped. To the front of where he sat. Hearing a portal open, his mind raced toward what would happen next.

A voice demanded, "Get up!"

Struggling to his knees, his balance was off. He felt a slight twinge of pain from his knee. He stood. Feeling the large gloved hand grab at his tied wrists. It was firm. Purposeful. The hand was forceful. But, it guided his movement. Without the erratic tugs, experienced before. It was calming to be lead.

"We will talk now." The voice sounded European. "Follow me."

The voice was soothing. It wanted to give the prisoner comfort. Before questioning. Harsh movement changed to the demeanor of quiet leadership. They left the space and glided down a hallway. Changing light was seen through the blindfold. His captor stopped.

"In here," he said.

Once in the new space, its size did not feel any larger. When seated, he heard the door close. The latching sound of a slide bolt punctuated with new words.

"Welcome to our home." A different voice, not European. But, just as soothing.

He felt hands untying the neckerchief that covered his eyes. When it removed, his eyes had to adjust. Brighter light flooded through his iris. He blinked many times. His tear ducts filled his lower eyelids. Eye sockets soothed by the moisture. While adjusting, hands moved to untying his wrists. He could see through teared eyes. His hands were free to move. Rubbing his wrists, he massaged the sleep from his fingers.

"What is your name?"

"I am Jaime Corea-Perez"

"Is there more to your name? A surname?"

"Yes. But I don't use it. My last name is Velasquez. My father's name."

"Your father was a Nicaraguan hero?"

"Yes." Jamie said with caution. Among some people he would admit that. With others, he wouldn't bring it up. Still others, he would do anything to keep them from knowing the truth.

"Well, Jamie Correa-Perez Velasquez, you are our prisoner. We will tell you when you sleep. We will feed you when it is in our best interest. We will guide your every move. You will become compliant." The interrogator across from him at table was purposeful in his delivery. He meant every word that was spoken.

"What have I done?"

"You are an enemy to your people. Not because you carried a gun against them. But, because of who your father was, as a Sandinista. Your people have suffered much. Your capture was an opportune moment. For resistance against the Sandinista government."

"But I have nothing to do with that," then he added. "Or, them."

"You are the son of the Sandinista hero. A valued asset. You can become more valuable in our hands." He paused, "we're going to let you think about that. My friend and I are going to leave the room. You may have your private thoughts. We will return."

The interrogator stood up. Motioned the man with European accent to leave the room. After which he followed. The door closed. Slow and quiet.

Jaime heard a locking mechanism slide into the door jam.

Toncontin – Constable Hangar
Thursday - PM

"Chief!" Jake's voice broke into Tom's silent space. "Team 2 mission is complete. H–34 dropped them at Danli. The bird should be on the ground here, in about 20 minutes."

"Thanks." Tom replied.

"Something you should know. Their prisoner, the boy is Jaime Velasquez."

"Who?" Tom's mind was processing three separate incidents.

"Jaime Velasquez, Son of Miguel Velasquez?"

"Well. What do you know?"

The machinery in his head began to turn. He nodded.

'There would be questions. I have questions. Not directed at this radio operator. Protocol was broken. Would have to sit face to face with the LRRP commander. See this prisoner. Take responsibility.'

"Col. Matthews is on his way here." Jake added.

"Does he know?"

"He said for you to wait for him."

Fred Matthews arrived fifteen minutes later.

"We've got to debrief Team 2. Take possession of their asset. Got to get ahead of this." Fred told Tom, with machine gun precision.

"I know. We can always depend on Murphy's Law." Tom replied.

"Bring me up to speed." Tom supplied as much information as given him.

"We'll turn the chopper." That would give Fred Matthews some extra time to wrap his head around this incident.

The chopper refueled on arrival at Outreach hangar. It was an hour drive from Toncontin to Danli. Fifty-seven kilometers. Turning the arriving chopper back to Danli would be quicker.

A mistake had generated an opportunity. Time would tell, on how it would play out.

Toncontin - Outreach Hangar

Latitude: 14.0342 N

Longitude: 87.1301 W

Central Standard Time (GMT -6)

Friday – Early AM

27 September 1985

Station Chief lay quietly. A Sleepless night preceded his workday. His thoughts alternated between family and Outreach developments. He rose from the cot. It was a place of rest. He had stayed at the hangar sorting through what he learned at Danli.

Still covered in yesterday's clothes. His focus was pulled toward documents that had been placed on his desk. The shut-down was looming. As he prepared to send the Provider into enemy territory.

The sun would rise soon. His team would be arriving. The King Air would be returning. He had decisions to be made.

Tom spent a half-hour on the overnight report in front of him. A lot of what he had read were pieces from previous reports. It being merged into a readable document. The actual sit-reps from LRRP Team Two was more abbreviated. It was in a combined military-agency interest. To establish what forces had camped along the border.

Monitoring Sandinista telephone communications was through another unit across town. The eyes and ears focused towards Managua were many and wore different stripes. This war centered on ideology. Tom was assured that the Soviets were performing the same activities. Soviets were using Cuban front-men to be there arms in reaching out to the local populace. The supply of weapons, ammunition and medicines was coming gratuitously from the island nation. Ninety miles south of the United States.

Testing. Probing. Financial aid masking psychological operations. It was a slow but sure means of gathering consensus. Little to their knowledge, it was being enacted on the populace. There were many forms of aid to be provided through military- and civilian-assistance commands. Both from the USSR and United States. There were other forms of psychological warfare that were not so pleasant.

Tom flipped to the pages of raw communication data. Hoping to pare something others might have missed. He was about to launch a re-supply mission. Staging equipment and supplies for a larger force to follow. Across the border. A designed infiltration plan against the Sandinistas.

"... Tracking 10+ man unit. Local boy supplied food. Friendly conversation. Plan track local boy. Report to follow." Tom put the report down. Went to get up. But, sat back down to finish the read.

He read, flipping back and forth to his dog-eared sections. The phone rang. Hoping it wasn't his wife, right now.

Boss is Not Happy

"Dammit Tom, your LRRPs captured someone!" The voice said in anger.

"Good morning, sir."

"Not much of a good morning." The voice came from nearly two-thousand miles North.

"Slow down." The two men knew each other well. "We talked to the LRRPs. They couldn't do anything else." His regional manager reported to the Director. They had passed on assignments since Tom's early military days. Many conversations with his boss at agency headquarters. This one not so pleasant.

"The Division Commander is going to see them hung by the balls!"

"I just reread the report. We don't snuff innocent civilians. Their leader was between a rock and a hard place. Situation was unfortunate"

"Just got off the phone with DIA." The voice paused, cooling his hot temper. "I know. But, you should see the shit storm it has stirred. All the way to the White House. You just got the first of many an ass chewing."

"There is nothing I can do after the fact."

"Fred Matthews has been tasked with finding a solution. For your own good, stay clear. Understood!"

"Yes, sir." Tom heard the phone line go dead. Sat mulling the broad stoked order.

Jake walked on the catwalk, between ops and the Chiefs office.

"You got a second?"

"Sure, come on in."

"The King Air crew will be on the ground," Jake looked at his watch. "In five minutes." He paused and looked down at the papers Tom had spread out. "See you're into the LRRP report." He continued, "the Contra team is in position at the drop zone."

Fred Matthews Interest

Col. Fred Matthews had a similar induction story to Tom McKay. He was a University of Virginia graduate. Couldn't escape the draft, like so many during the early Vietnam build-up. Attended OCS. One of the few commissioned Regular Army at graduation. Reserve officers could be ousted in a force reduction. Or, returned to enlisted ranks. Reduction in Force appeared after every major conflict. Much like base realignment and closure came with budgetary concerns. At the end of every major conflict. He was guaranteed his career, if he met his need to pass through certain gates.

Fred had settled into the embassy as a Military Attaché. Sent there by request through a Pentagon assignment procedure. Heavily influenced by The White House Chief of Staff. He completed all the requirements bringing him this far. His eyes were set on a military desk in the Executive Office Building. It was a short walk to the West Wing.

As light began to filter through the windows to his back, Tom had a major decision to make this morning. Between an ass-chewing, paperwork and building activity next door. The phone rang once more.

"What about the drop?" It was Fred Matthews.

"Pilots did acceptance flight. Mechanic and loadmaster worked out the kinks with the delivery system. Commercial pallets arrived. Supplies had been sitting on the hangar floor for a day or two. Build up is complete. Airplane ready to go." Saying it more as a checklist, than for providing information.

Fred interrupted, "Good. It'll be a first for you guys."

"Sent a message to Virginia. We launch today. Our guy told Danli, he's ready. They can get the supplies buried..." Tom stopped by his own interruption. Talking more about details Fred didn't want to know. "Well, we need something to go right."

"We're all hoping it goes well." Fred offered a part-confidence. "How are you doing?" He asked.

Having settled himself on all the questions he'd be asked later. Minding from across town. Knowing of Tom's family incident. And, how it affected Tom's fathering role from a distance.

"Got a call from my daughter. She wants me to come home. After we get past this rough spot, I'm going to take a couple days off."

"Rough. Been there. What are these kids thinking about? Kicks you in the nuts."

"Let's have coffee. Or, an adult beverage." Tom offered. It would be good to talk with another career military guy. One who understood. The only difference between them now, Fred had a chance to see his family more often. He could get a commercial flight anytime he wanted.

"That would be good." Ending, he hung up the phone.

Tom McKay had wanted one more overnight pass by the King Air Crew. Before he gave the "Go for Launch." Launch would depend on what he heard at the debrief. Fresh intel could help the mission.

The Provider would depart Tegutch into hostile territory. It would be a daylight drop. Murphy would know that his law applied here. Whatever could go wrong?

Lester Delivers a Box

One floor down, Lester entered the toll shed. A single gun-metal grey desk held position behind a row of open storage shelves. Left of the desk, a tall file cabinet hugged the corner. Tony sat behind the desk, back to the wall. No windows allowed for outside light. Above, a three-stick florescent fixture hung eight feet from the floor.

"Tony?" Lester called on entering the mechanics liar.

"Come on in." Tony yelled back. "Good morning." He greeted. "You ready for the big day?"

"As ready as anyone can be. Didn't want to interrupt. Is this a bad time?

"No." Lifting his intent from documents on his desk. To the gaze of a work partner.

"Aircraft is loaded. When you have time, I'd like to do a show-and-tell. It always helps me review my work. One final look."

"Sure." In a moment on redirecting thought, he asked "What you got under your arm?"

"This is the real reason I came to your cave." Placing the flat, twenty-four-inch-long box on Tony's desk. "It's my previous life. I carry it to remind me. Good people helped get here. Never want to lose sight of that."

"Ok, what do you want me to do with it?"

"Just hold it. When I'm back, you can return it."

"Anything I should know before I accept it." Good questions help prevent awkward future situations. Working for the agency carried extra personal responsibility.

"Just some personal history, legal files, pictures, letters."

Tony handled the box, "It's well wrapped. Shouldn't be a problem. I'll put it in the filing cabinet. Under lock and key." Touching it meant a tacit form of acceptance. Knowledge of what was inside.

"Thank you, Tony. You're a good friend."

Tony opened the bottom drawer of the file cabinet. Lester's box had its own space. Tony slide the long locking bar, top to bottom. Applied a lock.

"Now, let's go look at your masterpiece. The King Air will be here soon."

Walking out of the tool room, lights were extinguished. Tony locked the cage door.

They walked toward the Provider. Designation was Constable Outreach 35. Outreach 35 for short. Shortened designation made the callsign easier to speak during radio transmission. Lester displayed his hand-work. Walking Tony through the intended procedure.

Hearing the King Air approach, Tony began to open the hangar doors.

DZ Alpha

Thursday afternoon, Contra Team had arrived at the West side of the drop zone. Took up positions around the tree cleared field. Previous farmland, overgrown with small scrub. A road split the field. Length of the field from tree line to tree line was 1540 meters in length. Almost a mile, 5051 feet. The road surface had been cleared and widened. Tallgrass and scrub at road's edge had been pushed back.

This open field, was long enough to land a STOL aircraft. Designates Drop Zone Alpha. Long enough for three pallets, needed supplies to settle on. Most of the items delivered by air would be buried. Marked. And, retrieved later. The biggest need now was ammunition and food. The C-123 Provider would drop at low altitude by parachute.

The planned airdrop would begin on the North end of the field. Flying at about 2500 feet, the plane would dive to the Northern edge of the tree line. Dropping to 1000 feet above ground level. The chute released, pulling the pallets from the airplane.

The Contra force would stay off the drop zone. This would hide their presence. Radio contact could be made on a visual pass North to South. Established time for the drop not yet known. But, they'd be ready.

An Eastern perimeter was set 50 meters inside the tree line. This would prevent a surprise walk-up by any forces in the area. It would protect the Contra movement on to the field from the West. When the drop was complete, they'd wait to see if it attracted attention.

All the Contras would stay off the field. Until they knew it was secure to retrieve their supplies.

Safe working zone and passage afterwards were a priority.

Supplies would be buried, near where they came to rest.

If there was no contact with opposing forces, time was provided for item burial.

Burying the pallets, their biggest problem.

It could be done with luck and working fast before sundown. They could, then fall back to West side of the open area.

The Special forces operator moved with the Eastern squad. He had been supplied this way many times. On different continents. In different conflicts.

In position, they waited.

Tegucigalpa, Honduras

Toncontin International Airport (TGU)

Constable Outreach Hangar

Latitude: 14.0342 N

Longitude: 87.1301 W

Central Standard Time (GMT -6)

Morning

27 September 1985

Sun rose over the eastern mountain range. Tom McKay had been up. Having slept Thursday night on his office cot. He walked next door to refill his coffee cup.

"Good morning. Just want to let you guys know, how much I appreciate what you do."

Looking at the desks, papers were scattered. Left on desks overnight. His was reminded of certain OPSEC aspects. Operational thoughts, fresh in his mind pulled at his meandering thought. Other thoughts forced to the wings. Coffee would help him. Concentration this morning a must.

Jake drank from the overnight pot of coffee. When it was near finished, he'd brew another pot for the day crew. He appeared at the radio room entrance.

"Any more news on the King Air?" Tom asked.

"Taxiing to the ramp, as we speak." Jake replied.

"Anything that needs immediate attention?"

"There's a lot of chatter over the captured asset. Outreach 35 loaded, fueled and ready to go. Waiting on your decision to go."

"I want to see Jack Thompson and his crew first, as soon as they're in the building."

The information provided by the King air crew would be the latest intel he had before launch. Tom had requested a pass, over the drop zone. Any body heat signatures would register on their equipment. Pictures of the drop zone would help at mission brief. The files would also be transmitted to Virginia on black box download.

Tom looked forward to debriefing the King air crew. Airplane and crew had been on loan from the DEA in Panama. The electronic gear on board provided an excellent listening post. With photographic capability, eyes-in-the-sky.

They could intercept voice communications from radio transmission. Infrared cameras used in night surveillance helped track group movements under the Jungle canopy. The airplane was also outfitted with electronic jamming equipment.

The mission last night was to zigzag across the border between Honduras and Nicaragua. EL Guapinol to Nubarrones. Getting near the Jalapa area. Electronic data on the initial pass would be immediately analyzed by a person on the airplane. Any radio transmission plotted. Conversations recorded and checked for keyword transmission. On the second pass, the pilot would fly an alternate course. Any changes in movement by grid, detected by plotting second coordinates. Analysts could see direction, speed and distances travelled. Nonactive areas could be deleted by the operator.

On the third pass, the pilot directed his plane to a set of coordinates requested. Tom had given them to Jack for insertion into his covert flight-plan. A low-level pass made. Photographs were taken of the drop zone. The infrared sensing equipment would show any heat registration. Body activity on the ground. Overlaying the three types of signal reception provided analysis in threat determination. For this King Air crew, it was methodical and routine.

He called to Jack Thompson as he strolled across the hangar.

"Can I see you in ops?"

"Sure thing. I'll be right up."

He waited for Jack on the catwalk. Sun was now high enough. Airport was coming to life. Jack and his electronic officer came up the stairs.

"Coffee?"

"We could use some."

The three entered ops. A fresh pot of coffee was coming to life. The old, thirty cup pot provided liquid incentive to stay awake.

Its design, a fifteen-inch aluminum cylinder. A peg pouring spout protruded from bottom front. The pot gurgled and popped. The brewing cycle was just about over. Tom handed each man a paper cup with black fluid nearing the top.

"Today's our day." Tom started the conversation.

"The drop? Today?"

"Yup. Did you see anything that would cause me to scrub the launch?"

"No sir. Drop zone is wide. Almost like an airfield. Scrub to the East and West. Nestled in a 360° tree line. Sort of like the inside base of a bowl. There is one road entering from the South. Exiting North."

"How about heat signature?"

"Recorded some activity. But it could've been animals. Spaced far apart. No large groupings."

"Radio interception?"

"No. Pretty quiet."

"Good. We'll make the same pass tomorrow. After the drop. Thanks for helping us."

"Welcome," Jack said. He and electronics officer exited ops.

Tom stood in the middle of ops. "Jake?"

"Yes sir."

"Alert the crew. We're a go."

Drop Zone Alpha
Friday – Early AM

This morning, the Contra force held in position around the drop zone. A road ran through, near center of the field. It was previous farmland. The length of the field, 1540 meters. The road surface widened. Recent and intentional.

The vegetation was pushed back. Scrub, bushes and tall grass had grown up on its outside border. It's open area 750 meters wide. Tree line to tree line.

Plenty of space to bury supplies. Ammunition and C-rations for later. The biggest problem would be in camouflaging the pallets.

That was assuming no contact with Sandinista forces. Enough time provided for carrying out the task. They would stay off the field until they knew it was secure. With luck and fast work, they be could be done before sundown.

The Special Forces Operator had been supplied this way many times before. Different conflicts. On different continents. This area designated by long range patrols. Suggested as a landing or drop zone. Areas like this were scouted for possible extraction points. Searching for them when needed, was too late.

Outreach Ops Office
Local Time - 0930

"We've designated your call sign Outreach 35. We'll monitor your communications until you declare radio silence. Just a reminder, any cockpit chatter can be picked up. Keep it at a minimum. Here are the pictures of the drop zone with coordinates." Tom said, passing the copies.

"File your flight plan to insertion point. The DZ is 198 kilometers from here. Approximately 123 air miles. Roughly forty-five minutes to insertion point. One hour to drop and escape. You'll fly initial bearing 116.28. Turning to 116.33. A turn toward the DZ. You know what to do with the twenty or so minutes you go dark. Any questions up to this point?" The room was silent.

"Continuing. You'll drop North to South. Make your turn. Beat feet, low level back across the border." Turning his attention to Ops team. "All my personnel will remain on duty until the bird is back in Honduran airspace. Vigilance! Understood?"

Heads nodded, "Yes sir."

"There will be plenty of time for rest and relaxation this weekend. I'll even buy the first beer," he added smiling. "Good luck, everybody."

Shuffling broke quiet in the room, with purposeful movement. Bodies moving back to their stations. Flight crew departing. Heard in resounding movement through the beams, on the metal stairs. All the way to the concrete hangar floor.

"I knew a guy who flew this bird. They called him 'Black Axe.' Affectionately, of course." Lester commented as the crew walked. "During the early years in Vietnam, an Air Commando Group operated this bird out of Nha Trang. 317th Air Commandos. Covert missions. Ranch Hand operations. Their flight suits stripped of rank and insignia. That was 1965. This bird always brought the crew home."

The hangar doors were open again. Lester stood at the tail as Tony drove the tug. The other crew members on the left and right wingtip. Facing the nose into the wind, Tony stopped the tug. Crew went to work.

Lester stood fire watch. Forward of the nose, in line with #1 engine. Pilot turns on the collision lights. The prop turns.

Tony monitored engine start from airplane left. Halfway between body and wingtip. Adjacent to the pilot's open window.

Thumbs up. One of the Pratt…Double Wasp 18-cylinder engines began its start.

Its trefoil prop turned slowly, engine chugged to life. Spewing light gray smoke spun rearward, hiding the greenery behind its tail.

Co-pilot monitored the cockpit instruments while the engine cranked. Thirty seconds in, the pilot extended his arm through the open cockpit window. Having noted rising oil pressure and engine temperature. Indicating a good engine start. He gives Tony a thumb-up.

Tony crosses in front of the Provider's nose, along its right side to disconnect the power cart. Pushing it into the hangar.

With number one turning an idled prop, number two is started. Lester moved slightly left of the nose facing the copilot. Tony moved halfway to the wingtip. Tony signals co-pilot with high raised arm, one thumb up. The powerplant comes alive. Engine running. He rolls the fire extinguisher outside the right wingtip. Between hangar and airplane.

Lester entered through the crew door. It closes. Tony returns to a position far off the nose of plane. Raising both arms high above his head. Pilot flashes leading edge lights. Signaling "Ready to Taxi."

Tony marshals the airplane forward. Props bite the air. Momentarily, pilot holds brakes and releases in a test. RPMs increased, and brakes released. As the airplane taxis to runway, copilot obtains clearance for takeoff.

On line-up, all lights are on and checked. Seventy-five percent power applied. Brakes released. The plane lunges forward. Then props given a full bite of the moist, md-morning air. A third down the runway, Constable

Outreach 35 is airborne. Gear up. Its camouflaged flat belly could be seen from the barrio it flew over.

Tony watched from outside the hangar door. The Provider was out of sight.

Operations Office

Upstairs, coded orders came by tele-type. Placed in Tom's hands. It would be his responsibility to inform his crew.

"Have everybody gather in ops." He said solemnly.

He heard Tony walking up the stairs. The steel reverberated. Could also hear some milling around, in the radio room next door. He went to operations. Quiet settled on the second floor.

"Morning, again." The group responded.

"Constable Outreach is being closed. It's an administrative shutdown. They're consolidating two outstations. Each one of you will be informed of your next assignment. Just get ready. Protocol goes into effect now. While we have a bird in the air, our primary attention will be directed there. This will be the last op ordered from this station. When the plane returns, Tony will begin executing our aircraft disbursement plan. I personally appreciate all your efforts. Let's get to work. Sorry, folks." Tom walked from the room.

Aboard Outreach 35

In route – DZ Alpha

198 kilometers – 123 air miles

Initial bearing: 116. 28. 29

Friday – 27 September 1985

Ten minutes into the flight, Lester and pilot review drop procedures. Co-pilot flew while listening. Lester carried his picture of the drop zone for visual orientation. He returned to the cargo compartment for pre-drop inspections.

"Pilot, Load" Lester called on intercom.

"Go ahead Load."

"Pre-drop check, complete."

"Load. All remains as briefed. We'll go radio silent in five minutes. Reminder, no intercom until we're out. Across the border. Co-pilot will give a countdown to going dark."

"Copy."

Lester marked the time for silence. On the same picture, his own notes provided visual checkpoints. Estimated time by checkpoint was marked. As they flew, he visually checked landmarks. He estimated time to "Greenlight." His visual confirmation of the DZ, greenlight and time hack on his watch indicated drop time.

"Crew, Co-pilot. Counting down to radio silence. Ten, nine...four, three, two, one."

Lester removed his headset. It gave him freedom of movement. Prevented microphone keying. He re-checked his parachute. Reviewed emergency procedures. Crossed himself. And, watched for the greenlight to illuminate.

Without connection to intercom cord, he became acutely aware of the engine sound. Their vibrations through the airplane floor. The outside air rushed past the open ramp. He had been in this scene before. He felt the engine response to throttle pull-back. Nose went down, in a descent to low-level insertion. Below radar interception.

Nearing DZ, the pilot would pull up to drop altitude. That was Lester's cue to prepare for drop. Today's drop would begin at one-thousand feet above ground level. Dropping below that altitude before the drop was complete.

The front-end crew flew. He handled the drop. Watching for the tree opening on the DZ. He felt the nose pull skyward. Engine throttles tweaked to maintain drop airspeed. He was intent on watching for the green light. The tree-tops whisked rearward beneath the ramp. Terrain below sped by at 200 feet per second.

GREEN LIGHT illuminated. He checked for the tree line. Confirmed. He manually released the drogue chute by pulling the lanyard.

Nothing.

Pallets remained stationary. He pulled again.

Nothing. The drogue chute remained tightly bound in its green canvass outer covering.

"MALFUNCTION!" He yelled. But, he could not be heard.

RED LIGHT illuminated.

They had crossed the DZ on a Southerly heading. The plane began a descent for low-level escape. It made a right turn. Lester was without headset. Ran through the cargo compartment to the cockpit. It was hard to move with the parachute harness tightened into his groin.

"Co-pilot has the aircraft." Pilot pulled off his headset. "What happened?"

"Malfunction. Drogue chute. No drop." Lester replied in staccato. "But, we can recover. Do a modified LAPES. Fifty feet off the deck. I'll see to it that the pallets go."

"We didn't plan that." Co-pilot chimed in.

Lester bristled. "We can't go back without dropping. And, another attempt at drop altitude could draw attention. Who knows what else." Half shrugging, tightening his mouth to pursing lips. He barked, like orders from a drill sergeant.

"Low-level turns to that South-North heading. Tree-top level. Gear down. Flaps. Dive in and flatten out. 50 feet off the deck. Give me a 30° deck angle. Fly low and slow. Just above stall. And, screw the intercom silence."

Lester waited for pilot agreement. He nodded.

"After they're gone. Push the throttles against the stops. Clean it up. We'll beat feet back across the border."

"Let's do it." Pilot commanded.

The C-123, Provider was maneuverable at low speeds. It was an excellent tactical airframe. With high-mounted wings on the bloated body. The tail surface above and aft of the rear cargo opening. It was easy to load from the rear. It provided an excellent platform for airborne operations. With the ability for short field landing and takeoffs. Pilots working with it at stall speed was challenging. But, doable.

The Pratt & Whitney Double Wasp, 18-cylinder radial engines provided its power. It cruised at 150 knots. But, its stall speed was around 83 knots. In landing configuration, those speeds got much lower.

Lester scrambled back to the last pallet. The airplane was making swerving turns. The wingtips appeared to be touching the tops of trees. Resetting the pin to the lanyard, the drogue chute was ready. He put his headset back on.

"Loads ready."

The airplane made a hard bank to the left. Settling back into a South-North axis, picking up O64 heading. Lester watched the green foliage pass under the open ramp. Flaps extended. Landing gear went down. He felt the power pulled back. The airplane nose went down. He felt the airframe shutter as it pulled skyward to pick up desired deck angle. Props bit just enough air to keep the belly from flopping on the DZ.

Firefight at DZ Alpha

A Sandinista patrol was making their way through the forest area. They approached the converted farmland from the East. On the first pass to the DZ, they heard the approaching airplane. The patrol strained to see through the overlapping trees. Commander Pallais glimpsed a camouflaged airplane heading South.

It was impossible to determine size or type of airplane through the forest canopy. By the sound, he knew it was not a jet. The heavy throated roar of 36 cylinders keeping the airplane frame above the trees.

Contras, in position had waited overnight in a wide perimeter. Surrounding the drop zone. Special Forces operator had lead one contingent to the East side of the DZ. Part of the force which had set up 50 meters inside the tree line. They protected the East side from surprise intrusion.

Overhead sound of the airplane broke the concentration of the Sandinista soldier on point. He walked within 25 feet of a Contra adversary, dug into position. Contras deployed in an arc. In the path of the Sandinistas route of travel. The patrol had walked into the Contra perimeter zone of fire.

This was not a designed ambush. Sandinistas got to within 5 feet, when one Contra fired first. Killing the soldier on point. The first shot caused others fearful surprise. Turning their attention toward the sound of first shots fired. Sandinistas returned immediate fire in the general direction of that sound.

Rapid fire expended 50 rounds immediately. The surprise was enough to cause immediate trigger pull. Seeing the advancing Sandinistas, others on perimeter began to fire. Exposing their positions. The local patrol spread left and right of their path. They sought secure positions. Some opted for the camouflage of jungle greenery.

There was little area between opposing forces. The Sandinistas maneuvered around and among the wood. Locating the opposing Contras. Effective fire began to claim lives.

When the shooting slowed, those on the perimeter began to fall back. The firefight continued as the Sandinista force moved forward. The Contra force had reduced their numbers by one...then had lost two. Finally, three dead. The remaining Contras retreated toward the drop zone. Remaining insurgents reached the tree line.

Seeking distance from their approaching enemy, they moved through the scrub. Across the drop zone to the other side. They would meet up with their fellow Contras in the West tree-line. The Sandinista force only pursued them to the East tree line.

Sporadic automatic gun fire covered the Contra retreat. The gun fire was in their direction. But not aimed at them.

Modified LAPES

Outreach 35 made second approach to the DZ. At a much lower altitude.

"DZ in sight." Copilot called.

"Descending." Pilot was in control of the yoke and pedals.

Commander Abdel Pallais watched an airplane clear the South line of trees. It appeared to be landing. Landing gear was down. It descended. Its tail close to the ground. Fuselage lifted nose high. The engines roared. Producing a huge cloud of dust. The sound reverberating off the surrounding trees. The airplane danced fifty feet off the roadway. It was a huge suspended target.

The Sandinistas refocused their firepower on the slow-moving airplane. Aiming. Firing in bursts of six. At a slow, large moving object.

"Greenlight!" Pilot called over intercom.

He felt pallet-shutter, transmit through his feet. As the pallets exited, the Sandinistas watched three large objects fall from the airplane.

Outreach 35 was receiving incoming small arms fire. The Provider pilot pushed the throttles full forward.

"Load, were taking fire." The plinking of 7.62 projectiles against the airframe lasted five, long seconds.

No response came from loadmaster. Lester was not responding.

The first pallet exited the plane, dropping flat on the bottom surface. It skidded to a stop and remained upright. The corner of the second pallet dug into the dirt roadway and tumbled. It came to an abrupt stop. Three meters inside the brush. East side of the DZ. Scattering supplies as it came to a stop. Decorating the green shrubbery.

The third pallet carried Lester from the aircraft. It dug in immediately. As it first tumbled, it slammed to the ground.

Bouncing initially, Lester cart-wheeled to a stop. The pallet flipped end over end. Breaking the nets and spewing supplies over the roadway. Away from where Lester lay.

Escaping Outreach 35

Applying full power to the engines after chute release ensured altitude gain. Cargo was gone. Escape the only priority now. The fuselage cleared the trees at end of the open bowl.

From the ground, it appeared the flat belly drug through the tops of trees on the North end. Tree tops waved furiously. Outreach 35 had cleared the trees and disappeared.

Nose slightly up, the deck angle was decreasing. Gear and flaps returned to their stowed position. The pilot nosed his plane over for level flight. At low level, Outreach 35 was escaping. Heading back to Tegutch.

'*Those damned Americans,*' thought Commander Pallais. His men had interrupted a planned insurgent operation.

Sandinista patrol emerged from the tree line. Triumphant in their firefight, part of the contra party lay dead. Others had escaped.

On the other side of the field, the remaining Contras had listened to shooting at the airplane. They remained concealed. Looking out upon the DZ, they could see scattered supplies. And, a pallet reflecting in the sun.

They watched as the Sandinista patrol spread out on the field. Watching them move around the dropped supplies. Supplies and weapons dropped for them. They now belonged as property of the Sandinista Patrol. The men, sorted through these gifts.

The observing Contras fell back. Deeper into the woods. Slipping away through the wood behind them. This small group had lived to fight somewhere else. Their comrades gave the ultimate sacrifice. One dead in the East side wood. Two lying dead near the road. One of them the Special Forces operator. He had given his life.

Aboard Outreach 35

Drop Zone Alpha Escape

Latitude: 13.8990 North

Longitude: 86.1560 West

Central Standard Time (GMT -6)

Friday – 27 September 1985

"Load…" The pilot called for the third time. With more intensity.

"Hell," he said to the copilot. "We got to get out of here. I'll fly. You go check on the Load."

Still wearing his headset, the co-pilot unbuckled his harness as the pilot applied power. The copilot proceeded to the cargo compartment.

The cargo door remained open. Pallets were gone. No loadmaster on the plane. Copilot grabbed the seat supports to keep himself from rolling down the cargo floor.

He could feel Max power ordered from the engines. The plane banked left to pick up the return exfiltration point. It leveled in a high-speed retreat at 300 feet. The airplane had escaped the hot DZ. It settled into a smooth exit. The co-pilot hooked up to the intercom cord near the crew entrance door.

"Cargo is gone and so is Lester." He reported to the pilot.

"What? Say again!"

"Loadmaster was left behind."

Silence fell between the two pilots. The flight out of enemy territory was going to go fast. Assessment of the airframe damage from small arms fire could done at Tegucigalpa. Once in Honduran airspace, they would report the loss of Lester Russell.

Drop Zone Alpha

Surprised by his finding, a young rebel shouted for his commander. Keeping his weapon trained on the unconscious, face bloodied person. He waited for others to come to his side.

"Americano?" He asked his leader.

"Si." The leader replied. Then knelt to see if their find was still alive. Others gathered at the sight of this human finding.

Testing his carotid artery, the leader exclaimed "This hombre is alive!"

Commander Pallais thought briefly. "…*could shoot him here and be done with it. Or, not. What would my leaders, past or present do? More, what would they want me to do?*"

Commander Abdel began yelling orders in Spanish. "See if there are any medical supplies…You, find small trees…Ve! Ve! Ve!"

His medical knowledge limited. He knew first aid. Had performed life-saving on battlefields before. '*Assess the injuries. Stop the bleeding. Determine if there any broken bones. Immobilize those damaged areas….*'

He could not know if this captured American airmen had a broken back – or neck. That he would only find out after examination by a doctor.

Some of his men sifted through the delivered supplies. Those, sent to find medical items, returned. Rope netting from the pallets and the two small stripped trees were set near Lester. They would be used to construct a makeshift stretcher. One rebel returned with a canvas bag displaying a Red Cross on a white background. Another, brought a Jerry Can filled with water.

Lester was placed on the makeshift stretcher. They set upon working over their found prisoner. A bone was protruding near the neck but had not yet pierced his skin. The face covered with blood dabbed with water and gauze, found in the medical kit. Cuts and abrasions under his ripped clothing, would have to wait. Until examined by medical professionals.

"You, tend to him." Commander Pallais barked. "The rest of you, come with me." They returned to the scene of the firefight.

Commander Pallais returned to the deceased Contras. He went from body to body. Giving each of his men an assignment. He said, "strip the body. Take everything. We will bury the corpses. And, divide what we find."

Each man took a body.

"Comandante, tenemos un otro Americano."

Walking toward the voice, he looked down on the Special Forces operator. Shaking his head. He said, "do not strip this man. Go through his pockets only."

In his pockets they found a crucifix and religious medal depicting St. Michael.

"We will not bury this one." They did as he said. Finding nothing that would link him to the American army.

"You two," pointing at gathering soldiers. "Cut two trees about 7 centimeters thick. We will wrap him in the clothes of the dead Contras."

Following his orders, the two completed the tasks he had ordered. The Special Forces operator was wrapped in the clothing from the stripped Contras. They made a second stretcher to be pulled as a sled. Pulled by one man. The other bodies buried. One man pulled the sled to where Lester was tended.

Lester's battered body was placed on the constructed stretcher. Blood still pumped through his veins. His mind held in suspension. His soul somewhere in limbo.

The rebel leader knew the place he would take these bodies. One for recovery. The other for temporary burial.

'Rancho Perez was the only place within a reasonable distance from this area. It would take a day of walking with the stretcher and dead man on the sled.' He said to himself.

He assigned four stretcher bearers and one to pull the sled. His men formed for movement. Stepped out in the direction Commandant Adbel Pena-Pallais pointed them.

Constable Outreach Operations

"There's been an accident!" Jake reported.

Tom McKay looked up from his desk, "Where?"

"Constable 35 is coming back with unspecified damage. Delivered their load. Took fire."

"Notify the tower, will you?"

"That's not all. We lost the loadmaster."

"Dead?"

"Don't know. He's on the ground."

"What?" Tom questioned through a puzzled look. "How?"

"Mishap. Pilots didn't say. They were taking fire," he paused. Then said, shaking his head, "Don't know."

"Keep me up to the minute."

The station chief dialed the attaché at the embassy. Entire operation was looking at another international incident. If reported to the press, shit would roll downhill in a hurry.

'Hondurans already wanted us out of here.' He said to himself. *'Now we get caught dropping supplies across the border. And, I've got a kid in custody. This won't go well for the agency!'*

"Col. Matthews. Hurry." He waited. "Fred, we have an incident. Lost a man in Sandinista territory, near Jalapa."

Fred Matthews took the news in stride. "Don't tell me anymore. I'll get my folks to track your communications. Take this upstairs and we'll see how we address the situation. Get back to you."

Tom had lost one man before. In another operation in Beirut, one of his agents fell to assassination. Held by one warring faction. It was a time when they were getting ready to leave the city. Shutting down that office. Their operation had become compromised. Agents identified. It took all their exit strategy. Everything they had planned, to get out of the city. Before another tragedy hit. That one was too close.

This one could bring down the whole house.

'How do we handle this one?" He wondered. *"A beginning thwarted. Snuffed before taking hold. Loss of a human. Damage to an airplane….'*

He walked into the ops. Heard Jake talking into the phone. "Tony, you got to get up here. Our Provider is coming back with damage."

"What? How? I'll be right up." Tony replied. "Tell them I want a flyby to inspect for damage."

"Any word on the plane's location?" Tom interrupted. Now hovering at a desk in ops.

"Yes Sir. They radioed inbound. Arrival here in about 10 minutes. Tony requested a flyby to check the damage."

Station chief said nothing. Others in the room were intent on what they were working.

"Listen up folks." Tom demanded. "We got a real pickle now. I want you guys following all communication. Embassy is monitoring ours. Russell may be dead. If his body is found," he paused. "When he is found, it'll lead right back here to us."

Tony arrived from downstairs. "Heard." He said before anyone could say. "Going to scan for any obvious damage. Before they put her on the ground."

"Can we see…" One of the ops people interrupted.

Tony answered. "It won't tell us of any internal damage. It's the plumbing I'm worried about. But, we can look at the outside. Before they put her on the ground."

"Binoculars." Chief handed them to Tony. "I'll go with you."

The two bounded down the stairs and out the side door of the hangar. Toward the ramp. The chief brought a radio to communicate with ops. Tony had a hand-held multi-frequency radio. Between the two, they had communication with ops and tower. Ops could document their emergency. All that information needed later to extinguish the fires this incident would ignite. Airplane damage had to be determined. The next step would be putting the bird, safely on the ground.

A major accident caused by any aircraft at Tegucigalpa would be newsworthy. Toncontin only had one runway. A crash on the runway would send diversion notices. All the inbound flights would be notified. Commercial airplanes diverted. Some requests for delayed departures. In this case, any accident caused by agency equipment would be front page news. Tony listened to tower frequency on the hand-held.

"Tagucigalpa Tower this is Constable 35." Squelch trailed the message.

"Constable 35 this is TGU tower." The controller replied with a heavy Spanish accent.

"TGU, requesting low pass, flyby for damage assessment."

"Constable 35, standby." Controller answered. He could make no decision without a supervisor's approval.

Moments went by. Then pilot repeated, "requesting low pass, flyby for damage assessment. Declaring emergency."

That got the controller's immediate attention and interest.

"Flyby approved." He coordinated with other controllers.

The fire department rolled equipment to mid-point on the runway. The tower supervisor called the airport manager.

'This is no longer a closely held incident. Quiet and secrecy was removed. It will be reported to the State Aviation Agency. The entire aviation industry and the world will see. Know. Feathers ruffled. Attention called to the operation on our side of the runway. It is fodder for the Honduran President. Accelerating Constable's removal from the field.' These thoughts went in succession. Tom felt pressure building.

The Office of South American Affairs in the State Department was informed. A Special Officer, from inside the Executive Office Building would walk to the White House. Briefing the President of the United States.

Tony searched the sky to the south for the Provider. "There he is," pointing for Tom's benefit.

The plane seemed to fly normally. As it banked for the low approach, Tony had the binoculars planted to his eye sockets.

"Ramp looks up and OK. Cargo door open. No fuselage damage. None visible." In an afterthought, "Ask them how it flies. Hydraulic problems? If they've got control..." Tony thought aloud. "Do they have good brake pressure? ...We can check the rest on the ground."

Tom repeated the questions into the agency radio. Shortly, operations replied.

"Good aileron and rudder response. No hydraulic problems."

"Tell them no exterior damage noted. I'll see them here. Put it on the ground!" Tony said, displaying a look of disgust.

Tom repeated what Tony had said. Operations replied.

"Pilot reported, 'All OK. Landing'..."

Tony had no comment. His mind working on which aircraft systems to check first. Who he had to bring in for repair. All the thoughts arriving in his mind, simultaneously. He was the one to focus. This was his arena.

There was no crash to be. Tony just turned away relieved. Facing the hangar door.

Silence persisted. Seconds felt like minutes. Two minutes felt like an hour.

Toncontin – Outreach Hangar

Latitude: 14.0342 N

Longitude: 87.1301 W

Central Standard Time (GMT -6)

Friday Night

27 September 1985

It was late evening. Tom McKay was still in the office. The King Air Crew had arrived for their pre-flight and night surveillance mission set-up. The radio room was buzzing with fragmented messages. Everyone was tying the threads together.

The door opened slowly as not to disturb. Jake stepped in quietly, closing the door behind him. "We lost the Super King Air. They're being recalled to Panama, tonight."

"No more electronic surveillance?"

"Nope. Informed a minute ago. Citing the airplane incident."

"We really need those eyes and ears."

Tom thought of the drop that left Lester on the ground. He needed that nightly surveillance to keep the picture in view. It would give him comfort that everything was being done. But, not to be.

"Just wise protection of their assets." Jake paused. "If I can say…"

Tom interrupted, "Go ahead. We're all in this."

"With a man down in hostile territory. The Sandinistas will be watching for another incursion. We have no idea if…and where Lester is. He could be dead. On the other side, if he's alive we wouldn't know where to look."

"We know where to start!" Tom's frustration built. "Get me a secure line to Virginia."

'It was an appropriate hour to call my wife. I need to hear her voice.' His reasoning.

Dialing, he thought about the call received from his daughter. '…Rebecca pleading. Robert being arrested. Sally's strength through all this. All this, required of her. How lucky I am. No, blessed. To have married a woman with such strength. The entire well-being of the family rested on her shoulders. Now, I need to lean on her.'

The U.S. government had spent millions of dollars training him for this position. They told him how valuable he was to this and past operations. He knew, 'I am only one spoke in the wheel.'

The hub ran through the U.S. Embassy to its under-secretary for this region. From there, the line of communication got a little fuzzy. But, at some point it was combined into agency intelligence. And, passed on to the Office of President of The United States.

"Sorry, we can't take your call right now. Please leave a message. We'll get back to you. (Beep)...."

He did not leave a message. He, surprised that someone didn't answer. Tom checked the number. Even though he knew that was his daughter's voice on the recording. *'Maybe they are out. With our son? A family evening.'*

He dialed again. The same voice. The same message.

"Sorry... (Beep)."

"Hi, sweetie. I talked with my supervisor. He said it would be OK to take a few days off. Working on my schedule...Hello, anybody listening."

"(Beep). If you are satisfied with your message, press one..." He listened to the whole litany of choices. Pressed one. Hung up. It was a point of worry. Needing to be in two places at the same time.

'A substitute would have to be brought in from San Salvador. Given a major briefing. Brought up to speed. They were working on it. They had promised it before the incident. Who knew when they could make the arrangements? It would probably be after a few sleepless nights.'

He noticed a sink hole opening where his stomach should be. He rocked back. Looked at the ceiling. Breathed deeply. Closed his eyes. It was going to be a much longer night. Not being able to talk with his family. Agency activities pushed family to the side. Occupying his time. Mind split between country and family business.

His cot and blanket were part of his professional gear. When the call came back from his wife, he would be at the other end of the phone. Jake's replacement would have to transfer the call. He could sound fresh. Eager to talk with them. There would not be the opportunity to touch the liquor he had in his hotel room.

'That would only complicate any discussion they would have. The King Air crew departed. The whole building was quiet. No rushing wind through the

alley below. The birds nesting in the hangar kept their peace. He would have a talk with family. He would be semi-rested. All would be well in due time.'

Tom slept on bursts of twenty minutes. Nervous energy was still present within. Throughout the night he would awaken to the footsteps in the next room. Rolling over, he would go for another catnap.

Sun filtered through venetian blinded windows. It was his signal to rise for the day.

"Excuse me sir." A voice spoke, through the opening door.

"Yes. Come in. I'm awake." Lifting slightly. From the sagging cot.

"Got a message…The King Air has returned to Howard. Here it is," the operator said.

'KA 175 returned base…Mission terminated….'

On that night's departure, the electronic surveillance equipment was shut down. With exception to radar jamming capability. The King Air sped toward the coast. Flying West. Across the Gulf of Fonseca, it reached the Pacific coastline. Once in international waters, it turned to a heading of 150 degrees. Toward Costa Rica. Making a brief stop in San Jose for fuel.

The U. S. Embassy in Costa Rica had been notified. In the event they had small opportune cargo that would fit into the baggage hold. KA 175 continued into Panamanian airspace. The bird headed East toward Panama City. This asset and crew returned safely to the DEA. It had arrived at Howard Air Base in Panama.

"Coffee, sir?" The night hawk asked. Extending the paper cup filled with black liquid.

"Thanks."

"Any calls – overnight messages for me?" Tom sipped at his coffee. He hated himself for being anxious.

"No sir."

The door closed. Tom dressed.

Lester's Last Known Location
Saturday

It is 118 kilometers from Tegutch to those points west of Jalapa. Drop Zone Alpha.

The night had been quieter than most in the forest. Commander Abdel Pallais reassessed. His prisoner had not awakened on the trek East. Pulling a map from his side pocket, he calculated the distance to the only highway leading to Jalapa. Half a klick to the South, they could intercept Highway 29. It leads North and East. Passing Rancho Perez.

'On that road. At some point. Some time. A vehicle would pass.' He thought.

Informing his troop, they struck out for the Highway 29. Finding transportation for this injured prisoner. And weary stretcher bearers.

'Once depositing their prisoner. They would return to the field. The supplies, ammunition and weapons dropped on that piece of ground, would not go away. His men could get new weapons. Salvaging what else they could. The rest would go to aid the local militia in Jalapa.'

Commander Pallais decided to walk along the roadway. In plain sight. He would hope to discovery by local drivers. Walking for one hour. The faster he got his prisoner to Rancho Perez, the better. A stake bed farm truck approached from the West.

"Hola, Señor." The leader greeted the driver.

"Buenas dias." The driver replied.

"Our injured friend needs a ride to Rancho Perez. Can you help us?"

The driver became weary, when he looked at the men carrying weapons. He had heard that Contras were in this area.

'Where these Contras? Or were they the Sandinista Defense force?' The driver questioned

His question was not answered. It was not his business. He was only to provide the requested transportation.

The injured airmen and dead soldier loaded on the floor of the stake truck. Commander Pallais entered the passenger side of the vehicle. With all others on board, the aging truck labored under the weight of this party. It came up to speed slowly. Bounced down the road due to aging shock absorbers.

Rancho Perez

Senora Juanita heard the vehicle coming toward her house. She opened the screen door slightly. Reached for her shotgun. It was always loaded, near the front door. Leaning against the door jam.

She was never without a weapon. Away from the house she carried a snub nose .38 - concealed in some part of her clothing. Next her body. In the heat of the day, she would become aware of the heating gunmetal. Making her aware of its presence.

Juanita also carried a short survival knife. It was smaller than the N-40, Russian fighting knife. The shape of the blade, slight sloped forward. The point would draw blood like a pin. Black handle and no hilt guard.

In early marriage, her deceased husband had shown her defensive movements. And, offensive strikes. Used by Soviet Special Forces. The Spetsnaz and KGB.

She later trained in Sytema. The Russian Martial Art. She learned hand-to-hand combat, grappling and knife fighting.

As the vehicle lumbered toward the house, it became recognizable. A truck from a neighboring farm. But the speed at which it was traveling was unusual. She knew the owner. The driver slowed with squealing brakes. It came to a stop within five feet of where she was standing. She recognized the driver. Then Commander Pallais. Surprised to see the commander riding. Now exiting the cab.

"Señora." Abdel greeted. "We have an injured soldier. And, one dead."

She walked quickly to the rear of the truck. Issued militia clothing covered two lumps as they lie in the heat. Clothing used like sheets.

Pallais' Men removed both bodies from the stake bed truck.

"Where can we put him?"

"For now, take the corpse to the side of the house. The injured one, bring inside."

She saw *'this soldier'* was not wearing a uniform. His denims were torn from his lower half. Blood was covering most of the cloth. His face of dried blood. Scratched and gouged.

'...As though someone had dragged him face down. Across a rocky surface. To purposefully inflict damage. Draw out the blood.' Her thoughts led to further examination. *'Most likely he has broken bones.'*

She had been in firefights. People died and wounded. These were not wounds from bullets or shrapnel. She knew battlefield first aid. How to tend wounded soldiers. She also knew, when there was no use. For those who were about die.

"This man looks like he is about to die." Words came from her lips. "And, why did you bring him here?" She asked the Commander, with disdain in her voice.

Juanita's piercing eyes focused on Commander Abdel Pena-Pallais.

Toncontin - Outreach Operations

Latitude: 14.0342 N

Longitude: 87.1921 W

Central Standard Time (GMT -6)

Saturday – 28 September 1985

The pilots of Constable 35 were in debrief. Again.

"…We were in radio silence. No intercom."

"So, you have no idea how he left the aircraft?" Tom questioned.

"That's what I'm telling you." Pilot said.

"A well-planned mission. Something the three of you have done many times in the past. Turns to shit with one of our…" Tom collected his fluid thoughts. Roiling. Muddying the liquidity to slow his words. "One of *your* crew is left in enemy territory. And, we don't know how it happened?"

The pilot and co-pilot looked at one another. Saying in unison, "Yes." They made no mention of the malfunction. Leading to a second pass. The modified airdrop.

Tom did not question them any further. Saying with disbelief in his tone, "OK, guys. Write it up. Get some rest. You're flying the bird out of here. I'll have Jake give you a call."

Tony inspected the Provider. After his initial pass, he reported to Tom.

"Collected most of the rounds on the aft end. Tore up the skin on the bottom of the ramp. Couple of holes in the fuselage. It's more work than I can repair here."

"You notified people up your chain?" Tom asked.

"Not without telling you first."

"What's next?"

"I can patch it to prevent skin tearing in flight. El Salvador has a repair station. One-time ferry flight. We can send it to our hangar in San Salvador. The bird will be out of commission for at least two weeks." Tony paused. "If you want, I'll make the arrangements."

Tom nodded. Tony left his office.

The silent operation shutdown was progressing. With one less plane in the hangar. They would disburse two remaining choppers to Danli. The aviation side just got a little simpler.

This was not the only thing on the Tom's mind. On the personnel side, he had a man missing in Nicaragua. He wondered.

'No reportable radio interception. It could show many things… that the Sandinista government was not aware that we had been there… Or, it could mean they were keeping tight lips.'

There were separate and differing operations going on. Right inside their borders. Managua was fighting a war on three fronts. They left the Northern Border control to the locals…and, intelligence gathering to their Cuban partners. Fighting had not flared. But, it could at any near moment. Future time.

Cuba supplied a military officer and trainers to oversee. Action on hardened intel was coordinated through one military officer. He became responsible for training the local militia and recruitment of foreign nationals.

Managua only knew that the contra revolutionary force was a presence to deal with. Local commanders were in control. Cuban and Soviet counterparts acted in advisory roles with all the local units. Breakdown of counterrevolutionary forces was reported end of battle. Local militia and political education were handled from the mayor's office. There was activity persisting on the Mosquito Coast. The Southern Border with Costa Rica reported sporadic fighting. Yet, little on the northern tier with Honduras.

The agency had tried to turn Jalapa. Sending trained agency insurgents into the Northern town. They worked from within. It was a slow process. Nationalism had a hold on the collective thoughts of its citizens.

Long range patrols inserted at various locations. One would go in and another would come out.

Contras probed. Caused havoc for small communities. The force grew with disgruntled nationalists and mercenary volunteers.

Office of Military Attaché in the U.S. Embassy

Tom McKay and Fred Matthews spoke.

"I've taken full responsibility."

"You weren't there. Yes, the end responsibility falls on the section head. But, you didn't cause him to leave the airplane."

"There shutting us down. DEA pulled their surveillance. We have a boy, prisoner in custody. And, I got a man lost in Nicaragua." Tom said heatedly.

"It's only been twenty-four hours."

"I'm not supposed to second-guess decisions from Virginia. On anything," Tom McKay said.

"Nobody has made decisions about your man, yet."

"This is more than frustrating."

"I understand." Fred Matthews replied. He picked up the receiver, "OK. Tell him, I'll get back in five minutes." Turning back to the discussion, "There is another Central American fire. I need to consider."

Tom interrupted, "So, that's it?"

"I'm afraid so, let me think about it. I'll call you later."

The two men stood. Shook hands, signaling a finish to their discussion.

"I'll be waiting for your call." Tom exited. "Don't make me wait too long!"

He drove back to the airport. Travel time to the airport about 15 minutes. Time enough for private thought. Saturday traffic would pick up after noon.

Riding the roller coaster of emotions, Tom had regret. For sending Outreach 35, knowing of the impending shutdown. How thankful he was for his family. Even with the bumps, twists and turns. And yet, with regret. Piling on to his personal attachment, came the losses and operational mistakes creating them.

'The humanity of one person set other actions in play. Equal and reactive forces. Agency presence caused two international incidents. Well-meaning in the start. The dung was about to fling.'

On the personal side, there were three prongs to the fork. Each fit one of those differing emotions. The first was his wife. Second, his son. And third, the emotional appeal made by his rebel daughter. *"Come home, daddy"*

The fork drove deep. The sky was falling. Footing was becoming precarious. He wondered if his mere presence at home would have prevented his son from being arrested.

'Things happen over which most of us have no control. Would the things that he had control of, prevented that incident? His professional activity set a different view. His son could have made a better selection in friends? Was his being away the factor in marijuana usage? Was it experimentation or a regular occurrence?'

He tried to put blame out of his mind. Thinking of situation and family member affected.

'I am complicit, by fact. I am his father. There were things that I could've done. To prevent the set up for this incident... What have I done to my wife. Married after my first tour, she expected normalcy. What I gave her, something entirely different. Three tours later, we had two children. She wanted to be a mother. Wanted her husband at her side. I gave her something else. Single motherhood. Loving your children was not enough to make up for a husband away. My career choice failed our marriage. Our children. That's what she has endured!'

He said aloud, "I could've given her more of myself. I could've given my children more of me." To a chorus of honking horns.

He spoke to himself out-loud, when he expected a solution to come. In these thoughts, he was only speaking to himself. Punishing thoughts.

'Coulda', shoulda', woulda. The lament of all acts. Wishing they had turned out differently!'

"And, now my sweet daughter was pleading for me to come home." He said aloud, pulling into a parking space.

There was no immediate answer to his questioning. Being in two places. Dealing with the work created by ideology. Difficulty created by parts spinning out of control. He would have to go home.

It wasn't that he couldn't turn this operation over to another capable agency manager. He didn't want to. Seeing things through to their end. The way he operated.

'Caught in your own dichotomy. Two desires of equal import, coming together in the mind of one man. How does one choose? Commitments signed and sealed. Two wives at the same time. The wife and mother of your children.

The agency depending upon your best trained mind. Two things being true. Two lovers creating children of their own.'

The child from the other mother was operation Constable Outreach. He had people depending upon his proper management. Life and death sat on each side of the balance beam. Operational goals dependent on correct action. Superiors expecting certain outcomes. Not anticipating mistake, losses or failure.

He thought it strange to be verbalizing. But it was his only solace without answer. A complex situation.

'Where does one draw the line? Which is the most important of the commitments made?'

He sat. Not immediately exiting the car. Three minutes passed.

Tom climbed the metal, grate stairs to ops. He hesitated before opening door. All hands worked toward the coming closure of this station. Summoning all personnel to his office. Tony was the last to arrive.

"Okay," Tom said. "We should be drinking beer by the pool right now. But, you all know we have a situation. I need a recap. I want everything looked at. Provider pilot debriefs. LRRP and King Air reports. Radio chatter. And, I want Danli involved. Find out what they know from our 'boy prisoner.' I mean everything! We must know what went wrong. You must help the agency get ready. For whatever comes." He looked around the room.

"Yes, sir," came the response in unison.

"We've got a man down in hostile territory. We don't know where he is. If he's alive? But, we must go under the latter assumption. We must get him back. *We* leave no man behind!" He paused one moment. "Let's get moving. I'll check on your progress in an hour."

Tom had to let his crew do the work that they had been assigned. After their hurried departure, he sat in the relative silence of his office. His mind raced back to the last days in Saigon. Racing forward to his family accompanied tour in Berlin. He lost a man before. Beirut. He wasn't about to lose one now. At least, he didn't want to accept the loss of Lester Russell.

The ringing phone startled him. The surprise ended this mental trip. He picked up the receiver. Spoke expectantly.

"Tom McKay."

"Daddy?" The young female voice on the other end was immediately identifiable.

"Hi, Sugar, how are you?" He asked his teenage daughter. They spoke for ten minutes.

Nearing the end of the day, Tony knocked on Tom's door.

"The Provider is ready for its ferry flight. Call sign will be Albatross 35. The H-34 will be re-positioned to Danli. This afternoon. The only airframe left in the hangar will be the Huey. Expecting an agency bird this afternoon. It's bringing your interim Manager."

"Thanks Tony. Got a few minutes?"

"Sure boss."

"You know our situation. I'm going to go home for a few days. Family stuff. Don't know the ops guy they are sending. We'll meet him together."

"OK." Tony said, cautiously. More a question than answer.

"Give him all the support he needs." Pausing, "But, keep your ear to the ground. I'd like to be able to call you. You are *very* important here."

"Sure thing. Is there anything else I can do for you? Personally?"

Tom started to open the lid about his family. But, clammed up.

"No. Personal. Not really." He added, "Watch out for our people."

Tony sensed a conflicted person, "Looks like someone pulled the rug out from under you. I'll help where I can." He said, standing to leave the office.

As Tony reach for the door handle, Tom's phone rang. Again.

Rancho Perez

Latitude: 13.8955 N

Longitude: 86.1503 W

Central Standard Time (GMT -6)

Saturday – Late Morning

28 September 1985

The Commander's men lay Lester on the double bed. Tying his limp, left arm to the bed post. Right arm had been positioned and tied to his rib cage. Commander Pallais and Juanita Perez standing over their prisoner.

"I ask again." Juanita voice riled with anger. "Why did you bring him here?"

"You were closest."

"I have my own problems."

"Si. But, you are as much of a soldier as are my men."

"No!" She raised a stiff index finger to his nose. "Yo podria matar a este pedazo de estiercol. As hurt and angry as I am, I want to kill him!"

They left the room.

"We will call Major Sanchez. Your prisoner will be his responsibility." She said. Anger shooting, but not hitting it's mark.

Commander Pallais attempted to calm her. She pushed him away.

Abdel Pena-Pallais came from the town of Leon in Nicaragua. It was fast becoming second largest city in the country after Managua. A city of historic Spanish colonial churches. Located only 90 kilometers from Managua. It was a place where priests and professors made their discoveries. Founded in 1524. Abandoned in 1610 due to earthquakes.

He carried the name of a famous priest and poet. Did not know how he got it. The popular priest-poet of the same name had lived here until 1940. Noted for his words on social issues from a Christian perspective. After the Somoza family dictatorship took hold, he had a change of thought. After losing all his personal privileges.

Gangs with a profit motive fell. Gangs with the heart of Robin Hood stepped forward. Pallais associated with the former, reinvented himself as a soldier for the people. The person could change allegiance. But, inside remained a habitual part which desired personal gratification.

The commander was born in 1946. Reared in a poor family. Supported by the church.

In his own mind, he had developed his own brand of social justice. Socialist views combined with religious leanings. In his early years, food was a scarcity. The clothing on his back came from neighborhood handouts. He was a street kid. Following older children. Moved from Leon to Managua. Living his life among others like himself. Learning early that theft could get him what he wanted. Later becoming an enforcer for a gang.

His potential as a professional guerrilla realized. Living on the street, he connected with others holding similar thought. The uprising in Dominican Republic called to him. There was talk of turning that part of the island into a mini-Cuba.

At the urging of a friend, he traveled to get in the fight. Making his way there in 1964. "Constitutionalists" overthrew President Reid Cabral.

The Dominican Civil War started in April 1965. Four-and-a-half months later it ended. He had no viable income. Or, means for supporting himself. Able to evade capture and ultimate jail time, he slipped into Haiti and returned to Nicaragua.

He soon followed the Sandinista code. Having returned to Nicaragua he found himself reengaged through the Sandinista National Liberation Front. Participated in the uprising. Performing whatever the regional organization asked of him. He rose in the ranks of their rebel army.

That's where he had met Miguel Correa Velasquez. The husband to Juanita. Together they fought on the Mosquito Coast and the Costa Rican border.

Miguel Velasquez held his marriage in high esteem. Displaying a reverence toward his wife, Juanita. He talked about her to Abdel. Repeating the same story, twenty times. Soldiers held onto what they remembered of family life. Tattered pictures pulled from shirt pockets stood in for physical presence.

Being a friend and holding him in respect, he permitted Miguel to repeat of the same story every time. It was a fact that he had come to know Juanita without ever having placed eyes on her.

After returning to Managua, Abdel spent time with a woman. The young woman loved the stories that he told. Opened herself to him.

When she became pregnant, Pallais backed away.

He could not become the spouse of a woman from this barrio.

Her pregnancy caused much consternation among family. He was not ready to settle down. For that family, he would have to give up his war-wander-lust. He departed in the middle of one night. He did not seek knowing his child. Her memory became a distant nagging, of what could have been.

That was about as close as it came for him, to be carrying memories in his pocket. Most of his memories came from scars. The twisted mindset of a rebel living on the battlefield. He was not what the people of this town considered a normal man.

He knew '*there were no normal men. Only dead ones.*'

He transferred in the last declared State of Emergency, 1982. After the death of Miguel, becoming a commander of rebel forces in the region around Jalapa. The Jalapa district had become his domain. And, a chance to connect with Miguel's widow.

It was the place where Juanita Perez-Velasquez was awarded a living estate. A stake of land for giving her husband to the fight against imperialism. She renamed it Rancho Perez.

Her husband had been dead for two years. Abdel thought he and Juanita might settle down on her ranch. Pipe dreams. She wanted nothing to do with him. She tolerated him. And, at times shunned him.

Flyer meets Cuban Influence

The family farm was a remembrance to most in Jalapa. Families knowing one another. Giving in the community. Sharing the burdens of others. One family. One purpose. The Mayor was gracious, checking on Juanita. Giving her the feeling of safety. This had become a war zone of insurgents, brought by the United States.

Major Sanchez drove fast on the dirt road. A plume of dirt particles rose from behind the automobile. Dust collected on the trunk lid. His intent was to get the doctor to the prisoner immediately.

"This, my fine doctor was a find!" The Major said. "An American soldier. Placed in our hands."

"He will do you no good, if he is dead. Or, if I die in this automobile!" The aging doctor replied. Referring to the speed. The driver's manhandling of the car.

"Mis disculpas, if I have scared you with my driving. We are here." Flinging open the car door on arrival. Rushing into the house.

The doctor sat motionless. Crossed himself. Collecting his thoughts. Then checked himself for a wet spot. Sitting for a moment, before exiting the car.

"Thank you for coming, Doctor." Juanita greeted.

"Where are they?"

"The dead soldier is on the side of the house. And, the other is in my bedroom."

"I can do nothing for the dead. Have him placed in a temporary grave." The Doctor replied.

Commander Pallais and three men, carried the body to the edge of the pasture.

Near a lonely tree, his men dug a temporary grave.

Marking it with rocks. Placing them in shape of a cross.

Knowing the general location, could return to it.

Juanita opened the door for the doctor to enter. Ushering him into her bedroom.

"He is unconscious. He has broken bones. Cuts on his face."

"I will do what I can." The doctor replied. "Remove the rope restraints!"

Juanita and Major Sanchez untied the patient. Then stood at the foot of the bed. Doctor moved to the one side. Looked at the twosome watching his movement around the patient. He shook his head. Three Sandinista litter carriers crowded at the door.

Commander Pallais returned to the porch for a smoke.

"There is much to do here. Señora, please stay. Everyone else, out!" Doctor said, then added, "This is my domain. If he survives, it is God's will."

Juanita escorted Major Sanchez to the door. Her hand pushing in the small of the Cuban's back. She closed the door behind him.

The other men standing near the door had opened a hole for the Major to pass. The passage way filled by a closing wooden door. It closed on the faces of the litter bearers. Major Sanchez ordered the three to leave the house.

Doctor and Juanita

"I can't tell if there is any damage to the spine without an x-ray. The first thing we will do is stop any bleeding."

Juanita nodded. "What can I get for you?"

"Hot water and rags."

Juanita went to the kitchen. Started the water boiling. Returned, as the doctor finished his assessment.

"Will sheets do?" Juanita asked. Receiving a nod in agreement from the doctor. She began tearing the top sheet from her bed. Tearing it in large squares, setting them near Lester's feet. "I will be back with hot water."

Doctor discovered Lester's broken clavicle. His upper left humerus and ribs were also broken. A bone protruded through an opening in the skin. Near the clavicle. It had worked through the skin in transit from the drop zone. He would have to reset the clavicle and stitch the wound. The humerus he would also set. But, the broken ribs would have to heal on their own.

Juanita returned with a bowl of hot water, placing it on table next to her bed.

"What should I do?" She watched the doctor pull on latex gloves.

"Clean the blood from his face, while I prepare to set some bones." The doctor moved to the side of the bed, where the broken clavicle was exposed. He felt in and around the wound to see if the area was clean.

"Give me a rag with some water." He dabbed around the clotted blood obscuring the bone end, to expose the opening. The wound had begun to close. He would have to cut away the developing scar tissue to reinsert the clavicle. He went about the things of his learning.

Two hours after entering the bedroom, doctor and Juanita reappeared. Informing Major Sanchez of the patient's condition. Commander Pallais joined the circle.

"He will survive what I did to him. The extent of his wounds can only be partly seen, without further examination. He is in coma. We need to move him to the hospital."

"That is impossible!" Interjected Commander Pallais.

"If you want this man to live, we need to examine him. Take x-rays." The doctor retorted.

"We will do as the doctor says." Major Sanchez said. His curt reply a notice of his command presence. His stern look at the commander, let him know who was in charge.

Rancho Perez

Latitude: 13.8955 N

Longitude: 86.1503 W

Central Standard Time (GMT -6)

Saturday

28 September 1985

An aging ambulance arrived at the door of Rancho Perez. With help, the Doctor placed Lester on the stretcher. Driver and helper loaded Lester through the rear door. Quick and caring efficiency prepared him for the ride to hospital.

The doctor rode in ambulance with his patient. Major Sanchez followed. It was shortly after 4 PM.

The crunching rock in the dirt surface rebounded off the trees, left and right of the road.

Tunnel effect amplified the sound.

Moving away, engine sound became muted. Sound disappearing as they turned on the road.

Once at the road, the vehicles could not be heard from the farmhouse.

Evening was Juanita's favorite part of each day. But, not this evening.

She drank 2 cups of coffee per day. One in the morning and evening. Sitting on the porch with a strong cup of Café Bustelo. Permitting her thoughts to collect and merge with evaporating aroma. Yesterdays and today, each presented individual challenges. As they do in every day of life.

Four days had passed since Jaime's disappearance. Whatever trail he might have left, was long since blown clean. The forest and the jungle rejuvenated every day. The smell and tracks of humans went away with time. Dew collected each night. Falling from the trees. Bathing the forest floor. Washing away the human smell.

She sorrowed. It ate away at her heart. With American presence, mixed feelings created deeper thought. *'Contras in the area'* and now *'two American bodies brought to my door. One dead and one barely alive.'*

Their arrival added weight to her thoughts. A mother's pain of separation from her child. Mixed with anger toward an enemy who took away her husband. Layers of thought complicating the peace settling in at dusk. Sundown would come shortly.

She had brewed 4 cups of coffee. In anticipation of sharing with Major Sanchez. She could talk to him. He listened. They communicated. She felt comfortable in his presence. Their ties went through her land of birth. The stark opposite was true when near Commander Pallais. She felt edgy when alone with him. Uneasy at the sound of his voice.

"Senora," the Commander broke into her thoughts.

"Si."

"My men are settling in for the night. May I sit?"

With caution, she agreed. "For a little while. I have cleaning to do. The mess left behind."

"I was told of your son's disappearance. Saw him last week. He brought you the papers I gave him?"

"Yes. I passed them to Major Sanchez. Do you think the Contras killed him?"

"I am not sure, Senora."

"It makes me sad and angry at the same time. When you brought the American, I wanted him to die in front of me." She admitted, "I wanted to shake the American. Get him to tell me where my son is. To get him back."

"Revenge, Senora?"

"The Americans were cause of much pain to my country. My family. Me." Emotion built in her. From her stomach. It buzzed to her head. Cuban life affected by American retaliation. Starting before the Cuban Missile Crisis.

"I am sorry, Senora."

"How can you understand? You are Nicaraguan." Releasing moisture came to her eyes. Collecting in the lower eyelids. She became silent.

Gathering her strength. Stiffening her back. Standing. "I have work to do. Good evening, Commander." Juanita walked past him. Through the front door, closing it behind her.

In heavy jungle, tropic and high mountain areas, forests replenish themselves. The heat trapped by the forest canopy. Against the cold of the night air, pressing down. Trapping a layer of moisture like the troposphere. Dew droplets collected overnight. Would fall like a small rain shower. Much like tears. Gravity bringing them to earth.

As in the tears rolling down her face. Strengthening the resolve of this hurting mother.

Jalapa Hospital

Ambulance ride took 20 minutes at a slower pace. Removing Lester from the ambulance, lifting him on a gurney. The emergency room was a temporary stop. Doctor spoke with the nurse behind the desk, ordering x-rays.

"I am concerned about neck and back. We don't know how his injuries were sustained. We must use extreme care in moving him. I want the photos taken now. We may discover hope in keeping him alive."

Lester's condition was critical. He'd been moved many times. X-rays would tell of any bone damage. Doctor had set the shoulder. Before positioning him to immobilize his upper right quadrant.

Even though set, it would be x-rayed to ensure a proper knitting of the bones. Back and spine pictures might reveal other areas of concern. Where nerves might be pinched in the spinal column.

"When he is done, bring him back to emergency." Doctor ordered. "Monitoring his condition will be easier."

The gurney wheeled Lester to x-ray.

Major Sanchez appeared. "The Mayor has sent this guard to watch over our prisoner." He looked at the guard. The defense force guard nodded.

"We're expecting the patient back. In one hour." Doctor looked at his watch. "Thank you for complying with my wishes. He would not have lasted one night without extra scrutiny and care," Doctor said.

Time passed as they waited for the return of Lester to a quiet side of Emergency.

"They had to take extra photos. We had difficulty in positioning his body." The technician said, wheeling him into a designated room. An intern hovered.

Lester's unconscious state was of concern. His muscles would twitch. It could be thought of positively. A good sign. Body nerves reacting to trauma. But with each move, each movement ran the risk of doing more damage to be repaired.

Any bone protruding into organs perpetuated internal bleeding. If he survived the night, more pictures would be taken in the morning. Doctor added x-rays of his chest and stomach.

The intern was of Hispanic origin and U. S. Nationality. Had attended medical school in Grenada. Graduated the year before the invasion in 1983. On the island seeking internship when U.S. Army Rangers appeared at his door.

"¿es americano?" The intern asked. Checking the hasty written instructions by the attending physician. "How did he get here?"

"Brought in without identification." Replied Major Sanchez.

"How did his accident happen?"

"That is of no concern. His initial treatment was away from hospital. Brought here by ambulance." The major did not like questioning from a young, curious intern.

"Sorry, Major. Just interested. He's banged up. We'll change the fluids and dressings. Keeping a close eye on his condition. If your guard hears him move, he can notify the nurse."

Ops - Toncontin Airport
Saturday – Late Evening

As Tom cleared the top of his desk, Jake knocked and entered.

"Embassy called. They received a message from Jalapa. A John Doe brought to hospital by ambulance. American. His injuries pretty bad. Think it may be our loadmaster?"

"Call the Central American desk," Tom said. "Need to see what they know."

Tom wasn't sure it was Lester. But, partly relieved to hear the report. If Lester was still alive, they should do what was necessary. To get him back. Radio operator put the call through.

"I'm not supposed to get in the middle of anything." Tom started. "Pointing to our existence here. But, I can't sit back and do nothing."

"I understand how you feel. That's not the point. You know your operation is steeped in politics. It stops at the White House door." Voice on the other end was dismissive.

"You know how this works. He'll just be some forgotten piece of flesh. And, no one will take the responsibility to extract him. I don't want this guy to die in Nicaragua."

"We're not even sure it's him. There's not much I can order from this office. But, we keep pressing for more information."

"Information? How about some intelligence?"

"Your interim manager will be arriving tomorrow. Shutdown is ongoing. Once turnover is complete, you are free."

"I leave tomorrow afternoon for Maryland. Shutdown will be completed before I come back. Everything is in limbo. I need to be kept abreast of this situation."

"Your people know how to stay in touch, don't they?"

"Yes. But, I'm asking a favor. Can you keep me informed, as well? Don't know how much my folks will be able to tell me."

"If we need to talk, I'll let you know."

The tone might work well with someone else. Tom wasn't taking it from someone his junior. "I'll call your desk when I hit the ground in Baltimore." He hung up.

Tom was conflicted. And, frustrated.

This was the part of his job he hated. The loss of a man in enemy territory could not have been foreseen. Timing of Tom's family problems was not opportune. But on both accounts, they never are.

Perez – Velasquez

Connection

1940 – 1985

Juanita Maria Perez

Born in 1947. To an American-Jewish father and Hispanic-Cuban mother.

Her father, Jaime Perez was a musician who followed the Latin Band circuit. His percussive skills had taken him through many small clubs in New York City. The Latin music scene. His talent career progressed, arriving at The Latin Quarter Nightclub. He walked through its service entrance during the war years. It opened in 1942 at Times Square. The proprietor, Lou Walters. The father of Barbara Walters. "The Quarter" was in a historical wedge-shaped building at 1580 Broadway.

"The Quarter" known for its festive floor show that featured chorus girls. Can-can dancers brought memories of The Moulin Rouge in Paris. Headliners, played and performed. Frank Sinatra, Frankie Laine and the Andrews Sisters performed regularly.

The dashing Jaime also performed at the Copacabana. Somber times during the war could be forgotten at the two clubs. The Latin Quarter rivaled the existence of Copacabana.

The stage bands, exchanged musicians. Jaime dreamed. Saw himself in the rhythm section. On the Timbales, backing Xavier Cugat. He attended an open stage call when the band was auditioning

"Good afternoon," he said. "I hear Cugat is auditioning." Jaime skipped unnecessary banter with the stage door attendant.

"True." Replied the attendant.

"I'm here to audition."

Musicians had heroes, just like everybody else. For Jaime, some came as musicians. Others fought for the rights of his people. The persecuted Jews. Blindness in one eye prevented him going to the fight.

For now, he wanted the audition with the Cugat Orchestra. He needed the job.

Jaime Perez got his opportunity. Played 'The Quarter.' The band was leaving on a swing to Cuba. The Cugat band manager offered him a short time position to travel with them. He packed his bags and sailed with them to Cuba. When Cugat moved on, Jaime stayed planted. He furthered his career in Afro-Latin music. It would bring him closer to fatherhood.

...In September 1946, he worked the percussion section with a big band at the Hotel Nacional. There, Jaime Perez met a Cuban dancer. Her name Maria Delores Carballo. They dated for three months. Their time together was filled with magic.

Organized crime had expanded across the Florida Straits.

This was a time in Havana, when some families sought new territory.

When Lucky Luciano presided over a meeting of "businessmen from the United States." Reported to be the largest gathering of mafia in the Western Hemisphere. Hotel Nacional hosted Vito Genovese. Joe Bonanno. Frank Costello. Tommy Lucchese. Santo Trafficante, Jr. And, Meyer Lansky.

In a surprise appearance, Frank Sinatra sang with the house band. Declared to be his debut in Cuba. Jaime and Delores met him at a party later that night.

After a show on Christmas Eve, they had their first physical encounter. They had fallen in love. That was the night of Juanita's conception.

Yet, they both were concerned for the direction Cuba was taking.

There was labor unrest. Especially centered in the hotel industry. Many of Delores' friends worked at the hotel. Attempts at organizing the group had failed. But when time was right, the workers demanded an increase in wages.

American visitors continued their visits to Cuba. Coming to see famed fiestas. Still Catholic oriented. Especially during Lent.

In most Latin American countries, a good Catholic child was named for a saint. The Saint Day closest the birth date. Or, a family Patron Saint. This ritual of honoring saints of the church taken from the Roman Catholic calendar.

After the war, young Cubans went to the United States for schooling. Higher education. To New York. The place to be where you could converse in your native language. Those who were socially connected, would go to

France, Spain, Portugal, other European cities. They would later return to find an unsettling scene.

Contrasts were beginning to be seen. Education reflected the physical modernity of Havana. Some of the newer sectors of Havana looked like a smart American suburb. It was modern. Yet, the older sections of the city held the Spanish charm. It was the attitude of cultural protection. That caused some Cubano Citizens to begin pulling back.

One of those in the background was Fidel Castro. A developing political leader. He labored under the presidencies of Machado, Batista and Grau. Becoming exercised over the crackdown on student protest. Gangster style politics displayed on campuses by imitators. They saw this means of gaining financial success. Modeled after heavy-handed businessmen, taking over their city. Maintaining power over others. Some students spent more time developing their criminal enterprises than attending classes.

Many American tycoons would sail there. The rich and famous seen. Much like others in Palm Beach, Hollywood or Monte Carlo. The area was becoming less Cuban. More American. Only the language and the service people gave it a different flavor.

Castro opposed "American imperialism." His fear was that corruption between politics and illegal activities was invading his country. It was taking hold on his homeland. Visiting Americans put on blinders to what was going on around them. While The undercurrent was washing away the stability for the rich. A black hand controlled the uneasy surface conditions of the day. Going to Mass on Sunday was a way to cleanse their sin of inclusion.

Corruption from organized crime was well entrenched. Rum Running continued. But not all illicit activities dealt with alcohol. There was modern day slavery. A heroin market place. Assassination by untraceable foreigners. Gun running. Cuba was a transit point for many of the ills that were emerging in the United States.

Delores' pregnancy was normal. She worked through the first five months. When she began to show some weight gain, comments were made. But, she didn't tell a sole. She came from a devout Roman Catholic family. It was an outward sin to be having physical relations before marriage. Not to speak of the religious difference between her and Jaime.

In the early months of Delores' pregnancy, things were getting unsettled in Cuban politics. A new political party formed, known as the *Cuban People's Party.* Jaime and Delores became politically active.

It was not important to her, that others be pleased with her political action. Her parents did not approve of her association with Jaime. Her love for Jaime grew everyday of her period in motherhood. Jaime was an attentive mate. He had not mentioned marriage. But, she could see in his eyes. The love he was also building for her. Together they would make a good team, providers and parents to their newborn.

Later in 1947, they produced a child. They named her, Juanita Maria Perez. She grew and developed through the turbulent '50s. In her teens, Juanita met Miguel.

Miguel Correa Velasquez

A Nicaraguan. He left home early seeking his own way. Born in 1945, he became educated on the evils of the United States of America. He looked upon Fidel as the father figure.

He came to Cuba during their stand against the Americans. The Cuban missile crisis. He applauded the outcome of the Bay of Pigs. Learning of the South American Revolution, proposed by Castro. Supported by the USSR.

He trained in Cuba. Under the Soviet controlled Cuban military. At twenty, he served as a rebel. In the Civil War of the Dominican Republic. In 1965. One day, he would enter the fight in his own country.

He returned to Cuba. That was when he met Juanita Perez.

She had been turned away from the United States as a boat person. Now finding herself being indoctrinated in a reeducation camp. She became a member of the Cuban Revolutionary Forces. Her reacquainting with Miguel was by chance. But, the connection being instant. Thereafter, she would not sway from the communist way of life.

Together, Miguel and Juanita traveled back to his homeland. He returned to the family farm in Northern Nicaragua near Jalapa. He and his mate settled there.

Many nights ended in passionate lovemaking. Soon, Miguel and Juanita announced her pregnancy. In 1967, their son was born. Juanita and Miguel named the child after their parents. Jaime Correa-Perez Velasquez.

After the demise of Somoza, Miguel took his place as a rebel leader. He moved his wife to Managua while he was away. It provided a place where she could find work.

Miguel commanded men along the Mosquito Coast for the Sandinistas. Fighting alongside, Abdel Pena-Pallais.

When their son became older, they returned to the family farm near Jalapa. The boy was in his teens. They wanted him away from the streets. Found solace being around family in the farming area, eight miles West of Jalapa center.

In a firefight with Contras along the mosquito Coast, Miguel lost his life. Jaime was sixteen. Juanita mourned his death. Did not remarry. Protected her son at any cost.

Jaime Correa-Perez Valesquez

Named for his grandfather. Combined with a family name from his mother. Carrying the last name of his legendary father. His father, a Nicaraguan Hero. To the nation of Sandinistas, he was as much a hero as Che Guevara.

His mother had hopes of Jaime going to an American College. To learn the law. Much like Fidel Castro. But, Jaime was interested in music and art.

He was constantly drumming on surfaces. Even now at the age of eighteen, whenever he heard music. Latin and local indigenous strains of the Latin beat. He would be tapping his toes, drumming with his fingers and in some cases, singing along. He held his Grandfather's talent.

It was the case of being guided versus personal desire. This young man held close. Pushed into taking courses that would lead to a pre-law undergraduate degree. The subjects of sociology & psychology. Downplaying his talent. The artist which grew in his inner soul. She would write his name as Jamie. The American name.

His father had spent too much time away from home. Jaime had no relationship with his father. He knew of his hero status. Promoted it for the sake of his mother. He felt cheated that his father did not spend time with him. Other local children would be walked to school by their fathers. He could only point to his father's picture. Telling everyone what a hero he was. Parroting the words of his mother and others who knew the elder Miguel.

He had no personal experience with Cuba. He did not relate to the Sandinista movement. He sheltered himself from political discussions. Yet performed, as an organ grinder monkey. When around people who knew his mother well.

His mother knew there was another young man inside. But continued pushing him toward social issues. The fact that she wanted him to learn psychology, meant that she had a plan for him. To become a hero of his people.

The schoolmates would feign friendship. They did so out of respect. For his mother and their parents. He had become a lonely young man. Jaime had become an island outcast. He seldom smiled in pictures taken with his classmates. The only joy he felt was hearing the local music. Even at dances, he would stand alone tapping his feet. Drumming on his legs with his hands. Feeling the music from the inside out.

He was a good student. He learned well. Performed as requested. But, disappeared into his own thoughts when not prodded into some collective action. He lived the life of silence. When there was nothing to say that interested him. At these points, Juanita would prod him. To take part in the activities going on around him.

The young man learned how to resurrect a smile on command. Inside he felt like an actor. Performing for an audience. Maybe that was why, his mother thought he would make such a good lawyer. He could suppress his own beliefs and feelings for the sake of accomplishing the job at hand. Many a good, talented person would perform like that over the course of a lifetime.

Someday he would be able to do what was in his heart. Not the heart he gave to his mother. The one who protected him. But to the world. His creative brothers and sisters. With whom he had an affinity.

He did not know how he came about learning of Ray Charles and James Brown. Most likely knowing their names came from their oppression. The suffering of black people. These two respected, musician singers spoke through their music. Rhyme and rhythms, making their people temporarily forget their own plight.

It must've been so. '*In the cotton and rice fields of the South,*' he thought. The singer chanters, who helped their brothers slave in field labor. From sunup to sundown. Individually, each slave being his own person by thought. Yet connected, by the color of his skin and the stories of his past.

Stories of slave ships coming from West Africa to Cuba. And other Caribbean islands. The Afro-Indigenous music that came from their history. The combining of rhythms. Language. Feelings of oppression. By forces you consider to be stronger than yourself.

The stories of one strongman standing up to the oppressor. For the oppressed. On behalf of others. That was the historical movement of Cuban Savior Fidel Castro.

That wasn't the story he would write about himself. His heart was in music. The telling of his own story. Not being the story told.

Danli, Honduras

Battalion 3-16 Headquarters

Latitude: 14.0411 N

Longitude: 86.5704 W

Central Standard Time (GMT -6)

Monday

30 September 1985

Today, Jaime faced truth of a different kind. Questioning about a world, partly created by his father. He was held in a dormitory. Locked room. Fed twice a day. Questioned once. Not knowing where he was on the map. He had been here four days.

"Let's go." The voice of a man came from behind a full-face mask.

"Where?"

"You don't need to know. Quickly! Quickly!"

He stood. The American grabbed him by the upper arm. Shoving him toward the doorway. The voice was of low timbre. Authoritative. Determined. The man, taller than six feet in height. Stopping Jaime before going into the hallway. Placing a hood over his head.

Pulling him this way and that. Pushing him forward down the hall. Light shown through the burlap bad. The weave tight enough to prevent seeing any full image. Twenty paces in one direction. Turning left. Shoved this way. Stopping. Jerked a different direction. Hearing a door open. Pushed into a well-lit room. Directed and shoved into a metal chair.

His keeper grabbed his wrists. One by one. Tying them to something on a flat surface.

Jaime heard the booted footsteps walk away. The door closed. He was alone. Different location. But, the same inner loneliness. Until the door opened. Closing as fast as it opened. He felt a hand on top of his head. It removed the hood.

The room appeared to be 3.5 meters long by 3 meters wide. On the wall he faced, glass from the waist up. Couldn't see what was on the other side. His wrists tied to a ring, on a metal post sticking through a two-foot wooden table. The chair he sat in had a high, hard metal back. The body behind him moved to his right around the table. He spoke.

"Are they treating you OK?"

Jaime did not know how to answer the man in his forties. Yet, he cautiously said "Yes."

"I am Col. Fred. Last name is not important."

"You are Jaime Velasquez?"

"Yes. How did you know?"

"We've done some research." He paused, "Jaime? Are they feeding you enough?"

"Yes, sir."

"How's the bed. It OK?"

"I think so. Not like mine at home. Harder. But, OK."

"Good." Col. Fred said. Opening a folder with pictures and typewritten pages. "Is that you?" He continued, sliding a picture across the table.

"Yes, but. The sign I'm holding." He stopped.

"Read it."

"I denounce the Sandinista Government." Raised his head with a questioning look. "But, I never said that."

"I know. It's a trick. Interrogators use them. They use whatever necessary to confuse, separate or divide. It's about the side you're on."

"It's a trick?"

"Yes, young man. There are a lot of tricks. Methods. To get you to talk. Embarrass you. Get your family or friends to believe you collaborated with their enemy."

"Why? I've done nothing."

"I believe you." The man in civilian clothes paused. "But, would they?"

"I don't know. Hope not. There is nothing to tell you."

"You have more to say than you know."

Jaime had no response.

"You are in a bad place. It is a good thing for you that I am here. Without our interference, you would be beaten. You might have died. We don't want that to happen to you. See, you were just at the wrong place and at the wrong time."

"The last thing I remember at home was seeing my dog. Blood. Coming from his throat."

"Must have been hard to see that."

"He was a good dog. My best friend." Tears gathered in his eyes.

"Sad. I know." He readjusted his seating position. "I had a dog when I was young. Just about your age. How old are you?"

"Eighteen."

"I've got kids your age."

A tap came against the glass. Col. Fred gathered the file. All but the photo of Jaime holding the sign. Denouncing the Sandinista Government.

Standing, Col. Matthews said, "I'll be back." He walked out the door.

Within moments, the door opened again. Another man entered. Shined boots. Bloused trousers. Green fatigues. Dark skinned. Like the indigenous people who inhabited this land before the Spaniards.

"What did you tell him?" He asked in Spanish.

"Nothing. I mean. I don't know anything."

The man stepped close. Moving behind the chair where Jaime sat. Grabbing. Pulling a bunch of Jaime's hair. Making him look at the ceiling. "I'll tell you if you know anything."

"Yes, sir." Jaime replied.

"Where is your mother?" The interrogator asked, releasing the handful of hair.

"At home. I think. It's been days since I've seen her. A week, I think."

"Do you know a Major Sanchez?" The tall soldier moved from behind. Walked around the left table edge.

"Yes. I saw him last week also."

"Are they lovers?"

"What?"

"Are Major Sanchez and your mother lovers?"

"No! I mean, I don't know."

"He visits her. At your house. If not lovers, then what?"

"I don't know."

"Is she a whore?"

Forcefully, Jaime replied. "My mother is not a whore!"

"You are a teenager. Naïve." Pushing a laugh from his belly. Through his lips.

"Not a whore! Major Sanchez has never been with her. She wants what is best for me."

"How do you know?"

"I know." Jaime said, questioning his own knowledge. "Not a whore. She loves me."

"What is this picture?" Soldier said, sliding the picture to him. "You denounce the Sandinista Government?"

"I never said that. It was a trick."

"There is no magic here. You held the sign. That's you. Is that not you?"

"Yes. No. I mean, it's me. But, I didn't know what I was holding. I was scared. Confused."

"Are you scared now?"

"Sort of."

"Have I beat you?"

"No. But," He started. Stopping to think. "You are different than the Col. Fred."

"Do you like him?"

"He's OK." Squinting, pulling back. "OK, I guess."

"Are you a queer?"

"No!"

"Thought I'd ask. You like him. But, you don't like me. Why?"

"I guess you're a nice man."

"But not, OK? I had hoped you thought more of me than that." He stood, placing both large hands flat on the table. Looking into Jaime's eyes. "I thought we were making friends. You must be a selective queer."

"I am not a queer!"

"We'll see." Turning his large body. Opening and walking out the door. Closing it behind him.

Relieved, Jaime sighed to let out the nervousness of the moment. He sat by himself looking at the large glass in front of him.

Constable Outreach Ops

Tony's steps became more purposeful. Quickness added to his stroll into the Tool Crib. He could hear movement upstairs. The soft walking personnel usually did not plant their feet, as much as he heard now.

He stopped in the middle of the crib open area, and looked up in a questioning pose. *'Children stomping their feet?' When told to do something by their parents? While desiring to do something else.'*

The people upstairs were ordered to dismantle their nest. By a supervisor they didn't know.

Tony thought that he never made those kinds of attachments. Shuttled from place to place, living with bare necessities. His tools, simple reminders of his home and no quantity of gathered items. Moving from job to job. Simply doing the job assigned. Then moving on. No attachments.

'What to do first? Am I supposed to pack up all this stuff? Folks in our business, didn't build nests.'

He had his personal tools mixed with the station tools. Those which had been left behind. By mechanics before him. A slim accounting of personal effects was visible on the desk, to his far right. Walking with box at the ready, he immediately saw personal items that he could start with. The clipboard. The coffee mug filled with pens. The stapler.

Personal items were not seen on this desktop.

His pictures, handwritten notes and other memorabilia tucked away. Rarely shown to anyone else. One always had to think about the impression given when someone saw your personal things.

He scanned the floor. It was clean of debris. No loose items. There was no dust or dirt accumulation. One swipe by a shop broom would clean the place.

'It was the opposite of building a nest. You had to keep a place clean like this. Looking rather sterile. For someone in the agency, you had to think of impressions. Who knew what someone else could make of displays? Personal effects telling who you were. Female birds built nests. My job will be simpler than those upstairs. I do keep a clean work area.'

Complimenting himself in silence. Reverberating words from a support staff instructor. Instructions on how to exist in the agency. At times like this, the attentive company employee looks back. Unconsciously, to their initial training.

"What to do with all the company supplies?"

This wasn't an emergency shutdown. Just one of quiet, quick and intentional movement. The fax stipulated. "Lights going dark…Should be accomplished within 72 hours."

"Time to get to work." He said, louder. Looking up. Yelling, "Do you hear that?"

The operations office upstairs had a plan and checklists for such incidents. Occurrences. Happenings. Orders. Breech. A controlled movement. Whatever this was?

This morning, the folks upstairs had been told of the official shutdown. Through a lengthy coded fax from the embassy. No verbal communication came by phone. Nor had it been provided to the "night-hawk," just finishing an overnight shift.

The shutdown supervisor had arrived yesterday. Briefed by Tom McKay. It would be the "new guy's" responsibility. The NFG would inform the other two Communications Specialists. One was about to arrive for duty. The other, might still be lounging in bed.

The temporary manager walked to the radio room.

At the threshold, he said "On the way to the embassy. Stay with the cleanup. I should be back in two hours."

The soft, stealth operation had taken place just inside the Nicaraguan Border. The aftermath of Constable Outreach 35 was the primary concern. It needed to be monitored. Actively. And, without being supervised. All operations people would be briefed on the latest shutdown requirements when he returned. But, added to the regular job, now they had two. Local sanitizing procedures. Including papers to shred. And, personal effects to gather.

The shutdown manager returned at 1110. Walking across the hangar floor, he stuck his head in the tool crib.

"Need you upstairs." He told Tony.

Tony placed the handful of gathered tools in the top tray of his tool cabinet. Following the manager up the metal stairs. Stopping abruptly. Without command, behind the young manager at the top.

Opening the Ops door, the manager barked, "Everybody in my office."

Tom's old office measured 4.2 x 6 meters. They had all been together there before. But, now addressed by another agency guy. Some standard office equipment dotted the walls. The gunmetal gray desk was from Navy surplus. The blinds always remained closed. One could detect the lingering smell from cigarettes smoked in this room. Nicotine penetrating the painted walls. They hadn't seen this room without Tom. It looked different.

Five persons stood in front of the gray Navy desk. Its top, free of any paraphernalia. Only a gooseneck lamp sat near the phone. Other than needing wiped-down, the scene was rather sterile. Tom's personal effects had been packed. The new manager was here to provide the most current closure information.

"It's an administrative shutdown. They're consolidating two outstations. Word is that everything is being moved to El Salvador. No specific location, yet. Just get ready. The embassy will notify us when the movers will be here."

The staccato delivery of short sentences indicated the seriousness of the earlier received fax. Each man standing, began to develop his own personal questions. Some could be answered. But, others would not. This wasn't time to inject personal thoughts into this abrupt change. Soon to be, flurry of activity.

"Let's keep moving. I'll keep you informed."

Each member knew their assigned duties. They had checklists. Most drilled into them at initial training. Mentally they had practiced what had to be done. It was time for the game to begin.

The Honduran government had wanted this airport operation shutdown for months. The embassy denied any knowledge of what went on in the outstation. The denials were like a broken record. It was if the Deputy Ambassador didn't care what their host country thought. The United States was at war. Returned to the Cold War by their Russian adversaries. After the United States lost at the Paris peace tables.

The fall of Saigon was proof to those in the intelligence side, that no one could be trusted. The buzzwords, "Trust but verify" were hollow. Their President was giving them a new faith in the system.

Not this, "namby-pamby, do whatever feels good" attitude. Held by some previous American administrations. This was purposeful. In protecting our Southern border.

There was strength in the Oval Office. President Reagan escalated the War on Drugs. He increased military spending. His "Morning in America" notion brought him a landslide victory in 1984. He wanted to end the Cold War. It was, "striving for peace through strength." That phrase brought smiling support from the United States military. Throughout the world, intelligence folks felt a new sense of meaning.

Yet, the Honduran political mood was turning liberal. An election to be held this year. It might reshape the cooperative agreement they fostered to now. It had become a dance. Between the strong-minded National Party of Honduras. And, the liberal factions that worked their way into the government.

The Honduran military was becoming tired of the fight. To which they were called on their borders with Guatemala, El Salvador and Nicaragua.

Potomac, Maryland

Latitude: 39.01796° North

Longitude: -77.20884° East

Eastern Daylight Time (EDT)

Tuesday – 1 October 1985

Phone rang at the home of Thomas McKay in Potomac, MD. Sally McKay answered in the kitchen.

"Fred. So good to hear from you."

"Good to hear you too, Sally. Is Tom Available?"

Tom's wife held the phone away from her in the kitchen. The long cord allowed her to step into the hall. Keeping the receiver at arm's length. Tilted her head and faced the upper staircase. Sally called.

"Tom, the phone is for you." She heard footsteps.

"Tom McKay."

"Tom, Fred Matthews."

Yelling downstairs, "I got it honey." He waited to hear the receiver click, as the handset settled on the wall cradle. "Tell me we got something."

"We found him. He's in hospital. In Jalapa."

"How do we know it's him?"

"Finger prints. Our source took his fingerprints."

"He provided finger prints?"

"No, he's unconscious. Our source is an intern. He went in to check on him. While in the room, he took the finger prints on a cup. He met one of our people to pass it."

"Let's go get him!" He perked up.

"Not that simple." He paused, "The source said they plan to move him. Didn't know when or where."

"We also have an asset belonging to them."

"Yeah. Clueless kid. Sheltered. Even if we tried a trade, initiation would have to be back channel. I'm working on that. But, it doesn't look plausible."

"What then? We let them whisk him off to a prison. Torture. Assuming he wakes up."

"Let's not get too far ahead."

"Damn it, Fred. That's my guy. It was my call to send the plane."

"For now, just take solace in fact that he's alive. One step at a time."

"I know. Might be getting too old for this," He paused. "Call again with any updates."

"When are you coming back?"

"Robert's hearing is tomorrow. Plan leaving on Saturday. Booked already. BWI-Miami-TGU."

"OK. I'll call you if anything else develops." Fred ended the call.

Jalapa, Nicaragua

There was little activity in Hospital Emergency. Nurses moved around their station as they attended to walk-in injuries. A guard sat outside one room holding patient "X – John Doe". Allowing those in white coats and nurse uniforms to enter. Recognizing anyone else of import, he would allow them to pass.

"Good morning, Commandant." The guard standing, half at attention

"Any trouble overnight?"

"No, Major."

Major Sanchez walked into the room where Lester Russell lay in coma. "John Doe" as he is known to all them. The attending nurse startled by the opening door.

"You startled me, no one should be in here."

"It's okay. I am Major Sanchez. This is my prisoner. He is a guest under your care."

"Yes, Major."

"Any news?"

"He's shown signs of responding to Doctor's stimuli."

"Reviving. From the coma?

"Too early to tell. But, his vital signs are improving. He wiggles his toes. Responds to touch in various places. All good signs."

"How much longer, before we know? He's must be moved soon."

"Again, too early. Why don't you speak with the Doctor when he arrives?"

The nurse finished her work. Passing by the Major on her way out the door. Major Sanchez stood looking at his charge. Intravenous fluid dripped. Hanging bags with lines ending at the left forearm.

The right arm bandaged all the way to the shoulder. Crossed bandages made an X across his chest. Betadine stained gauze covered his scapula region. His right arm immobilized, bandaged to his torso. Gouged skin was stitched. Cuts and abrasions were starting to heal in the open air. The room smelled of chlorine and Betadine.

Major Sanchez left the room. Walked out of hospital. Driving to the Sandinista Training Facility.

Today, ten new recruits would graduate from the guerrilla warfare school he commanded. The trainers worked at forming volunteers into fighting men. It was the first class. The school, a thumb on the nose to the CIA. Their attempts at changing the minds of the mayor and people of Jalapa had failed.

Hardening of Rancho Perez

An early model Ford pickup pulled up to the front of the ranch house. Juanita Perez exited the front door. Standing on the porch. Near her shot-gun. Recognizing the blacksmith exiting his vehicle.

"Hola, Senior."

"Buenas, Senora Velasquez." He had not seen her for near a year. Was not aware that she dropped usage of her married name.

"Major Sanchez said you would come today."

"I brought the grate for the window and the metal door. You will have to show me where he wants them placed. I also brought my strong son." Turning to him. Forcing the younger man to introduce himself.

"It is a pleasure to meet you, Senora. I am Miguel. The same name of your husband."

She exchanged the required pleasantries.

"Please, follow me." Leading them to the side of the house. "We will place the grate here." Pointing to the window of her bedroom. Leading them back to the porch.

"Por favor." she said. Ushering them inside. "And the metal door will go here." Pointing to the interior door leading to the same bedroom.

"Thank you, Senora."

Juanita watched the two exit the front door. Returning immediately, carrying the metal door.

"We will install this one first. If you must leave, the window grate can be done without you being here."

"Thank you, you are kind." Juanita watched them install the metal door.

The door had flat metal sides that would bolt to the inside of the door frame. Sturdy metal hinges, that didn't squeak. The door face covered by crossed, grate material. Welds made at many points on the sides, interior and back. The added touch was paint. Painted black. It did not match her interior. But, it had its own purpose.

An hour later, the job for the blacksmith and his son completed inside.

"Thank you, Senora. You bring great honor to our city." The elder man said.

It was approaching the time when she should leave for the ceremony. The dedication of Miguel Velasquez Training Facility. Closing the front door, she entered her bedroom. Admiring the steel door that was just installed.

She prepared. Putting on a dress. Touching her face with makeup. None required. But, that the lady thought so. Splashing perfume on her fingertips. Applying it to the pulse points of neck and wrists.

Miguel Velasquez Military Training Facility

This school was one of pride for the people of Jalapa. The first graduation ceremony took place today. Attended by the Mayor, families of the recruits and others. Juanita being the special guest. For whose husband, the school named. "Le Academia Militar de Miguel Velasquez." His widow, Juanita Perez-Velasquez would speak at the graduation.

It was 117 air miles Southeast of Tegucigalpa. The Sandinista Revolutionary Front planned to train many more fighters. These trainees prepared to fight. But, there were no divisions massing across the border. Only guerrilla fighters. Trained like them.

Being far from Managua, the Sandinista Government was realizing a new battle front. On the Northern forest border with Honduras. Small groups of opposing forces slipped through the porous border with Honduras. Supplied by the United States of America.

Establishment of this training camp was response to CIA. Their failed attempt at changing hearts and minds. This facility located outside the city limits, to the West. Local women cooked the food for the trainees. While their husbands went about normalcy in Jalapa. It was a community effort organized by the Mayor. Under the urging of Major Adolfo Sanchez, the Russian trained Cuban military officer.

Major Sanchez became Commandant of the Academy. Relocated here months before, he met with local groups in church. At holiday outings. In the town hall. To promote the need for a training academy. Shoring up the war effort against the Contra-revolutionary insurgency.

He had the Mayor's ear. The Mayor had the aging heart of a patriot. He would fight for the homeland. With the local militia, if needed. A reserve force, gathered to support the small police force. Citizen militia.

Mixed among today's graduating patriot trainees were young students. Their acceptance of taught beliefs. Being taught the historical truth about America, would help them in their fight. Should the Contras knock on Jalapa's door. Again.

They would meet their new leader, Abdel Pena-Pallais. He had just returned from an operation with three kills and one enemy captured. That captured soldier was lying in hospital. Known a Patient X – John Doe. Awaiting questioning. When he woke from his coma.

Commander Pallais was a proud man. He carried the banner. He wore the title of Nicaraguan and professional soldier. Up from the streets of Leon, he followed many Marxist inspired revolutions. In the Caribbean, Central and South America. Participating at the side of Miguel Velasquez on the Mosquito Coast.

He returned North. From the Mosquito Coast. Taught tactics, when not in the field. Would take the first graduates on a live patrol.

"Saludos, mi companero patriota." Pallais opened. "Es un dia glorioso para la revolucion!"

"Vive la revolucion!" The trainees responded.

Two other men standing with him were the Mayor of Jalapa and Major Sanchez. Seated behind them was Juanita Perez.

"Mis hijos de Jalapa," The Mayor began. "You are the future of our beloved Nicaragua. You embark on a historic day for our country. You will spearhead the beginning of our Northern Defense Force." He paused to the cheers of these volunteers. "Never has so much interest been paid to us of the Northern tier. To our President Daniel Ortega. Our representatives in Managua. Our national military leaders and our friends from Cuba. We say thank you!" He raised his right arm. Fist to the sky. "May God bless this emerging defense force and our nation – Nicaragua!"

Cheers of elation came from the men who stood before him. A mix of college students, urban workers and farmers. Training on weapons, tactics and first aid. And, military history. Of various nations. Well-rounding a soldier in these forms of training.

Major Sanchez had built this training academy. He planned to pass 1000 men through it in the first year. It was a matter of pride for the Cuban attaché. To stand before the first class of Sandinistas in this Northern Civilian Defense Force.

"Es con gran honor," he began, "that I stand with the illustrious Mayor of Jalapa. And, with a great warrior. Man, for our people, Abdel Pena-Pallais. He was trained in Cuba - for which I am proud. He fought along the side of great rebel leaders. At the side of Miguel Velasquez." He paused as the trainees erupted with cheers at the name of their national hero. "A man, I add," He paused for the cheering to subside. "Who was also a son of Jalapa…Carry the memory of this hero with you as you embark on your first mission in our region. Viva Nicaragua!"

He stopped. Allowing the audience to continue the chant "Viva Nicaragua."

"And now, allow me to introduce Senora Juanita Velasquez. The surviving widow of our great Miguel." As she came to the podium, cheers for her erupted. Tears fell from the eyes of women. They knew the hardships of their sister. They wept for her at Miguel's memorial service.

"Gracias, mi Alcalde. Gracias, Mayor Sanchez, militar cubano adjunto. Gracias Comandante Pallais. Gracias Gente de Jalapa." She waited for the people to get quiet. "Gracias a todos. I am proud that the name of my husband will live on through this academy. His loss was painful for me. Not only a loss, to my family. But, it was also a loss for our people." She stopped.

"My son disappeared a week ago." Saying it caused tightening in her throat. Tears formed. She maintained her composure.

"We believe my son was taken by the Contras. Looking out on these graduates, I see my son. I see him in your faces. Sons of the revolution. Protectors of our great town and region. You are trained well. You will be led by a man who is a Nicaraguan hero. Major Sanchez and our Mayor honor us, by establishment of this facility. I thank you for allowing me to speak on this grand occasion. Viva Nicaragua!"

Trainees filled with pride. Ceremony ended. Men standing before the mayor, Major Sanchez and Abdel Pena-Pallais accepted handshakes. Pats on the back. They were fired up. Ready to go. In one hour, they would leave. Their first stop that night, would be Rancho Perez. Before striking out on a seven-day mission.

Nicaragua

March to Rancho Perez

Latitude: 13.9120 N

Longitude: 86.1386 W

Central Standard Time (GMT -6)

Tuesday – 1 October 1985

This small unit struck out after the congratulations and tearful good-byes of females. Hugging and kissing. Departing with Commander Pallais in the lead. These new trained soldiers moved West on the Highway 29 toward Rancho Perez.

For a rebel like Abdel, using the highway to enter or leave a battlefield was for movies. Forbidden. Here, he realized that expedience was a sure way to get home out of the minds if his men. He could use this departure as a symbol for all in Jalapa to remember. As in the troops marching victorious through town after battle. He would march this group of young men out of Jalapa with pride and heads held high.

He planned the six-kilometer march. To stop in late day. Giving the men time to relax and reflect on this great day. It would be the cementing of those feelings of pride. Building on those feelings day by day, created great confidence among fighters. On this evening, they would stop at Rancho Perez. It was Velasquez Family land. Juanita's Residence. She, the widow of Miguel Correa Velasquez. The honored female of this region.

They addressed her as royalty. Had many Sandinista politicians visit the ranch. The ranch was a life estate gift from the country of Nicaragua to the Velazquez family. She renamed this plot of ranch land, Rancho Perez. She agreed to host soldiers and other para-military personnel on her property. Camping overnight. Welcoming them on behalf of the Velazquez family.

"Me gustaria aprovechar esta oportunidad," she started. "...To welcome you to the ranch of Miguel Velazquez – my deceased husband." The patrol remained quiet and reverent.

"Gracias, Sra. Velasquez," Commander Abdel Pallais said. "We are honored to stand on the ground graced by Commandant Miguel – my friend."

The men were directed to a small plot of ground, 100 meters from the house. While they set at making their camp, Abdel followed Sra. Juanita Velasquez into the ranch house.

The building was 900 ft.^{2} on the exterior. It contained a living area opening into the kitchen. Two bedrooms on the backside, with the cattle pasture 50 meters off the back wall.

Electric was present and used only when needed at nighttime. Phone lines ran from the city. To those who could afford the service. Or, others who were daughters of the state. The Mayor of Jalapa saw to the ranch having its own line.

Previous cooking was done on a wood-fired stove, still standing in the kitchen. But, she now used a small gas range. Gas delivery spoke to the importance of this ranch and the woman who resided here.

She opened the back door to the kitchen. And, the windows in the front of the house. The front door stayed open most days from sunup to sundown. It allowed the cooling air to whisk away the heat created by cooking.

"Como estas?" Adbel asked.

"I am well. You?"

"Beautiful speech today, for my men."

"I had difficulty delivering it. When talking about Miguel."

"He was a great man and husband."

"I have his memory with me every day. My son Jaime helped with that memory. His presence gave me strength." Pausing. "Now, I have no one on this ranch. He did his chores without question. He was about to go to college."

They chatted while she continued with her cooking. The festivities of the day, loosened her distrust of Commander Pallais. She talked of her plans in Jaime's departure for college in Managua. As his mother, she wanted him to start there.

But, finish at an international university. The state would pay. It was another perk for being the son of the war hero. Hoping he would make his own mark as a man.

"He was the man of the house," Juanita added. "I cry for him every day."

"I am so sorry Senora."

As the sun dropped below the western trees, lights were turned on.

"Have you thought about re-marrying?" Abdel asked.

"A woman always hopes her white knight will appear."

"Have you seen him."

"No. Raising my son became everything."

"I neglected that part of my life. For the good of Jaime."

Commander Pallais stood, "Maybe he stands in front of you. Yet, you do not see."

She said nothing. He was embarrassed by his forwardness. Thinking it would be a good time to exit.

"I must tend to my men. Good evening, Senora." He walked out the door.

Rancho Perez
Morning – 2 October

The sun had not broken from behind the Eastern tree-line. Haze from ground fog filled the air. Commander Pallais' men had broken camp. Gathering at the South end of the pasture. They awaited the return of their leader.

Juanita sat on the porch with her cup of Café Bustelo.

"Good morning, Senora."

"Commander. You move early."

"Yes. Training continues. We build on the acquired learning to strengthen each man."

"Travel with care."

"Senora. One more thing. I stand in front of you. Asking you to consider that I might be the man you seek."

She thought about his words before leaving her place last evening. The words today had similar overtures. He had interest in her. He kept his desire muted. But, spoke to her from his building feelings. A man would not contain those feelings for a long time. They would boil over. Or, he would whimper away.

'Which man was he?' She questioned.

"Good day, Senora." He marched toward the gathered fighters.

Hospital - Jalapa, Nicaragua

A nurse passed by the guard at patient's door. Entering. Something was different. Patients sheet kicked away. Partly covering one leg. The fluid bag was near empty. The intravenous tube disconnected from the syringe. The patient had moved since last checked.

Going bedside, she looked at his face. Then back at the bag. He moved. Eyes fluttered. His face grimaced. Then his body calmed. He was waking.

Moving back and opening the door. Excited, she told the guard to summon the intern.

"Qué es lo que necesita, enfermera." The intern asked as he entered.

"Se trasladó. Él está despertando."

The intern lifted one of "John Doe's" eyelids. He could see the pupil in reaction to his light.

"He is coming out of coma. Call the doctor on duty. We need confirmation of my assessment"

The nurse hurried to her station. Dialing the operator to summon doctor on call. Five minutes went by. The doctor walked with a purposeful gate. Down the hall. Rounding the corner near her station.

"Our John Doe is waking. Slow. But, a good sign. The intern called for you."

Doctor followed the nurse into the patient's room. Touching patient's foot with a pen. Pinching skin on the opposite leg. Sliding the pen top along his forearm. Nerve reaction to all three stimuli was a good sign. He too checked the pupils.

"There may not have been any spinal swelling. Nerves reaction is normal." Doctor said to the nurse.

Again, a grimace appeared on the face. Eyes partly opened. The body tensed. His upper body wrapped, to keep the arm and shoulder in place. With movement, nurse could see the pain transmitted through his facial expression.

"Can you hear me?" Doctor asked.

Lester opened his eyes. Moved to nod. Try to lift his head. But stopped by pain. Fell back limp, once more.

"Are you in pain?"

"Yes" He answered in a whisper. He closed his eyes again. Nurse covered his naked body with a sheet.

'Where am I?' He questioned. 'How'd I get here?' The pain increased. This person now realizing, feeling pain. Pain level description masked before, by his comatose state. Now increasing. His internal questions forming. Some answered soon. Some answers coming later.

"Good morning," the female voice said. With a heavy Spanish accent.

"Where am I?" The words taken from his internal script.

"You are in Nicaragua." Replied the doctor. The intern fidgeted.

The intern said, "I'll call Major Sanchez." Departing the room.

Activity around the waking patient increased. The tube connecting to a bagged solution reconnected. Shoulder dressing checked. Drapes were pulled back. Nurses came and went in a relay. One never leaving his side. Watching the hurried activity, Lester had trouble concentrating. The movement around him was confusing. His pain fluctuated.

The door opened to a brown shirted male.

"Good morning." The Cuban Officer spoke. "How do you feel?"

"Not so good."

"You have been with us for five days."

"How did I get here?" He asked again.

"You were found on a dirt road. An American airplane was dropping cargo. Supplying Contras. Your injuries severe. We rescued you. And now, you are my prisoner."

Lester's thoughts went back to what he could remember. '...Combat off-load. Pleiku. Vietnam. These men and women did not look Oriental. When *confronted always think first. The situation may not be what you think....'* A matron, woman, his mother whispered from his memory.

"It's fuzzy." John Doe said, from Lester's body.

"The Contras left you to die."

"Contra what?"

The aged doctor entered the room with the intern on his tail. Interrupting Major Sanchez. Sliding between him and the patient. Saying, "Disculpa."

"You must be in pain. We will give you something mild for now. You'll want more, shortly. Not too much at any one time. You have been in coma."

Lester had more questions. But...He recalled what he could remember... *'Name. Rank. Serial number. Lie. Lie. Lie.'*

The pain medication would take a while to act. Major Sanchez did not want one minute waisted.

"That was quite a load, they dropped ... What base did they come from? ... How many teams do you have in the area? ... We'll get the answers...." Questions seemed like rounds bursting from the muzzle of a weapon.

Lester heard the man's voice rattle. The Major's words purposeful. But, Lester heard only part of them. Slow to his own comprehension. Yet, hearing the sinister tone of their delivery. The man's demeanor was one of a seasoned soldier.

The pain medication began to take effect.

Jalapa, Nicaragua

Hospital

Latitude: 13.9214 N

Longitude: 86.1268 W

Central Standard Time (GMT -6)

Thursday – 3 October 1985

Overnight, the hospital staff had increased Lester's pain medication. After the increase, he slept through the night remainder. With the meter level of pain around two. He was experiencing managed discomfort.

Lester was now addressed as John Doe.

"Your doctor and I have arranged a trip for you." Major Sanchez announced. "We're transferring you to a prison hospital in Managua."

John Doe said nothing.

"The ambulance will be here soon. A doctor will ride with you. The six-hour trip may give you something to think about."

He exited the room. Insuring the nurses knew of his plan. John Doe was his charge. He needed to place him in a controlled atmosphere. As the patient felt better, frequency of interrogations would increase.

'Six-hour trip.' Lester thought. *'Managua? Prison hospital. None of it makes sense. They know my name. Is it John Doe? Name. Don't remember my rank. Or, serial number. Lie. What about the rest of the crew? Where are they? Hot LZ. Pleiku. Firefight. I'll have to tell them at some point.'* He thoughts mixed.

'Escape? How far would I get? Where would I go? Might even be a trigger-finger-pull away. Officer was right. Some things to think about. I'm tired. Hurt.' He drifted off into a drug induced slumber.

In the short period, he drifted in and out. He remembered walking in the briefing room. Among his own.

'Marines were holding their own. But, without the Combat off-load. Their ammunition would run out.' He drifted off again.

'He needed to slow his own thought. Thought created tension. Tension generated pain. Be more purposeful. Taking on the position of deniability.'

'North Vietnamese will get nothing out of me. Name. Rank. Serial Number. Date of Birth. Lie? Hell, I don't know anything. How long can I hold out? Before they kill me?' Drifting.

'Escape. Evade. Where the hell am I?' The thoughts changed. *'Freedom. I'm John Doe. Can't remember my serial number. I will be interrogated. May be tortured. They will attempt to twist my mind. They will turn my words*

against me. They will be relentless. They will come again and again. My strength will last if I believe in America's position.' He wasn't sure in whose body his mind had settled. He drifted on the sea created by the morphine given him.

Lester *was* going to be interrogated. By the Sandinistas. At a place determined by their schedule. When and where it suited them. He was a hated man.

Ambulance Ride

A military ambulance backed into the emergency bay. Two Cuban soldiers exited. Opening the rear entry, pulling the ambo-gurney from its locked position. Wheeling the gurney through the swinging metal doors.

"Hola, señores. Te puedo ayudar." The Intern greeted the two in uniform.

"Estamos aquí para satisfacer Mayor Sanchez."

"He is in that room. I'll take you in." Leading the attendants into John Doe's Room. Guard, at the door spoke to the soldiers in Spanish.

"Stand-by." Major Said. "The doctor is on his way."

He went to the two soldiers to confer. They discussed travel plans. The doctor arrived with a nurse right behind.

"We are going to give him something to relax." He nodded at Lester. "It will take effect almost immediately."

The nurse disconnected the intravenous line. Inserting a needle into the port. Pushing the plunger. Nurse placed a small piece of gauze across the needle entry port. Taping it to his forearm.

The Intern, Nurse and two ambulance crewmen placed Lester on the gurney. Wheeled him out. When loaded, the Doctor and Major Sanchez met them. Doctor and one crewman rode in the back with Lester. Major Sanchez sat on the passenger side. The five of them drove away. Only the Intern left standing on the loading dock.

Once outside the city limits, the driver pulled over. He went to the hood. Opening it. As if he was checking something. Major Sanchez exited. Opened the rear side door.

"Why did we stop?" The Doctor asked.

"Driver is checking under the hood. I'm making sure we weren't followed." When sure, signaled the driver to close the hood. Once more, they were on their way.

"Drive seven kilometers. Slow down. Make sure no one is behind us. Got it?"

"Si, Comandante Sanchez." He continued driving. The ambulance travelled Westward on Highway 29, seven kilometers.

"See anything?"

"No, Comandante."

"There is a road on the right. Take it."

The ambulance slowed to make a smooth turn. Driving onto a dirt road. Treetops touched from left and right. Forming a tunnel through overhanging greenery.

The Doctor yelled forward. "What now?"

"Do not be concerned Doctor." Major Sanchez yelled back. Turning back to instruct the driver, "Follow this to the farmhouse. Back in."

"Si, Comandante."

Upon seeing the farmhouse, Major Sanchez saw Juanita step onto the porch. When the driver turned around, Major Sanchez exited the vehicle. He went to the driver's side in the rear to guide the ambulance back.

"Hola, Senora." Talking over his shoulder.

"Major Sanchez. On time, as we planned."

They could hear the Doctor's voice outside the ambulance. When the rear door was open his voice was much louder. He continued.

"No se trata de un hospital."

"Yes, Doctor. There has been a change in plans."

The two ambulance attendants helped the doctor. The step down, with no loading platform was two feet. He wasn't expected to jump. Immediately, he started questioning the Major.

"What are we doing here?" Turning to Juanita, "Hola, Senora."

"This is where we are going to keep John Doe. You can remain his doctor. We will see that you are transported, as necessary."

"But, there are no nurses. The things that will be needed for changing his dressings..." He stopped short of finishing his thought. Major Sanchez interrupted.

"We have prepared as best we were able. The room prepared by our medic. If you don't find what you need, we will get it for you. Now, let's get him into the room." His words being final. He motioned for the attendants to do their job.

Carrying him through the front door. Through the open, steel hardened door. Into Juanita's bedroom. Placing their "John Doe" on her bed. Using leather restraining straps from the ambulance, securing Lester's both ankles to the bedposts. Securing his free left arm to the headboard post.

"That will keep him from thrashing around when he wakes up." Said one attendant.

"I protest!" The Doctor said.

"He will be OK. Senora Perez will see to it." Slowing his delivery with purpose. "Breath Doctor. Now, tell the Senora what regimen she must follow. She has provided medical help on the battlefield. She is capable."

"Qué clase de porquería es esto."

"Breath." The Major repeated. "Tell her what you want her to do. Now!"

"I protest. I don't like being part of this."

"Protest noted." Major acknowledged, nodding at Juanita.

Juanita touched the Doctor's arm. Her gentle touch calming. "Let us go to the kitchen. You can write down what you want me to do." She said with calmness in her voice.

"I don't see how this will help in his recovery." The Doctor said to Juanita.

"The Major is afraid for the life of this prisoner. We don't know who his is." She was interrupted.

"OK. But, I need my bag from the ambulance."

She told one of the ambulance attendants to retrieve it.

As Major Sanchez came out of the room, he closed the steel, braided door. Sliding the locking pin into the metal door jam. He sat with Doctor and Juanita in the kitchen. The attendants prepared the ambulance for travel.

Doctor pulled three vials of pills from the retrieved bag. Placing them on the table.

"This vial is for inflammation. He has swelling around the spine. No more than two per day. This one for infection. His shoulder. Every four hours. This one for pain. No more than four per day. Instructions are on the labels. He does not have any broken bones in his back. But, he may have ongoing pain caused by swelling around the spinal canal."

"What about other broken bones?" Juanita asked.

"His whole body was x-rayed. We set his shoulder. The broken bones set by us will heal in time. Broken bones in his hand and arm will heal. We immobilized the shoulder and right arm. The way we wrapped it. The coma caused by blunt force trauma. As he comes out. Begins to make a full recovery. He may not remember some things. Realizing his situation, he may become unsettled."

"How will he relieve himself?"

"He may need help in the beginning. That unfortunately, will be left to you. He must be bathed. Wounds kept clean. That will fall on you. But, as he gets stronger. He'll be able to take care for his own needs."

"I'll leave one of the ambulance attendants to help overnight." Major Sanchez added. "When I come back tomorrow, we change out the guard."

"I will come back with Major Sanchez." The doctor looked for the Major's acknowledgement. "That way I can assure I've done my work. Here is my private number. If you have a question about anything, call me."

When the doctor had finished, he was asked to sit on the porch.

The ranch given by life estate to the family of Miguel Velazquez. The state controlled what happened on this property. Dictated by the Sandinistas. Fulfilled by Major Sanchez. The keeping of this prisoner was an award to the state. Extracting the right information would be invaluable. It would make great propaganda against the continuing insurgency perpetrated by contra revolutionaries. And, the United States.

"We have no drugs to make him talk." Juanita commented.

"One thing at a time. I will get what we need. Su ayuda es muy apreciada. Senora." Major Sanchez bid farewell. On the ride, he spoke to the Doctor with forcefulness. Compelling his silence. Insuring that he would not repeat what had happened. The ambulance brought five. Left with three.

Danli, Honduras

"Code." The agent said into the receiver.

"Purple grass."

"Number of the day?"

"Two-six-four."

A moment went by as two in the office confirmed the code. Agent prepared to write everything transmitted over the phone line.

"How can I help you?"

"John Doe moved by ambulance to Managua."

"Hold on." The line went silent.

Another voice came back. "Where in Managua?"

"Don't know. Loaded him up an hour ago. Nurses told he was taken to prison hospital. That's all…."

"We'll tell your sponsor. He'll call you back, if he needs anything. Thanks."

Call ended.

The agent wrote notes on the call: "1300 hrs. Call short. Intern at Jalapa Hospital. Bits of information. John Doe moved to Managua prison hospital. Transmission recorded for review. Call ended at 1303 hrs. Estimated Exposure: Four."

Rancho Perez

Latitude: 13.8955 N

Longitude: 86.1503 W

Central Standard Time (GMT -6)

Friday – 4 October 1985

Major Sanchez stepped out of his vehicle.

"Buenos dias, Señora."

"Good morning to you, Major. You are early."

"Yes. I came to see the physical condition of our captive. Brought the guard, I promised."

"He breaths. Through the night he moaned. Yet he only woke once."

"You look and sound distressed." The conversation took a turn.

"I am. The thought of where my son may be. Alive or dead. Covers my mind."

"Senior Jaime would not have wandered off." He paused, placing his index finger to his chin. "I reviewed the final report. In the area where your dog died, the vegetation immediately revived. No signs there. Approximately 500 meters from this spot their trail was found. Our inspection of a known coyote trail showed heavy boot prints. Boots soldiers wear. They went for a Kilo. Toward the Nubarrones. Smaller footprints also. Tracking movement to the North and East. Lost the signs among a rock stream bed. He may be kidnapped. It has been eight days. No sign. I am sorry, Señora."

Juanita appeared strong on the outside. Yet, waves of uncertainty rolled through this mother's body. Waves created muscle tension. Put her stomach in knots, when she was reminded of her missing son. Unsettling fear for her child within her whole body. Thoughts generate into body response. Her love for Jaime was at the base of this mother's instinct. Her reactions generated from the emotions. Held within her.

Juanita felt twice betrayed by the Sandinista cause. Yet, she felt grateful for the life estate on this property. Giving her and Jaime a place for him to live. Where he could continue his schooling. Grow and graduate high school. Having graduated in Jalapa, the previous Spring.

Jaime was a child unaffected by the war. His mother preferred it that way. It kept him from seeing the horrors that come from man's greed. Need for control. For that, she was grateful. But, the bond that a father's attention develops, was missing.

Now, her son had disappeared. She felt he was taken by a force. Forces manipulating the Contra-Sandinista War. The Sandinistas would not have taken Jaime! Commander Abdel and his men fought the Contras at the opening in the forest. Two bodies brought to her doorstep. American soldiers. One buried on her property and the other lay in her bed.

"Do you think it was the Contra Revolutionaries?"

"It is hard to say, Señora." He paused. "It may have been. Suspicions are there."

"Who else, then?"

"Banditos? Smugglers? Americans soldiers? I do not know."

A shrill sound came from within the house. Both Juanita and Major Sanchez, startled. They moved through the front opening to the house. The only other human awake in the house was an ambulance attendant.

The rifle carrying guard followed them. Brought by the Cuban Major that morning. The guard left to protect Señora Juanita. Also, to prevent the escape of their captive.

A cause for patient concern sprung the ambo-attendant to John Doe's bedside. His surprise noted by his speech. He spoke.

"El prisionero grito."

"Did he move?" Asked Major Sanchez.

"An arch in his back." The attendant responded. "It was like he was having a bad dream."

Juanita had gone to the opposite side of the bed. She touched his bandaged arm. His body reacted. His eyes opened.

"This is the sign I wanted to see, today." Major Sanchez said. "I will call the doctor. Go get him." He left the room, taking the ambulance attendant with him.

"Can you hear me? See me?" She asked.

"Yes. Who are you?" Lester replied.

"I am Juanita. I am taking care of you." She replied, with mixed emotions. "You are safe here." She heard the Major's car start. Gears grinding. The crunch of rock as it drove away.

Lester tried to get up. Realizing he was shackled to the bed. A new face came near. Pointing the muzzle of his weapon toward her prisoner. He said something in Spanish and spit in Ward's direction.

"Imbecil," she blurted out. "…Escuchas en mi piso!"

Lester didn't need a translator to see the fire in her eyes. Or, the subject of her exclamation. The guard backed away.

Turning her glare toward Lester, her face softened.

The interrogations could begin. Lester could speak. He could move his head. Look around. His surroundings were not that of a hospital. He was in a bed.

'How did I get here.' One of his many thoughts.

'How long have I been asleep. What day is this?' He did not know what caused his pain.

"Are you a nurse?"

"No, mi compadre." She said with caring concern. "We found you. You are safe here," she repeated. Leaned his way.

"Are you ready for some solid food?" She asked, in a soothing voice. "I will make you something soft."

Lester nodded. He could not remember the last solid meal.

'…breakfast. Before take-off. Flying. Low level. A firefight? How many days ago?' He was not asking for the count. Just wondering. Watching the petite woman walk away. Turning his gaze to the soldier with the gun.

"He's going to stay with you, while I get the food." She said to her prisoner. Smiling.

Baltimore-Washington International
Saturday – 5 October 1985

"Thank you all, for seeing me off." Tom said to his family of three.

"Your welcome, Dad." Robert was the only one to reply. "Thank you for being with me in court." His sincere thought. Embarrassed for his father. Sorrowful for days of angst he caused his mother.

"When will you be back?" Jessica, his daughter asked. "Can we go somewhere, just us?"

Tom began to tear. Caught it before a tear dripped. "I promise. Your Mom and I will plan something. Soon."

The announcer called ticket holders for the American flight to Miami. Boarding began.

"Give me thirty days. Or, less. I'll be home. We can work on things together." Kissing his wife on the mouth. Placing hands on both children. Pulling them to his chest. Hugging them. Kissing his wife one more time. Turning and walking to the gate.

His thoughts mixed.

'...leaving again. My most important achievements were here. Behind me. Our man in a place so opposite this scene. Experiencing...who knows what? Love standing behind me. Comfort of a family who cares. Returning to the loneliness of a hotel room. Going back into the hot box...'

As he boarded and took his seat, the curtain fell. He was walking back into a black hole.

'...my mind has to be on Lester. Getting him back. Finding a way....' He hadn't talked to Fred since Thursday.

Rancho Perez

Juanita enjoyed cooking for someone. Other than herself. Returning with a plate of food and drink. Setting them on the night table. A flat surface turned to feeding table. She removed some items from the table-top. In a bit of housecleaning. Lifting and placing this feeding station to the side of Lester's bed.

"Ahis...." She said in Spanish.

She undid the leather restraints. Removing those securing his ankles to the bed posts. The guard stood. Grasping his weapon with both hands. Stepping one pace closer. Holding the weapon at ready, across his chest. He said nothing.

Then she moved to the secured wrist. Undoing it.

"Can you sit up?"

"Think so." As he tried, he winced with pain. Juanita helped swing his legs off the bed,

"How does that feel?"

"OK." He said, through lessening sharp shoulder and spinal pain.

She turned, looking at the gun holding rebel. "Ver. No representa una gran amenaza."

"We have some chicken and rice and agua." She announced, cutting into the chicken thigh. "You can't eat too much. All you've had, has been liquid. From the bag."

Juanita feed him in silence. Twice looking over her shoulder at the guard.

"Do you remember Patty Hearst?"

"Yes," Ward replied with caution.

"She was one of my heroines. Kidnapped to extract a ransom. Turning her allegiance to the SLA."

That was not how Ward had remembered the whole story.

"...Granddaughter to William Randolph Hearst. College student. Kidnapped in Berkeley, CA. 1974. Joined the SLA to keep from being killed. Robbed banks. Fugitive. Caught about the time of Paris Peace Talks. Claimed brain-washing. Tried in 1976...." He did remember. Beyond the Pleiku hot LZ.

"I was in Cuba. My husband," she stopped, crossed herself and touched her thumb to her lips. "He was sent to Angola, fighting with the Popular Front."

Lester listened, nodded and chewed. He discovered a new area of pain in his mouth. Wiping his lips with the back of his free hand. He tasted blood. On the back of his hand, a blood streak. It seemed more appropriate to eat than complain. Continuing the ingestion of solid food. He would need his strength.

"My son," she stopped again. Her lips quivered, "My son. He is missing. Eighteen years old…." Her body stiffened, the previous smile turned to a face of anger. Yet, she was hurting inside.

Thinking this would be a good time to engage, Lester asked, "Missing?"

The guard tightened his grip on the forward rifle stock. There was a cloud overtaking the room. Her tense stance had broken into the meal setting.

"Yes. We can only assume, some *Contras*," she added emphasis on the last word. "*Contras* kidnapped him from my ranch!" She became quiet. Body rigid. Standing as the soldier she was.

Lester did not know what to expect next.

'She had a son. Where was her husband? She wore no ring. This house. Metal grate on the window and door. Not a military setting. But, the guard…These few pieces of information did not fit.'

"Are you sure? Kidnapped?" Lester asked. Tasting the blood in his mouth.

"You know!" She said, with anger trilling her words. "I think your meal is over!" She continued. "What were you doing? What brought you to the open field where you were captured?" She thought she knew the answer. What she heard from Commander Pallais. But, she was trying to get him to admit it.

"I remember falling," he said. Then he stopped. His mind a jumble of thought.

'What would Yoda say?' Triggering other thought. *"When questioned, admit nothing… You will be out of the house soon. Away from your father."* The thoughts mixed. Confusing.

"What *would* Yoda say?" He asked aloud.

"Is that some code? Yoda? What is a Yoda?"

He did *"remember falling…looking at the sky. Feeling the excruciating pain. Hearing the gun fire,"* before there came a long black period. It was too much, too soon. Unfamiliar surroundings. Not knowing. Disconnected thought.

Danli, Honduras

Latitude: 14.0411 N

Longitude: 86.5704 W

Central Standard Time (GMT -6)

Monday – 7 October 1985

Agency contractors were in meeting with their lead interrogator, an agency employee. Three contractors, military trained.

"The Agency is going to put feelers out to locate Lester Russell. We got the call on his movement to Managua. Since then, nothing." The leader prefaced discussion. "In a separate communication, our Embassy has developed a memo. Referencing the youth, we have locked-up here. It is to be spread among the Central and South American Embassies. Each Embassy tasked with reaching out to their Nicaraguan, Cuban and Russian counterparts."

"What is our part?" One asked.

"We're to sift through photos and significant interviews with the boy. Come up with some plausible story on how we obtained him. Show our concern. Interest in returning him – unharmed, fed and happy. He has become a distraction. We've got bigger things on our plate."

"Sandinistas are really going to be pissed. When they see. Young, Mr. Perez holding up that sign." One contractor added.

All laughed, but the leader. It was a trick that they had played on many before. During training situations. Yet, they had used it on this unwitting high school student. It worked. They had pictures.

"He had no idea what he was holding up." Laughter.

"Besides patting ourselves on the back," their leader interrupted. "What kind of input do we have for Tegucigalpa?"

"We got the location. Background on the area where he was nabbed."

"It wasn't far from the DZ. Half way between where our man went missing...." The third contractor interrupted.

"Where Russell was finger-printed in the hospital. Sixteen kilometers up the road."

"Got those from our source in hospital. An intern."

All three contractors had commented. One rustled through files on the round table. Pulled a file. Reading agency notes on the inside flyleaf.

"Our contact. Intern. Had attended the medical college in Grenada. American students who weren't accepted to U.S. Medical Schools. Rescued in 1983. Found an internship in Nicaragua. Finishing his residency in Jalapa. Loyalty is to his medicine. Hippocratic Oath – Do no Harm. Indebted to Rangers who protected him. Got him off the island." Contractor reading from the provided information.

"The Sandinista patrol interrupted the staging of supplies." One lowered his eyes to papers and pictures scattered on the table.

"New training camp in Jalapa." Second contractor pausing, then said. "Not relevant. But, intel."

"Prisoner's mother is the widow of Miguel Correa."

"What else have we got on video and recordings?" Lead asked. "Tom McKay will be here shortly. We got to give him something to work with."

The conversation at round table, bounced for discovery to implication. From implication to usability. Jaime's physical condition was good. His mental condition played into lines of questioning. Cracking someone who knew little. Thinking they knew less of what was sought. The purpose for their discovery was raw material. To be used later. As it could fit into a much bigger picture. What Jaime thought he knew could fill a thimble. What he knew, could help them save his life. And, that of the loadmaster.

The plan was to use an information gathering technique. Good cop established a form of comfort and openness. In the second phase, an interrogator questioned using an opposing tactic. 'Bad cop' left the room when 'good cop' arrived. Back and forth it would go. Sometimes spelled with long periods of silence.

Tom McKay walked into the room. "Good morning."

Pleasantries and hand-shakes exchanged amongst the intel folks. Tom pulled up a chair. "What have we got?"

"Told that our man was moved to Managua."

"Managua? Yeah, no location. A prison hospital in Managua." Lead said. "The folks in Virginia are working up background on Nicaraguan prison hospitals."

"That surely complicates things. But, that tells us he's alive." Tom showed surprise. Yet, thankful. "When can I see the boy?"

"He's in the box now."

"Let's do it." Tom said.

"Who's up?"

"That would be me." The tall dark-skinned contractor raised his hand.

Tom looked at the man, saying, "I'll follow your act."

"No biting." Lead said, with a chuckle. They walked the thirty paces. Three went into the observation room. The tall interrogator, entered the box. Followed by Tom McKay.

"Stand up!" Interrogator yelled. "Show respect!"

Jaime stood immediately. Handcuffs had replaced the normal rope restraint. Secured, but with more civility.

"That's my good, little queer. Sit down!" Shouting orders. "Another associate joins us." Pointing to Tom, standing back to the closed door. "We won't play today. But, our time is coming. Right, sweetheart?"

"I am not a queer!" The thought was repulsive to Jaime. Yet, he was afraid of the large, indigenous looking man. "When can I go home?"

"When you've told us everything." Tom said.

"And, after our date." The tall one added.

"What do I have that you want me to tell?" Adding, "I'll tell you anything you want to know. So, I can go home."

"What do you think?" Interrogator asked, turning to Tom.

"Sounds kind of sincere to me." Tom replied.

"He is sweet, though. Yes, sincere. Like a girl." Pausing for effect. "I can't wait." Walking around the tables' edge. To a position directly behind their captor. He began stroking Jaime's head. "*Very* sincere."

Tom settled in to his chair. Leaning forward to make eye contact with Jaime.

"What do you have to tell us?"

"I am Jaime Velasquez. Live with my mother. Father is dead. A war hero."

"What war hero? I never heard of him." Tom egged Jaime on.

"He died fighting for the Sandinista cause. Mother said he died on the Mosquito Coast. I don't remember much about our time together. He was always gone." He stopped. "And, I don't like this man touching me!" He exclaimed, pulling away from the hands that touched his hair.

"I live on a farm. Where I was captured. I like riding my motorbike. My dog died."

"That's all interesting. But, we need more concrete information. Let's try this. What do you know about the Cuban contingent in Jalapa?"

"They arrived about two years ago. Major Sanchez visits my mother. And, no! They are not lovers."

"What of this Major Sanchez. Why does he visit? If they are not lovers."

"I don't know. They always talk by his car. Seldom does he enter the house. My mother is always home. Sometimes she goes into town. But, never at night."

"Does Major Sanchez run the Sandinista Training Camp?"

"I've never been there. I don't know."

"How often are you visited by Abdel Pallais?"

"He stops by with other men. I met him in the woods. They were..." He paused searching for a word. "Hunting. The day before I was captured. He gave me some papers for my mother."

"Hunting?"

"Yes. I think so."

"What was in the papers?"

"I don't know. They were for my mother. When you take me home, you can ask her?"

Tom wanted to laugh. Keeping a straight face required turning away. "What were these men hunting?"

The tall interrogator was having a problem in controlling his amusement. Containment was key to effective interrogation. Perception was everything. It was good that Jaime couldn't look directly at him. Though his reflection was seen on the glass wall.

"You're not going home!" The tall one barked. Getting back into character was the only way to further the interrogation.

This interview would continue until the team became satisfied. Actionable intel came by effective questioning. Response or reaction. Communication twisted to meet objectives.

Rancho Perez

An automobile broke through the opening between the trees. Juanita did not recognize it. As it came to a stop at her porch, she could see the face of the Doctor in the driver's seat. Stopping near where she stood. Exiting the car.

"How is our patient?" The doctor asked.

"He is awake. He ate. I gave him a pill for his pain."

Major Sanchez extracted himself from the passenger side. "Is my guard awake?"

Doctor walked past Juanita. Following Doctor, Major Sanchez stopped at her side.

"I'm not riding with him anymore." He said in quiet.

Man with the medical knowledge had reached bedside of his patient. Saying to the guard, "That will be enough for now!" Motioning him to leave the room.

Juanita followed the doctor and Major Sanchez. They danced with the guard at the door. As he tried to leave the room.

"You two, out! Doctor's orders." Waiting for the major and Juanita to leave. "And, close the door behind you. Por favor."

Ten awkward minutes passed. Juanita and Major Sanchez having to make small talk. In the kitchen. Most of what they shared involved passing intel reports. Without something specific to talk about, like two teenagers on their first date.

The Doctor reappeared. His concern over bone infection. This was not the most sterile of locations.

"Señora, no sé lo que hiciste. But, he looks better today. Maybe, being around you is good for him." He thought. "But, I'm going to leave the IV port in his arm one more day. If his fluid levels are low. We can hook him up again. If he's better tomorrow. I'll take it out."

"Good. When can I question him."

"Now. Briefly. I'll check his vitals when you are done." Turning to Juanita, "You, young lady can make me a Café Bustelo." He smiled.

Major Sanchez entered the bedroom.

"I am Major Sanchez. The military attaché to Jalapa. You had an accident. At the same time materiel was falling from an airplane. We have provided you with excellent medical treatment. This doctor," motioning toward the kitchen "will be coming back every day. Until you no longer need his services."

"Jalapa?" He questioned. "In pain. Would like to feel better."

"You are American? Commander Pallais brought you here. He said you came from the airplane. Is that true?"

"I remember the plane. Falling." Lester replied as John Doe.

"The airplane was dropping supplies. But, you are a mystery. Who do you work for?"

"Things I remember. Nurse said I was in Nicaragua. Is that true?"

"You are in Central America. Do you work for the American Government?"

A lull falls upon the conversation.

'I am in Central America? Where? Lester asks himself. *If I escape, which direction would I go?'*

Through his foggy thought, Lester replied "I don't remember." A pause. "Any of it."

"Do you work for the United States?" The second time that pointed question was asked. Lester's training was to give a name and some story. "My name is Lester Russell. I don't know how I got here. When I first woke up. In the hospital. Thought I was in Vietnam."

"You seem to know your name? You have not lost your memory. Must know where you came from?"

"Major," Lester returned "I don't remember. I wish I did. Things flash in my mind. Vietnam. Lots of night firing from a gunship. Hundreds of rounds. I remember falling. End over end. Then, things went black."

The questions persisted. The Major voice got louder. He became heated from Lester's repeated responses. Juanita and Doctor could hear shouting from behind the closed door to the bedroom.

Juanita was uncomfortable. Conflicted. Two thoughts intersecting. Her son, only God knew where. Maybe questioned. And, the questioning of this prisoner. Horrible thoughts of what her son might be subjected to. She stood. Displaying extreme nervousness.

"I do not like this. In my home. In my bed. The place where my son and I lay our heads. Before…." She stated, "You can stop this now by going in. Please."

The elder Doctor felt her uneasiness. "I'll stop it." He said, walking to and opening the bedroom door.

"That's enough!"

Reluctantly, Major Sanchez left the room.

"Are you in pain?" The Doctor asked from the doorway.

"Sort of," Lester replied, using American slang. "I was okay until he showed up!"

Major Sanchez had exited. The Doctor left the doorway. Returning a couple minutes later. Entering the bedroom.

"Terse nature of that questioning could bring on pain." Doc said, handing him a pill.

"Thanks." Lester was given a glass of water.

Doctor tested his memory. "You remember how this happened? An accident induced coma would create selective amnesia."

"I told them as much as I know. I don't know anymore."

"I am just asking. Because you were in a coma. A hard bump on the head. Swelling in your spinal column. I am concerned for your health." The Doctor replied.

"Just remember phrases, 'What would Yoda say?" He paused, "And, others that don't fit." Their conversation could be heard through the open door. Lester faked being unable to recall any more.

His interrogator was now in the other room. He had attempted pressing the truth from Lester. Those interrogations would continue. Both he and the Doctor knew that much. Doctor left the room. Coming face-to-face with Major Sanchez.

"Go easy. He is not fully recovered. He can still die. A stressed patient can tell you nothing, if he is dead!"

"Yes, doctor."

The Doctor fumbled in his bag. Grasping a vile, looking at the markings on the top.

"Here," he said. Handing Juanita the vile filled with pills. "If he experiences a great deal of pain, crush one of these. Mix it with water. Have him drink it. He will calm down. It will make him sleep."

The doctor left the house. Major Sanchez in trail. They drove away. Lester's interrogator reserved the right for questioning him another time.

Following instructions, she crushed two pills. Set them aside. Both she and Lester would sleep well this night. With the Doctor's help.

Tegucigalpa, Honduras

U.S. Embassy

Latitude: 14.0723 N

Longitude: 87.1921 W

Central Standard Time (GMT -6)

Tuesday – 8 October 1985

INTER-AGENCY NEWS -
INTERNATIONAL INCIDENT:

Cuban Assistant to Deputy Ambassador – Panama. Apprehended in DEA operation. Tocumen IAP, Panama. Connection to transport of cocaine. $5 million street value. 72-hour detention - DEA Ops, Panama City. Panama Government denies involvement. Immediate transmission: POTUS. NSA. SECDOS. SOUTHCOM.

"Morning Jerry." Fred Matthews' call was not unusual. Yet, the subject didn't fit normal discussion involving Honduran military topics.

"Fred? How can I help you?"

"Did you see the daily briefing?"

"Yeah" Jerry replied. An Interagency Coordinator. Desk for South and Central America, main State Department building. "What specifically are you referring to?"

"Panama. DEA detention of a Cuban diplomat."

"Quite an incident. Damned if they do. Damned if they don't! $5 Mil is a lot of stuff."

"How about we run with this. It's only going to get bigger. We got about 2 hours. Gather what you can. Send it to my secretary." The phone call was short. Implications bore international ramifications. Never reaching the pages of newspapers in the United States

Cubans discovered that their man was in DEA lockup. On a 72-Hour Hold. Telephone channels would be abuzz. POTUS/Chief of Staff, would be on the phone to the Secretary of State. NSA would conference with agency heads operating in Central and South America. Other unidentified offices would smell blood in the water. The Russian Embassy in Panama would be in a long discussion with the Kremlin. It would only exacerbate tense relations. Between two adversarial nations. Between cold war enemies. And, among nations within this region.

Undercover operations and resources could be compromised. Surfacing, affected by rumblings through embassy channels. The news media had a special interest in Central America. Congressional Committee knowledge would send staff to cover it like a blanket. They'd be all over it. Interagency squabbling would go on below. The CIA would quietly look for value for any on-going mission or operation.

Everyone used information to identify their target. Pawns exploited in a much larger game.

Panama had become a hub for drug transit to the world. It had seen its difficulty in trying to maintain a zero-tolerance stance. The law was clear. Order was on shaky ground. Sticking its thumb in the eye of the United States, whenever it could. Panama was ripe for dictatorship. It could never go to war. It served many masters. Bending to desires from the outside world. Failure assured.

The canal was the only thing keeping Panama in the eyes of all world powers. Ships transiting the canal flew flags from every nation. The canal remained open. Because of the revenue it brought to this Central American nation. Control of the canal was being attempted by the Chinese. In a finance move with Noriega.

The banking industry had found an ease of operation in Panama. So much so, that this state was becoming an international banking center. Trafficking of every kind flourished. With it came subterranean money-laundering for that illegal drug, human and weapons trafficking. Out of reach. Close at hand.

Fred wanted to read the material Jerry would send. Ending his conversation.

"I can see the headlines. **'Panama Caught in Middle of Drug Sting. Noriega denies Involvement.'** The White House is sending an envoy here. Expected to arrive this morning. I'm sure the subject will come up. I don't want to be flat-footed. Call me back." Fred said.

"Okay, will do." Jerry hung up.

It was five-hundred-forty-five nautical miles between Tegucigalpa and Panama City. 1010 kilometers. Across Costa Rica, through Nicaragua into Honduras and on North. Cartels had staked their holds in each nation. A hold on poorer segments of Society. The arterial flow through each state. The drug trails marked. Thanks to DEA and it's aviation department. King Air watching and listening posts.

Toncontin Airport

Tom was reacquainting himself with traffic in Tegucigalpa. He had taken a leisurely country drive to Danli, yesterday. City driving today demanded more of his attention.

It was a fifteen-minute drive from his hotel to the airport. The place he last supervised an agency operation. While away, tending to family matters, the operation had ended abruptly. Not unusual for the agency. He waited for his next assignment.

Today, he needed to return to the hangar to collect his thoughts. Seeing the physical location would get him back in tune. Return his gaze toward the problem. One that needed solving.

'Wow! Looks spacious. Without planes on the floor.' He thought. *'Clean. Tony did a great job. Tremble at the thought of looking at OPS office. Probably looks like a bomb hit.'*

He climbed the stairs. Footsteps reverberating sound on the empty concrete floor. Movement transmitting through the bolted, metal connections. Catwalk groaning at any weight across its aged surface. He opened the door to Ops. Nodded his head with pursed lips. "Not bad." He said aloud.

Stepping around the corner into the radio room. Fixed his sight on the door that had been hidden by equipment. A door that led to his office. Trying the doorknob, he opened the passageway. Stepping through to what was once his office.

"These guys did a great job." Saying aloud. He being the only person hearing his own words. Floors were clean. Any sign that it had been recently used, erased. What was missing?

'Forgot about my pro-gear. Probably in storage somewhere in the city.'

The sound of a jet in taxi was getting louder. Curiosity led him out on to the catwalk. Voices speaking in Spanish bounced off the interior hangar walls. There were others in the building.

'Had the Honduran government seized the hangar so quickly?'

A Lear Jet made a 180-degree turn, facing West. It stopped in front of the hangar. The voices got louder. Hangar doors began to open. The abandoned ramp, empty ten minutes before, now was flurry of activity. A tug. Power cart. Black SUVs. Honduran soldiers marshalled. Ringing the concrete pad, front of the hangar door

Turning toward the stairs, Tom planned a quick exit. Moving down the stairs. He faced a suited man pointing a handgun. He immediately raised his hands. Man motioned with the pistol pointing at him. Tom moved right. He stopped to face the wall.

"Hands on the wall."

"I'm an American."

"You have ID?"

"Front pants pocket."

"Get it."

With right hand on the wall, Tom pulled his ID wallet from left pocket. Handing it over his shoulder.

"Tom McKay?"

"Yes."

"Turn around." With handgun held at arms-length, Secret Service Agent compared photo ID to Tom's face. He lowered the weapon.

"Can't be too careful."

"I get it." Tom replied. Other security personnel moved to where they stood.

"Stand down." The agent commanded. "What are you doing here, Mr. McKay?"

"I had an office upstairs. Family emergency took we away. My folks cleaned it out while I was gone. Just came back to look."

"Come with us." They walked back the length of the hangar. The hangar doors were fully opened.

"Check this out." Agent said, handing Tom's ID to another agent.

"Tom, is that you?" A voice came from the crowd surrounding the distinguished visitor.

"George. How are you?" Traveling in government circles always bore possibility of seeing someone you knew. From the past.

"It's OK," George said. "I know him."

"What's going on?" Tom asked.

"Envoy for POTUS. I'll introduce you." Taking his arm, guiding him toward the envoy.

"This is Special Envoy Peterson. Here on fact finding."

"Mr. Peterson," Tom greeted. Extending his hand. "Tom McKay. Office of Central American Studies."

"Barely get on the ground. And, I find a guy who can answer some of my questions."

"Here's your ID." A voice interjected. "He checks."

"That's a good thing!" Mr. Peterson paused. "We're going to see Fred Matthews at the Embassy. You know him?"

It would have been a silly response. Tom just nodded.

"Why don't you join us? Unless there is something more pressing. The President would appreciate your input. Don't think you should refuse." Mr. Peterson had a pointed way of making it mandatory.

Agents ushered the envoy into one black Suburban.

"You can ride with me." George said. Directing Tom to another vehicle.

Tug hooked to the Lear, began backing the plane into the hangar. Power cart pushed behind the closing doors. Once again, the hangar doors closed. The arriving plane hidden from view. Two guards stood in front of the hangar. Honduran Military Guards dwarfed by the enormous hangar doors. Vehicles sped away.

U. S. Embassy

"Envoy Peterson, a pleasure to meet you." Fred Matthews stuck out his hand.

Mr. Peterson shook the outstretched hand. "Col. Matthews. Pleasure mine. May I call you Fred. Let's dispense with all the formality. I'm Al." Short for Albert. To him time was a commodity. Less waisted on formality. More time to dig in.

"You know Tom?"

Fred expressed surprise at Tom being in this presence. "Yes, we know one another." He said with the coldness that might be shown to an underling.

"Fred. How's the wife?" Tom played along. But, got no response

"We'll be in the conference room. Security protocol in place." Fred ushered them to a high-ceilinged room. Electronic equipment tucked into one corner. "Coffee. Something else." A staffer took orders. Then walked out. Closing the doors behind him. One of the Secret Service Agents stood at the door, outside.

"The President is interested in accelerating our presence. Now, that we have the formal agreement with El Salvador." Looking at Fred, said. "He expressed his pleasure that Constable Outreach Operation was disbanded. Too much visibility. This close to Nicaragua. Your hand in its shutdown much appreciated."

Tom was blind-sided. Couldn't show the emotion he wanted to express. His outward demeanor like that of a soldier. Stone-faced. Eyes ahead. Attentive to surroundings.

"Thank the President for his confidence." Fred replied. Knowing that he had screwed a good friend. Fucked without a kiss.

"I brought Tom, because we know his work. Strange, running into him at the hangar." He continued, looking at Tom. "You still have a man down in Nicaragua. Am I right?"

"Yes." One-word replies would not leave an opening for tag-along questions.

"Let's get to your briefing, Fred. We'll hold questions until after."

Rancho Perez

Latitude: 13.8955 N

Longitude: 86.1503 W

Central Standard Time (GMT -6)

Tuesday – 8 October 1985

Juanita had slept well. She in the bed of her son. Her new bedroom. The guard for Lester, sleeping upright in a chair next to his prisoner.

She lounged in bed. The sun rising much earlier. Expected the return of Major Sanchez. Maybe the Doctor would come later.

She lay, eyes wide open in Jaime's bed. Thinking how she had been co-opted by the state. How her husband had given his life.

'The use of this property to provide safe passage, shelter for drug movements. Sandinista soldiers coming and going. This place isn't mine. It's a way-station. A stopping place for people to rest. Now, an infirmary for a captured American. Yet, to we don't know why he was on the road. Is he a soldier? Up to now we only know his name.'

Sunlight took darkness away from her curtained room. The bedroom with a Western exposure. She had to gather and rise. Be ready for the next visitation. As she pulled on her clothing, her words came together. Her thoughts many.

'It was unusual to watch Abdel. As he mixed that powder with water. A sign he had done it before. Heroin or cocaine? How much lay buried on this property?' Flipping from one subject to another.

'It was like the doctor said. Crushing. Mixing. Spoon feeding our prisoner. Did they have that mixture, when my husband lay dying? After the battle?'

'This property lent to me as a show. I am the face. It provides a stopping place for drugs to pass through. The Sandinistas use it as a campground. The meat we grow feeds soldiers and their families in Jalapa. The Contras kidnapping my son. What haven't I heard or seen involving this property?'

Lester had slept through the night. She exited to the living room. Hearing a vehicle arrive. Looking to confirm that it did not bring a threat. Opening the front door.

"Good morning Señora." The words coming from Major Sanchez, as he approached the house.

"It is not a 'good morning!' I am thinking of my son. This American lies in my bed. Causes hate and distrust in this house. How can that be a good morning?"

"We are sorry Señora. But we must do it this way. If it is uncomfortable for you, we can provide you meals and quarters in town." Major Sanchez offered.

She pushed past him stopping at porch edge. Arms folded across her chest. Surveying the space opening out from the porch. To the left, a point where Jaime entered the line of trees. To the right, a sloping area where soldiers camped for the night.

Major Sanchez continued into the house. Telling the guard to leave the bedroom. After closing the wooden door, he picked up where he had left the questioning. The evening before.

Lester, through a drug induced fog was stirring. Strapped to the bed. Vulnerable. Questions similar. Delivery different.

As Juanita reentered the house, she heard the major imploring his prisoner to answer.

"…I know you remember," the Major demanded.

"I told the doctor. And I told you, I don't know." He said the last three words in slow deliberation. "What I remember has nothing to do with Central America."

A shooting pain emanated from his lower spine. Running to the base of his neck. He arched his back. Pains shot through his shoulder and down his arm. His grimaced facial and body reaction told Major Sanchez that he had to stop.

"When was the last time she gave you medication?" He was asking a man who was fighting pain. Shuddering his body.

Opening the door, Major Sanchez yelled at Juanita.

"Get him something for his pain!".

Juanita ladled the gritty syrup from a coffee cup. Fed, by the spoon to the patient-prisoner shackled to her bed. The fact of her being in the room calmed Lester. Soon, the liquid began to mask his pain. It took Lester on a sleigh ride. His body became less tense. Limbs relaxing as the liquid mixed in his stomach. That pill powder transferred through his veins. Within minutes he would relax. Lester's pain was under drug management.

But, the Major would have to wait. He could question Lester in the afternoon.

Neither Juanita nor Major Sanchez knew what each tablet contained. There was no label on the vile. It had no pharmacy label. The vile a clear plastic container. The drugs could have been supplied through a pharmacy. Maybe the mixture was not meant for humans. She set the vile on the table and walked away.

Embassy Conference Room - Tegucigalpa Mid-Morning

Monthly, embassy staff would be corralled in the conference room. Minimum security credentials, required. To attend a State of Host Nation Briefing. An overview of current regional activities. Areas to avoid. Reports on crime for staff to be aware of. Today being special with the presence of Al Peterson, Presidential Envoy. Briefing to be broader in context.

All reminded of the security clearances needed for each part of the briefing. Many would stand against the walls. Some were fortunate to have acquired seating.

"Much of this may be redundant. This overview is required. Present day activities will be briefed to the Security Clearance level held." The young staffer prefaced. He introduced the presenter. A man from the Intelligence Office took the podium.

"The government of Nicaragua was held from 1936 to 1979 under Somoza family control. Anastasio Somoza holding power...." The history lesson heard before. Presenters always talked to basics first. As subjects required higher security clearances, the room would be thinned.

"The Sandinista national liberation front (FSLN) is a democratic socialist political party. They won the Nicaraguan election in 1979. The term Sandinista came from Augusto Cesar Sandino. Leader of the nationalist rebellion. Assassinated in '34. The term resurrected in '81, after the election."

"In 1981, POTUS condemned the FSLN. Sandinista government had joined with Cuba in supporting various Central American Marxist revolutions. El Salvador had become a target. At the request of its government, CIA armed and trained a combatant force. Saw the remnants of Somoza's National Guard fill their ranks. The term anti-Sandinistas took the moniker *"contrarrolucionarios."* Shortened to *Contras.* Indigenous guerrilla forces joined the fight."

Some hadn't heard previous briefings. The subject line jumped across time and nations. It was not a history lesson. The information passed again, as a reference to host nation status. To inform the staff of trending politics and alliances.

"Nicaragua declared an official state of emergency in 1982. In response to attacks by the Contras...."

That part of the briefing ended. "Those not holding Security Clearance above SECRET must leave the room." Milling of bodies headed toward the door. "Managers, check the staff remaining. The remaining part of the briefing with be TOP SECRET...."

Within five minutes, the room settled to hear the rest of the briefing. Eighty percent of the staff exited. The intelligence briefer continued.

"Under their law, the Nicaraguans could hold suspected revolutionaries without trial. We think that may be the auspices under which they hold Lester Russell. Our loadmaster. But, we have not been told of his capture. Hospitalization. Or, their reported movement of him to Managua"

"In Nicaragua, there are few civil liberties. Nicaraguan homes entered without cause. Property seized. People conscripted to do the bidding of the government. Freedoms suppressed. Illegal activities used to further any goal. Nicaragua has folded into the Narco-State Consortium. All for the good of their regime."

"State of emergency continues, never rescinded. This year the Sandinistas broadened the '82 emergency law, suspending more civil rights. Giving military and guerilla forces the mandate to protect drug smugglers. As they pass through, on their way North."

"Our means of push-back is through the Contras. They operate out of camps here in Honduras. Background checks start at Danli. Weapons & Tactics training conducted in the Southern mountainous region. Location named La Laguna de Guam Buco. Thirty-five kilometers from Danli. The HQ of Battalion 3-16."

He paused. "And, before anyone mentions atrocities perpetrated by previous Batt 3-16 members. I know! I have files in my office. Claims from Honduran citizens on human rights abuses. I won't go there."

"Our primary means in the Sandinista fight was via economic sabotage. Yet they still hold the hearts and minds of their own locals. Seen at our last attempt to turn Jalapa to our favor. A well-planned operation. But, failed. Our systematic campaign to undermine and disrupt never took hold." He droned on with slides in support of this presentation.

"...We've received widespread murder, rape and torture allegations against the Contras. Reported from both sides. Other guerilla tools used to terrorize communities into supporting the Contras. As in reports of Battalion 3-16, many human rights violations counted."

"Unfortunately, some Contra Revolutionaries became more mercenary than liberator."

"Turning to regional concerns and connected activity. We look at connections between warring groups and their inter-connection within the drug trade."

"The CIA developed and cultivated a working relationship with General Manuel Noriega. Panama Canal, a strategic interest for the United States. Each government agency doing business with Panama turned a blind eye. To the corruption and drug dealing of Manuel Noriega. It was reported that he is a key player in the Medellin Cartel."

"That's where we look deeper. The drug trails lead from Columbia through Panama. Costa Rica and Nicaragua. Protected by regimes in those places. We've got the biggest Army. But, can't use it. Congress prohibits our interaction in Central America's regional politics. The 'war on drugs' is mostly fought on U.S. territory."

"Which brings me to my final point. The President of Honduras wants to distance himself from our fight. As appeasement, the Ambassador lobbied for and got the closure of Constable Outreach. Some have thought it was a mistake. With politics as it is, El Salvador now becomes our place from which to launch future operations. Using existing Contra training facilities in Honduras. Under the radar."

"I'm sure I missed specific points. You came here to find fact." Acknowledging Al Peterson's presence. Our office will attempt to answer any questions you may have. They will be answered. You are welcome to come to our office. This ends the TOP-SECRET portion of our briefing."

As the room began to fill with low level murmuring, Tom turned to Fred.

"Where do you stand in all this?"

"My position is to support the administration. As they find ways to roll against these Narco-Nations." Addressing it more to Mr. Peterson than Tom McKay.

"All that historical background, can help analysts formulate plans. I worked one small segment of the total operation. Overseeing coordinated ground and air operations. But, that has gone away."

Fred acknowledged the operation shut-down. Tom continued with his thoughts.

"To be honest, I took this assignment because I needed to fill a square. Get that job in Northern Virginia. Keep me closer to home. But, now I'm invested." Looking at Fred, he continued. "While away on a family emergency, the rug pulled from under my feet. Lights turned out. Doors closed. Our fledgling air operation. Constable Outreach. Snuffed. In its infancy. Would it grow to be a viable operation? Probably not. There were limiting factors." His tone stiffening. Delivery forceful.

"But, one thing I do know. I've got a man on the ground in Nicaragua. You and I put him there. No one has eyes on him since Sunday. Is he in Managua? Who knows. But, we have a responsibility to him. We have a responsibility to our code of conduct. We never leave a man behind. I didn't hear anything about how we plan to get him back!"

Fred and Al Peterson look at one another. Fred wondering when Tom would stop.

"I make it my responsibility. You can do whatever you want with my career. But, you can't take away my need to get him out. You won't take that away from me!"

Tegucigalpa, Honduras

Latitude: 14.0723 North

Longitude: 87.1921 West

Central Standard Time (GMT -6)

Wednesday – 9 October 1985

"I took the liberty of having your things brought from the basement." Fred addressed.

"Thanks." Tom was being short. Only one-thought answers. His head was throbbing. Eyes couldn't stop watering. "Where?" He hadn't been this drunk in a year.

"Quite an impressive speech, you gave."

"Yeah. Guess I stepped on it." Tom was forced in replying with a longer sentence.

"No. Quite the contrary. POTUS has directed that we give you what you need." He looked directly into Tom's bloodshot eyes. "Our briefing, must have been too basic. Mr. Peterson was more knowledgeable of current affairs. Cerebral to a point. Apparently, Al's patriotic approach bent more toward what you had to say." Adding, "And by the way, I apologize. The shutdown wasn't my idea. I just made it happen faster."

"So, where's my stuff. I'll get out of here. Go nurse my body." He rolled his head. Attempting to loosen his neck muscles. "Please?"

"Follow me." They walked toward the conference room.

"Are you trying to make me suffer? Couldn't you have dropped them at the reception desk?"

"No." Returning his thoughts to a purposeful one-word utterance. Stopping short of the conference room, facing right. "Here they are."

"Where? Stop fucking with me!"

Fred opened a door on the hallway. "In here." Tom's office lamp was atop the desk. His cot was assembled. Tucked in the corner behind the door. A few of his personal pictures now sat on top of this desk. Not tucked away in desk drawers at the hangar.

"What's this?"

"Apparently, you didn't hear me. We are to provide you every bit of help you need. Within the scope of the Ambassador's reach." Patting Tom on the back. "You're welcome."

Tom looked around the room. Recently painted walls. Plenty of light. A view on the street. The wide Avenida, with a tree dotted median. Greenery shading the grounds of the embassy complex. Manicured by a local force. Holding the beauty of its white buildings settled on a canvass of green.

"What can I say?"

"Tell you what you can do." Fred pushed Tom toward the cot. "You can lie down. I'll find something for your head." He walked out the door.

Rancho Perez

Major Sanchez arrived late to the ranch. Lester had eaten breakfast. Remaining behind the closed steel door. The duty guard rotated. A new conscript sitting on the porch. Lester lying, uncomfortably on his back. Both he and Lester listened to all goings-on in the house. Coming from a space between them. Juanita was anxious.

"It's been sixteen days since the disappearance of my son. Neither Managua nor our intelligence has been able to tell me anything. You did not report it! Why?"

"Senora, we have tried to discover his whereabouts. I am Commander in this region. First, we could not admit to his wandering off."

"Wandering off?"

"Bad choice of phrasing. 'Disappearance.' What I meant to say."

"Why wasn't Managua told?"

"It was my decision. I knew that eventually we would have to tell them."

"But, it has been six-teen-days!" She let a string of Spanish cursing fly into the air. "Now! Managua knows. They are sending someone. To discuss this whole mess!"

Major Sanchez had no retort. "Did you tell them about our prisoner?"

"Yes, I did. I felt it my responsibility. Your way failed. Now, we will see what comes of this. I want my son back!"

Major Sanchez, said nothing further to her. His male ego, in-control position was usurped. He marched to the steel door. His heals planting on each step. A purposeful show anger for what Juanita had done. His next discussion would be with Lester.

"Well, apparently your host has brought the Nicaraguan government into our cozy mix."

Lester said nothing.

"Your fait will now be in their hands."

Shortly before 1 PM, the silence held between Juanita and Major Sanchez broke. An automobile crunched its way on the gravel road. Sound approaching the ranch house. When it came in view of the porch, Juanita exited to receive her guests.

"Hola, Senora." A Colonel from the Sandinista government addressed her. Exiting from behind the wheel.

She watched two other bodies exit the vehicle. From the passenger door. A Cuban Colonel. He nodded to her with familiarity.

The other from the right rear. "Good afternoon, Senora." He said. Touching the brim of his fedora with an index and middle finger. She remembered him from a visit, two weeks earlier.

"Buenas Dias." She replied. Major Sanchez exited her front door. Taking a position to her right.

"We would like to see the captured soldier. Your call gave us much to discuss on the trip here. To say we were surprised, would be an under-statement. More like a blind-side." The Cuban Colonel said, glaring at Major Sanchez.

"Of course, Colonel." The entourage walked past the standing guard. A local from the Mayor's Reaction Force. Standing at the front door. His attempt at position-of-attention, lacked full military bearing.

Juanita opened the heavy metal door. Led the foursome to the leather shackled prisoner.

"We are told, you are Lester Russell." The Nicaraguan Colonel addressed. "This is Colonel Mendez," pointing toward the Cuban. "And, this is Alexandr Dutrov our Soviet Regional representative."

"We hope Major Sanchez has treated you well." Said Colonel Mendez.

Comrade Dutrov added nothing to the conversation.

"Yeah. OK, I guess. They could do without the leather. It reminds me of an S&M movie I saw." There was no laughter at this wry humor.

"Senora Perez tells us that you have come a long way. In…" He paused looking at Juanita. "…fourteen days." Cutting a glare at Major Sanchez. The Major was beginning to get the message. "We will talk with your doctor. See if it may be advisable to transport you to hospital in Managua. For complete recovery."

"You are a unique find. In this small rural region." Alexandr Dutrov broke his silence. "We would not want anything to happen to you. Mysteriously. It is in our best interest to keep you alive."

"Alive would be better." Lester quipped.

"I'm sure Major Sanchez has extracted much information from you." Col. Mendez added.

"I don't know what he could have gotten." Lester replied. "I don't know much. Can't remember how I got here. I can shed no light. As I told Miss Juanita, I didn't know my name…." He said, looking at her.

"Let us agree, you know more. You just haven't been given the right opportunity to tell us." The Soviet returned. "Colonel Mendez, shall we let him rest?"

The Colonel nodded. The group of five exited the bedroom. A room modified to be a prison cell. Major Sanchez closed and slid the locking bar on the metal door.

U.S. Embassy - Tegucigalpa

Tom stood looking through the open blinds. Knock at the closed door. An aide to Colonel Matthews entered.

Without turning, Tom said "I forgot how beautiful this city was. Avenida la Paz has a charm. Different from the look of the barrio." He mused.

"Sir, Col. Matthews sent this box." The aide placed the box on the corner of the desk. "If there is anything you need, call extension 4105. I'll be available."

"Thank you. Tell Fred, thanks for the hangover remedy." He still felt the effect of the bottle he consumed. "There's a lesson somewhere in there."

The aide backed out. Closed the door. The security tape on the box was broken. Tom lifted the top on the container. Security warnings pasted on four sides. The type of box that he had seen during many years in Army Intelligence.

On the top was a memorandum. "To: Ambassador John A. Ferch. From: Albert Peterson, Special Assistant for Central American Affairs, White House. Subject: Aiding Special Representative Tom McKay – Office of Central & South American Studies...." It delineated the desires of President Reagan. From the envoy, he blindly met at the hangar. Whom he owed gratitude for putting him in this position.

Lifting the items one-by-one from inside. He scanned each folder. Three dossiers. One labeled Major Adolfo Sanchez, Cuban Regional Representative. Another, Abdel Pena-Pallais, the slimmest of the three. And, one full folder labeled Juanita Maria Perez-Velasquez. The heaviest one capturing his interest. Other loose notes and pictures covered the bottom of the box.

He set the box behind his desk. Placing the large folder top desk center, in front of his chair.

'Who was this female? Why was her file larger? What role did she play? Time was ticking away. Twelve days since the airdrop. Each day added difficulty in obtaining Lester's return. Only a few days more, and the trail would go cold."

His afternoon passed as he read the dossier of Juanita Perez. Picking up the other two to establish his own foggy connections. Going back and forth between files.

At five o'clock, Fred's aide knocked and entered. "Anything else I can get you before I head out?"

"No. Thank you for this." He knew from where it came. By-passing many in the chain between him and the White House door. "I need to make a personal call. How do I call out?"

Aide instructed him on switchboard protocol. Then departed. Tom placed his call.

"Hi sweetie."

"Hold on, I'll get Mom."

"Wait. Before you go, I've got something to tell you." He prepared to admit a likeness in attitude toward his daughter, Rebecca. "I know it has been hard on you." She was the oldest child at home. "I understand some things better. I did something yesterday. That you could have done."

"What's that, Daddy?"

"There's no doubt. My image as your father can be a negative one. You want a closer relationship. It's tough with my being this far away. I've seen you rebel. It's tough on your Mother."

"No, Daddy."

"Just listen. There are a lot of reasons. But, I want you to know, I understand."

"Daddy, I love you."

"Yesterday, I did something. Took a page from who you are. The person who carries my genes. We're closer than you think."

"How's that?"

"I blew my lid. In front of some powerful people. I rebelled. Against the system."

"How so?"

"The facts aren't important. I'm not able to say. But, yesterday I was you. When you see something wrong. You rebel." He paused. "You may not know what you're rebelling against. But, you speak out. Telling everybody, there's something wrong. I understand that."

"Daddy, I'm sorry."

"Don't be. You taught me something. What's important. I want to say, 'Thank you.' For being my daughter. Being strong for your Mom."

"I love you," she replied. "When are you coming home?"

"Soon, pumpkin. *Very* soon."

Tegucigalpa, Honduras

Latitude: 14.0723 North

Longitude: 87.1921 West

Central Standard Time (GMT -6)

Thursday – 10 October 1985

"Tom, can you come to my office?" Fred spoke into the telephone handset.

"Be right there."

Fred Matthews' career spanned the same time frame as Tom McKay. Starting with a bit of difference. But, assigned to Army Intelligence. Then moved to the Defense Intelligence Agency. He worked Black Ops in Thailand. Serving as DIA coordinator, South East Asian Desk in Vietnam & Cambodia. Now, in the military attaché slot at the U.S. Embassy in Honduras.

Planted by senior members of the White House Staff. He had been in Honduras before the departure of previous Ambassador John Negroponte. His purpose, to discover military need that could exploited. To build a better relationship with generals in command. Ones that would see a North American perspective. In the administration's efforts on the war against Sandinistas. Studying and reporting directly to an office in the Executive Building. Next to 1600 Pennsylvania Avenue.

When Tom arrived, Fred was on the phone.

"I don't care about the approval process." Fred said into the receiver. "This comes from an office tied to the White House. You can check. But, make it quick." He ended the call.

Tom had asked Fred to spread photos and a video of Jaime Velasquez. Throughout the Central and South American Embassies. For embassy persons to pass selectively to their Nicaraguan counterparts. It would be the first admission that they held Jaime Velasquez in Honduras.

"Have a seat. I had this call on hold. Be just a minute." He told Tom.

"…We have an American that's gone missing. The idiot was studying narco-flow through South America. A writer working for the Times. Notified by his editor that he went missing about fifteen days ago." Stopping to answer questions. "Yes. A newspaper reporter. We need to find him. I know our resources are thin. But, any thought and action you can provide, will be helpful…." He hung up.

"Wow, Fred. That was good. Off the top of your head?" Tom said.

"No. But, not bad. If I say so myself. That should start the questions coming. We'll see what surfaces." He paused to turn his thought. "I forgot that I had this file." Said, handing Tom a personnel file labelled Lester Russell.

"Where'd you get this?"

"It's a copy. But while you were gone, I requested it be sent. Needed to know about our Loadmaster. Interesting background. Seems he was working with us in Thailand. Never crossed his path."

"Thanks." Tom replied. "For this and the box you sent yesterday. How long has DIA been tracking Juanita Perez?"

"When I arrived, the file just appeared on my desk. Seems she's DGI. You read her background?"

"Yes. That's quite an extensive workup."

"My take is that she – silently – has applied a great influence on the Mayor and City elders. Her husband being Miguel Velasquez. And, his family being from Jalapa. Deep roots. Cubans thought exploitable."

Rancho Perez

Col. Mendez, Cuban military attaché from Managua was quartered at the training facility. He would arrive, unannounced. Stay for a few days. Then leave.

Today, he drove out to Rancho Perez to hold a private conversation with Juanita.

Cuban government had given her time to grieve the death of her husband. Two years. Time with her son, on the land once owned by her husband's parents. Now, they were intent on reactivating her official status.

"Senora, Major Sanchez has been unable to break Senior Russell. The man who lies wounded in your bed. We have ordered the Major to stop. He will follow your direction."

Juanita interrupts, "In his defense, he has taken all able measures."

"Yes. But, you have developed a bond with the prisoner. His doctor has noticed. His recovery comes along well. Commander Pallais has mentioned it to Major Sanchez. But, we suspect for different reasons."

Juanita had become the only one Lester trusted. Became Lester's surrogate nurse. Tending to his wounds. Bathing and attending to his most private needs. Making Pallais jealous of her attention toward him.

"Now, you will act in two capacities. For the Sandinista cause. You have gained his trust. Can converse with him on his level. Become the Trojan horse. Get on the inside. A soldier using means only a woman could apply."

"I appreciate your confidence Colonel." Juanita paused. "But..."

"The doctor thinks it will help him further to recover. Without the seeming negative approach of a male interrogator. He will open to you. Major Sanchez could not break through the amnesia. We need to know if he's faking or just can't remember."

"And, what can I look forward to?"

"Once this is over, we will return you to Cuba."

"Not without my son!"

"Yes, Senora. We are working diligently. On your concern."

"What else can I do? Circumstance makes me a willing participant."

The quiet of this ranch played a melody. In the Nicaraguan countryside it punctuated the Town of Jalapa. Folks from town would drive out. To visit with Juanita, immediately after her husband's death. But, it dwindled to nothing now. Except for military automobiles. And, cattle trucks. Moving, adding, deleting cows from the pasture.

After Jaime's disappearance, Juanita noticed a marked increase in vehicular traffic. There were many coming and going at Rancho Perez. She was appreciative for the company. Yet felt constrained to one point of view.

As the Colonel drove off, cattlemen arrive with a wagon. To deliver weened calves. Branding the new calves with the Rancho Perez mark. Picking up aged cattle for slaughter.

Lester had drifted in and out of sleep. Due to the medication prescribed by the doctor from Jalapa. Partly due to drugs given her but not filled in a pharmacy.

As he lay there, he heard calves expressing their displeasure at branding. Juanita moving about beyond the jailer door. She awakened Lester with a call. Strolling into the bedroom.

"Are you ready for lunch?" Juanita asked.

"I could eat something."

"Let me loosen these." She said, undoing the leather handcuff holding his left arm above his head. "You were very convincing yesterday."

"When?"

"The Sandinista visitors who came to see you. Yesterday." Juanita moved to the ankle restraints. Loosening the left one first.

"That was a lot of brass. They came to see me?"

"Yes. You are quite a celebrity. The American with amnesia. They came from Managua. A five-hour trip. Here to our little corner of Nicaragua."

"Yeah, sure." He replied. "Did they bring you any word about your son?"

Juanita tensed. But, kept it hidden from her captive.

"No. Unfortunately. I miss my son. He is such a sweet boy." Loosening the last ankle restraint. "Can you sit up?"

"Maybe, with a little help." She gently, with surety assisted Lester in sitting.

"How does the shoulder feel?"

"Sore. But, it feels good to sit." She helped him sit erect.

"The men who were here yesterday will make inquiries about you. It is possible that will help us know why you were found on the farm road."

"Really?" Lester wanted to put the pieces together. He did have amnesia. Nagging knowledge of his identity. Thoughts masked by his brain fog. He questioned if their search would be good or bad.

"I will move the table close." She said, leaving the room.

The guard was not to seen. Lester sat on the edge of the bed. The first time left alone. Without restraint. Door open. Hearing her move dishes in the other room. Listening to her footsteps, as she re-entered the room.

"Where is your guard?"

"He's on the porch." Nodding in that direction with her hands full. "He misses his family too." She set the dish and glass on the small table. Lifting the table and moving it bedside.

"After you eat, I want to help you. Maybe you can remember. Even the smallest detail."

Lester was thankful for the care this woman was giving him. He could have died on that road. He strained in remembering. It wasn't easy. There was nothing that came willingly.

'Flashes of jungle seen from the air. Long lines of tracers stretching to the ground. The sounds of bullets hitting the airplane body. Plinking. He had been there. This wasn't that place.'

Juanita broke into his search for a recent memory. While she fed him, the conversation continued.

"We know someone was here the day before you arrived. Do you know who they might have been?"

"No clue." He said. "I barely knew my name was Lester three days ago. Wait."

"What?"

"I really don't know anything. I don't know where I am. I don't know how I got here." He replied, in staccato.

"So, you say."

"Yes! I say!"

"Please, don't be upset. We will work together to help you."

"What would Yoda say?"

Juanita looked puzzled. "Who is Yoda?"

"Nobody. Just a character in a Star Wars movie."

"You remember that."

"Yeah. But, I don't remember seeing the movie."

"How is that you can remember a character from a movie. But, you turn up a blank when it comes to your recent history?"

"You sound just like my mother." Having said that, he went inward to family memories. "She was a strong woman. Could do anything needed, around the house."

"She apparently meant a lot to you." Juanita enticed him to continue.

"Some bad memories shadow what I can remember." With that he said nothing more.

Lunch conversation was interrupted occasionally by cattle expressing painful displeasure. Two adversaries in the house were beginning to connect.

Tom's Office - U. S. Embassy

Tom had been sent photos, audio tapes and video briefings on Central American Narco-Traffic. A new item would arrive every day. Seemed anything he requested, appeared without haste.

US Embassies were making their contacts relating to the agency's youthful prisoner. Feedback collected and forwarded to Tom. It was important that they documented the humane treatment of Jaime Valesquez. Daily reports and pictures sent to him from Danli.

The narrative developed, in discussions with Jaime was altered. The content modified and recreated to aid certain people to notice. To assist in the discovery. Creating interest, building discussion. Enticing the Sandinista Government to bite.

Now that Fred had sent them, the world would see. He expected that they would hear from their operatives soon. By whatever means the intelligence is collected.

Tom listened to a taped recording on an intel briefing. Linking the Sandinistas to Noriega. Read the evidence of a Panamanian link to drug mules. Moving through Nicaragua to Honduras.

Looked at King air photos, unavailable to him before.

Read the latest reports on DEA's arrest of a Cuban embassy aide. Drugs seized. The crate moving under diplomatic document cover. DEA suspecting a connection to surges in Miami drug activity. Causing the street price to change at the dealer level.

The weekly amount of cocaine, arriving in Miami every week fluctuating. DEA suspecting a tie to traffic through the Cuban Embassy.

Inter-agency reports of turf battles between Mexican and Columbian Cartels. Creating possibilities of larger turf wars. Unrest on the streets.

Gangs doing in Miami what guerrilla forces did in Central America.

Reading of other agency discussions on espionage and interdiction within Central American Region.

There was more information than one operative or analyst could absorb. But, he was trying. Educating himself. Placing tabs on certain pages that linked to other related – and, unrelated material.

Deep in thought, he startled to a knock at the door. "Come in."

"This secure package just arrived by courier." An aide said, handing him the file.

Thanking the aide, Tom opened the secure package. He was beginning to feel comfortable in these surroundings.

The folder reads. "Top Secret."

It contained high altitude aerial photos.

Connected verbiage read, "Cubans suspected of building runway near Jalapa... Purposes unknown." In the next written sequence. "Air Force Combat Control/Special Ops team inserted. Investigate runway construction. (13.899058 N; 86.156099 W) Findings: Compaction tests consistent with unimproved runway construction. Strength assessment: Runway able to support STOL aircraft. i.e., AN-14 Pchelka & AN-72 Coaler. Detailed report available."

Danli, Honduras

Agency Facility – Battalion 3-16
HQ

Latitude: 14.0411 N

Longitude: 86.5704 W

Central Standard Time (GMT -6)

Friday – 11 October 1985

The third series of interrogations began with a difference. Jaime stood in the corner where he was placed. He was told not to move. One of Battalion 3-16 interrogators would be in to talk to him. His compliance was out of fear, isolation and the onset of loneliness.

Prisoners are subject to many forms of mood altering conditions. Jaime had not been alone from the day he was born. Without some form of familiar company, until fifteen days ago.

In a final attempt to extract usable information, the interrogators changed their tactics. Initially he was treated gingerly. And placed in a barracks room given to NCOs. When his minor wounds healed, the interrogation team moved him.

Now, he was being kept in a closet sized room. He slept on the floor with only a blanket. The overhead light burned 23 hours a day. That one hour when the room was totally dark, was the most fearful for him.

Twice a day, they would provide some sort of sustenance. But, to this young man it was not food. It was the scraps that one fed to pigs. The scrapings of non-eaten food, left from soldier's plates. When brought to him, the door was opened. The plastic dish thrown like a Frisbee. Sliding towards him, across the concrete. Some food would escape the bounds of the plate and wind up on the floor.

The floor that he slept on had dried food left from other prisoners. Bugs shared the living space. Primarily of the cockroach family. These cellmates found their way to this food splattered floor. The insects seemed not worried at the human mass that shared their dining room. Hundreds of sizes smaller than the human body sharing this space. A boy prisoner being held. This was isolation for counter-intelligence collection.

This space was used for Battalion 3 – 16 prisoners. An infamous location used to store political prisoners. Not too long before, there had been reports of a special unit. Members of this unit did horrible things to their fellow countrymen. Those who created problems of political dissent, mysteriously disappeared. Bodies to be found in neighborhood gutters, where they had lived. It was a means by which control could be placed on the populace. Psychological warfare perpetrated on their own people.

A well-lit interrogation room was three times brighter. The interrogation room three times the size of the closet he stayed in. The closet light bulb was not a luminous match for florescent lamps. A piece of glass, one third the size of one wall hid monitors.

Behind the glass stood two agency contractors. No sunlight showed through it. A table took most of the floor space. There were only two chairs.

The door was scarred. In the space between the bottom of the door and the floor, light could be seen. Through the door, movement could be heard on the outside. Heavy boots walking left to right, then back again. Most of the footsteps did not stop at the door.

Hearing an approaching set. Stopping. The door opened.

"What are you doing standing in that corner?"

Jaime was stammering for an answer.

"I don't want you standing there. Stand over there!" The hardened voice commanded in Spanish.

As Jaime moved to where he was pointing, another order rolled out of the bull-horned mouth.

"No! No! No! Not there," the voice continued. Pointing to the opposite corner, "Over there!"

Jaime went to move around the table. The green clothed Honduran soldier intimidated his subject. He moved in his path. Jaime stopped.

"Are you breathing on me? You eat with the cockroaches. Your breath smells like a cockroach!"

"No, Senior. I'm trying...." Cut short. His reply was one of nervousness

"Have you been kissing cockroaches? Did you find a girl friend?"

Jaime did not know how to reply. "I'm... I am...."

"You don't know what you are! Whoever you thought you were, you are no more."

Jaime began backing, with the interrogator two inches from his face.

"Stop breathing on me!" Inching forward as Jaime backed up into the wall. The glass wall at his back.

"You are a cockroach. The lowest form. You are nothing!"

"I am Jaime Valesquez." It was the first time he had used his name as a shield.

The interrogator backed away, crossing his arms. Looking at his subject, he tilted his head to the left and then to the right. "And, that should mean something to me?"

Jaime slid sideways. Down the wall to back away from his minder. The interrogator was a step behind him. Backing Jaime into another uncomfortable corner position. The interrogator stepped closer. Chest to chest.

Grabbing Jaime with the u-shaped hand. Thumb to the left. Pressing hard on his throat. He squeezed and lifted the young prisoner off the floor. By upward force. Against the jawbone. Jaime peed.

"What have you done to my floor?" The Honduran yelled.

Jaime felt a warm liquid on his leg. The hand still felt around his throat. It squeezed. Tighter, until his Adam's apple pressed on his windpipe. Unable to breath. Fear shooed all thought from his head. This moment without thought brought peace.

Peace without oxygen.

The hand released. Allowing Jaime's feet to touch the floor.

He gasped to inhale.

His trousers were wet. The warm liquid was turning cool. Jaime knew life as air entered his body. Fear returned.

U. S. Embassy

Tom was finding many non-related pieces of paper in the bottom of the boxes delivered to him. Amongst the papers, newspaper articles. Clippings added a piece to the Central American puzzle. From The New York Times, Wall Street Journal and Washington Post. One had been pasted to a hard back of an empty legal pad.

Lead read, "Honduran General Mentioned in Drug Case." He moved it closer for a read. "José Bueso Rosa, a General in the Honduran Army. Named as a co-conspirator for his alleged role in smuggling drugs. To the United States through Florida and Louisiana. The same being person, earlier named in an assassination plot. Against the Honduran President Roberto Suazo Córdoba in 1984. The general is suspected of having ties to Contras, fighting in Nicaragua. The named individual was tied to $40 million of cocaine seized. A joint operation between the FBI and DEA intercepted the shipment in Miami. Administration officials commenting said, 'The General could not have been involved. It was a dis-information campaign perpetrated by the Sandinista Government'...."

Other loose articles covered the bottom of the box. One article head-line read, "Contra Commander Found with Drugs." Another article tied to "Southern Front FDN Units Protecting Drug Smugglers." No names. Innuendo. "Sources said...now involved in drug running out of Panama."

"...Suspected covert foreign connections supplying weapons. Person in the Panamanian Government tied to trading drugs for weapons. Cuban connection to Noriega suspected. U.S. Drug Enforcement Administration fighting uphill battle...."

Tom called Central American Desk in Virginia. "...Is there a drug connection to Constable Outreach? I wasn't aware of?"

The voice on the other end replied, "It's impossible to say. Lots of media reports. Connecting Contra Operations and drug trafficking. But, nothing involving you. That, I can say."

"What can you tell me?"

"The Assistant Director overseeing South American activities has cautioned us in discussing possibilities. 'Stick to the facts,' is what we're told."

"Can you call me if any 'facts' cross your desk?"

"You know, I can't promise that."

"Well, I got my own situation going on here. My man is being held somewhere in Nicaragua. Got a boy in custody belonging to a Sandinista Queen. I'm a little bit on edge. What can you promise me?"

"Tom, I know your situation. Just can't go beyond what I'm told." The call didn't end well. There were loose ends. Tom felt outside the agency loop.

U. S. Embassy - October 12, 1985

Tom arrived his temporary office at 8 AM. Questioning a connection. Between articles he had read and ties to the missing Lester Russell. The call with Central American Desk didn't end well. Fred was dumping new information on him every day. He had no idea what to do about getting Lester back. The young man in holding at Danli was providing no usable information.

One dossier held on his desk covered what was known about his mother. Yet, Jaime Velasquez had no knowledge of her past. Other than he was heir to the heroism of his father, Miguel Correa Velasquez.

He picked up the receiver, on the third ring.

"Tom McKay."

"Morning Tom, Jack Simone. Danli."

"What can I do for you Jack?"

"We have a problem. Your boy is experiencing some difficulty."

"How so?

"We tried a different tactic. Thinking he would respond to Honduran interrogators. It got out of hand. Sent your young man into a state of depression. Crying. Not eating. We may have pushed him too far."

"How bad is he?"

"Jaime's mental attitude had already started downhill. Thought we could crack him."

"Get to the point."

"He tried to hurt himself last night."

"What?"

"Yeah, we found him this morning with marks on his wrists. Tried to cut himself with the plastic plate. One used to feed him."

"We can't...be seen hurting children. For God's sake."

"Where is he now?"

"Moved him from Honduran side back to the barracks. Doctor looked after him. He'll be OK, physically. But, right now his mental state is not good."

"No more interrogations!"

"Doc says, he doesn't trust anyone. Won't let them near."

"You will not let anything happen to that boy! Understood!"

"Understood." The call ended.

Rancho Perez

Latitude: 13.8955 N

Longitude: 86.1503 W

Central Standard Time (GMT -6)

Sunday – 13 October 1985

"I have some business to attend, in town." Said Major Sanchez.

Commander Abdel nodded. "I will stay with Señora Perez. Ask our guest a few questions. When do you expect to return?"

"I must meet with the Mayor and Colonel Mendez. Visit the training camp. If I am not back by sundown, be back in the morning."

"Commander Pallais will stay here?" Juanita asks.

"Please Señora. If I do not return, I'm sure you will be a gracious host."

The major was gone. Lester's guard had been silent and unseen. Returned to his post at the steel barred room entry. Commander Abdel touched his arm as he looked in at the prisoner.

"I will take a combat nap. Get me when our prisoner awakens." He settled onto the floor. Using only his fatigue jacket as a pillow. He was asleep within minutes. The guard resumed his sitting position in the prisoner's bedroom.

Juanita paced on the front porch. *'My God'* she said silently, for no human to hear. *'I am placed in a situation. None of my asking, but through my family's connection. A man lay recovering on my bed. Strangers come and go in my house. My son is gone. My only hope. God, give me strength….'*

The pacing helped calm her. That was, until the next round of interrogations.

Commander Abdel slept for 20 minutes. Rising and walking to the porch, found Juanita sitting. She looked out toward the place where her son disappeared. Pallais touched her shoulder. It startled her.

"When we get the information we seek, I will take your prisoner out and shoot him."

"And, who put you in command at my home?" She said angrily.

"He will be a casualty of war."

"Not with my knowing!"

"He came from the airplane, Senora."

"He does not shoot at you. He lies in bed. Recovering from his accident." She paused to think. "And, there is no evidence that he fell from the airplane!"

"Senora, I saw it with my own eyes."

"What man or woman could survive a fall from an airplane? Without a parachute?" Then added, "You must have been taking those drugs you hide."

"The parachute." Commander Abdel said. "He was wearing a parachute."

"What? Why did you not bring this to our attention?"

The commander said nothing. His thoughts went to the day of the firefight.

"You and I cannot settle this." He said firmly. She had touched an exposed nerve.

"You don't know who is in charge, do you?"

"It is Major Sanchez."

Juanita shook her head slowly. Said no more.

"All will be well Señora."

"How can you say that? My house has become a battlefield hospital. You will not stop until you get the words you want. You are an unwanted guest in my home. What rights come with my husband's estate? This property?"

"Señora, you are upset. Rightfully so. But it will be over soon. And you can get back to living. We will go on."

"And what of my son? Where is he? Can you get him back?" Tears came from her eyes.

The guard interrupted their conversation.

"Commander, he is awake."

The commander and the guard returned to the bedroom. Closing the door behind them. Occasionally, Juanita heard screams. She assumed Pallais was inflicting pain. She covered her ears.

'Is my son being subjected to such torture? When will I know that he is alive? This is painful – listening and waiting!'

The sounds diminished. No screams of pain. No loud voices. Commander Pallais came through the bedroom opening. He had a shoulder satchel in his hand. A bag made from green canvas.

He said, "I carry sedatives that will help us keep him both quiet and talkative."

"I know torture is a means to get information. Those sounds take my mind elsewhere."

"I gave him something to sleep."

"What did you give him?"

"Heroin. For our fight, injured soldiers need medication on the battlefield. I carry this satchel." Commander Abdel said. "I gave him something for his pain. To quiet *your* prisoner."

Ten minutes passed. Her bedroom door opened.

"He sleeps again," the guard said. The use of heroin was to quiet the prisoner. Not relieve his pain.

Her disgust expressed through her facial expression

"Would you fix us dinner?"

"Yes! It will pass time until the Major returns."

Commander Abdel sat at the table. He watched Juanita boil rice. Her refrigerator was small. She removed a package of beef, brought by the cattlemen. Other items left from previous meals sat neatly on the shelves.

"Tendremos carne con arroz." She said as she continued her preparation. "We will have brewed tea."

The commander fumbled to retrieve a pill vial from his green bag. Juanita paid no attention to him. He removed one pill from the vial. Set the pill on the table near where he sat. Then he placed the vial back into the bag.

He watched her walk away, with two plates in hand. Eyes of desire followed her movement. Carrying the food into the prisoner. And, one for the guard.

While she was away, Commander Abdel crushed the pill. Sprinkling the particles into her glass of warm tea. Watching the particles descend as they disappeared. Juanita returned to the kitchen.

"Your guard said he was grateful."

After eating, the Commander went to the living room. Sitting on the couch, he beckoned Juanita to join him in conversation. She was feeling a little more relaxed. Conversation was light. They shared some laughter. His eyes watched her intently. When under the influence, he would approach her.

He saw her falling into his arms. She would give herself to him. Juanita and Abdel sat on opposite ends of the couch. Abdel's desire for interaction came from a guttural need for female attention. Not remembering the soft touch from his mother.

"I feel light-headed," she said to Abdel. Juanita was feeling the effects of the crushed pill sprinkled in her drink.

"Too much activity?"

"I am not sure. Maybe." She stopped. "The disappearance of my son. The American in my bed. More traffic through my house…since I can remember. You."

"Me?"

"You know what I mean. How different we are." Feeling more relaxed. Waves of dizziness rushing, from the base of her neck. Fighting the waves only made her tired of trying.

"I think I'll go lie down."

"Can I help you?"

"I have it." When she stood, a wave caused her to list to the right. Catching herself by the couch arm. She made her way to the door of her bedroom.

'Can't go in there, my bed is already full. Turn left. Bed in my son's room.'

In two steps, she fell against the wall. Guard watching Lester, opened the door. Abdel moving toward her.

"Let me help you." Abdel said, lifting Juanita from under her arms.

'Her underarms were warm. Her breasts firm. So soft, her skin.' Abdel thought.

Abdel walked her to Jaime's bed.

Lying her on the bed, he knew this would be his time. He kissed her on the mouth. Juanita pulled away. Her eyes opened wide, as he touched her beast. Sliding his hand down her stomach to her crotch.

With a jolt, she sat up. Her head knocked him off balance.

"What do you think you are doing?"

"You want me. Actions show, your desire for me." He pushed her upper torso back down onto the bed.

"No!"

"If you won't admit it. Maybe, you are confused." He said, applying more force, holding her down. He went to climb on top of her.

"I said, 'No'!" She leveraged his weight. Throwing him off the bed. Rolling to arrive on top of him. Her knife at his throat.

"What would prevent me from driving this knife deep. To your spine?"

Her words slurred. But, her actions completed with precision.

Rising, she spoke one word.

"Out!"

Abdel scrambled to his feet. Embarrassed. Taken down by a woman. Juanita backed him out the door.

"Out!" She screamed. She was wobbly. Adrenaline shooting through her body.

Repeating again, "Leave. Get out!"

Hearing the clamor, guard opened the door. She pointed the knife at him.

"And, you! You get out too." Looking at the startled guard. Pointing toward the front door. "Get out of my house!"

"But, Senora."

"Sali. Saca tu cuerpo de mi casa!"

The guard moved around Juanita. Never taking eyes off her. He backed out the front door. Following him, she closed and locked it behind him. The effects of the drug overpowering her adrenaline. Stumbling toward her bedroom door. Knife held low and to her side. Entering the room holding her prisoner.

The activity had awakened Lester. She continued toward him with knife in hand.

"My dirty American!" Slurring her English. "Would you try to rape me?"

"No!"

"Where's my son?" Hoping he would tell her.

"I don't know where he is." He said. Nervousness heard in his reply. Left hand and ankles secured.

"I would do anything to get my son back" Tapping the knife blade on her leg.

Lester said nothing.

"My name is Juanita Maria Perez," she exclaimed. "I am the widow of Miguel Correa Velasquez, a Sandinista hero. Killed by your Contra forces." She paused. "I am a mother." She began to cry. "You took my son."

He listened to every word. She was a woman suffering in her own pain. Her anger expressed in her words. Her sorrow the subtext to the war in which she was involved. Not a sad woman. Proud. With motherly instincts.

She moved closer to the bed. The anger on her face clearly seen. Her disheveled look, spoke of the confrontation. The knife she held in her hand became his concern. She stumbled, touching the bed. Movement of the bed, reminded Lester of his pain.

"And you," she said. With the anger of a vixen. "You will suffer for taking my son."

He tried but could not pull away.

"You will give me what I want." She exclaimed, holding the knife point toward the ceiling. Grabbing one corner of the sheet covering him. She pulled it toward the footboard. His naked body exposed.

"This can't be good," he said to himself.

"How does it feel to be vulnerable?" The tone of a witch came from inside her.

"Not good," he replied with nervousness in his voice. He could imagine the knife going South into his body. Slicing through his skin. Or, genital removal. His body a target for any placement of the knife.

The room became quiet. He could hear his raised heart-beat. Only the light from adjacent room pierced this darkness. Juanita Maria turned with her back to him. She straightened herself. She removed her top garment. Exposing her long lean back. She released the fork that held her hair in a twist. Long dark hair fell to the middle of her back. Her dark hair seemed trained to go where it was needed.

Turning, she began to expose the front of her body. Her breasts firm. Barley exposed by limited light. As she moved closer, he watched for the place of her knife. In the open air, he saw goosebumps. She did not speak. Removing her clothes in silence.

"What the heck is going on here," Lester thought. His testosterone acting like a block to the pain he experienced before. His penis becoming hard.

'Oh, no. *Think of something other than her body...*' It was no use.

He got harder as she moved closer to the bed. The knife in her right hand. His back stiffened. The muscles in his legs tightened. His tight buttocks raised his back. He felt a shooting pain.

Wielding the knife. Cursing Pallais. Talking to him throughout about her son. Understanding little of the Spanish she spoke. Touches Lester on his stomach with the knife. Slides knife toward his penis. Touches it with the flat side of the blade. Sliding the flat blade across his leg.

She dropped the knife.

The warmth of a hand touched his penis. Causing it to get harder. Fondling it. Kissing him gently on the stomach. Looking at him. Face resting on his stomach.

"Ahora," kissing his penis. Her mouth was warm. His cautious excitement enjoyed the stroking. He held back the pressure from building sperm. The longer he held it, the harder he got. Finally, he could hold no longer...

"Meirda! En un día anterior, que habría montado aquello."

Juanita lifted her head. Comes close to his face.

"These are things that do not mix. People who should not be together. Acts of violence that solve nothing. Sex with a man you hate."

She gently kisses him on his cheek. Walks from the room.

Rancho Perez

Latitude: 13.8955 N

Longitude: 86.1503 W

Central Standard Time (GMT -6)

Monday – 14 October 1985

Lester heard an automobile engine start. Half-awake in his state, had listened to talking voices on the other side of the door. Willing himself awake. Vague memories of a satisfying encounter.

'Did I imagine. My wet dream was real. Maybe the medication. The shot given me by a soldier. Pain was real enough. What information are they looking for?' The thoughts escaping through a foggy memory.

A vehicle engine sound changed and was moving. It idled for a moment. Then picked up RPM. Fading away from the house. Whoever was driving changed gears and kept moving away. Another gear-change. The sound muffled. He strained to listen. There was nothing left there to hear.

'Was he alone?

Moments passed. He drifted. Awakening to footsteps. They moved from left to right. Stopping somewhere in a far reach forward to the right.

'I am not alone.'

The movement seemed purposeful. Walking in a pattern. Like someone pacing.

'...like someone anxiously waiting to use the bathroom. He had used those facilities. Under the watchful eyes of a guard.'

Beyond the closed wooden door, coffee brewed. Aroma of a Central-American blend. Its smell floating above him. The earthy smell he remembered. He missed his medium-ground American coffee. He could drink it all day. Without stomach flips.

'...stomach rebelled. High caffeine and acid with thicker brews. Food took it away. Food. Dammit, I'm hungry.'

The pacing person on the other side of the wall, made one final swing to the left. Rebound to the right was slower. A stop-framed picture put to sound. Stopping at the door.

'OK, here we go.' The door did not open. *'One-thousand-one, one-thousand-two, one-thousand...'* It opened.

Juanita Perez, his *'vixen jailer'* stood, silent in the doorway. Looking through the room. Past him. He pulled his head back, as far as the moderate pain would allow. Looking to his right and left. Then he looked back in her direction. She hadn't moved.

"Are you ready to eat?"

"Yes!" Half choking on his saliva. Pushing the words from his mouth That was all that would come out. Clearing his thought was difficult lying on his back.

"Do you feel like sitting at table?"

'What the hell is she up to? He asked himself, without speaking.

"Aren't you afraid that I'll rape you?" His dream rolled from his lips.

"No. There is no fear of that." She replied, immediately. "I take care of myself."

"Then, yes. It will be good to get off my back."

Juanita removed both ankle straps. Then undid the strap holding his left wrist.

Bringing his arm to his side required effort. The joint resting in stretched position, did not respond. It temporarily locked. He needed help bringing his body erect. Any jerking motion sent shooting pain up his back.

"Swing your legs." She assisted the turning motion, lifting both legs. Gently toward her. Releasing them. To grab his arm, assisting Lester toward the sitting position. Grabbing his wrist.

Once sitting, he watched her pick up clothing from the floor. Looking her up and down, without trying to be obvious. She moved away. Dropping the clothes at the edge of the wooden door. Turned. Approached the bed.

He was watching this female. His eyes fixed on her waist. Attention drawn to a slightly fashionable belt. Holding a scabbard, knife handle protruding from it.

'Deep breath. Breath…breathe.'

"Do you like what you see?" She paused. "Or, was it this you were looking at," Patting the scabbard.

He half-nodded. *'Yep, she's got it.'*

"The doctor said, your pain was probably from inflammation. If your back or neck was broken, you wouldn't move."

'Thank you for that diagnosis! And, when the hell did a doctor examine me?'

"We're going to stand now." She prefaced each movement with a command. "There. Okay?"

"So far."

"Small steps. Don't worry. You'll make it." She stopped, selecting her words carefully. "You only have 20 paces to the kitchen table."

He moved slowly. She, half-supporting him. Let him do all the work. Keeping her right arm free. Hanging toward the scabbard. She was a professional. Her husband was professional. He needed her to lead when the time came. This was one time.

Her count of the number of paces was nearly correct. The pace count was twenty-two. He didn't move like a gazelle. His moves were more like a comedic version of Frankenstein. With each step, the knee discomfort upon rising was lessening with movement.

Seated at table, his back felt less pressure. Moving into that seated position was almost as difficult as swing off the bed. Muscles used to sit, were different than those used to rise.

"OK?"

"Thanks." He had genuine feelings of gratitude. The first time without the rough handling guard. Or, others poking to cause pain. Walking to the kitchen table was a small victory. However small, it was knowing that he was not incapacitated. He would get better.

"Huevos envueltos en hojas de plantano, pan y café." She laughed. "Let me translate. Eggs wrapped in banana leaves, bread and coffee."

'Juanita the jailer, had a sense of humor.' Through her Spanish accent, she spoke clearly. *'Where did she build such a command of the English language?'*

A plate was put before him. He only had one arm with which to eat. He was right-handed. Banana leaves tied with plantain fiber, were a challenge. Trying to untie the fiber with his left hand presented manual dexterity problems. The neat squares looked like Christmas packages. She stopped him.

"Don't you say grace first in the United States?"

"Yes?" He offered, "But, not since I was a child."

"Well, here we give praise for the food put in front of us!"

He bowed his head. Juanita offered a prayer in Spanish for the food they were about to eat.

She unwrapped his eggs. Scraping the banana leaves clean. Removing them from his plate. He looked up at her.

"Where's the guard?" Lester asked, covering his fascination with her. *'She was a beautiful woman....'*

"He is not needed anymore…Eat."

There was no conversation. She watched him intently. He ate all on his plate.

"The doctor said you are recovering well. He took the IV port from your arm. Your shoulder and back will take the longest."

"When did he come?"

"A couple of times. Mostly to just look. Bring supplies. And, give me instructions."

"I don't remember."

"It's okay. You have come a long way."

Lester thought about the words forming in his head. "Last night. The soldier gave me a shot. I heard…" He stopped. "I heard you yelling. Is he your boyfriend?"

"No," She said. Laughing, then turning stern. "He was a friend of my husband. Soldiers. He won't be back."

"Now, you. Lester Russell. Why are you here in Nicaragua?"

"This is…I'm in Nicaragua?"

"Yes. The soldier, last night. He found you on a road, West of here. He found you in this condition."

"I remember. Falling. Vietnam. Gunships. Low-level." He searched for another thought.

"Doctor did say you took a jolt. May have amnesia. Result of hitting you head hard."

Lester said nothing. Staring at her.

"Well?"

"I remember – or, dreamed. Walking. A long walk."

"That's good!" She was genuinely pleased. Her actions showed it. "You were walking, from where?"

"I don't know. Just walking. Trees. And, a road. Near my house."

"Okay, it'll come to you."

His body experienced physical trauma. Being swept from the airplane. His shoulder remained immobilized. Arm tied across his chest. He experienced shooting pain in his spine. From his coccyx, up to his neck. Quick movement brought it on. Face was scarring. His mind settled in the past.

"What would Yoda say?"

Juanita gave him a puzzled look.

Working Group - 41
October 16, 1985

Working Group 41 had been in Tegucigalpa for two days. Fred's working story had not generated any feedback from other embassies in the region.

Sunday was spent setting up WG-41 situation room. When Monday rolled around, they were ready to dive in. They reviewed documents of significance, as selected by Tom McKay. Establishing a written time-line. They decided that the position of scribe, recorder would rotate. Everyday.

Two-sided boards, for writing with chalk arrived. Boards on which notes could be pinned, sat on easels. Files and boxes containing Constable Outreach reports repositioned to the basement room. Team members sifted through the boxes. Searching for additional connections to exploit.

After hours of work yesterday, each member knew the agency position. And how it affected future relations in this region. Other members offered contrapuntal points of view. The one holding reserved opinion was from the DOJ. His would be a legal opinion researched overnight in Washington DC.

When Tom arrived. Anne was placing a packet at each member's position.

"You're early." Tom said, thinking he would be the first to arrive.

"Had a fitful night. Food didn't agree with me."

"It takes a while adjusting."

"Got this off the fax this morning." Pointing to the packet she held. "It might be something we can use later."

"What's that?"

"Your Memorandum of Understanding. DOJ drafted one we can plug and play with."

"I'm impressed."

The other three working group members came through the door.

"Morning everyone." Tom greeted.

"Where are we?" Rich Rubenstein asked.

"Talking about a MOU. Anne got this off the FAX this morning." Holding it up for everyone to notice. "But, we're not there yet." Tom said.

"What's your guy's name? Lester is it. Last seen in Jalapa hospital. Then driven by ambulance to Managua. That would mean somebody with clout ordered it. The Sandinista government has to know his whereabouts." Hank questioned

"Talked to my guys in Panama. We're correct in assuming there's a whole pipeline. Through Costa Rica to the States. The pictures we looked at yesterday, are only part of what's available." Sam Maddox said.

"Have we got any feedback on the pictures sent of boy?" Ann asked. "That would be a good place to start."

"Fred even greased the skids by the cover story sent out. The Times said they'd play along if questions arise. What about this Cuban Embassy employee?"

"Talked with the agent who busted him. The Panamanians let him go before the 72-hour hold was up. They had him dead to rights. Cubans said they'd be glad to clear up the misunderstanding. Didn't release the crate. It's in DEA storage. Won't let it go. Creating quite a diplomatic flap."

The room door opened. Fred Matthews stepped in and closed it behind him.

"Morning everybody. We got a hit through the Panamanian Embassy. Said their contacts in Managua might know where our guy is. Just wanted to deliver that news myself."

"That's a start." Tom said, cheering the news.

Fred waited for more comments. None came. Then he left the room.

"We need something more concrete than that. We need someone to bite on the kid's picture." Anne added.

"We're farther on than I was seven days ago." Tom added. "Let's do a review."

Tegucigalpa, Honduras

Latitude: 14.0723 North

Longitude: 87.1921 West

Central Standard Time (GMT -6)

Thursday – 17 October 1985

Tom started the position statements for those at table.

"Anne and I are going to work in tandem. We come from the same house."

"Constable Outreach, conducted its first aerial delivery. It was to resupply and position supplies for future incursions. The recipients, the Contra Revolutionary Forces operating in Nicaragua. The supply delivered by a C-123 Provider plane. The means of supply, by airdrop. The plane flew into Nicaraguan space low level to prevent detection. Once at the DZ, the crew performed the drop. At some point during that offload, the cargo handler – our loadmaster – was swept from the airplane. He was the only person in the cargo compartment. We do not know how that happened. Discovered missing afterwards. During high speed escape. The plane was damaged. But, it did recover to Toncontin airport." He paused, then Anne continued.

"The Contras were neutralized. We lost a Special Forces Operator in the fight. Three days later we received notification from a hospital employee. An American was treated in Jalapa Hospital, Nicaragua. Subsequently, our source obtained fingerprints. Confirming that American was Lester Russell, our loadmaster. In another unrelated incident, forces attaining intelligence around the Jalapa area, captured an asset. Described as a young man associated with the local Sandinista defense force. He remains in custody and is being questioned..."

Tom stood. "Reported, that Russell was moved by ambulance to Managua area prison hospital. Since then we have no intel. Through Embassy channels, a cover story was developed. Placed at all our Central & South American Embassies. Since, feelers have gone out. Seeking more information about our man. All we know at this point is that he was alive sixteen days ago. We want the him back. And, we need to retrieve the body of our Special Forces operator. Are there any questions?"

Questions were handled by Tom for clarification purposes.

The next person to present was Sam Maddox. DEA agency perspective and position.

"Thanks Tom. Anne. In an unrelated situation. Our agency personnel in Bogotá had been tracking drug shipments. The operation was routine. In one movement, the shipment of drugs tracked to the Cuban Embassy. Over the course of two weeks, more drugs found their way into the

Embassy compound. An unnamed source informed us that a large crate was to be shipped to Panama. Under Diplomatic Courier transfer to their embassy there. I cannot divulge any operational details that may compromise our source..."

"The crate arrived at TAM cargo. To fly on a passenger plane bound for Panama. A Courier escorted the crate. The agents in Bogotá suspected that the crate contained cocaine. They observed high-level attention paid to the Cuban Courier and the crate itself. The agent-in-charge called his counterpart in Panama..."

"Under the suspicion that the crate contained an inordinate amount of cocaine. It was traveling under diplomatic transfer. The agents in Panama made a judgment call to detain the Courier. And, confiscate the crate. It created the situation which has had international implications. The Cubans would like to clear their Courier and have the crate released." He paused. "But, I don't see how quoting my agencies activities in Panama affect this situation."

In the absence of Fred Matthews, Hank Thoreau then laid out a scenario. "We're presented with the opportunity to return all playing fields to normal. The USSR has agreed to work with us. Presentation pictures and doctor report was a positive sign."

Hank continued, "Normal reaction is to call fowl before we get here. Where we are. They never called fowl. Our position is to maintain the working relationship with the Honduran Military. Fred Matthews has his hands full every day maintaining the status quo here in Honduras. In a letter from Special Envoy Al Peterson, he sees a workable solution. His letter available here to be read." He turned to the next speaking point.

"We asked the Soviet Embassy to contact Cuban and Nicaraguan government officials. We have not heard from them up to this point. Yet, we are to assume that they can apply enough pressure for us to begin a dialog."

The group sat silent for a few moments. DOJ Attorney Rubenstein stood. He presented a legal position on behalf of the White House for the President of the United States.

"You have seen the MOU in your packet. It is an instrument used between agencies of the federal government. To trade resources for budgetary concerns. But, it has been used between adversary states to accomplish a desired outcome. Tom was involved in an agent trade where the MOU was successful. In that case, it was not a magic document. Hard diplomatic work between the USSR and U.S. Embassies made it effective..." He paused.

"We have an opportunity here to drag it off the shelf. Insert wants, desires and outcomes to meet opposing state goals. Let's turn our attention to findings within recent interactions. In there, we may find how we can get our guy back. In trade for the boy captured in Nicaragua."

Platform was set. Each agency representatives went about reviewing their files for input keys. Knock came at the door. A female embassy employee beckoned Tom.

Call for Tom McKay

"There is a call for you."

"Put it through." He said, not thinking it would be of a personal nature.

"I think you want to take this in your office."

With a puzzled look, Tom followed the employee up one flight of stairs.

"Tom Mckay."

"Alexandr Dutrov. You may remember me from Berlin."

"Alex. To what do I owe the pleasure."

"I'd like to invite you for a drink. With an old friend."

"Sure, where and when?"

"Say five o'clock. Café La Plata. A local establishment near the airport."

"Five o'clock. Look forward to seeing you. Friend." When Tom hung up, his thoughts went to their meeting seven years prior.

'The voice had familiarity to it. A little older. But, the recall was pleasant. Outcome positive. It would be good to catch up. What brought this call out of the blue – the ether covering the planet? Got to report this contact. Documentation would have to be within the embassy logs. Date. Time. Discussion. Fred Matthews....'

"Fred, got a minute."

"Sure, come on in."

"How are things on the home front?"

"Supposed to talk with Betty and lawyers on conference call this afternoon."

"Think positive. There might be something to work with." Tom paused. "I have a foreign contact to report. You're the best chance for getting it on the record. Immediately."

"In person? Or, phone?"

"Phone. KGB agent I worked with in the past. Prisoner swap. All, sort of routine. Documented on both sides."

"Who was it?"

"Alexandr Dutrov."

"The KGB regional guy?"

"Yeah, lot of water under the bridge since then. He wants to meet at five."

"Do you need assistance?

"Don't think so. He proposed it as a friendly meet. I can't say no now. Got to show."

There was no time for getting electronic surveillance in place. Chances would have to be taken. Contact was reported. If a nefarious act was being planned, it would be on the record.

Interrogation Office – Danli

The section supervisor waited for all affecting parties to arrive in the ready room. Battalion 3-16 Commander was on his way. The rest of the team mulled in personal conversations between them.

"Commandant, thank you for coming." The two shook hands. "This is my team. Some you may know in passing on the base."

"It is my pleasure to be in this company," the Commandant replied, looking around the room.

"Please. Sit here." Supervisor gave him a seat next to him at the head of table.

"This concern is about one person in our custody. One Jaime Velasquez."

The Commandant was aware of the young boy. Carrying the name of a Nicaraguan Guerilla Leader. His mind raced to incidents where his men had lost their lives. "What concern do we have for a person in your custody?"

"Orders came down from my superiors. And, this applies to all personnel in this room." Turning to the Commandant, "We wanted to make you aware of these orders. In the spirit of openness, being on your compound." He paused to pick up the document before him. He read directly from it.

"TOP – SECRET"

"Dissemination Only - By and Between Cooperating Agency Partners

"TO: Agency Personnel & Contractors, Sub-Station Danli, Honduras

"THRU: Supervisor, Interrogation Team

"CC: Agency Headquarters, Virginia; Commandant, Battalion 3-16, Danli

"FROM: Tom McKay, Constable Outreach, Tegucigalpa, Honduras

1. This memorandum establishes a no contact rule. Between interrogators and Jaime Correa-Perez Velasquez. Held in detention at Danli Sub-Station.

2. Under no circumstance will Jaime Velasquez be interrogated. He is to remain in the custody of agency personnel under 24-hour guard. He will have no contact with anyone outside this office. Or, the agency sub-station, Danli, Site 16.

3. Request this order read to Commandant, Battalion 3-16, for informational purposes only. Providing needed explanations.

4. This order carries with it the full support of the Agency Director.

5. Information supplied based on need to know.

Signed //S//Thomas F. Mckay."

"TOP – SECRET"

Quiet held the room. Until the Commandant spoke.

"This is the son of our enemy."

"Yes, sir. I know. But, I will not go against orders. Written or verbal. This memo states the official position of our agency. A copy delivered to your office."

"I will speak to my superiors!" The commandant pushed his chair back. Leaving the room.

Tegucigalpa, Honduras

Latitude: 14.0723 North

Longitude: 87.1921 West

Central Standard Time (GMT -6)

Five PM – Café La Plata

Thursday – 17 October 1985

"Tom. Over here."

Tom McKay walked toward the table near the alley. The umbrella flaps wavered in the light breeze. Back to the wall, sat Alexandr Dutrov. When Tom got closer, Alexandr stood and extended his hand. Tom scanned the area for observers.

"Alex. A surprise to see you. Your call, totally unexpected."

"Good to see you Tom. You were a pleasure to work with in Berlin. Hope we can start with that attitude. Much has happened between our nations since then."

"What can I do for you?" Tom wanted to get straight to the point of meeting.

"What no small talk first?"

"I apologize. A lot going on right now. Some with family. Mostly with the job. You know."

"Yes. The job takes its toll on the family."

"See you are regional security director. Long way from Berlin."

"Yes. Comes with the territory. You move up. Or, they move you out. There is no middle."

"So…," Tom was interrupted. By a waiter.

"Dos cervezas? O, habrá algo más." The waiter asked.

"Dos Imperial y dos tragos de vodka." Alexandr ordered.

"Sí. Ahora mismo." The waiter walked away quickly.

"You did that well."

"I've learned a few things. How about you?" It was a leading question.

"First, to what do I owe the honor of our meeting here?" Tom asked.

"We have interests in common. We hear you are looking for a journalist. Da?

"I believe the embassy put out some feelers. Your point of contact would be the U. S. Embassy."

"Our friends contacted us about a person who could be that man."

"Any details?"

"You always were a man who got right to the point." Alexandr said with a laugh.

"It's always good to work with someone who knows you so well."

This form of open flattery is a constant. It reset the stage for coming discussions.

The waiter arrived with the beer and two shots of vodka.

"¿Habrá algo más?" The waiter asked.

"No. Gracias." Tom replied.

Alexandr lifted his glass of beer. They clinked glasses. Both taking the first sip.

"I came with pictures. You can tell me if this is the man you seek." Alexandr said, sliding three color pictures across the table.

Tom reminded himself not to alert Alex, with facial expression or body language, movement.

"This could be him. I'd have to pass them to my embassy contact for verification."

"If you are interested, a doctor gave me this." He added, pulling a folded document from his jacket pocket. "The pictures and document are yours to keep."

Alexandr took another sip of beer. Raised the small glass of vodka. Tom followed suit.

"To our working together, again." Alexandr toasted. Drank the vodka.

Tom downed the shot. Then said, "Is there anything we can look at for you. Or, someone you may be seeking? We have connections throughout Central America."

Tom expected one reply. But, got another.

"Always to the point." He replied. "There is a young man. Barely out of school. His mother worries about him. She cries. I have a soft heart. Would you help me find him?"

"I always do my best." Tom was aware that both agencies - KGB & CIA - were keeping tabs. Knew what goes on with the other. With this visit, the specifics pointed to solving regional concerns. The surprise was in pinpointing the exact agency contact to make. Both parties surmised that the other was involved. Caused both nations a covert meeting. On the sly over alcohol.

Meeting on the battlefield would have much more a devastating effect.

"There is one more thing." Alexandr said, waiting for an opening to discuss the second point.

"You always come prepared. Shoot." Tom said, "But, I didn't mean that literally."

"A figure of speech." He wanted a slow delivery. With words that were non-implicating. "There is a certain crate In-Bond on a U.S. Government hold. DEA has interest. I think my friend said, in Panama."

'There it was! The drug issues the DEA said had no relevance to Constable Outreach.'

"I wouldn't know about Panamanian Customs. But, I will inquire." Tom replied

"I can't ask for any more than that. To you, my friend. Saludo!" Alexandr held his glass of beer high for another clink. "One more. Then, back to work. Yes?"

"Absolutely!" The meeting lasted an hour. Tom knew that somewhere on the crowded street, two agents were photographing the meeting.

Hotel Elegante
Seven PM

Tom walked through the lobby. Taking a brief look, into the hotel bar. He spotted Fred Matthews on a stool. He looked like a beaten man. Back slumped forward. Elbows on the bar.

"Looked for you when I came in." Tom said as he approached. "May I sit?"

"Of course. How'd the meeting go?"

"Got some interesting photos. Among the discussion of other topics. I'll share later."

"What are you drinking?"

"Scotch on the rocks."

Fred called the bar tender. "Johnny Walker Black sobre hielo."

Bar tender returned with the drink and fresh bowl of fried plantains.

"By the way. Thanks for sending the photographer."

Fred raised his glass, slightly.

"He wasn't the only one. Glad I registered the contact with you." He wanted to ask about Fred's telephone conference. There was only one way. "How'd your conference go?"

"Sobering. That's why I'm here."

Tom waited for Fred to continue. He didn't want to press.

"Seems Betty has been thinking about this for years. Her third attempt with the same law firm. I never saw the signs."

"In our business, the signs are sometimes hard to see. Family is totally foreign to what we do. Until it affects us."

"She always was busy. Canasta Club. Women's League. The homeless shelters."

"All worthy ways for a homemaker to get out. Without being on the arm of another man."

"Yeah. But, I almost wish she had. At least she would've had some fun. Apparently, the fun ran out of me fifteen years ago." He looked at Tom. "You know when someone is busy, it masks all sorts of things going on below the surface."

"Never thought about that."

"Yes, sir. It's doublespeak. She wanted to matter. To me. Yet, she wanted to recapture her past. Before me. Her independence. She thinks it's too late."

"It's never too late." Tom said, thinking of his own situation. "You just have to re-engage."

"After John went off to college this year. There was nothing for her to do in the evening. But, sit in the house by herself. All her friends were busy with family or husbands who were at home."

"That's the sad thing about us being gone at this age. If our women were younger, they might try a night out or two."

"What's sad, is I've been mirroring her action. Keeping busy because I feel guilty. No quality to life. Just quantity. Doing more. Taking on more. Afraid, you'll be put out to pasture."

"Happens to all of us."

"She is deserving of being a priority in my eyes. Sacrificed a lot."

Tom was beginning to think that too much talk was leading to excuses. He had none.

"All our wives are subjugated to the needs of the job. It makes me think. I could be where you are." He fidgeted with a decision. "I'm going to go upstairs. Call my wife. Thanks for the drinks. See you in the morning."

U. S. Embassy - WG-41 Work Room
Friday – 18 October

"We have pictures." Tom announced to the working group.

The other members each took a turn looking at the three pictures. Tom was saving the doctor's report for a crowning moment.

"And, this. It's a report from the doctor who treated Lester in hospital."

"Where'd you get this stuff?" Hank asked.

"It won't become a surprise. Pictures were taken of the meeting. Alexandr Dutrov." Tom replied.

Two members knew the name immediately. From regional study. Sam Maddox and Rich Rubenstein, were left wondering at the name.

"KGB Regional Intel Director." Ann offered.

"How did that happen?" Rich asked. Thinking of other implications over the meeting of two foreign operatives.

"Called me. We met. I brought you the intel. That simple." Tom said. As if to say, *'You don't want to know any more.'*

"Okay." Hank said. "We got a positive turn here. Let's not blow it."

"There's more. They surmise we have Jaime Velasquez. And..." Turning toward the Sam, "They know about the crate. No surprise. But, they want their drugs back. Cuban embassy employee cleared."

"No fucking way!" Sam blurted immediately.

The first casualty in the negotiation was going to be the DEA position. The Russian had held the last for effect. Their bargaining position was good.

"We, at least have to consider it." Ann added.

Sam was fuming. "So, we take it in the shorts!"

"There is a greater good here. Without admitting the agency was gearing up for a guerilla war. We can get our guy back. Get rid of the albatross delivered by well-meaning, conscience-following U. S. soldiers." Said Rich Rubenstein.

"And, we all go home for everyone to fight another day." Added Tom McKay.

"I got to get some air!" Sam stood. Knocking over his chair. Fuming. Walked edgily, out of the room. Slamming the door.

The room was silent. Group remaining wondered what other requests would have to be considered. Who would be the next to balk?

"Been there." Tom said.

"Well, we have something – and, someone – to work with." Hank was the last person to speak.

Tegucigalpa, Honduras

Latitude: 14.0723 North

Longitude: 87.1921 West

Central Standard Time (GMT -6)

U. S. Embassy - WG-41 Room

Saturday – 19 October 1985

"Before we get started." Sam Maddox was the first to speak. "I'd like to apologize for my outburst yesterday. Spoke with Headquarters. They faxed this position statement. Having read it, it is something to which I must adhere." He said, handing the faxed document to Rich Rubenstein.

"Been there," Tom said. Looking around the table. Everybody nodded.

His emotional stance was common. Each had been in situations where their personal outburst had disrupted meetings. Silence followed, until Rich broke it to move forward.

"We had a skeleton staff working through the night. I was called twice from Washington."

"Where do we stand, legally. With the desires proposed by Dutrov?" Tom asked.

"They checked international law. Customs and practices of similar legal precedents. Nothing could come back to us. But, the law regarding diplomats is specific." He paused to pick up an opinion. "The most fundamental rule of diplomatic law is that a diplomatic agent is inviolable. Diplomats may not be detained. Arrested. They are completely immune from criminal prosecution in the receiving state."

"So, the DEA in Panama has no grounds on which they can prosecute?"

"There is a tenet of diplomatic law. It is that a diplomat cannot be prosecuted under the laws of a state in which he finds himself. The agent is bound by the laws of the state he serves. Diplomats may not be detained. Arrested. They enjoy complete immunity from prosecution." He paused. "There is a remedy. Panama could declare the courier a 'persona non-grata.' That way, Panama can expel him. The United States would not be involved."

"What about the crate held in-bond?"

"Let me quote: 'The private residence, papers, correspondence and property of diplomats is also inviolable… agents of the receiving state cannot confiscate, open or tamper with items belonging to the diplomatic mission…' Without their consent. But, there are exceptions."

"We're in process of obtaining permission from Panama." Sam said.

"Yes, Panama can approve. But, they must conduct the search and seizure. Not a third party. In this case, not the US. It's agents or assigns are prohibited."

"This is bull." Sam retorted. "If we don't seize that product, it will wind up on the streets of Miami."

"Is Panama willing to go that far?" Anne asked.

"All indications are that they have been complicit. Allowing previous shipments to transit their airports bound for the United States." Hank commented. "We've been on the periphery. But, have knowledge of previous contraband shipments going through Tocumen in the past."

"So, the DEA has no legal stand to seize, hold or enter the crate for further inspection?" Sam asked. His inner emotion beginning to build.

"I am afraid that is the case." Rich surmised.

"Okay." Tom said, turning to Sam. "Like you, I don't want that shit on my streets. For the possibility of my kids getting a hold on it. We've got to move on."

"We can return the 'crate in question' as part of the agreement. We just need to stall that from happening. Until we've completed the asset swap." Hank offered.

Silence held the room. Hank continued.

"My folks in DC have two points. Mostly administrative." Hank was about to change the subject. "Rescind the letter of reprimand for the LRRP Team Leader. Clean up his 201 personnel-file. Allow him the right to continue his career, without that black mark."

"We can do that without making it a part of the MOU. A Presidential Executive Order can fix that." Rich provided.

"One more thing," Hank added. "There's the body of a Special Forces Operator. He was working with the Contras. Command believes he was KIA on the drop zone. We need to get those remains for a proper burial in Arlington. His family needs closure."

"I'll have to bring that up with Dutrov at our next meeting." Tom said. "Let's move on."

"The swapping of prisoner assets has been common amongst major powers. The position of the White House is clear. We don't recognize the Sandinista Government nor Cuba as parties here. Only their promotion of socialism for their benefit. I'm sure a Kremlin lawyer is advising his comrades the same thing. But, for different reasons. To do so would bite us later."

"So, it has to be a deal between the USSR and the US?"

"Yep. When the document is written, it will be between the two majors in this conflict."

"We can make the swap. Place to be determined. Naming the assets to be exchanged?"

"It all depends on how specific you want to be. Implications for the future. Ultimate document declassification."

"What I'm referring to is the cover story concocted by Fred Matthews. 'The Times Reporter at the wrong place at the wrong time, etc.' Tom took a sip of water. "We don't want Lester Russell outed as our loadmaster. No connection to the airplane. Constable Outreach. Or, our Contra operations." He further stated.

"Nor do we want our military guys tied to the CIA. The LRRP team specifically." Hank added. "We got to make it look like the boy was wandering and lost his way. Hell, pin the capture on the Honduran military. I don't care. Just leave our military activity out of it."

"What about the Special Forces operator?" Anne asked.

"I think I can work something out with Dutrov." Tom said.

"Have we got enough for the first draft?"

"I can have it by 2 PM."

"Good," Tom said with a pleased tone. "I've got to put out another fire. Meet back here at three?"

All agreed.

Tom's Office - One Floor Up

"How's our boy doing?"

"He's not getting any worse." Jack Simone said. "But, where can we move him?"

"Why?"

"There was an attempt to do him physical harm. Might even have been an assassination attempt. Got lucky. Stopped the Honduran in the act. These Battalion 3-16 troops answer to a different code." Jack stated.

"I don't want anything to happen to him!"

"I know."

"We're working on an exchange. Young Mr. Perez for one of ours."

"How'd they get one of ours?"

"Don't ask. We're in meeting now to make it happen."

"Got to move him soon. I don't have the manpower to provide for his security."

"I'll work on it. Meantime, clean him up. I'll get back to you this afternoon."

Rancho Perez

Lester was beginning to experience freedom within the hardened confines of Juanita's bedroom. The wrist and ankle straps had been removed. Allowing him to get up and down from bed, at his own will.

He was sure that there would be no rescue attempt in saving his life. He was having to make the best of a situation that he partially created. This emotional bonding with Juanita was something he was questioning of himself.

While a prisoner, this short time in his life he would have to make the best of it.

It was a foregone conclusion – in his mind – that he was expendable. The US government would deny his existence. Other than in classified meetings, he did not exist.

The agency's grunt work was kept from Congress. And, the American people. The support of their contra force was being withheld from everyone.

There was no mother, wife or girlfriend who would be looking for Lester's return to the United States. Those who cared, were aware of his activity in aviation. His friends thought that he worked for an airline. His long periods of absence were normal. His return to the States would be for a short period of time. Then he'd be gone, again.

Lester had shunned the development of any relationships. There were occasional affairs. The times he had sex, only because the female was looking for satisfaction. Not necessarily from him. But, as a servicer. After a night of hard and rough intercourse, the female would disappear into the crowd. Not to seen again. Much like the encounter one would have with a prostitute. The sexual act completed. No payment exchanging hands.

He thought of his approach to romantic relationship as one to avoid. Dismiss until a later date.

His escape was possible. Yet, improbable. By resisting, it would increase his chances of survival. Any information they sought would be useless. Any given, would be worthless. Thus, his life would be of no use. Become worthless. They would have no more use for him. He would be executed. And, forgotten.

This short-term interpersonal relationship with Juanita had started an attachment. Being in the presence of a woman while captive, was an anomaly. Her hard and sensitive sides clashed. A rough agate seen for the gem it was. Her beauty was enticing. Her control of him came as a fact of his being secured to her bed. She would not leave him. A prisoner in her home. After all, he was a guest.

In his thought, he questioned his comfort. Someone might ask him, *"Was he attracted to a hardened, female guerrilla figure?"*

He would have said, *"absolutely not!"*

Assuredly, she was using him. The question arising, *'for what purpose? The return of her son? A block to the advances of the Sandinista soldier?'*

'Was she attempting to extract needed information from him? A nefarious unseen motive? Was it because of the lack of physical attention she received?

Before his being a prisoner, guest in her home? Was there some other reason? A psychological induced reason for her erratic treatment of and toward him?'

'Was her previous sex life wrought with rough encounters? Was she damaged by men who took away the only private part of her? That part which only should be given. And not just to anyone?

That range of thought, rolled over in his pain controlled thought process. This is what one did while in captivity. Attempting to sooth your situation by taking your mind off it. Talking to yourself. Between bouts of questioning, one sought a sensible conversation. In this instance, he was having one with himself. The captured becomes the child. He eats, drinks, sleeps, performs body excretions when and where the captor tells him.

Habitual activity changed. This new kind of "captor-parent" relationship molds you. Into something that deals more on a primal wave than what is considered as sane treatment. A person's habits can change in twenty-one days.

'All infants became attached to a caregiver. One that provides for them… She could be considered a 'safe choice' in dealing with this enemy. In this case, I considered myself like an infant. Looking to this female as my caregiver. This was not a secure attachment. But, it could be considered an attachment secured through an adversarial position. Laced with punitive action, there were times of comfort given by this vixen.'

Lester was anxious to know which of these thoughts bled the truth.

'Discussions with her were becoming friendly. From them, I see a person. A mother. A different way of life. I have empathy for her. She's good with a knife. But, I don't think she'd purposefully hurt me. I'm not afraid, when I'm around her. I sympathize with her. Her plight in life.'

'In survival school, they trained me to interact in this fashion. With enemy minders or interrogators. But, never a woman. Not sure what to make of her kindness. Is she using it to gain my trust. There had not been harsh, painful interrogation since the soldier. No guards rotated now. No constant flow of persons through her small house. Just a barred window and jailer door containing me.'

'The terror generated from the unnamed Nicaraguan, wanting to beat my exposed body. The arguing of Juanita and others heard through the wall. In a language, I barely understand.'

'It all seemed to turn on one night. That night when he feared this woman jailer. Feared the knife she held close to my penis. Not being able to control my own man part. Or. body functions. Resisting was futile. Seeing her naked female form. There was no resistance to prevent physical desire. Only an active participation in the sex act would have been better.'

'I recognized that I am a prisoner. Of a war that no one in Washington wants to talk about. My memory is returning. I held information that would be damning if presented in the media. My health is improving.'

'The doctor had come last evening to check on my condition. Inspecting my wounds. Feeling for the correct positioning of my shoulder. The securing bandage for my right arm to my torso, removed. Changing it out, for something less constrictive. Dead skin against rubbing cloth had created a rash. Replacing the bandage that held my arm in place, took away the wrapping. Providing me with a sling for my forearm. Allowing more movement. Mobility.'

'Lying on my back for days, had caused sores to develop. Flesh ripped away from body. Doctor provided salve to heal the open sores. Juanita rubbed it into my skin. My left wrist and both ankles had become swollen. She removed the restraints. Having me tied to the oversized bed frame. Now removed. Telling me to move around more. It all seemed so civilized.'

'Was I developing emotional ties to Juanita. Even though she harassed me. Threatened. Intimidating me with an object. Creating fear with her knife. Then turning that fear, 180° to an act which should have been pleasurable. After losing control with my phallic member. The pleasure response planted. The captor bonding through the act that should have led to sex.'

'...and, what of a willing and passionate evening in bed with Juanita Perez. Was that a possibility?'

"Must hold my emotions in check. Through this masked recovery from amnesia. Denial many times. Knowledge on how I arrived in Nicaragua. Misleading my captors, a must! Remember methods and practices learned in survival school. Shun initial fear to find strength. False evidence appearing real....'

Lester was playing a new game.

Rancho Perez

Latitude: 13.8955 N

Longitude: 86.1503 W

Central Standard Time (GMT -6)

Sunday – 20 October 1985

The jailer's door was locked. Standing there looking out, Lester saw the front door was open. Breeze filtered house air, with sweet smell of moist greenery. Breeze coming from West to East. Through the open window with bars across it.

Juanita was not heard. Lester couldn't see her. Just the smell of her perfumed soap detected. Other sound punctuated his present thinking. He heard a car in the distance. Coming closer to the house. Then seen through the vertical bars.

He saw Juanita step into view on the porch. Open the front door. Place her hand on the barrel of the gun, leaning on the door jam. Pulling it to her side. Stepping off the porch.

"Hola, Senora." A voice greeted the woman standing at the porch.

"Buenos días, coronel." She only addressed one male exiting the car.

"How is our newspaper reporter this morning?" Colonel Mendez asked.

"Seems much better. He eats well."

"Senora, we have good news." Major Sanchez interrupted that thought.

The two Cubans approached where she stood.

"I can always use good news."

"We have pictures of your son."

She did not know how to react. Wanting to see her son. Yet, not knowing what images were captured in the photos. Reluctantly, she held out her hand.

"Mi bebé." She said. Tears coming to her eyes. "Ve bien."

"Yes, he looks unharmed. That is good Senora."

"Where is he? When can we go get him?" She fired anxiously. "I can leave now!"

In her excitement, she gave no thought to that of circumstance. Preventing immediate retrieval of her loved, young man. The son she protected.

"We're working on that."

"Colonel Dutrov is minding his return. He took your pleas to his heart."

She had a hundred questions. But none would come from her mouth. Only gratitude.

"I had prayed he would stay safe. He's been gone twenty-six days. I've counted, every-one. With morning, noon and night prayer. Where is he?"

"The facts are less than specific. But, we have been assured he is well. In good hands. Unharmed."

"Thank you." She said. Kissing the hand of the Colonel. "May I keep these?"

Excitement and pragmatism met with the coming words.

"Si, Senora. But, there is something else."

"What, Major?"

"Commander Pallais has gone missing. Have you seen him?"

"No!" She said, with emphasis. "He is not welcome here."

"You are adamant. Is there something we should know?"

The explanation took a few minutes. Attitudes toward Pena-Pallais changed. His actions spoke to questions of his character. Her words cutting through the respect, he had developed as a soldier. He would become discredited. Thought lesser of a man. Ostracized at hearing of his attempted rape. Become a *persona non-grata*.

Café La Plata - Tegucigalpa
Mid-Afternoon

Tom greeted Alexandr Dutrov. The seating positions changed. Tom sat with his back to the wall. Alexandr would have to sit with his back exposed.

"I took your information to the embassy. They were appreciative of your concern for the newspaper reporter."

"Seems we have developed a reconnection." Alexandr replied.

"There may be questions. Answering them will bring us closer. But, I feel that this document has answered most of them." Tom said, sliding the typewritten document across the table. As the Russian touched the document, a waiter appeared.

"Qué puedo conseguir para usted."

"Dos Imperial y dos tiros de Scotch." Tom ordered. The waiter departed. "My Spanish is less than desirable. But, good enough for ordering drinks."

Alexandr skimmed through the Memorandum. It contained all the concerns he had brought to Tom on Friday evening.

"You work quickly."

"When we have a gentlemen's agreement, it is easy to translate to written form."

"So, you have the young man?"

"He is in safe keeping. Unharmed. Ready to go back to his mother." He paused, then added. "And, our reporter?"

"He is returning to good health. Anxious in returning to the US."

"What is our next step?"

"We must consult with our partners. I can see them tomorrow. Depending on their stubborn attitude. Dealing with their nemesis. We should know something mid-week. Okay with you?"

"We can ask for nothing more. Changes to this document may add time. But, all sounds good."

"Thank you, Tom."

"I am appreciative that you extended your hand first." Tom replied. The drinks arrived.

"To your health." Tom toasted. Lifting the glass of beer. Touching it to one held by Alexandr Dutrov.

"Just like old times. The beirgarten. Near your American, 'Checkpoint Charlie."

The meeting ended. Tom returned to the embassy. He had one more thing to do today. Returning to the questionable movement of Jaime Velasquez from Danli compound.

"Yes, I got it worked out."

"I've got my men pulling four-hour shifts. Watching the kid." Replied Jack Simone. "His attitude still stinks."

"Appreciate your efforts. I'll be down in the morning. Bringing a transfer document. Taking that responsibility off your hands."

"Thanks Tom. See you in the morning." The call ended.

Rancho Perez - Sunday Evening

The afternoon sun had gone West. Light still shown thru the trees. On the East, it had become night.

Lester was permitted more time out of room. Attitude toward him had changed. Thoughts of his being a combatant, swayed. He ate at kitchen table. Had conversations with Juanita that were substantive. Her pain of losing her only son, her only child was not diminished.

Yet, she displayed strength. Resigned that her superiors were taking action.

Thoughts of Lester as the wayward reporter, set new light on the man he became. In her mind, he was not a threat.

"After dinner, we will sit on the porch." Juanita said.

"That'll be a first."

Gathering two cups, she poured the Café Bustelo. They went to the porch. Upon sitting, Juanita handed Lester a cup of her evening elixir.

"Your physical condition has come a long way."

"Still have some pain in my back. Can't move well with my knee. But, I can live with it."

"Tell me, why does a reporter go off by himself?"

Lester wasn't sure what she was talking about. "I don't know."

"You were found on the road. Where the airplane dropped supplies. Why were you investigating drug trails?"

"Drug trails?" He replied. He had no thought to what she referred. "I can't remember being there. How I got there is a blur."

"To some, you are an enemy. To others, your activity in finding truth in noble."

"Reporter?" Lester was still stuck on that one word. This, a new type of questioning.

"We have been told that you are a reporter. A writer for The Times. The newspaper printed from New York."

"I must have taken quite a bump on the head. That I don't remember."

"Commander Pallais." She stiffened at speaking his name. "He was convinced that you fell from the airplane."

"I do remember falling." He added. "But, it does seem a stretch that I would survive a fall from an airplane. That is, without a parachute."

"Not to worry. He is not here to tell his story."

"You mean the soldier?"

"Yes. He thought you were from the American Air Force."

"No?" He answered with a questioning tone. "Things I remember about planes..."

"It will all come to you. The doctor said amnesia is a tricky thing to diagnose. It takes trained psychologists to work with someone who has amnesia. Help them to remember."

"You have been *very* kind. Nurturing me back to health. At least this far."

"Now, I hear your words. Like a reporter, a writer."

Sitting in the evening air. Cooling atmosphere allowed humid air to settle. Ground fog built in the low area. An area used for soldier encampment. This side of the fenced pasture.

"I love the evening. And, the morning. The heat of the day, not so much." Juanita said.

"It is quiet. Peaceful. Just the sounds of birds settling for the night." Lester said. "Why don't you have a dog?"

A statement that brought back memory of her heart piercing. "I had a dog. He and my son played right out there. The dog was killed. My son disappeared."

"I'm sorry." Space between comments showed reverence. "You kept asking me about your son. How did he disappear? What killed your dog?"

"We don't know the whole story. I thought you were with them. The Contras. Hopefully, we will know soon."

Lester sat thinking. Wanting to remember all her words. Hoping to work them into his story. Flashes of scenes danced across his brain. He would steal glances at her. Tying the words to the way she looked at this moment. Sensing his gaze, she would smile. They sat quietly together. Sitting in the evening air. Warmth discovered in their light conversation.

"Let's go in, we can sit in living room." She said.

"The evening air is starting to get cool." Lester added. "Thank you, for taking care of me."

"De nada."

"No sure why I was brought here. The connection you have with uniformed soldiers."

"That should be of no concern. My husband was a soldier. The Sandinista say a hero. To me, a man I fell in love with. The other side of being a soldier."

"Never stayed in one place long enough to fall in love. Find a woman."

"You would be a fine mate. Strong. Able to withstand much pain. Recover from injury fast."

"Can't say I ever had feelings…those kinds of feelings about any woman." He replied. "The only woman I loved was my Mom."

"She must have meant a lot to you."

"Yep."

"You never found a woman who measured up to her?"

"No, never did."

Tegucigalpa, Honduras

Latitude: 14.0723 North

Longitude: 87.1921 West

Central Standard Time (GMT -6)

Hotel Elegante

Monday – 21 October 1985

The dining room was a sea of bright-white table clothes. The tables nearest the entry had clear vases containing flowers. Color dotted on a white pallet. Fred Matthews sat near the window.

"Thought I might catch you here." Tom said, approaching with a folder under his arm.

"Breakfast?"

"Think I will. Wife says I need to eat better." Not thinking before the words rolled from his mouth.

"I'd be fortunate if my wife talked to me. We seem to be talking through her lawyer."

Tom seated himself. A waiter arrived. Motioning toward the Continental Breakfast Bar.

"Café?"

"Si." Turning toward Fred, said. "MOU given to Dutrov last evening. Expect to hear in a couple of days."

"Forward progress. You seem to have pissed off a few people. In the process."

"Keeping my eye on the ball. Sometimes fixed agendas go down. DEA wanted that big score. DOJ wouldn't have let it happen, anyway."

"Can you send me the MOU? Like to look."

"Sure, when I get back from Danli. Or, do you need it sooner?"

"No. Anytime. Just like to see what you came up with." He wanted to know about Tom's road trip. "What's going on in Danli?"

"Seems someone tried to get at our youngster." Tom replied.

"Assassination?"

"Don't know. But, I can't take any chances. He's a key to our working plan."

"What are you going to do?"

"Made arrangements with embassy housekeeping. They have an open room in the guest house for a week. Going to bring him here, for the swap. Marine contingent will guard him."

"What if the trade doesn't take place?"

"I'll have to deal with that as it comes. Can't leave him there. Can't, really keep him anywhere. He brings meaning to the original word, 'kidnapping.'"

Coffee arrived. A silver-handled container with pouring spout. Cream in a lipped porcelain cup. The breakfast of breads, yogurt and fruit, there for the selecting. Conversation light as each man prepared for activities of the day.

Tom drove East out town.

Diplomatic Dance

Alexandr Dutrov started the MOU discussion within the walls of the USSR Embassy. The initial mark-up circulated. Copies sent from Tegucigalpa to their embassies in Washington, Managua, Cuba and Panama.

Agreements were best worked out in person. Sometimes parties are not afforded the travel to meet. Time wasted can cause your deal to be pushed aside - be muscled out. The next flap taking priority in the mind.

This contract by memorandum would be meaningless to lower level embassy employees. Low on scale of importance. Yet for individuals concerned, a fire that needed extinguishing. For others, opportunity to add items from their country agenda.

Soviet under-secretaries discussed this Memorandum of Understanding. A review by each would be based on their status, between the nation in which their embassy stood.

The next step would be a mark-up. Sharing thoughts with governments of their host nations. Cross-referencing immediate activities. Then sharing all the collected points of interest. Thoughts exchanged with other party embassies in their locale.

The process met with telephone exchanges. Current state status. Reminders of the stakes. Some arm twisting. Parried with state and regional desire. Despite some requests for inclusion and anonymity. A real dance of intent, using words instead of bullets.

The outward appearance was of civility. Internal viewing was a messy cacophony.

Tom McKay - Danli Sub-Station

When Tom pulled up to the gate, the Honduran guards walked around his vehicle. One held a long pole. With a mirror attached to one end. He swept under the front, sides and trunk area.

Tom passed his ID to the gate guard. Guard walking into the shack, checking with superiors in another building. A phone call cleared his entrance. He drove to the building housing agency interrogators. It faced the parade field.

"What's the threat level today? Tom asked of Jack Simone.

"They bumped it up last night. Nothing credible we can see. But, whenever command feels skittish, it goes up."

"Brought the transfer documents. You'll need them. When the Commandant gets wind of the transfer."

"Where are you taking him?"

"Back to embassy for now."

"Follow me. We'll get you on your way."

They walked down the corridor. Up one flight at the end of hall. Short walk to where a civilian clothed guard sat at a door. Jack and his guard exchanged some private words.

"Seems the kid had a fitful night."

"He's okay, I hope?"

"Let's see." Jack said, unlocking the door.

"Jaime, tienes un visitante."

"¿Quién sabe que estoy aquí?"

"I'm Tom McKay. Remember me?"

"Si. Long time ago. What do you want?"

"Let me look at your face?" A swollen knot below his left eye and abrasions to his right cheek, were the only visible injuries seen. Turning to Jack, he said. "How'd this happen?"

"Told you about the Honduran."

"I definitely, am taking him out of here." Turning back to Jaime. "We need to move you from here. I'll tell you more, later." He said with concern in his voice.

"When can I go home?"

"Soon, Son." Tom replied. "Soon." This could be Tom's son. But, for the position in which he existed in the States. He was not happy with the treatment that Jaime underwent. His body language and terse comments after, would tell Jack more. His concern now, only in moving the young man to a safer place.

"Do you have a fatigue shirt and a baseball cap!" He asked Jack.

"Yes, sir." Jack replied. "I'll get them for you." He left the room.

Tom sat down on a chair near the bed. "Sit. Por favor Siéntate, por lo que podemos hablar."

The boy did as he requested. He had a quizzical look about him. Not knowing what to expect next. "Please, senior. I've done nothing."

"Yes. I know. We're just trying to make the best of a bad situation. I'll take you somewhere you'll will be safe. A place where I can look in on you. Until we can return you home to your mother. Do you understand?"

"No hay más lugares como éste. Por favor,"

"No more places like this…I have a son a bit younger than you. It would hurt me. No, I would be devastated. If he was treated this way."

"Promise?"

"Yes. I promise."

Jack returned with the fatigue shirt and Army baseball cap. "It's got some subdued rank on it. Will this work?"

"Yeah. I've got to get him out of the gate. Without suspicion from the guards."

"Take off your shirt." He told Jaime. "Put this on." While Jaime changed, Tom and his agency counterpart discussed his plan.

"Okay. Now the hat." Tom adjusted the shirt. Tilting the baseball cap forward to cover his black and blue cheek bone. Putting his fatherly hand on the boy's shoulder. Stepping behind, asking "How's he look?"

"From a distance, he can pull it off."

"Let's just hope the gate guard doesn't want a closer look."

Jack thought for a second, then said. "I've got an idea."

The three left the room. Tom thanked the guard at the door. Went down the stairs and out the side door. A black Chevrolet Suburban with tinted glass sat below the four-foot stoop. The supervisor started the SUV. Placed Jaime in the back seat.

"Go get your car. I'll follow you out the gate. Hopefully, the guard won't question my leaving the compound."

Jaime's Move to Tegucigalpa

Tom started his car. Said a prayer. Met the black SUV. It pulled out behind him. The guards were as attentive on departing vehicles as they had been inbound. Tom arrived in the serpentine row to exit. Concrete barriers directing vehicles. He waited his turn.

As he approached the guard shack, a guard walked out in front of his vehicle. A guard walked around the vehicle, peering through the windows into the back and front seats.

"ID, por favor."

Tom handed him his Embassy pass. The guard looked at it. His intent not determined. "Estás con la Embajada?"

"Si. I'm a Cultural Affairs Officer."

The guard held the ID. Walked to the rear of the vehicle. Then back to the driver's side. Handing back his ID. Waving him to exit. The Black Suburban was next.

"No puede ser de cuidado." Jack said through the lowered side window.

A second guard signaled for him to roll down the passenger side window. Reaching across the front seat, did as he ordered. Guard at the driver's side looked in, as did the other. They both stepped back. Waving him to exit. Both vehicles drove in the direction of Tegucigalpa.

Outside of town, Tom pulled over. The Suburban followed.

"Close." Tom said to himself, with relief in his voice.

Bringing Jaime to Tom's car, Jack commented. "Usually not that much security. I don't know what to think?"

"Best you don't think. Just go back. I'll call you when I get to the embassy."

U.S. Embassy Compound - Tegucigalpa

Honduran Security stopped Tom at the vehicle entrance. The guard put Tom and his vehicle through a similar security experience. Jaime wore the hat as Tom had instructed. The boy had no ID. A convincing story would prevent extra scrutiny.

"Senior McKay. Hola." The guard approaching remembered him. "Did you have a nice drive?"

"Yes, thank you. Had to go to the airport hangar. Pick up my mechanic."

The guard leaned down to look in the driver side window. Saying something in Spanish to Jaime. Tom tensed. But, did not want to give away his nervousness.

"Si. Tuvo que limpiar. Gracias." All Tom understood was "Yes. And, Thank you."

The metal gate began to open. Tom waited until it was clear for him to proceed. Inching away from the standing guard. Driving toward parking.

"What did he ask you?"

"Asked if I was working hard?" Then said, "Yes. Had to clean up. Thank you."

Tom chuckled to himself. *'Maybe this kid has a career in the spy game.'*

Tegucigalpa, Honduras

Latitude: 14.0723 North

Longitude: 87.1921 West

Central Standard Time (GMT -6)

Embassies Dance to MOU Arrangement

Tuesday – 22 October 1985

Two Embassies of United States worked on the Memorandum of Understanding Draft. State Department and an office in the Executive Office Building reviewed it for content. Input was provided by the Black Site at Danli. In part, the draft read:

"In consideration...the United States Government agrees to release the Cuban Embassy Staff Member...Return of the Diplomatic Crate from Bogotá...for the release of Lester Russell...place to designated in a future communication."

The USSR, Cuba and Nicaragua calculated exploitation of the overt DEA action in Panama.

Three adversarial embassies coordinated their response to the memorandum.

It read:

"...Whereas, the United States and its Drug Enforcement Administration, did detain an embassy staff courier of the Cuban Government. Delaying the work transpiring between countries of the region. Seizing a crate of documents destined for the Cuban Embassy in Panama. Cuban Council of State and The Partido Comunista de Cuba, condemn the United States for such action. And, demand made for the release and return of the items belonging to the Cuban Government. Further, clearing the name of Cuban staff member. The issuance of a formal apology is hereby demanded."

Not a mention made of the agency's holding of Jaime Correa-Perez Valesquez.

"Typical arrogance of the Soviets and Fidel's minions." A staff member said at the U.S. Embassy in Panama.

"What do you expect? They got caught with their pants down. Pretty blatant."

"The Ambassador summoned the DEA supervisor."

"Would love to have been a fly on the wall."

Embassy - Tegucigalpa

Col. Fred Matthews coordinated the input from Honduran perspective. An agency representative and one other embassy staffer sat with Colonel Matthews.

"Have you seen the pictures sent us from Danli?" An agency staffer asked.

"Yes. One is pretty well staged." Col Matthews added.

"But, it may get the Nicaraguans to move on their position." The other staffer added.

The picture shared amongst the two agency offices in San Salvador and Panama. One delivered to Tom McKay. The agency response and input to the memorandum read:

"We are in possession of a Sandinista valued asset. The young rebel apprehended and brought to Site 16-Central America. Questioned and held. Intelligence gathering continues. One, Jaime Correa-Perez Valesquez held pending direction from the Office of Director. The added photograph taken during a friendly conversation between interrogator and subject."

"Once that picture is forwarded to the KGB, Cuban DI and Nicaraguan DGIN, their tune will change."

That was the consensus. Staff and agency personnel in all three embassies agreed. Thought the picture added weight to the memo. Working response to the Soviet and Cuban demand would add an extra dimension. The negotiated release far from settlement. Between Cuba and the United States.

No country wanted one of its heroes, or family members to denounce their own country. A statement made by the son of a rebel hero would carry weight among the people of the country. Picture or not. Nicaraguan hero, Miguel Correa Valesquez died only two years earlier. Now his son was denouncing the Nicaraguan Government. The Sandista Regime. Through this photograph.

"I denounce Nicaragua and the Sandinista Government," the sign read. Held under the chin and over the chest of Jaime Perez. The only son of Miguel and Juanita Valesquez.

It was not a photograph that would bring comfort to the governments of Nicaragua and Cuba. Their efforts raised Miguel Correa to a list of revolutionary heroes. A hero of recent revolutionary activity in Nicaraguan history. With the likes of Che Guevara and Emiliano Zapata.

Cold water doused on the tended flame from the son of the most revered.

The Honduran government was being slow to respond.

Tom's Office

"Fred, what has the embassy heard from Honduras?" Tom asked. The phone call slipped through. A personal visit prevented. Anxious to proceed with the trade. Time running out for quartering Jaime in the Embassy Guest Quarters.

"With respect to what?"

"The Memorandum? Our swap of assets?" Tom was focused. Single-minded.

"Don't know. I'll check into it."

Fred Matthews had other issues with which he was confronted. The separation with his wife. A call from Al Peterson. Embassy staff questioning about the Nicaraguan boy. Guarded by Marines in the guest quarters.

"Al Peterson called yesterday. Seems the DEA mess landed on his desk. Noriega called the President. He wants the Cuban crate thing to go away." Fred added in explanation.

"We're working on that. We've heard from all the players but Honduras. They're dragging their feet."

"Did you have an altercation with the Commandant at Danli?" Fred asked. His pointed question bordered on scolding.

"No." Tom searched his thoughts for anything which would have been construed as an altercation. "My guys invited him to a meeting about our boy. I was told, he stormed out. That may be what you refer to."

"Those Batt. 3-16 guys run their own army."

"Know the history. But, the boy had nothing to do with their past."

"They seem to think so. His father has been on their radar for years. Told they have proof Juanita Velasquez is a Cuban agent."

"Still, nothing to do with our memo." Tom added.

"Wouldn't be so sure. Memories are long in this culture. People who wield power in this society, control more than an elected President."

"I'll check with our analyst. See what she can come up with." Tom stood, preparing to end the conversation. "And, see if you can put a fire under the Hondurans. We need to move. Our window of opportunity is closing."

Tom left his temporary office. With the Juanita Perez file. Then went to the basement meeting room.

"Anne, see what the agency may have generated on Juanita Velasquez, recently." Handing her the file retrieved moments earlier.

"Sure, Tom." She added, "Hank has something. It might interest you. Relevant to our work. He walked out for a smoke."

Tom was getting his exercise. Had wanted to visit with Jaime. But, got caught in tracking down fragments of stories. And, thoughts from his counterparts.

"Hank. Walk with me." He said, finding the DIA rep at the outside smoking area.

"Where we headed?"

"Over to the guest quarters. Going to introduce you to Jaime. The young Nicaraguan."

As they walked, Hank lit another cigarette.

"Anne says you're privy to something involving our Memorandum?"

"Yeah. One of our people overheard thoughts on an assassination. Lots of times, it turns out to be nothing. Bluster. Bully talk. But, this has ties to our work here."

"Tell me."

"An exchange intel officer mentioned a female. The only name heard was Correa. But, a female in Nicaragua. From that relayed, a Cuban female. It didn't register until I looked at my notes. It could be nothing."

"What's nagging you? Do you think it might be Juanita Perez?"

"Nicaraguan. Female. Girlfriend of Miguel Correa...Velasquez."

"How did your exchange officer come to this information?"

"I can ask." Hank took a deep draw on his cigarette. "I'll call when we get back."

They had reached the guest quarters. Tom only had a few minutes to check in on Jaime. It would be his first meeting with a different American.

Garden of Catholic Ministry - Tegucigalpa
23 October 1985

Alexandr Dutrov sat waiting for Tom to arrive. The bench was one of three. Facing the statue of The Virgin Mary. Tom approached from his left.

"Good that we found another spot. Too many meetings over alcohol might get someone to talking."

"Good morning, Tom."

"What was important?"

"Seems the only sticky point is a delay from the Hondurans."

"I know. The attaché and I talked about it yesterday." Tom added.

"What do you suspect that they are holding out for?"

"Their President is not a fan. They want our money. But, not our cultural exchange."

"Some might see that as an opportunity. We have faced similar attitudes."

"We've got a long diplomatic history. Just not with their current administration."

"Noriega is making noise. Getting some press. Cubans are less than happy. Hear the Chinese are making inroads. Bad for everybody." Alexandr said.

"What have your people got that we can leverage?"

"There was an incident in New York. Between a Honduran Deputy Ambassador. Something about a hooker. Couple of weeks back." Alexandr offered.

"That would take a long time. We haven't got weeks to build the story."

"The hooker. One of ours. They had interesting talk during foreplay. The video and recordings could surface."

"You are a son-of-a-bitch. Aren't you?" Tom laughed.

"All is fair. You must remember what we do for a living. There are bigger things at stake. A little embarrassment is nothing."

Tom stood. Patted Alex on the shoulder. "Call me." Then walked off.

Rancho Perez - Early Evening

"Your meal was delicious." Lester told Juanita.

"It is good to have an appreciative man in my home. One I can share a meal with." Juanita stopped, then added. "And, my thoughts."

Lester was becoming more appreciating. In mass, these few discussions stimulated his thought. His desires were being met with kindness. Those episodes of kindness brought dreams during his sleep. Reality being more mundane than the fantasies occupying his resting mind.

"Tell me again, how they found me." His night thoughts did not coincide with what he was being told. Saw. Heard. Remembered.

"Again?" Juanita replied. "Do you not remember what I told you last night?"

"I'm just trying to remember. My thoughts are hazy. Up until…" He stopped.

"Up until what?"

"Did I dream that you came into my room. I mean the room with barred windows. That one," he said, pointing with his left finger.

"Yes." She said, with a twinge of embarrassment in her voice.

"You came at me with a knife." He paused. "Then you took off your clothes."

She wanted to hide her face. "Commander Pallais drugged me. Something I had not experienced before. Think they call it Devil's Breathe. Like Ecstacy."

"You mean the date drug?"

"He must have put it in my drink." Her embarrassment turning to a slow boil of anger.

"I saw you, naked?" He asked. "My wet dream was real?"

"Do we need to talk about this?"

"I'm sorry. It was just something I remembered. Please forgive me."

Juanita was surprised. Here was a man, apologizing for something she had done. Drugged. Desiring a man. Just not Commander Pallais.

"You shame me."

"You don't need to be ashamed. Embarrassed. Or, feel like an object. I meant no harm." He said, searching how he could say the next words. "You have beautiful hair. A beautiful body."

She said nothing. Listening to his words. Parsing the compliment for its hidden meaning.

"If we had not met under these circumstances. Your being my jailer and nurse. We might have kicked off a chance meeting with a date."

"You would ask me to go on a date?"

"If I knew who I was, you might like me. We could have started there."

Juanita became warm with these pleasing words. Flushed, before pulling herself back into their conversation.

"I would have liked that." She paused. "But, for now I must clean the dishes."

Tegucigalpa, Honduras

Latitude: 14.0723 North

Longitude: 87.1921 West

Central Standard Time (GMT -6)

Office of Tom McKay

Thursday – 24 October 1985

The window of opportunity was closing with the setting and rising sun. A sleepless night followed by waiting for something to happen. All activity had slowed. Anticipation was high. Expectations called into question. Tom picked up the phone after the first ring.

"Tom McKay."

"Tom, Alexandr." The voice said. "We placed the video in the hands of a Honduran Presidential aide. Now, we wait."

"Alex, we're running out of time. The curtain is closing."

"Patience, my friend. Calculation says we will hit our target today."

"I sure hope so. Any thought why our host has been dragging their feet."

"One name. Fred Matthews."

"We can't talk about this over the phone. Every conversation recorded."

"I will say no more. But, if you look there. You may find the stumbling block."

"Stumbling block?"

"I'll call you when we have something positive to report. Good day." Alexandr Dutrov hung up.

Tom sat questioning Alexandr's motive. But, it presented enough of a question. To look at all who were playing the game. When an agency operative is presented a twist, it is better to go back to square one. Look at all activity with unjaundiced eyes. Look at the pieces. Rearranging them to fit alternative scenarios. Eliminating those that are cancellable. Seeing where they lead.

"Fred Matthews?" Tom said out loud.

Tom needed to speak with Fred. Question him on an alternate line of thought. Glean answers. That would help him understand why Alexandr outed Fred, as the road block.

"Fred, you have some time? Like to review with you. Get your thoughts on the MOU. It'll help me gain a better perspective."

"Sure. Got nothing on my calendar until one o'clock. Come on up."

The walk was purposeful. Not desired. Just something Tom had to do.

"Here is the latest MOU draft with all the additions, deletions and mark-ups. Changes highlighted. Still can't figure why Honduras is dragging their feet. Any thoughts?"

"I've been talking with the General Martinez. There's a question of military aide. President Cordova is cutting their military budget. The deep recession has taken away money needed. It's a stalling tactic. Their looking for us to make up the difference."

Tom would accept that as a plausible explanation. Had it not been for the question mark placed after the name of Fred Matthews. The KGB was good at making others look hard at themselves.

"Have you talked to Al Peterson?"

"He says there are funds that can be moved. But, it will take a few meetings with friendly Congressman on the Hill. And they're out of town, Visiting their districts."

"How fucking convenient!" Tom blurted. "What can we promise the President to get this moving forward?" Then continued, leaving Fred limited space for interjection. "But, it's more complicated than that. Their old ties with Argentina and Peru implanted ideas that are hard to kill. Look at Danli. Battalion 3-16 HQ. How fast did they ramp up the threat level? After someone. Don't know who. Leaked the détente over our downed loadmaster." Tom set the snare.

"Leaked?" Fred got in a one-word response.

"More like openly informed." Tom paused. "Intel got that El Presidente had been trying to disband 3-16. But to do that, they'd have to eliminate half the political establishment. Attitudes espoused by the opposing political party. President Cordova only won by a slim margin."

"Politics!" Fred said. "The Commandant at Danli has a first hand, battlefield experience against Miguel Correa Velasquez. Lost many men. It's personal with him."

"Jaime is just a boy." Tom reasoned.

"Yes. But, a symbol. And, his mother is a DGI operative. That's the trifecta."

Tom wanted to ask a pointed question. Thought hard before letting the words come from his mouth. "Where is the White House in all this? You have some powerful people pulling your strings. Clue me in."

"The White House sent me here. All indications are that Honduras is ripe for going the way of Nicaragua. People tire of being pushed around by special interest. The money clan. Using the people as pawns for their game of amassing wealth. It's an uphill battle."

"If we're not willing to fight this fight, then where?" Tom asked.

"El Salvador."

"That's why Constable Outreach closed down so abruptly."

"A sort of retreat to safer ground. And, you were just caught in the machinery to make it happen. That is, until Al Peterson went to bat for you."

This line of thought was not why Tom had come to Fred's office. It didn't answer the questions generated by a KGB spy. Alexandr was looking at the big picture. Tom was down in the dirt. Solving a difficult situation involving real people. It was the macro view versus the micro view.

'Was I being played?' Tom asked himself. *'Was there another move planned? International chess players always looked seven-or-eight moves out. What was the end game?'* He brought himself back to ground level.

"What can we do to make this asset swap happen?"

"I think your friend, Dutrov has played the right card."

"You know about that?"

"NSA got wind that the Soviets were setting up the Hondurans for a move. They just played that card to solve another problem. It was a good move for the right reasons. For them and for us."

"Guess I was just too close to see the big picture. Do you think it will work?"

"We expect you'll have their cooperation by the end of this day."

Tom stood silent. Flabbergasted. Embarrassed. A man with emotional ties to a child, not of his making. Caught in the weeds. Held out of the loop. Performing the right actions for the circumstance. Moved by righteous thoughts of preserving the anonymity of his agency. Attempting to return the status quo by saving two humans in this trade. Displaying his own humanity in the process.

Working Group – 41: Mid-Day

Anne Larson, CIA Analyst had discussed Tom assertions with Virginia Headquarters.

"Tom, spoke with a knowledgeable section head."

"What did you find out?"

"Juanita is a DGI mole. She got to Jalapa through some hard turns in her life. She's just been dormant there while mourning the death of her husband. Now we know why the Cubans wanted her safe passage back to Cuba. That was a specific stipulation along with the crate and other demands."

"Her son didn't know. Wonder how people in Jalapa knew?"

"Apparently, she's been a fixture in town politics. Using the guise of grieving widow. Supporting the activities proposed by the mayor. May have even put a few thoughts in his head, along the way."

"There are many things that have become clear to me, today."

"How does her being a DGI agent fit into the MOU?" Anne asked.

"We have local vendettas. Generals who think they are in control of the country. Embarrassment and hurt feelings surfacing. Political games being played between our host, the U. S. and our adversaries. Savvy people on all sides playing cards. Making moves and setting up situations, for handing in the future. The only straight shooters are the Nicaraguans. My hat's off to them. For whatever reason, they provided medical care for our loadmaster. Been nurturing him back to health. While our partners have done what they could to hurt and harm the whole process. Returning both Lester and Jaime to their rightful place of existence. And, we sit here doing the hard work. Using our intellect and knowledge to make that trade work. Those nefarious minds can only think of how it will harm them. Or, their position in the region. Saving face." He stopped. "Sorry, what was your question?"

"The MOU? Her being a DGI agent?" Anne repeated.

"Think it brought the Cubans to agreement." Tom replied. "Never know what is going on behind the scenes. Now, my request for your research seems meaningless."

Tom's Office

Tom gathered all the files and loose papers. Placing them back into the DIA transit box. He and the working group had gathered all their tools in one basket. Offering the expertise of their given station. Drafted a document, marked and modified by others party to the incidents. Now, they wait on one holdout. Honduras.

Tom was dejected. Played by powers bigger than his agency. The fight creating waves which might affect his future. His only solace being within family.

"Will you place a call to the states for me?" He asked the embassy operator.

He waited. Staring at the phone. Wishing it would ring. Call was ready.

"Hi, honey."

"Is anything wrong?" Sally McKay asked.

"No, just wanted to hear your voice."

"Are you alright?"

"Relatively so. I'm just spent. Missing you and the kids."

"You don't sound so good."

"This past two weeks has drained me. Got in a situation involving a young boy. Not much older than Robert. Every time I look at him, I think he could be my boy. Would someone, on the other side care as much about what happens to him?

"Where people are involved, the job gets doubly difficult. When you get personally involved, your humanity shows."

"Just wanted to hear your voice. The wisdom you always provide. How are the kids?"

"They're fine. Missing you. Ask when you're coming home."

"Soon. Once this situation is resolved. My time in Tegucigalpa will be ended."

"Be safe. Come home to me. Love you."

"Love you." Tom ended the call.

The receiver had barely hit the cradle when the phone rang again.

"Tom, we got an agreement." Rich Rubenstein said. "Can you come down?"

"I'll be right there."

Rancho Perez

Latitude: 13.8955 N

Longitude: 86.1503 W

Central Standard Time (GMT -6)

Friday – 25 October 1985

The early morning air was moist. Dim light had not pierced the room. Sun had just begun to rise. Sweet smell of flowering vine lifted through the open windows. Lester lay in bed awaiting the sound of Juanita's rising.

As she passed the open bedroom door, peered through the bars covering the opening. "Buenas dias, senior."

"Good morning," Lester replied. He noticed she was still wearing her night shirt. He listened as Juanita rustled in the kitchen. Soon the smell of coffee reached throughout the house. He watched her cross again in front of the spaced bars.

It was time for him to rise. With one limb hanging by sling across his mid-section, he used his left arm to push away from the bed. Swinging both legs, he was now able to enter and exit the bed without help. Dressing was a bit more difficult. But, manageable.

Walking toward the open door, he saw that the breakfast table was set. Coffee and conversation, followed with some prepared sustenance. It had been a day or two, since the bolt and lock had been set on the iron-barred door. It swung easily with a push.

"Did you sleep well?" Juanita asked. She was smiling more this morning.

"This shoulder always presents a challenge to sleep. But short catnaps suffice. I'm rested." He noticed her shapely legs, exposed to her thighs. "Lounging in your nightshirt?"

"I'm a little lazy this morning. You don't mind?"

"Interesting look." Another thing he noticed was her long hair. It reached the middle of her back. A scene he remembered from a week earlier.

"Just like an old married couple." He joked.

Juanita poured his coffee. Then returned to preparing food.

He looked at her slim figure. Black hair with hints of auburn at the edges. The solid calves. Olive skin at the bend in her legs. Nightshirt reaching the middle of her thighs. *'She was a Hispanic beauty.'* He thought.

Turning, she saw this man looking at her. It made her self-conscious. Straightening her nightshirt.

"The food will be ready soon."

"I'm in no hurry. Just admiring your natural beauty."

She experienced that feeling of feminine flushing, once more. The warm flow which rises from the inside, working outward. A natural body reaction when appreciated by the opposite sex.

"Why do you look at me like that?"

"You are easy to look at." He said. "I may have trouble remembering how I got here. But, I haven't forgot how to appreciate the fine form of a woman."

"You were travelling on the road, when the airplane dropped those supplies."

"What?"

"You asked me to tell you, again. Yesterday." She explained. "You are the reporter, the embassies are looking for." She said, with a soft delivery. And, looking directly into his eyes. "They've been talking about you for over a week."

"Thank you. That helps me. I want to remember. How did you know that?"

"Colonel Mendez informed me three days ago."

"If you know who I am, then why am I here?"

"Arrangements are being made to send you home. Does my hospitality offend you?"

"No. That's not what I meant. You are a gracious, lovely woman. I am enjoying our time together. Just wondered."

"When you are gone, I will miss having to take care of a man. I forgot the small pleasures that come with bathing and caring for a man. You were unable. It was my duty."

"I could have died. Without you I wouldn't be here."

She knew that within days he'd be gone. It was the information sent by the Cuban embassy. That told her of this man.

'A reporter following drug trails for a story he was writing.' She was okay with that.

For a short period, they did not talk. She prepared food. He drank coffee and watched her. His thought being on the story. Made up. About his arrival in Jalapa.

Juanita displayed a desire for his affection.

He wanted her. Yet, denied acting on his sexual desires.

"We can't. I can't." Lester explained.

"Why?" Juanita asked.

"I heard you say, 'These are things that do not mix." He hesitated. "Sex with a man you hate. Acts of violence that solve nothing. People who should not be together'...."

He could not voice aloud his other thoughts. *I am not a who she thinks I am. Her kindness should not meet with that truth. It is best for us both. Truth is a knife that cuts both ways.*

Juanita parrots back "And, what would Yoda say? To this?"

U. S. Embassy

"We have all the pieces. And, a tentative agreement."

"Multiple crises. Face saved. Death averted." Sam Maddox summarized.

"Not quite that simple. But, a demonstration of what can be accomplished. When all parties come to the table." Rich Rubenstein stated.

"So, how will the final document read?" Tom asked, anxious to move forward.

"We need to look at each point. Precedents reviewed. Brainstorm the implications and tweak the language."

Tom had delivered the DIA transit box with his arrival this morning. Dropping it in the corner with other like material. All classified to some level. The files and document sort would take place. By a knowledgeable staffer, with appropriate security clearance. Once the prisoner swap was completed.

"This morning, I'm going to step back. Allowing Hank to discuss the logistics." Rich added.

Hank, the DIA representative passed a packet to each of the working group members. Then began his presentation.

"The site selection for the transfer will be," he paused to look at the marked photo he held. "Drop Zone Alpha. Between Jalapa and Ocotal. Site has significance. Place of original airdrop. Where Mr. Russell went missing. It is also the alleged place where The Times writer was reported missing."

"Why there and not at the nearest border crossing? To Managua?" Tom asked. "Isn't Lester held in a prison hospital. Near Managua?"

"We don't know where he's being held. We're still operating under the covert premise. No photographers. Nothing which draws attention to this agreement. We have photos of the drop zone, compliments of DEA. Knowledge of that site. That's where they agreed. To make the swap."

"Let's move on," Rich prodded.

"722nd Transportation will supply one UH-1 Iroquois. Tail flash blacked out. Numbers and insignia scrubbed. Depart from Toncontin. Fly 70 air miles, 133 kilometers…to the determined coordinates. Stay on the ground approximately five-to seven minutes to deliver Mr. Velasquez. And, retrieve Lester Russell. Then fly back to TGU."

"Any air-cover?" Sam asked.

"Corporate has a Sandie we can use." Anne added.

"The point here is we don't want to draw attention. It is a friendly swap of assets. No guns. No military. Just an in-and-out. They get the boy back. We get our loadmaster. Or, correspondent. However, you want to refer to him." Hank added.

Tom sighed deeply. Pushing air from his lungs, out and across his lips. The tension in his lower abdomen building with each day. He wanted it to go well. No blazing firefights. No one getting hurt. Just a simple exchange.

"We're still waiting for them to tell us if he'll brought on a stretcher. Or, ambulatory. Got to be ready for each condition. On the ground at Toncontin, Mr. Russell will be met by an AeroMedical Evacuation unit. A C-130 will fly him to Panama."

"Still feel better with air-cover." Anne added.

"Okay. Any other discussion?" Rich asked.

"Transfer will be easier if he's ambulatory." Sam said.

"Again, checking on that…Iroquois has a range of 274 nautical miles. That's 507 kilos. Allowing for extra time on the ground."

"Do we know how he's being delivered. Vehicle? Or, on foot by the militia?"

"No." He said abruptly. "As we get closer, I'll keep each of you informed."

Rich stood. "Now, a quick review of points on the memorandum…." He went through each section highlighting the final language. The entire document being transmitted. Everyone in the room did not agree with specific points. Embarrassments to their agendas. But, the document fulfilled the purpose for Working Group-41. It solved minor points of diplomatic concern. Ensured the return of two adversarial assets. And, reset the field for continued ideological battle.

The lawyer ended this final presentation.

"…First, we expect the final transmitted around noon. Embassies will coordinate the signing. We should have it back in our possession by close of business today. Second, Tom will meet with Dutrov with the final document. Any last-minute additions will push the day and time of the swap. We want no surprises." He paused, taking a breath. "Third, the Attorney General sends his appreciation to you all. This has been closely watched by the White House. You may be contacted for a de-brief. I, personally thank you for your cooperation."

Café La Plata

Alexandr Dutrov requested they meet at the café. Tom arriving last.

"You had to arrive first." Tom stated.

"I like it, when my back is against the wall." The two shook hands. "I've ordered. It is in appreciation for the work your group performed."

"We all had a hand in the Memorandum."

"Yes, but all that secretarial work. My fingers tire, thinking about it."

Tom laughed. "It's set for Sunday."

"Good. We all can get back to what we do best."

"Here is the final document. Without signatures. Just a formality for my old friend." Tom said, handing him a manila envelope.

"Do I need to read it?"

"You can. But, it's boring stuff. Let's just agree. When we've accomplished this goal, we'll meet to burn the agreement…"

They both laughed. The drinks arrived. A standard for closing the deal. Two Imperial and two shots of Vodka.

MEMORANDUM

of

UNDERSTANDING

T O P - S E C R E T

MEMORANDUM OF UNDERSTANDING

BETWEEN

The United States of America on behalf of

The Honduran, El Salvadoran & Panamanian Governments

AND

The Union of Soviet Socialist Republics on behalf of

Cuba & The Nicaraguan Government

1. Parties. This Memorandum of Understanding (hereinafter referred to as "MOU") is made and entered under Security Classification of TOP SECRET; into by and between the State Department of United States ("USA"), whose address is Washington, DC, and the Council for Foreign Affairs, Union of Soviet Socialist Republics ("USSR"), whose address is Moscow, Russia; NO DISSEMINATION OF INFORMATION IS PERMITTED OR ALLOWED.

2. Purpose. The purpose of this MOU is four-fold:

a. To establish the terms and conditions under which the mutual release of captives held by Nicaragua (NI) and Honduras (HN) will take place; the conditions for their return; caveats established to facilitate this action; and, actions to be prevented during and after the action has been concluded. Whereas a U.S. citizen is being held in Nicaragua against his will; and, one Nicaraguan citizen is held in the Department of El Paraiso, Honduras against the will and desires of the individual, family, Nicaraguan Government and Cuba.

b. In consideration for the foregoing "mutual release of captives," the Drug Enforcement Agency, an agency of the United States, agrees to release a Cuban Embassy employee – described to be a diplomatic courier – from further and future criminal action. Whereas, the "diplomatic courier" was detained during a routine drug operation. In addition, one (1) crate – measuring 4ft x 3ft x 3.5ft – said to contain "documents," was seized during transit between Cuban embassies. Confiscated by Panamanian & U. S Drug Enforcement Personnel.

c. To return the human remains of any U. S. citizens currently held by the Nicaraguan Government;

d. To prevent an international incident; embarrassment to the parties hereto; reestablish proper working relationship between the undersigned countries; and, to return diplomatic relations to cooperation within the Central and South American Region.

3. Term of MOU. This MOU is effective upon the day and date last signed and duly executed by authorized representatives of the parties to this MOU; the governing bodies of the parties' respective countries or municipalities; and, shall remain in full force and effect for perpetuity; or, until this MOU is amended or modified by the parties at a future date. This MOU may not be terminated, with or without cause, by either party upon or until all caveats have been met; written notice is provided of either party wishing to amend or modify the agreement; and, which notice shall be delivered by hand or diplomatic courier to the address listed above.

4. Responsibilities of Undersigned Country Representatives.

a. The USA (on behalf of HN) will fly one UH-1 type aircraft to the point of release. The coordinates and general location of the release point will be 13.89905 N and 86.15609 W; a country road running North-South; marked to a point of recognition; and, in an area near the Nicaraguan Town of Jalapa;

b. The NI representatives will travel to that location from a point between the Towns of Ocotal and Jalapa, NI; in a hospital supplied ambulance; other vehicles will not be permitted on the ground at this specified site;

c. When it has been determined that a safe exchange can be made, the USA will release their NI captive to ambulance personnel present; and, the same personnel will release the US Citizen to the exchange team aboard the helicopter;

d. Reasonable means of protection for the exchanging parties is hereby allowed;

e. Once the exchanges are considered complete, the parties to this agreement, their operators, assigns and support will depart;

f. In a humanitarian gesture, Juanita Maria Perez-Velasquez will be permitted to emigrate to Cuba; in the company of her son, Jaime Correa Velasquez; to complete the mourning of her late husband & father, Miguel Correa Velasquez;

g. It is imperative that all support personnel be thoroughly briefed to this agreement; placing initials on the document upon departure of; and, sign off the agreement upon their return to their base of operation.

5. Responsibilities of Parties for Which this Agreement is Made.

a. The Countries of Cuba, Panama, Honduras, Nicaragua and El Salvador are held to this agreement by fact;

b. They, or any member of their government; those holding power, as in – The Presidency, Cabinet Positions, Intelligence or Military Services – of or to that country shall be held accountable; and responsible for this agreement;

c. Any parties participating in the exchange; or, the released captives – subjects of this agreement – will also be held responsible for this knowledge; held responsible not to disseminate any information relating to this agreement;

d. Any party participating in the exchange; the released captives; or, families of the released captives disseminating any information relating to this agreement, shall be dealt with to the highest extent allowed by law.

6. General Provisions

a. Amendments. Any signatory party may request changes to this MOU. Any changes, modifications, revisions or amendments to this MOU which are mutually agreed upon; by and between the parties to this MOU; and, shall be incorporated by written instrument, effective when executed and signed by all parties to this MOU.

b. Applicable Law. The construction, interpretation and enforcement of this MOU shall be governed by pre-written Fairness Doctrines & Accords Existing between Countries and States; and, International Law. No court in either Primary Agreeing Country; or, Courts in Countries on behalf of which this agreement is made shall have jurisdiction over any action arising out of this MOU; and/or over the parties; punitive action will be unnamed; that future action to be determined. Initials for the country representative to this document:

(Initials) ___/___/__ /___/___/___

c. Entirety of Agreement. This MOU, consisting of five (5) pages, represents the entire and integrated agreement between the parties and supersedes all prior negotiations, representations and agreements, whether written or oral.

d. Severability. Should any portion of this MOU be judicially determined to be illegal or unenforceable, the remainder of the MOU shall continue in full force and effect, and either party may renegotiate the terms affected by the severance.

e. Sovereign Immunity. The Embassies of The United States of America and the Embassies of The Union of Soviet Socialist Republics and their respective governing bodies do not waive their sovereign immunity in entering into this MOU; and, each fully retains all immunities and defenses provided by law, with respect to any action based on or occurring as a result of this MOU.

f. Third Party Beneficiary Rights. The parties do not intend to create in any other individual or entity the status of a third-party beneficiary; and, this MOU shall not be construed to create such status. The rights, duties and obligations contained in this MOU shall operate only between the parties to this MOU; and, shall inure solely to the benefit of the parties to this MOU. The provisions of this MOU are intended only to assist the parties in determining and performing their obligations under this MOU. The parties to this MOU intend and expressly agree that only parties' signatory to this MOU shall have any legal or equitable right to seek to enforce this MOU, to seek any remedy arising out of a party's performance or failure to perform any term or condition of this MOU, or to bring an action for the breach of this MOU.

8. Signatures. In witness whereof, the parties to this MOU through their duly authorized representatives have executed this document on the days

and dates set out below, and certify that they have read, understood, and agreed to the terms and conditions of this MOU as set forth herein.

The effective date of this MOU is the date of the signature last affixed to this page.

(Signature Page and initials by all parties)

Top-Secret
Guest Quarters - U.S. Embassy Grounds
25 October 1985

Tom walked into the guest quarters. To where a Marine guard sat outside a door. The guard jumped to his feet. Standing squarely in front of the door.

"Good evening, Mr. McKay."

"Evening. How's our charge?"

"Quiet sir." The Marine stepped aside. "You think that boy never watched TV before."

"Who knows. Might not have TV where he's from."

Tom knocked on the door. Opening it. The young man could have been his son. Lying on the bed. On his stomach. Chin in his hands. Propped up by elbows holding his head erect. So engrossed, he did not hear Tom enter.

"Jaime?"

The boy slid off the bed. Standing five feet from Tom. "Si."

"I've got some good news." Tom went to the TV controls. Turning down the sound.

"What news?"

"You're going home."

Jaime stood motionless. The words initially fell on unbelieving ears. "Home?"

"Yes. I said, you're going home. We've got it set for day after tomorrow. Sunday."

He bounded to where Tom stood. Hugging him. Joyful. Happy.

Tom put his arms around Jaime. A hug that he would give his son. If he was here. He felt warmth for having granted life, back to the young man. Holding back the emotions that would come from his tear glands.

"Here is my phone number. These folks can track me down. I want to know how you are getting along."

Jaime pulled back. Tears in his eyes. Asked, "Does my mother know?"

"Not sure. That's why we have it set for Sunday. The arrangements are still in process. But, you're going home to your mother."

"I wish I could talk to her, now. Tell her what a good man you are."

"A lot of people worked on this." Tom said in return.

"But, you rescued me. Brought me here. Came many time to check on me. I got to watch television."

"Yes. TV helps pass the day."

"When can we tell my mother?"

Tom thought. *"What would be the ramifications of letting this boy talk to his mother? All the hard work is done. One more foreign contact to report. What the hell!"*

"What is your home number? I'll have the operator dial for us." He said. Called the night service number at the U. S. Embassy. Then told the Embassy Operator to dial the number Jaime gave him.

"Hola. Senora Perez. Tenemos una llamada de larga distancia para usted." The operator announced.

Tom handed Jaime the phone.

"Momma, estoy llegando a casa…."

Rancho Perez

Latitude: 13.8955 N

Longitude: 86.1503 W

Central Standard Time (GMT -6)

26 October 1985

Activity returned to Rancho Perez. The relationship between Juanita and Lester, marked with formality. The chance of intimacy passed. Mood within the ranch house walls surfacing with cautious optimism and happiness.

Juanita, happy for the returning Jaime. Sad at closure coming between her and Lester. A return to normalcy. A chance at intimacy forbidden. Jaime Velasquez changed by experience within the world of warring parties. Lester knowing his real identity. All masked for the protection of everyone. The exposure of truth known by each would affect their interaction.

"Under different circumstance, I would have approached you. Sexually."

"There is nothing to discuss." Juanita replies.

"I'm happy that your son is coming home. That I am going back to what I do."

"There are people who cannot be together. I see that. But," she stopped.

"But, what. What is the question?"

"If we were not who we are," she paused. "Would there have been a chance?"

"Not for us to know. We can only go on. Back to who we are."

They were having two different conversations. She is questioning life choices. He is settling for the next events that would rule his life. Both futures uncertain. Both willing to move forward.

Touching his hand from across the table, Juanita changed the subject.

"Colonel Mendez and Major Sanchez will be arriving within the hour. They have information. Details for us. Information on my son." She stood, walking to Jaime's bedroom.

Lester watched her. Seeing her disappear into the room farthest from the kitchen. Watching, as she walked back to the table.

"I have something for you." Juanita said. She handed him a coin. "Lady Liberty. A symbol. The other hero in my life."

Lester did not understand the significance of her statement. "It's a Silver Dollar." He turned it over twice looking at the date of minting. "Where did you get this?"

"My father gave it to me." Her attitude turning somber. "He was a U.S. Citizen. A musician. Came to Cuba. Met my mother there."

"I don't know what to say."

"Take it. Remember this time in Nicaragua. This hour. Day. Me."

Lester has no words. His inner-being, touched by this cap to her kindness. The scene will remain in his recovering memory. Silence filling the space around them. He turned the coin slowly, in his left hand. Juanita moving the air as she cleared the table.

A vehicle approached breaking Lester from inner thoughts. Turning to see the advancing vehicle. She wipes her hands. Straightening herself. Composing. Putting on armor to cover the softness she just displayed.

"Buenas dias, colonel." Juanita greeted the men exiting the vehicle. "Major Sanchez."

"Hola, Senora." Major Sanchez says.

"Our good news continues." Colonel Mendez adds.

"Come in." Juanita directs them through the front door.

Both officers were surprised to see Lester Russell sitting at the kitchen table.

"You look well, Mr. Russell." Col. Mendez addresses.

"Not 100 percent. But, much better than before I can remember."

"You will be pleased to hear that your editor awaits your return."

"I'm sure he got along well, without me."

Juanita placed their hats in the living room. Returning to take a seat at table with the three men.

"We came to tell you of the arrangements."

"What about my son?"

"He is fine. Assured that he is taken care of." The Colonel replies.

"Tomorrow, you will see." Major adds.

"You sir, still have medical issues. Before you leave tomorrow, the doctor will have one final look. Our insurance that we have done everything for your safety, health and security."

"The doctor and ambulance will arrive around eight AM. Plenty of time to check you. Before we drive you to the release point." Added Maj. Sanchez.

"The Americans are flying a helicopter. They will deliver Senior Jaime. And, pick-up your charge, Senora." Colonel Mendez explains.

"The Colonel and I will arrive here with the ambulance. I will wait here. The doctor, ambulance attendants and Colonel Mendez will ride with the Senora. To the place of transfer." Maj. Sanchez, turning to Lester. "You will be on a stretcher. Secured."

"What time will the transfer take place?" Juanita asked. Her voice showing the expectation of a mother.

"We have set the hour at eleven AM." Colonel replies.

"You will have your son back. Senior Russell will go back to write his story. All will return to normal." Major Sanchez announces.

Toncontin - Constable Outreach Hangar

The briefing for prisoner transfer was set for nine AM. A gun-metal gray UH-1 Huey sits as a backdrop, in the expansive hangar. Doors removed. No fin flash or markings indicating unit or country of nationality. A single red cross adhered to the nose. Two pilots from the 722nd Army Aviation Battalion flew the helicopter. It arrived late afternoon on Friday.

Others are present for the mission brief. Tom McKay gives the overview. Two Marines from the Embassy Security Team stand to the back.

"Our point of retrieval is between Jalapa and Ocotal, Nicaragua. A Cuban airstrip. Dirt and unimproved. Latitude: 13.8990 North, Longitude: 86.1560 West. We'll be operating as an air ambulance. Clearance given through diplomatic channels."

Looking at the pilots, he continues "File a normal flight plan. Using Diplomatic Number 41-6334. That clearance tied to your call sign. There will be another plane on our frequency. It's a Sandie using a Panamanian Call Sign. I'll pass more information tomorrow…"

"It'll be the five of us on the first leg. Pilots, our Marines, and me We'll have a young Nicaraguan in tow. Please limit your conversation with him. Upon arrival at transfer point, we will escort the young man to a point forward of the chopper."

Addressing the Marines, "You'll be armed with M-16s and a pistol each. Eyes outside on arrival. You see something, call it out. Once the chopper is on the ground, we'll make the transfer for our asset. He'll be on a stretcher. You guys will carry him back to the bird. Again, once onboard outside vigilance is essential. Not expecting an ambush. We have air-cover. But, be prepared."

Tom continued, "When we return, a C-130 Air Evac will meet us here. At the hangar. Once the chopper has shut-down, a team will come to our bird for his transfer to the one-thirty. Our asset will be transported to Panama, under the care of Med-Evac personnel."

"Showtime will be 0700. At the hotel lobby. Pilots will determine takeoff, flight time and time on the ground. Time of transfer set for 1100 hours." Addressing the entire group, "Final briefing by our pilots in the morning. Any questions?"

Body and foot movement was the only sound. "Okay guys, get some rest."

This military briefing set the stage. Only Murphy's Law would now be in control. Anything discussed outside of this briefing would be a violation of agency code.

Hotel Elegante

The room phone rings as Tom enters his hotel room. Door swung closed on its own, as Tom moved toward the phone.

"Tom, Jack Simone."

"What can I do for you?"

"One of my guys overheard two Batt 3-16 guys talking."

"About what?"

"An assassination. In Managua. A Cuban DGI agent. That mean anything to you?"

"No. First mention from you." He paused. "But, wait. I heard the same thing from another source."

"They didn't talk long. My guy walked out of earshot."

"Thanks for the call." Tom hangs up.

He thinks for a moment. Dials a number in the hotel.

"Fred, sorry to bother you on a Saturday."

"It's okay. Just watching a soccer match."

"Got a call from Danli. There's talk of an assassination. In your contacts, you hear anything about that? Or, something that might clarify?"

"No. You remember me telling you how angry the Commandant was over the transfer? Maybe that has something that might explain what was overheard."

"No. This was more specific."

"Can't say I know anything about it."

"Thanks, Fred. Again, sorry to bother you on Saturday."

Tom's gut tells him something is not adding up.

'Working Group-41 comes through in record time. Settling three separate incidents. International points of diplomatic discussion. A prisoner transfer set for tomorrow at eleven. All that lines up. No matter how fast. Hondurans drug their feet. Supposedly, over military funding. They came through when the Russians applied pressure. Now, the talk of an assassination we're not privy to. Who's zooming who?'

'It was surprising how fast this prisoner exchange had been designed. Scheduled phone calls between security personnel on both sides had been tense. Driven by local Embassies in Tegucigalpa. Going back and forth. A means by which each side tried to gain an upper hand.'

'Phone calls were short. When negotiations started for the exchange, Jaime was being exchanged for a news reporter. A person considered to be of high value for the paper which he wrote. If Fred doesn't know. The embassy is outside the loop.'

It bothers him. No one to talk with about it.

'We've got a rogue Commandant playing God. No way to break into those discussions. Guess he feels like we slapped him in the face. Should we have allowed him into the discussions of transfer? I will have to notify the folks in Virginia. Maybe they can make some sense of it.'

Jack Simone gave no date. Timeframe. Or, other intel to work with.

'And, still puzzled about what Alexandr knows of Fred Matthews.'

Tom picks up his keys and departs the room. He needs to find a secure line in the Embassy to talk with management in Virginia.

Tegucigalpa, Honduras

Toncontin Airport (TGU)

Latitude: 14.0723 N

Longitude: 87.1821 W

Central Standard Time (GMT -6)

27 October 1985

Jaime had been prepared so that he heard as little as possible. Navy flight-line ear protection muffled the voices of others. Hearing loss prevention was not the goal. He had been kept in silence at the outstation. The only place that he heard voices of other humans was where he slept. Where he was questioned. The interrogators changed out depending upon the proposed discussion.

The move to embassy exposed the boy to knowledge of his whereabouts. The hour drive from Danli to Tegucigalpa. His safe keeping more like a luxurious vacation. Mental conditions set aside.

Taken from isolation was Tom's idea. Throwing him into a modern living existence with communication alternatives. Doing what boys do. Regular food delivery. Freedom to remain awake long after sundown. Watching TV until falling asleep. This sheltered young man had experience three styles of existence in the last thirty days. Today he was being returned to an existence where love was the primary motivator.

The Huey lifted tail first, as power was applied. The fuselage showed its age. Primer painted over its gray body did not totally hide the symbols on its fuselage. This bird might have been seen on the flight deck of a U. S. Navy troop carrier. It possibly came from a Navy helicopter attack squadron stationed aboard a ship in the South China Sea. It had seen action off the coast of Vietnam.

The Bell Iroquois was nicknamed the Huey. Because of the original designation, Hotel Uniform – One. An inversion of UH. During the war, UH-1 troop transport frames were often called "slicks." Gunships were referred to as "frogs" or "hogs." The "slicks" had two door gunners. One of which was usually manned by the flight engineer.

During the war 7013 UH-1s served in Vietnam. Of these, 3305 were destroyed. 1074 pilots were killed. Along with 1103 other crewmembers.

UH-1 flown today is powered by a General Electric T700 engine providing 900+ shaft horsepower. Producing a Maximum speed of 135 mph. Cruise speed of 125 mph. With a range of 315 miles. That is 274 nautical miles. Or, 507 kilometers.

The U. S. refit the remaining UH-1Bs. Some were sold to countries friendly to the U.S. This chopper had been sent to Honduras for training exercises. And, probably would not be returned to the United States.

The transverse bulkhead provided a backboard for people to lean into. Fuel tanks were under the floor. The two-bladed overhead design creates the "Huey Thump." While in flight it is particularly evident during descent and in turning flight. The landing gear consists of two arched tubes. Skids. A four-man bench seat faces rearward behind the pilots. Another five-man seat, sits opposite in front of the transmission bulkhead. Bench seats facing outward from the transmission, on either side of the aircraft provide seating for door-gunners. One being the flight-engineer position. On this bird, the doors are removed.

Distance between Toncontin and Drop Zone Alpha is 113.6 kilometers. 70 miles on the ground. 73 air miles calculated for 117 kilometers flying.

On takeoff this morning, the turned-up skids, skimmed about a foot off the ground. Until forward speed was gained. In about 800 feet, the chopper lifted skyward. It set a flight plan course towards the landing zone near Jalapa.

Six souls were lifted from the concrete taxi-way. One being the non-combatant, Jaime Velasquez. Tom carried a Springfield Arms .45 Cal pistol. The two Marines had M-16s and .45 Cal side arms.

Wind whisked past the door openings. Blew through the open cargo compartment. Once outside the ten-nautical mile Critical Flight zone, pilots would transition to cruise altitude. A flight level of five-thousand feet would be held. Radar contact maintained and monitored under the diplomatic, air-ambulance flight plan. Flight time to destination, 45 minutes.

An A-1J Skyraider had been tasked to provide fire support, should it be needed. Brought in for Huey pilot comfort. Designated callsign, "Blanket 15." It flew East-South-East from an undisclosed base. Entering Nicaraguan territory at tree-top level in radio silence. Flying an azimuth of 102 Degrees and at 220 Knots Airspeed…

"Outreach 15, this is Blanket." The Sandy pilot radioed.

"Go ahead."

"Estimate overhead in 10 minutes."

"Copy, Blanket 15."

It approached the LZ from the North West. The chopper from the North. Both expected at the LZ at same time. The Huey would make one pass identifying the road. Once both birds were in area of operation, the Skyraider would pop up to 3000 feet.

Then fly a holding pattern around the landing zone. Watching and waiting. It gave the UH-1 crew relative comfort that air-cover was being provided by a Sandy.

"Will stay with you until curtain falls." Sandy pilot added.

Both parties heard the mic-button click twice, indicating that Outreach 15 understood. The A-1 pilot had not been at the mission briefing. Any reference to the word "hot" would indicate their need for his intervention.

Cuban Dirt Strip: DZ – Alpha

A LRRP Team with Air Force Combat Control and a PJ lie in the woods. West of the dirt strip. Their insertion originally planned for other purposes. But, tasked with overseeing the prisoner transfer. They monitored the UHF band being used for the flight. There was no contact with the LRRPs. They did not exist. This exchange of adversarial assets witnessed. A boy for a loadmaster.

Jaime fidgeted on the canvas seat. With his back to the longitudinal bulkhead, he sat lateral dead-center of chopper cargo area. On either side of him sat the armed security members. Facing rearward, Tom sat watching him from a position, back to and between the pilots. He reached forward and touched Jaime on the knee. The fidgeting stopped.

Descent started. Pilots could see the North-South road. The Cuban unimproved airstrip. DZ Alpha. Now a Landing Zone for Outreach 15. A brown stripe cutting through the center of a green circle. Ringed with trees.

The treetops were getting closer to the belly of the chopper. The pilot and co-pilot monitored separate frequencies – the pilot the flight designated UHF frequency; and, the co-pilot on Guard. Radio chatter broke the silence in pilot's ear. Verbal communication between pilots confirmed aircraft status.

The rotating blades cutting into the air provided a most distinctive sound. Which any Air Mobile Soldier could identify. The conversation of passengers held to the essential.

A road wide enough to land a C-130 skimmed below the helicopter. At a distance on the South end, sat a white Cadillac ambulance. Red cross on the roof. No human activity was seen anywhere in the bowl. The chopper cleared the North tree line, continuing South. Making a banking maneuver to the left. Circling. Lining up with the brown dirt landing zone.

The pilot began to slow the forward movement of this mercy angel. The nose of the Huey lifted slightly to allow the rotor blades to catch the air like a parachute. At a higher angle of attack, the fuselage was slowing to settle its skids on the roadway. With both skids on the ground the lift was reduced to zero.

As the chopper settled on the ground, one of the security team crossed himself. Heightened awareness reduced the sound that each could hear. They prepared for exit by removing seatbelts. Cautiously moving outboard to the edges of their canvas seats. Facing out toward the door openings. Pilots reset flight switches in preparation for takeoff.

The Huey had set down in the middle of the LZ. Blowing dirt and sand outward from blade downward force. Giving it near equal space to lift. Gain speed. And, take-off before reaching the trees on the South end. Where the ambulance sat, shaded by the trees.

The 5000-foot hole in the middle of the forest, was probably a planting area for indigenous people. Indians that had previously dotted this region. The Miskito Indian territory extended from the Eastern Coast to Rio Grande. The Chorotega, Cacaopera and other tribes inhabited the Central & Northern Pacific Areas of Nicaragua. This land used by other farming people before lying dormant.

The landing zone had a North-South orientation. Heavy forest started fifteen-hundred feet off the road to the East. The terrain sloped gently downward to the West. The scrub slightly heavier, led to a tree line the same distance from the road. Bushes allowed for concealment. On the North end of this straight stretch, the road curved slightly to the Northwest.

All eyes were looking outside the chopper for any movement. Everyone aboard was on heightened alert except for the exchange prisoner. Armed security moved selector switches from safe to firing position. Tom touched his forty-five-caliber handgun. Slid his hand around the grip and undid the retaining strap on the holster.

The LZ was a ripe place for an ambush. If something went wrong with the exchange, firepower could be applied to take out the chopper. Any Sandinista force would then be in a firefight with those remaining alive. Murphy's Law hung in the balance, hovering near the fulcrum. The slightest wisp of air could move it.

'Whatever can go wrong, will go wrong. Great place for an ambush,' Tom thought. But no words were spoken.

Nicaragua

Landing Zone Alpha

Latitude: 13.8990 N

Longitude: 86.1560 W

Central Standard Time (GMT -6)

October 27, 1985

Once the chopper sat down, the two Marines exited. Taking up positions at each door. Tom exited from the left side with Jaime in hand. He guided the boy near the nose. Followed by the Marines.

Huey blades whirling above. A moderate form of dust generated from the whirling helicopter blades. Minutes began to mark this planned prisoner exchange. All movements seemed in slow motion. Chopper blades synchronized to move by the count of each second passing.

The Cadillac-Ambo moved forward. Stopping 500 feet off the chopper's nose. Two bodies exited. The driver and passenger. Disappearing behind ambulance. Shortly they reappeared carrying a stretcher. Two other bodies following the stretcher bearers. They moved to positions each side of the stretcher. The four with stretcher moved forward toward the awaiting chopper.

Tom motioned the Marines to take up positions to his left and right. Jaime was immediately to Tom's left. Between him and a Marine. They ducked to move under the slinging helicopter blades. Four walked from the North. Four with their stretcher patient walked from the South. Meeting mid-distance between chopper and ambulance. A hundred feet between them.

At a closer distance, Tom could see three men and a woman.

'Was that the woman? Dressed in green Cuban fatigues. The female, Juanita Perez?'

The agency knew that women were much involved in the fight against oppression. Their retold stories had become modern day myths. There had been many female communists who fit into that playbook. But, Tom had not expected that a woman would be part of this exchange party.

'The calling for her to be here – her returning son!'

Tom sees a hand reach out from the stretcher to touch the woman. The body on the stretcher, holds the woman's hand. Momentarily. The grasp released, as the two stretcher bearers walk away from her.

They walked forward. Whirling chopper blades punctuate their gate. Tom hears the Sandy overhead. His gaze intent on two statues standing behind the ambulance attendants.

Stretcher bearers stop. Half way between. Setting the stretcher on the ground. They backed away.

Tom recognizes the uniforms to be Cuban. He and Jaime move forward toward the stretcher. His arm over Jaime's shoulder. Preventing him from bolting towards the awaiting party.

At the stretcher, Jaime looks at Tom. Tom looks down to confirm the patient to be Lester. Tom nods. Then, looks at Jaime with a smile. Releasing the hold of the kidnapped. Jaime moves quickly away from him.

As Jaime reached the woman, they fell into an embrace. Arms wrapped around the young Nicaraguan. Her green fatigues becoming a stark contrast to the boys bright clothing. Clothes Tom had purchased for Jaime. Like shopping for his son.

'The woman bared her emotions. An age difference between the woman and the young captive was also noticeable. It was Juanita Perez-Velasquez. The mother. Different from the person depicted in her dossier.'

Mother and son reunited. He held her tight in a display of affection.

With Tom facing the five to the South, Marines come to the stretcher. Tom looked at Lester. Marines pick up the stretcher. He motions for the Marines to start back, toward the chopper. They moved on Tom's command.

He remained in position. Focusing on the woman. She, looking back at him.

'Juanita Perez-Velasquez, the Cuban DGI Agent.'

He checks the time on his watch. Tom salutes. The adversaries began backing away from the transfer point. Tom watched them enter the ambulance. He turned, walking purposefully to duck below the whirling blades.

'Time of transfer 1110. UTC 1710. Face to face with Cubans. Juanita Perez-Velasquez'

The ambulance backed to the South end tree line.

Departure: 1115 Local - Destination – Toncontin

Aboard the Huey, one Marine sits on the canvas seat, back to the pilots. Securing the stretcher to D-rings on the floor. Tom takes a seat abreast Lester. The other Marine comes aboard last. Both Marines face outward, toward the five-foot openings. M-16 muzzles pointing out.

Tom grabs Lester's left hand. Clasps his other hand around, enveloping the hand of his loadmaster. The exchange, one of joy for Lester. Happiness and relief communicated by Tom McKay.

"Blanket 15, transfer complete." Co-pilot informed the Sandy pilot. Two clicks heard in co-pilots headset.

The Huey began to power up. Power then applied to whirling rotor. Tail lifted gracefully. The change in blade pitch sounds vertical lift. Nose titled forward toward the South. Forward movement. Skimming the roadway. 25 knots…liftoff. Flying toward the ambulance. Belly of the Huey skimmed the treetops above it. Red cross visible on the ambulance roof below.

Marines focused on the horizon. The Huey turned East. Then North-West toward Jutiapa, Honduras. The ambulance was not seen. It was gone.

'We need fifteen minutes to be out of harm's way. Baby, don't fail me now.' Tom's thoughts were now of the air-evac transfer.

"Blanket 15, we're outbound. You can follow us to the border."

"Copy, Outreach."

Three set of hands touched Lester's extremities. A smile turned to three faces making eye contact with their repatriated American. Lester tried talking over the air-rush and whine of the turbine. Talking without the use of a headset would force him to shout.

The doors had been removed from this Bell chopper. The rushing air created its own barrier to normal conversation. The overhead turbine provided escape power. The rotating blades transferred power to forward movement. Vibration felt through the fuselage floor.

The combined sound of the turbine was constant. The air-rush, lulled its passengers into their own thoughts. No words spoken. What little pain Lester felt by movement, could not dampen his gratitude.

The kilometers clicked by under the chopper. With full power and cruise speed set. They flew toward the boarder. Constable Outreach 15 banked left for a turn toward Toncontin. Tom and the two Marines sat back in a release of tension.

Crossing into Honduran airspace, co-pilot makes the radio call.

"Blanket 15, thank you for your service today. Next time we meet, beers on us."

"Copy that, Outreach. I'll collect soon." Seen off the left of the Huey, Sandy gave a wing-wag. Its pilot pushed the power lever forward. Then it was gone.

"Tegucigalpa, Constable Outreach 15 has airfield in site." Pilot radioed.

Copilot placed a radio call to the waiting C-130. The airplane staffed with air-evac personnel. That would take Lester Russell to Panama.

"Air Evac 6407, Outreach 15"

"Go ahead, Outreach 15."

"ETA Constable ramp in ten minutes."

"Copy, one-zero minutes. We'll be ready." Squelch crackled on the tail end of message.

Landing clearance requested. "Copy all, Tegucigalpa Tower."

Approaching the airport from the Southeast, the Huey skirted the East end of Runway 20. Flying parallel to it, on a runway heading to the ramp.

After the turbines shut-down, the pilot turned over his right shoulder. "On behalf of the 722nd Army Aviation Battalion, welcome back to Tegutch."

Air Evac 6407 - Destination Howard AB, Panama

A sedative given to Lester by the aero-medical nurse. It held him in a state between ultimate rest and presence aboard this ship.

The C-130 was empty. Lester was the only passenger, secured to a litter strapped to the floor. A nurse, doctor and med-tech were tending to this single patient. The hum of turboprop engines was sound that he could recall from his past. He had traveled on many C-130s, sitting upright in the canvas seats lining each fuselage wall.

The pain from his broken clavicle was nonexistent at this point. His twisted knee would need surgery to repair the torn ligaments. The laceration on his left arm caused by the extraction cord would reopened. Scar tissue removed. Repaired and sewn back up. Scars on his face would eventually disappear. Blending with others from the ring.

"How you doing, bud," a med-tech asked.

"Flying man," Lester replied. Both chuckled.

He lapsed into the warm comfort of the morphine induced state. Occasionally, opening his eyes. He looked for the beauty in the face of the only female. The nurse scurrying around him. She was not Juanita. The nurse smiled, knowing he was watching her.

Doctor in attendance, had just returned from the flight deck. He had called ahead with instructions for the hospital and ambulance crew. The flight would take another hour.

Lester had no idea the destination of this plane.

The C – 130 touched down at Howard Air Force Base. The taxi back to parking would take approximately 3 minutes.

"Glad to have you back," the loadmaster said, as he moved rearward to open the cargo doors during taxi.

"Where are we?" Lester asked. He searched for anyone around him to answer his question.

"Panama," the med-tech replied. "You'll soon be at the hospital. How are you feeling?"

"Still loopy."

"Morphine. The Asian serpent. Brother and sister to heroin." He paused. With that, he patted the forearm where the IVs had been placed. "You take care…."

With cargo doors open, the plane came to a shuddering stop. Checklists were being run. Engine shutdown. The loadmaster directed the ground medical crew to approach the ramp. He lowered the ramp and medical transport personnel came aboard. Some discussion between med-techs took place, before they all surrounded him.

"You ready to go soldier?" A med-tech asked.

"I'm at your mercy," Lester replied through his drug-induced speech and thick tongue. "Thanks for the ride."

Four bearers lifted the liter - one on each handle. A nurse held the saline bottle high above the liter. They carried him through the cargo compartment, down the ramp into the waiting ambulance.

Rancho Perez

Latitude: 13.8955 N

Longitude: 86.1503 W

Central Standard Time (GMT -6)

28 October 1985

The Memorandum of Understanding agreed between six Nations. It allowed Juanita Velasquez and her son emigration to Cuba.

Juanita loved her son above all else. She would do anything to keep him safe and close to her. The rural atmosphere they lived in, did not provide the education she sought for the young man. She wanted him educated, grow to marry and produce grandchildren. The way she saw it, none of that would happen outside the small town of Jalapa.

She was to move from Jalapa with the help of Colonel Mendez. He was doing so under orders from their Embassy in Managua. The message read:

"Asistir a la Señora Juanita María Pérez Velásquez en el embalaje, transporte y regreso a esta Embajada. No debes discutir ninguno de estos acontecimientos durante el último mes. El transporte aéreo se ha arreglado para ella y su hijo. Deberá llegar con los bienes a más tardar a las 24.00 horas del 28 de octubre de 1985."

Colonel Mendez had arrived at Rancho Perez shortly after 7:30 AM. It was coming close to eight that morning.

"Señora, we must hurry. Tell your son to pack lightly. We have less than 16 hours to be at our embassy. In Managua."

"Yes, Colonel. We are hurrying!"

"We do not know what faces us on the road."

"Si, coronel." She said in response to his pleading. Her quick reactions to verbal stimulus demonstrated her focus. Turning to Jaime, coming out of the house. "You can't take that," she said to her son in Spanish. "Clothing only!"

When the packing was complete, two small suitcases sat at the front door. Colonel Mendez was opening the trunk. He turned and walked in the quick military posture to where the suitcases sat.

"This is all!" He said, declaring what they would take.

"Yes! Yes, Colonel." Juanita replied. "Go, Jaime…" she added, pushing him out the door.

Juanita turned and looked one more time at this ranch house. Two-bedroom, 900 square feet. The life estate given to her after the death of her husband. With memories of the man that recovered in her bed. It would revert to Property of the State upon her departure. Continuing to supply beef for the Sandinistas. And, people of Jalapa. The farm a stopping point for soldiers and drug mules. She pulled the front door closed.

Battalion 3-16 - Danli Military Compound

The information that Jaime had provided was not of any military significance. But, he had provided enough extra background to locate his mother. The loving son had given the agency interrogators enough answers. The agency wanted to locate her.

Batt 3-16 interrogators had their chance at Jaime. He was lulled into a false sense of security by men speaking his dialect. That comfort of familiarity lowered his natural resistance. He had no military secrets to divulge.

Locating his mother would complete the information the Hondurans needed. Resurrecting the horrific scenes from a previous battle, stirred the Commandant's passion. The pictures told of the horror perpetrated by men under the command of Miguel Velasquez. The Commandant pursuing a Honduran Military Vendetta to eliminate the Velasquez bloodline. It came closer with information provided.

Maintaining secrecy, set actions in motion that would be far-reaching. LRRPs hiding their presence had abducted Jaime Velasquez. The coordinates of the abduction were also on the LRRP Report. Shared by the agency. Part of the cooperative agreement between the U.S and Honduran Militaries.

Honduran Intelligence had tied her to the Cuban government years before. Her husband had an unofficial bounty on his head. Before he died in battle. She would slip away again. She had sought refuge within the Cuban community in Managua, in the past. Had been under the radar. Recently residing eight or so miles West of Jalapa.

The final MOU was shared with high ranking politicians. Brotherhood allegiance between politicians and general ranked officers, paved way for information sharing. It provided a location where the prisoner transfer would take place. Told that she would get a free pass to Cuba. A copy of the Memorandum was given to the Commandant, Battalion 3-16. It's headquarters in Danli, Honduras.

It also provided the possible location from which Juanita Velasquez would depart Nicaragua. She would never cross into Honduras to escape. Her nearest Cuban Embassy was in Managua.

A surreptitious check of registered passengers departing Managua was underway. As a DGI Agent, she would most likely travel at government expense. Aeroflot, TACA and others served Havana City. Some also provided limited availability for Cuban government officials at no cost.

The Commandant had dispatched a team. Sympathizers would aid in the search. They would find her. One dedicated soldier would kill her and her son.

Agency Ops – Danli Office

Across the compound, two contractors talked with their agency supervisor. The shut-down of Constable Outreach at Toncontin was now official. The agency had retrieved their loadmaster. Agency operations sought a new location. Warranting that Danli Operations would be the next facility closed. It was a systematic pull-back. For the foreseeable future, they still had a job. That could end at any day for a contractor.

"I have one job that needs to be done." Jack Simone said. "Both of you speak Spanish?"

"Part of the job." One replied.

"We're tasked with retrieving the Special Forces Operator, KIA at DZ Alpha. You two are going to drive down to Jalapa Hospital and get the remains. We have a mandate under Special Orders. Created by the Embassy. I gave them your names. Passport numbers. Here is the Special Order. A packet that will get you across the border. And, hopefully back."

"What?" The other interrogator keyed on the word 'hopefully.'

"Just kidding. It'll look good in you file. Agency hires from our pool of contractors."

"When do we leave?"

"In the morning. Retrieve the body. Back by sundown."

There was temporary glee in their step. Until it sunk in, that they were going after remains of a Special Operator. It would never be stated that he died in a covert operation. Or, where. He would be honored only by special operators who knew him. His name marked is a solemn ceremony at a building located on Ft. Bragg. And, by family members who could only surmise the involvement of his death.

Hotel Elegante - Tom's Departure

Tom closed his hotel room door for the last time.

He would catch a military flight to Panama. There, he would sit with Lester Russell. They would talk. He would give his sincere regrets for putting his loadmaster in an untenable position. He would let Lester say whatever was on his mind. They would connect man-to-man. Something that they had not done, before launching Outreach 35. Sending Lester on that injurious flight.

"Buenas Dias, Senior McKay," the desk clerk greeted.

"Good morning. Checking out." Tom said handing her the key to his room.

"How was everything with your stay?"

"I couldn't have asked for more from the hotel."

It is with other things, that Tom was asking more. At this moment, he felt a freedom not experienced since the early days of his joining the agency. The agency operations would go on. He would fly to Panama, to make his 'amend' with the captured and returned C-123 loadmaster. It was closing the book on Constable Outreach.

The agency had moved all equipment and operation personnel to Ilopango, San Salvador. The operation at Hangar 4, Toncontin Airport, Honduras was closed. The government of Honduras had won their fight with the US Embassy. The offices wiped clean. The cleaning crew supervised by two embassy employees. The cleaner had gone through each room. A white glove would show no sign of dust.

The tool crib downstairs – office of Tony Mercado – needed little cleaning. The hangar floor, swept and mopped. Kitty litter used to soak up a few standing oil stains. With the hangar doors closed, the Marines escorted the cleaning crew out the side gate. The pathway led to the street. It was as if, no one had used this space in the last six months.

Flight to Panama

The C-130 had landed. It had made its way from Panama to 'Tegutch' with supplies for the Embassy. The return trip to Panama would carry a single pallet of Embassy security documents. Embassy personnel would walk the documents on of the plane. Placing them on the military pallet. Included on the pallet was a large wooden box labeled and for receipt at the embassy, agency desk. In it contained the personal effects of Lester Russell. The edges lined with security tape.

Aircraft loaded. A sequence of timed event. An embassy employee watched every hand touch the embassy shipment. Under those watchful eyes, one would ring the loaded items with red warning tape. It placed in such a way that any movement of those items would break the tape. Indicating tampering.

Two loadmasters would net and secure the boxes to the pallet. One load-master manifested the escort at plain side. Tom McKay was a second passenger, manifested with her.

"Y'all can sit anywhere." The load said. He completed the read briefing from his handheld checklist.

"Tom McKay," he introduced himself to the young lady escort.

"Barbara…" She replied, extending her hand.

The airplane cargo ramp raised. The black SUV circled to the left, away from the tail of the plane. The whirring motors of the hydraulic system played a tune in the background. The cargo door closed and locked. One loadmaster placed the bags belonging to Tom and Barbara, in line with those of the crew. He secured the baggage to the floor, threading a 2-inch strap through the handles.

The air cart started. And within two minutes the number two engine was turning. Sound of the one turbo-prop coming up to speed heard through the crew entrance door. Vibration felt through the floor. Taking their seats across from one another, the passengers buckled their seatbelts.

Four engines turned. Checklists run. The C-130 blocked from the ramp. Close to the runway, near the end. They would soon be airborne. Tom's connection to Tegucigalpa would end, when the wheels came up.

Managua - Cuban Embassy - 4 PM

Colonel Mendez, Juanita and Jaime arrived at the vehicle gate to the Cuban Embassy. Within a minute the guard allowed them to pass. A declared Cuban with passport, Juanita sought refuge for return to the island. It might take a day to produce a Cuban passport for her son. She was unaware of the status she had attained – marked for death.

Quartered in the Cuban Embassy was step one on her return to Cuba. Already having feet on Cuban Diplomatic territory. A Cuban intelligence officer would debrief them. She and Jaime would share a room in the Embassy. Passage booked on a flight to Havana. Returning to her home-land. She wanted for the education of her son.

Panama

Hotel Intercontinental

Latitude: 8.983333 N

Longitude: 79.516670 W

Eastern Standard Time (GMT -5)

October 29, 1985

Tom McKay had a restful night. Knowing that his immediate concern was fulfilled. The return of Lester Russell, to the hands of the United States. Other caveats listed in Memorandum of Understanding were in process. Arrangements were underway.

This morning, he would take breakfast in coffee shop at street level. A swing by the embassy. A visit to the hospital where Lester would reside. Where his loadmaster was under diagnosis. Yet, locked in the secure section, on the third floor of a Black Site Hospital.

Moving around his hotel room was a different experience. Another place to hang his clothes bag. Open his luggage. Using it as a dresser from which to select his daily wear. Before retiring, he had given the Embassy and Central American Desk his contact number.

"Wouldn't be here long enough to stow my undies and socks in the drawer. Visits. Tying up loose ends. Mostly ensuring Lester was well cared for. Hospital was off the grid. Only talk. Secrets kept from the American Public. Had heard of two hospitals. One in Panama and one in the Philippines. Black sites. Run by the government but funded separately. A budget item hidden under National Institutes of Health. A place where, soldiers went. Who contracted diseases unknown – or, incurable. Where they would live out their lives."

Stepping out of the shower, Tom heard the hotel phone ringing. Towel wrapped around his middle, he moved purposefully toward the sound.

"Tom, Al Peterson."

"Good morning, Mr. Peterson. What can I do for you?"

"Information for you. Your LRRP patrol leader is restored to the honor he deserves. Presidential order."

"That's good news."

"Danli is working on retrieval of Special Operator body. Maybe, you could call them."

"I will. When I get to the embassy."

"One more thing. The President wanted me to share his appreciation for your efforts. Keeping this off the radar was important. Your team. The Memorandum Folks, did a hell of a job."

"Thank you, sir. Maybe each one of them would like to hear that personally. Can you arrange that?"

"I can." Al Peterson paused. "How's your boy?"

Tom had to think about who he was referring to, *'Lester or young Jaime?'*

"Lester Russell." Al Peterson added.

"Sir, he's hardly a boy. But, I'll tell him you asked about him."

"Okay. If there is anything you need, call me."

"Thanks…." Hanging up the receiver. The phone sat on one corner of a large blonde dresser. He stood staring into the mirror above the dresser.

'If there is anything I need? How open-ended was that statement? Is there something I don't know? What you don't know can kill you!'

U. S. Embassy - Panama

Tom entered the U.S. Embassy shortly after 10 AM. Went to the agency desk.

"Good morning." He said to a Hispanic, outer office employee.

"Good morning. How can I help you?"

"Tom McKay. Here to check in."

The young lady, knocked at a door next to the small alcove. Entering. Closing the door behind her. Within a minute, the door opened. A tall, squared jawed man walked through the opening with his hand extended.

"Tom, it is a pleasure to see you again."

"Roger. I didn't know you were stationed here. Good to see you." Tom replied.

They shook hands. Tom led into the office. The female backed out the door. Closing it.

"Heard you were coming to sunny Panama. Read the daily briefing. Been following the DEA case with the Cubans. Good work your people did."

"Let's put some truth to that. The situation was ripe to solve many problems. Yeah, everybody did one hell of a job. But, it all seemed to go too smoothly."

"What do you care? The job got done. Understand POTUS is happy. Time to move on. There's a lot more work to do."

Tom smiled, "You were always going after the next big thing."

"What is it that my office can help you with?" Roger asked, sensing an immediate need.

"I need a secure line. Calling Danli Operations."

"We can do that." He stood, "Anything else?"

"Yes. You have tabs on Alexandr Dutrov?"

Roger looked at Tom. With a gaze of questioning. "He's here. In town. Came in two days ago. Staying at the Russian Embassy. Why?"

"We have some business to conclude."

"Anything I should know?"

"I'll let you know when I make contact. You can put it in your records." He stood, "Now, how about that phone line?"

"Follow me."

The two walked down the hall to the communications section. Entered. Introductions given. Tom shook Roger's hand as he was leaving. After which, Tom was led to a small cubicle. Where his phone call could be made.

Tom's Secure Call

"Tom McKay."

"Yes, sir. How's the loadmaster?" Jack Simone asked.

"He's in good hands. I'll see him later today. Thanks for asking." He took a deep breath. "Where are we on the body retrieval?"

"My men left this morning. Should have been in Jalapa by nine. Assuming there were no snags. Crossing the border under diplomatic sanction should have paved the way. Expecting them back no later than four."

"Are you in contact?"

"No. But, if they run into a problem. They'll call."

"Here's my hotel phone number." He read it off a hotel card. "If there's a problem, call me. I can also be reached through the embassy."

"There is one more thing." Jack prefaced.

"What's that?" Tom expected something about agency business.

"Mentioned how I angered Battalion 3-16 Commander."

"Yeah, what about it?"

"It surfaced again."

"How so?" Tom asked.

"All our transcripts and files involving Jaime Velasquez boxed and taken."

"That's normal when a case officer closes an operation."

"This isn't normal." He paused. "The Commandant has them."

"The files sent to the Battalion 3-16?"

"Guy from another agency showed up with an order. All the files relating to Velasquez we taken. One of my men watched. Think they went across the parade field."

"That's a breach. Who was the guy?"

"Someone from DIA." He paused, "Hank Thoreau. You know him?"

"Son-of-a-bitch!"

"We wanted the files gone. But, not that way. Couldn't stop him."

"Not your fault. Just keep this quiet. I'd like to see the Order." He read the fax number off a laminated card pinned to the wall, above the phone. "Call me after you send it."

"This is the shit that ends careers." Jack added.

"One more reason to call me!" Tom said, understanding his own uneasiness.

The call ended. Tom stretched his analytical thought. *'What office wrote such an order? Why were these files such a high priority? Who was recipient? Where were the orders coming from? DIA usurping agency authority! Over a Honduran embarrassment? Or, something else?'*

Lester's New Prison

The third floor of this U.S. Government hospital housed 80 patients. This level held four wards. In one section of this X shaped building, a hospice provided for patient last days. One extension held persons who had contracted infectious diseases. The third, a military brig for injured prisoners. And, one for patients under psychiatric care with serious injury or illness.

Each segment of this floor sealed. Each ward had its own ventilation system. Which scrubbed the air – in and out. Each room sealed from the other. Electronic emissions trapped inside the exterior walls. The walls and roof hardened to prevent escape or intrusion. Telephone calls in and out monitored at a remote location. Television reception limited to Armed Forces Radio & Television Service.

One elevator went to this floor. Only accessed from a shaft, separate from the hospital building. The shaft itself sealed to prevent the transfer of air. Normal power came from an outside source. In emergency, the elevator and this floor had its own generator. It too hidden, to prevent tampering.

Security prevented entry and exit. Once a patient entered this sealed area, he was prevented from leaving. Servicemen who had contracted untreatable venereal diseases, lived out their lives on these floors. Those contracting unknown virus' were used as laboratory specimens.

The only way out, by legal expulsion or death. Lester was considered in this category until cleared. Blacklisted pending investigation.

Through a series of checkpoints, Tom navigated his way to where Lester was held. Security first. Elevator ride. Additional security. A desk where names were held for permitted entry. Nurses station. Secured room. Electronic locking mechanisms securing each space.

"You look like the boxer, I'm looking for." Tom said.

"Wow, I didn't expect to see you." Lester surprised at the visit. "So soon."

"Actually, you're going to get tired of seeing me. Treating you okay?"

"Food could be better. When you get a taste for Central American cooking. None of this institutional stuff seems to cut it."

"How about your injuries?"

"Orthopedics is planning a surgery or two. Straighten a few things out."

"How do you feel?"

"Ready to get back to work." Lester added, "After the surgery and psyche evaluation."

Tom knew there would be more to his return than that. "Let's take it a step at a time."

"I didn't tell you. How much I appreciated you coming after me. Personally."

"I never left a man behind."

"Don't know what you did. What the agency did, to secure my return."

"There will be time later, to fill you in."

Lester was itching to ask about Juanita. Prefacing it with, "What about my jailer?"

"The Sandinista Prison?" Tom asked.

"No, the woman who nursed me back. She's a real hero." He paused to dampen his interest in her. "She went to bat for me. Heard her take on one, really bad guy."

Tom knew who Lester was talking about, "You mean Juanita Perez?"

"Yes." Lester sought more information. "Will she be okay?"

"Think so," Tom replied with a non-committal response.

"You must take care of her," he told Tom.

"We are considering what needs to be done." Tom replied.

"She saved my life. That ought to be worth something."

But, Lester was thinking, *'Saving my life was her means to gain the return of her son. In her words, "I would do anything to get my son back!'*

"Yes. She saved your life. We saved her son's life. It was a concerted effort by many people."

"Where is she now?"

"As far as we know, she is in Managua. That was part of the deal. She would repair to the safety within the City of Managua…" Tom said no more.

'Knowing something doesn't give that person the right to openly use it in conversation.'

Some thoughts Tom held to himself. His careful execution of conversation with Lester would not reveal known facts.

"She was kind to me. She kept the soldier from hurting me. For that, I am truly grateful."

"How is your treatment coming?" Tom asked, changing the subject.

"I am alive. Take my medication four times a day. Have seen an army of doctors. They ask a lot of questions, too." He returned to thoughts of Juanita. "I don't want anything to happen to her."

"You keep getting better. We'll work on everything else." Tom said standing, "I'll be back to check in on you."

Managua, Nicaragua

Juanita Found in Managua

Latitude: 12.136389 N

Longitude: 86.251389 West

Central Standard Time (GMT -6)

October 30, 1985

It had been three days since the prisoner swap in Jalapa. Cuban Embassy personnel booked Juanita and Jaime on a Cubana de Avicion flight to Havana.

Agency personnel were traveling on two different tracks. Cubans and the Honduran military managed the ending of this situation. Also on different tracks. Opposing views were being held within a virtual structure. Previous standing declarations would have fulfilled. New activity would take a back seat. At some unseen point these dynamic forces would collide.

"Think we have something." An operations manager reported. Calling from Virginia.

"Where?" The voice on the other end asked. Coming from inside a U.S. Embassy.

"In Managua. She spotted coming out of the Cuban Embassy. Getting in a vehicle. Returned about an hour later with a garment bag."

"Is it a positive ID?"

"Yes. We have pictures."

"That's good work. Let me pass it on." Closing that conversation, Fred Matthews dialed another.

The call placed to Intelligence Battalion 3-16 in Danli, Honduras. Phone rang at their contacts desk. The conversation was short.

"... Podemos hacer que algo suceda. Me pondré con nuestro equipo en Mnagua. Le mantendrá informado.

Through combined agencies efforts, they had located Juanita. An opposition cell in Managua, 282 KM away had found a key figure in the Honduran vendetta.

The administration and Honduran Intelligence agreed that she needed to be neutralized. An American would stick out. A Honduran operator would better blend among the locals. He would pass through into Nicaragua. Driving to Managua. Driving would be less conspicuous.

Memorandum of Understanding was an old document by now. Shared only with a few. Everyone had orders. The MOU could not erase standing orders. Even when they conflicted.

Eyes on the Cuban Embassy would watch for any movement Juanita made. They mostly saw the comings and goings of persons to the consulate involving visas.

On occasion, a limousine would enter the gates. The consensus was that Juanita would return to Cuba as soon as was possible. Getting her away from this Central American affair was becoming more important. The date of her travel with Jaime marked for November 1st.

Panama - Telephone Conversations

Tom arrived at the Hotel Intercontinental. He checked for messages at the front desk.

"Good evening, Senior." He paused for the clerk to acknowledge him. "Any messages for Tom McKay?"

"Si. There are three." Handing him pieces pulled from a key pigeon hole.

"Gracias." The pink note heads read: "While You Were Out…." He leafed through them as he walked toward the elevator.

'One from Danli Operations. One from Central American Desk. And, one from Fred Matthews. Wonder what he wants?'

In the room, Tom places the first call to Danli Operations.

"Tom McKay here."

"Yes, sir." Jack Simone responded. "Two things. The remains of our Special Forces Operator were delivered to the local mortuary. In preparation for movement back to Dover. A C-141 will make an op-stop at Tegutch. That's set for November first."

"What's the second?"

"The rumor of an assassination is confirmed. It's Juanita Perez and her son Jaime."

"What? They were given diplomatic sanction to return to Cuba!"

"Don't know the details. But, our operations office upstairs got the call from our Honduran landlords."

"What supersedes a Presidential Order?"

"Previous written agreements for intelligence sharing and our military assistance to Honduras."

"I can't believe this."

"Maybe they'll make it…."

"Every child should get to know his grand-parents." Tom said. Thinking of promises made to Jaime. Equating promises he had made to his own children.

"Hate to be the bearer of bad news."

"I've got to go." Tom hung up.

He looked at his address book. He hadn't used it since he left Honduras. Searching for the number Jaime had given him, under Velasquez, Jaime.

He punched the country code and number on the house phone. It was not a secure line, but he dialed the number anyway.

It rang. Three…five…ten rings. No one answered.

"Come on. Pick up." His frustration was building. "Damn it! If anyone can hear me. Pick up damn it!" His heart sunk deep. No answer. He hung the receiver on the cradle.

Thinking, 'Who would know about this? Al Peterson? Fred Matthews? Central American Desk in Virginia? What can I do to stop it?"

He punched in another number. Hotel Elegante in Honduras.

"Fred Matthews, please." He waited. The room phone rang five times.

"I'm sorry Sir. Mr. Matthews doesn't seem to be in his room. Can I take a message?"

"Just tell him, Tom McKay called. Ask him to call me…." He hung up.

He dialed a third number.

"Central American Desk. Code...." All calls in and out had to meet procedural specs.

"...Tom McKay. Need to talk with a supervisor." The phone went silent for five seconds.

"Yes sir. Tom?"

"We have a problem. An elimination order is being executed. The subject is under diplomatic sanction. It's a mistake. Confirm it. Call our desk in the Executive Office Building."

"I am not at liberty to discuss this over the phone."

"Someone is going to die. We spent weeks working through diplomatic channels. This needs scrutiny. Must be elevated to your boss. To the highest level."

"Sir. I can take the information. Pass it up the chain. But, I cannot talk about this over an open line!" The last words forced an end to the conversation. Tom listened to a dial tone.

Tom turned and sat on the bed's edge. He didn't know who else he should call.

'I need a drink.' Standing and reaching for the bottle in his baggage.

He placed the bottle on the dresser. Plastic cup ready. But, the motivation to pour a drink had gone. Ten minutes went by as he lay, spread eagle on the bed. Phone rang.

"Tom, Fred Matthews."

"Fred, we have a problem."

"How so?"

"There is an elimination order. On our subject. Juanita Perez."

"Really? Where did you hear that?"

"From our operations interrogator at Danli."

"And, how did he get involved?"

"Hondurans. Battalion 3-16 Command. Overheard conversations. Somehow the Commandant became privy to sensitive information. I don't know."

"We do have an intelligence sharing agreement with them."

"But, to work in concert with us."

"We don't control what they do with that information."

"Even if it hurts our cause?"

"What is our cause? What is your job?"

"You have to help stop this."

"No, I don't." Fred Matthews stunned Tom. "We don't get involved in squabbles between two warring states. At least, without being ordered to do so. If you recall, your operation wasn't supposed to be here."

"Cut the crap, Fred!"

"What crap?"

"A mother and her boy are going to die. We promised safe passage."

"What we promised was, that we would not do anything to stop their emigration to Cuba."

"Shit! You sound like a politician. Were you privileged to this piece of information?"

"That's unfair."

"Did you know about it?"

"I won't answer that!"

"You're making it hard for me to understand."

"As a member of the Embassy Staff, I cannot interfere in the affairs of the host state…"

"What about stopping their rogue generals?"

"Who says it's a General? Or, that he went rogue?"

"So, you do know something."

"Knowing a piece of information doesn't give me the right to share it with someone else!"

Tom caught his own words thrown back at him. The thought crossing his brain earlier. Slapped in the face with a code that spelled silence. A code of the clandestine force.

"You still there, Tom?"

"Yes." He quieted. "If this happens, their blood is on my hands. Just as sure as if I had pulled the trigger."

"The business we're in, is not easy."

"I know that. But, all the good work…."

"We have to think of the big picture. We don't have all the knowledge. See all the pieces. We can only execute on what we know. I know it sucks! The 'good work' will be counted in the end." He paused, to slow his delivery. "Think maybe you got to close?"

"Maybe." He breathed in. "I promised. I made that promise to a boy about my son's age."

"Sorry, Tom. It's out of our hands." Then he added, "Al Peterson asked me to oversee the cleanup of this mess."

"Now, it's a mess."

"For POTUS it is. I'll be coming to Panama in the morning. When I check in, I'll give you a call."

Managua Nicaragua

The Honduran operator arrived in Managua.

He contacted operatives watching the Cuban Embassy.

He had one job to fulfill.

Before Juanita and Jaime had a chance to board her flight.

End the lives of the Cuban woman and her Nicaraguan son.

Panama

Black Site Hospital

Latitude: 8.915 N

Longitude: 79.519 W

Eastern Standard Time (GMT -5)

31 October 1985

Tony Mercado walked onto the hospital ward. He checks with a nurse on duty.

"Good afternoon, I'm looking for Lester Russell."

"He's in isolation room eight, halfway down on the right-hand side."

"Thanks."

The door locking mechanism buzzed. Tony pushed the door open. Stepping toward the bed, the door closed and locked behind him.

He was visiting Lester for the first time after the accident. Under his right arm, he carried a box. The box that Lester had given him the day before Constable 35 took off.

Tony had talked with Tom McKay. Briefly. Long enough to locate his friend. Wasn't sure of how much Lester knew. He didn't want to be the one who spilled any beans. Didn't want to upset. He would have to feel his way through the conversation. Yet, he wanted to see his friend.

Lester was sitting up in bed. His right shoulder in a cast. Arm supported by a metal rod. The lacerations to his forehead and jaw had healed over to scar tissue. His lower half dressed in blue military lounging pajamas.

"Well, you look like hell." He said approaching the bed.

"What are you doing here?" Lester asked, shaking with his left hand.

"Came to see you. Heard you had a tumble."

"Yeah, I did. Still trying to fix the broken parts as you can see."

"How about the parts we can't see?"

"I'm OK. Had a few sleepless nights. But, getting better."

During the pause in conversation, Tony handed Lester the package. "I got transferred to Howard air base. This was in my file cabinet at Tegutch. Remember giving it to me?"

"Yeah. Wow. Thank you." He turned the package end-to-end. He noticed immediately that it had been opened. "Did you open this?"

"No. They got their hands on it before I left the hangar."

"What did they want with it? And, who is 'they'?"

"Some security personnel from the embassy. There's an investigation after every accident. Although, we're not directly under FAA jurisdiction. The IG wanted as much background on the crew, airplane and maintenance as they could get their hands on. Damage control, you know."

"There shouldn't be much to investigate. I just fell out of the airplane. Rookie mistake."

"The director's office ordered it. The Pentagon had a few queries. Foreign journalists working in Nicaragua smelled a story. Somehow, the story got squashed. US press never got hold of it."

Lester opened one end of the box. The end that Tony had re-taped. He pulled papers and photos onto his lap. "At first look, everything seems to be here. And, by the way. Who took over your spot at Tegutch?"

"Guess you hadn't heard. They shut down the hangar operation. After the flight."

"When?"

"A few days after your accident."

Lester paused before continuing, "Wasn't much of an accident. No one's fault but my own. I just tumbled out of the plane."

"Feel like talking about it?"

"Don't remember much. There was a malfunction on the drop. The pilot and I cooked up a plan. Do a low approach – wheels down, nose up at stall speed – to roll the pallets out of the plane."

"That's sort of nonstandard."

"Yeah, but it was our only way to complete the mission. Supply the troops." Pausing, then asked "What about the plane?"

"There was some small arms damage to the fuselage. All the systems were intact. No damage to the engines. And, they were able to retract the gear." Tony paused. "Pilot felt pretty bad. Couldn't get him out of the bar."

"Last thing I remember was hearing the plinking of lead hitting the fuselage."

Fumbling through the papers and photos, Lester commented. "Something's missing."

"Not surprised. With as many hands on that box, I'm surprised the box is still intact."

Lester changed the subject. "What did they do with the plane? The Huey? The Sikorsky?"

"Moved the Provider to Ilopango. The Huey and the H-34 sent to Danli. Reserve Combat engineers built a helipad and parking ramp. They were on their two-week Summer Tour. The Hondurans felt pretty special."

"What's at Ilopango?"

"Combined operation. There was a support station for the Salvadoran insurgency. They just combined equipment. They support the Contras from there. Guess it's more efficient use of agency equipment."

"That's a long pull – to Nicaragua. Shortens time over the target."

"Mostly overwater. But, they do some Honduran overflight."

"So, what happened to the stuff in my locker?"

"I'm sure it was bagged and tagged. Col. Matthews oversees the investigation. You remember him. Saw him this morning. Have you seen him?"

"Nope. You're the second visitor." He paused. "Tom was here. Two days ago."

"You can expect to see Col. Matthews. Maybe others."

"Thank you for the warning." He paused, "At least, I got to see two friendly faces before the black hats get here."

A nurse from the duty desk entered the room. "Everything okay, Mr. Russell?" She checked the water carafe on his bedside table. And pulled back the drapes. "It's a beautiful day. Need to let some sunshine in here." She said, as she headed out the door.

"Good lookers here, huh?" Tony commented.

"It's good to be back among females who speak my language." Lester chuckled.

"What would Yoda say?"

Laughter between the two, caused the conversation to drop off. The silence in the room broken only by the parrots nesting in the palm tree, below Lester's window. Tony struck up the conversation again.

"You Remember the King Air?"

"Yeah."

"I work for that group now."

"Smaller airplane. Less to go wrong. Easier to tow. Newer equipment."

"You like it?"

"Yes sir. The DEA has three that they use in combined operations with other agencies. It's a great aerial listening post. The PT-6 engine is a work horse. Great engine to work on. A lot different than the radials." He changed the subject. "By the way, what was in that box?"

"Personal history. Photos of my golden glove days. Letters from my mom. Court Orders. And a letter of instruction, for anyone who opened it on my death."

"Well, thank God we didn't have to read from that last part." Tony wondered, "What's missing?"

"A legal document. Court orders."

"A 'get out of jail free' document?"

Lester thought before answering. "Sort of," changing the subject. "So, you been here the whole month?"

"No. Got a chance to go back home – Aquadilla. The P.R. Visited with family. It was good to see them. The only hard part was getting back to Miami. L-100 both ways."

"What happened to Jake. Did he go to Ilopango?"

"Briefly. I think he went home. And, heard he was reassigned here on base. You know, those commo guys can show up anywhere. But, I haven't seen him."

A long silence, fell on the room. Tony broke it.

"Anything I can get you?"

"Out of here!"

"Sorry man, can't do anything about that. My expertise is with the airplanes. If you need anything, here's my number. You get better."

"I'm working on it."

"You got to get your ass in gear," he said with a smile. He moved to the left side of the bed. Their hands clasped.

"Thanks for the visit."

There was much surrounding this incident. From the tumble, capture and what transpired during his internment. Disappearing documents from his personal effects. Internally, agency supervision was questioning procedures. Tony wasn't privy to all that was being deliberated. Lester had not seen Fred Matthews. But, he was sure that he was on the way. Tom and Tony were the first familiar faces he had seen since hospitalization.

Tony exited the room. Lester had many questions.

Lester's Private Thoughts

Lying in this hospital room. Seeing the occasional nurse. He was alone. He hadn't tried to navigate the television control. Only his thoughts kept him amused.

'What happened to the things in my apartment? Where's my stuff? And, what happened to the manila envelope with my legal documents?'

'What would anyone want with an old court document?'

'The record had been expunged. At least, that's what they had told me. But, that was so long ago. Only my mother knew the truth. And she was dead.'

'Wonder who has it? Could they reopen the files? Someone with some juice, would be the only person to reopen an expunged file.'

'My mom protected me. Doing it at great harm to herself. The old man – son-of-a-bitch, that he was. Self-concerned. Jealous of any affection mom *showed toward someone else. Even her children. What the hell did she ever see in him?'*

'Love is blind. But I don't think she was blind. Think the mothering instinct was just directed towards him. He was so needy. Always seeking attention. She gave him that. While trying to fix him. The only thing it got her, was three children with their own set of flaws. And I'm one of them.'

'The things we do. In the name of love. Bite us in the ass in the end!'

'What of Juanita? Protecting her son. From the person, his father had become. By protecting him, shielding him from the truth. Will only make him eventually become the thing she shielded him from. He will want to know. Without forethought, her son will grow to idolize his father. Maybe, becoming just like him.'

'The hours of conversation we shared. Made me understand her plight. A woman trapped. Wanting her son to have the education she was denied. The way of the mother.'

'Always wanting more for your own children, then you received for yourself.'

'In a different day. Different time. Circumstance. She was my mother!'

'Sacrificing herself, the best way she knew how. Protecting. Fighting off the den robbers. Like she did for me.'

'I feel sorry for her. I lied. Cheated. Used the information I was fed. To protect my own ass. Protect the secret that I had to keep. While she goes back to the only world she knows. How the hell, is that fair?'

'Me here. Taken care of. In my own brokenness. While she masks the true person, she showed me....'

Lester was startled from his own thoughts. Hearing the door buzz open. An orthopedist and a nurse entered. Coming toward him to question about their hand in his physical repair.

Managua, Nicaragua

Augusto C. Sandino International Airport (MGA)

Latitude: 12.0829N

Longitude: 86.1005W

Central Standard Time (GMT -6)

1 November 1985

Drive from the Cuban Embassy took thirty minutes to *Aeropuerto Internacional Augusto C. Sandino*. Named after Nicaraguan revolutionary Augusto Nicolás Sandino. It was the main and joint civil-military airport serving Managua. Located in the City's Sixth Ward - *Distrito 6*. Eleven km from downtown Managua.

Its interior was modernized. New equipment. With air conditioning, background music, loudspeakers and conveyor belts for baggage handling. A restaurant served passengers and flight crew on the upper floor. Patrons could see airport activity while they dined.

Airplanes displaying many different carrier colors were seen on the field. Pan Am, Taca, Iberia, KLM and Varig airplanes transited this airport. In stationery gate parking, movement on taxi-ways and during takeoff.

The long building housed the main terminal. Built in the shape of a Quonset. A building designed using a semicircular cross section. This building modified to provide a modern look. Roof supporting arches reaching out on one side. Providing a canopy for arriving and departing passengers. Palm trees and shrubbery lining the open area fronting the structure. A long arching drive led to the passenger departure section.

A black, four-door Audi 4000s pulled up to the center of the terminal building. Followed by a second. Each had four passengers. Stopping curbside. Then, two bags retrieved from the lead vehicle trunk. Juanita Perez exited from the lead vehicle and Jaime Velasquez, the second.

The men in dark suits, covered the woman and young man. Suit jackets hiding the shoulder holsters carrying Makarov 9mm pistols. Six people would enter the terminal. Juanita, Jaime and four in the DGI detail. They moved through the opened doors of the building as a unit, with mother and son surrounded. The two drivers would stay with the vehicles.

One guard went to the Cubana de Aviacion ticket counter. He slid an envelope to the attendant. The other five moved to a secluded area. Juanita and Jaime sat on a bench, flanked by the men in suits. The guard at counter retrieved tickets for the flight. It scheduled to leave in an hour. Juanita stood, as the returning guard handed her the tickets.

"Gracias Señor." She said. Her tone more nervous than thankful. This was a big step. Returning to her homeland, she had left twenty-some years before. A place of fond memories with her parents. The departure spot for her attempt at escape. Across the strait toward Florida Keys. Turned back by U.S. Coast Guard. The reeducation camp where she pledged allegiance to Fidel Castro. The chance meeting of Miguel Correa Velasquez, the father to Jaime.

"Señora, tenemos que pasar a la puerta 10A."

"Vamos, Jaime. Sigamos a estos hombres."

Few passengers milled in the terminal. Dotted here and there. DGI agents looked at each person. Assessing the possibility of threat coming from that direction. The walk took them half-way through the terminal. To a passenger lounging area. The gate was well marked. Attendants to take tickets had not arrived.

The Cubana airplane sat outside the gate. Seen from the lounge area. Men loaded small cargo and passenger bags. A fuel truck sat off the left. With a hose leading to the plane. Soon, the gate would open. Juanita and Jaime would be on the tarmac, walking toward the airplane.

Shortly, a flurry of activity signaled the time was getting close.

"Señoras y señores, anunciando la salida del vuelo 3482 de Cubana. Servicio directo a La Habana."

A single guard took the tickets and envelope to the gate attendant. Behind him many passengers arrived from differing directions. Men with narrow brimmed, straw hats covering their heads. Varying colored guayaberas, fitting each torso. Sizes of people in many shapes. A few in dark suits with open necked shirts. Contrasting colors melting in one small throng.

Juanita and Jaime stood at the motion from DGI agent at the desk. Moving toward him with the other guards on their heels. The two would soon be among the crowd pushing toward the attendant taking tickets.

A Hispanic male brushed by one of the guards, pulled a handgun and turned toward Juanita. He fired once. The bullet struck her shoulder. Guards behind her lunged at the man, knocking Jaime to the floor. The shooter continued to move closer, he shot twice more.

The guard near the counter pulled his weapon and shot the intruder.

Screams came from woman in the crowd. Men were diving away from the gathered line. Jaime lay covered by one security guard. One DGI agent had hold of the assassin, as he fell to the floor. The other two faced out scanning the scurrying crowd. Pointing their weapons. Expecting other persons to draw and fire.

Jaime stood, seeing his mother lying on the concrete floor. Blood spilling from her chest and abdomen. She, reaching for him with on hand. Eyes wide. Sorrowful look as she lost consciousness.

He knelt and held her hand. Tears beginning to flow. Screaming, "Mamá no te mueras! ¡Por favor no te mueras!"

One DGI agent knelt at her side. He touched her neck. Feeling for her carotid artery. Looked at Jaime. And, shook his head. Saying, "Ella se ha ido. Ella está muerta."

Jaime released his mother's hand. Stood. Turned toward the shooter. Looking down at the dying Honduran.

"Mataste a mi madre. ¡Quienquiera que te envió encontrará un hecho peor que su muerte!

Panama - Hospital
Tom gets Lester's diagnosis

Tom walked to the glass door separating the corridors. With the buzzing sound, the door opened with a crack. He pulled it and stepped into the hall. The door closed and latched behind him. Walking down the hall, he stopped at the nurse's station.

"Can I see the doctor on duty?"

"One minute, Sir."

A minute passed. A doctor appeared at the nurse's station. Tom extended his hand. Then, he saw Fred Matthews standing in the office doorway.

"I was going to ask if we could talk. About Lester Russell. But, I see you are already in consultation."

The doctor nodded and turned toward Fred Matthews. Looked again at Tom.

"A lot of interest in this patient. Please come in."

"I am Lester Russell's supervisor. You already met Fred Matthews." he said, showing his ID to the doctor.

"Fred, didn't expect to see you here today."

"Just following up."

"I was told you'd be around today." The general practitioner said to Tom. Turning to Fred, "I just thought there had been a change. Speaking to the two of you keeps me from repeating myself." He paused, "There aren't any others I can expect, are there?"

"No," Fred said. "I came alone. Thought Mr. McKay had another meeting."

"Both of you understand that I can only give an overview. Orthopedics has not completed their report after surgery. And, Neurology has not delivered their findings. Psychiatry, is a whole separate story. You'll have to schedule a meeting with Dr. Wong."

"We want to know what physical injuries he sustained." Tom took the lead before Fred could speak.

"Lester's Injuries are consistent with a fall and tumbling. And, diagnosed by the Nicaraguan doctor. Coma, he transited. The concussion has lasting effects. Orthopedics found his clavicle and humerus bones broken. They started to heal. But, a shift occurred during trauma from later beatings and movement. Ribs broken. He'll need minor surgery off and on. Preventing any possible future damage. His cervices sustained a crushing injury. That was a major concern. The lumbar and sacral area was a concern with swelling around the spinal cavity. Any questions?"

"Of course, neither of us is a doctor. But, we can understand most of what you've told us." Fred Matthews started. "When can he be questioned?"

"What Mr. Matthews is trying to ask, what can we do to help in his recovery."

The doctor sensed a rift between the two officials sitting in his office.

"I'll answer both questions. You can help in his recovery by being positive around him. As stated, psychiatry has not completed a full work-up. Until that time, I would hold any serious interrogation. Until their report is completed. But, it is my opinion that you can help him by remembering. By answering to things, he would know. What he knows now. Not what went on before his release."

"Did they use drugs on him?" Fred asked. His position less than attentive to physical condition. More the watch of a Rottweiler.

"There were traces of heroin and other opiates. It was strange that we found methaqualone in his system. Something we haven't seen in years. Used as a recreational drug, Quaaludes were quite the thing in the seventies."

"How about pentothal? Truth serum?" Fred continued his questioning

"No. Not that we were able to find in his system. But, some drugs move through and out of the system faster than others."

"So, we know drugs were used. But, not for what purpose. Right?" Tom asked.

"Yes, you could say that."

"When will the psychiatric report be complete?" Fred asked.

"No telling. They can give you an overview. From which you can draw preliminary conclusions. But, I wouldn't hang your hat on preliminary findings."

Phone rang of doctor's desk. "Yes. Tell the nurse I'm on my way." He hung up. "Gentlemen, I have a patient who needs me now. We can talk more after the other reports are in. Let me show you out."

Tom and Fred walked back to the nurse's station. They continued their walk to the security door. The nurse buzzed them out.

"Listen, Fred. I know you are here on a witch hunt! But, leave my guy alone until he's well enough to know what he's saying."

"Let's get something clear, Tom. You are not in charge here! I have a mandate that goes all the way to the President's desk. I'll do what I must. Don't get in my way!"

Panama

Hospital

Latitude: 8.915 N

Longitude: 79.519 W

Eastern Standard Time (GMT -5)

2 November 1985

"Lester Russell?" The embassy attaché addressed. "Fred Matthews, US Embassy." Showing him his State Department Credentials.

"Good morning sir. What can I do for you?"

"I've got some questions. Do you feel well enough to talk?"

"Sure, what's this about?"

"I was with the Embassy in Tegucigalpa. At the time, you had your accident." Fred moved around the foot of the bed. Walking toward the window.

"What does the embassy have to do with that?"

"I'm now an envoy of the Executive Branch. Leadership has concerns that need putting to rest. You can help me."

"If I can shed some light, I will."

"I met with your doctor. The one overseeing your hospitalization." He reached for the curtains, to pull them closed. "Mind if I close these?"

"No." Lester wondered, "Which doctor?"

"The general practitioner on call for this ward. He is concerned about my questioning you."

"Why? I have nothing to hide."

"More about your mental condition. Psychiatrist hasn't provided a full diagnosis." He stopped. "How many physicians have you seen?"

"I've seen so many. Lost count. Orthopedics. Neurologists. Psychiatrists. Which part of me were you seeking information on?"

"Not so much your physical condition. More a query into release of information." Closing both pull-curtains, he turned to Lester. "That's better. Less distraction."

"Sun shine, sort of makes me want to be outside." Then Lester stated, "You're one of many who has wanted me to discuss what I know."

Fred reversed his flow through the room. Around the foot of the bed. Pulling a lightweight chair to the right side of Lester.

"How many others have been here asking questions?"

"I think, four. Not to include Tom McKay and Tony Mercado."

"Agency personnel?"

"Yeah. Each with a different set of questions. Wanting my knowledge of certain individuals and activities. Where I was held. That sort of thing."

"You were a captive for thirty days. Were you tortured?"

"Yes. Up to a point. Minor roughing up. Beaten? Not really. Juanita stepped in before things got too rough. Then it stopped. Most of it was a blur."

"How so?"

"I don't remember much until," he paused. "One night, a Nicaraguan soldier gave me a shot." He paused. "There was a commotion. The Nicaraguan soldiers were kicked out. Things changed." He stopped. "The Sandinista guerilla was physical. The Cuban Major, not so much. Others in uniform threatened. They didn't have to beat me to cause any pain. All they had to do was move me. Shift my body. The pain just followed."

"Where did all this take place?"

"On a ranch. Cows heard morning to night. A lot of activity. Coming and going."

"Did you tell them anything?"

"I didn't know anything to tell. Was in a daze. But, the pain was real."

"Didn't know anything?" Fred paused. "Or, just don't remember what you told them?"

"Didn't know…if I told them, I wouldn't know." He shifted his weight in the bed. "It wasn't until after the fight with Juanita. The guerilla. He injected something between my toes. They fought. She kicked him out of the house. That jolted my memory. It got better. If I answered his questions before that, I can't remember."

"Fight?"

"Yeah, he did something stupid. Wanted more from her than she was willing to give. You know. Sex. She never said."

"Let me get put this in perspective. Someway I can understand...." He repeated back most of the facts Lester had given him.

Lester had given Fred Matthews facts he could remember. Omitting the embarrassment, he experienced after Juanita's fight with Pena-Pallais.

Pallais drugged her. He attempted to rape her.

"You okay with this line of questioning?"

"Sure. Why?"

"Your body language." Fred pulled back, to get a bigger picture to put in the frame. "It tells me there might be something you're holding back."

The questions continued. Lester answered truthfully. And, to the best of his recollection. Supplying pieces that only the doctors may have been privileged to. Psychiatrists would delve deeper. Pulling out. Beckoning Lester to reveal his recordable mental state.

Fred changed the subject. "There's been an incident. We need to know as much as you can give us, about Juanita Perez."

"She was on your radar?" Lester questioned. "You had a file on her?"

"She was. Quite a dossier on her as a matter fact." Fred paused. "She and her husband."

"Then, what can I tell you that you don't already know?"

"That's what I'm here to find out."

Discussion went all the way back to the C–123 takeoff, from Toncontin.

Lester went back over the whole story. How he was swept from the plane. Didn't recall much until waking in a bed. The pain and interrogation. His day by day recovery. And, ultimate release.

He wanted to tell someone about the embarrassing event. His ultimate ejaculation. Empathetic conversations between him and Juanita. Afterward. Desirous, but subdued feelings. But the implications, could be far-reaching.

He could be charged as a collaborator – aiding and abetting the enemy. He would, permanently lose his security clearance. Could remain in holding somewhere. For an unlimited amount of time...Tried...Imprisoned at Leavenworth...He, could in effect, lose everything.

"When you were released, do you recall who transported you? Anything unique? Anything you can tell me about your captors – Ms. Perez?"

"She seemed to walk out of the fog. Like a vision. Took care of me. Protected me. What I can remember."

Lester was coming to believe there was more. He wasn't told the true purpose of this questioning. Rehashing the story, didn't change anything he said. Repeating what he knew sounded like a stuck needle, on a damaged record.

Fred wanted to know something he could use. The doctor cautioned him about pushing Lester too far. Most interrogators would exit. Allowing another to enter, changing the tactic. But, he wanted it all.

He began again, "...you must know this. Juanita Maria Perez-Velasquez was a spy for the Cuban government. She participated in your interrogation. She extracted information from you, without your knowing – being aware of her methods."

Disbelief and the urge to fight caused Lester's adrenaline to spin up. His body tightened. The shock by movement caused Lester to feel pains in various parts of his body.

"I don't believe it!" He said, "How could you know that?"

"We know many things. Like, I know about your juvenile record. It was supposed to be expunged. But for a flaw in record keeping, it would have been."

"What does that have to do with this?" He asked, with anger in his delivery.

"It's all part of the record. Of who you are." Fred slowed his delivery. "We also knew who Juanita Perez was. Before you met her. I'll let you think about that. Maybe, in our next meeting you will be forthcoming. About your conversations with her."

Fred stood. Replaced the chair where he found it. "Have a good day, Mr. Russell."

The deals governments make to save face, are not always what is in the best interest of the individual. The collective good, code for something else. Spoken in discussions, speeches and filibusters. Always leaves loose ends.

Those loose ends need tying up. That was not the business of politicians or heads of state. It was the active business of lower level operatives. It was the business for individuals, far removed from the upper echelon. Those away from public view. The worker-bees, correcting mistakes caused by executive decisions.

"No! No! No!" Lester shouted, as Fred Matthews left the room. "Wait a minute! Come back here!"

Hearing the clamor, a nurse rushed toward the shouting noise. She brushed by the departing Fred Matthews. Keying herself into Lester's room....

Another Visit for Lester

Tom McKay greeted the nurse at the central station. She looked at him with disdain.

"Going to see Mr. Russell." He said.

"Not without clearance!" The nurse replied.

"What?" Tom displayed a look of puzzlement.

"Hold on." She punched the intercom. "Someone else to see Lester Russell."

The doctor immediately opened his office door. Marching toward Tom.

"What did I ask you yesterday?"

"I'm sorry?" Tom replied with a question. "I am aware of your request." He added. His inner senses feeling the building anger.

"I said, 'No interrogation' until Mr. Russell is cleared by his psychiatrist!"

"You've caught me at a loss. I haven't seen him yet."

"Well, Mr. Matthews was here. He didn't..." Doctor caught his temper. "He, apparently did not listen to what I requested."

"Fred was here?"

"Yes. And, he sent Mr. Russell over the edge. Had to use sedatives to calm him down."

"Is he okay?"

"Now, he is. But, now his psychiatrist will only permit a ten-minute visit. Under supervision."

"Can I see him?"

"Yes. Ten minutes. Then you're out!" Turning to the nurse, points at his watch saying. "Go with him. Ten minutes. Then he's out!"

Tom was about to tell Lester something he knew. Something he had gained through a top-level communication. It would have to wait. That information was not to be shared, in front of his nurse-minder. Tom's visit lasted nine minutes.

Tom McKay & Alexandr Dutrov

"Understand you've been here for a few days." Tom said, approaching the KGB agent.

"Yes, been like a mini-vacation." Alexandr shot back. "No one has died. Here at least."

"Sad about Juanita Perez." Tom offered. "Rogue generals. Politicians out of control."

"You always know the right thing to say."

The two had agreed to meet in this park. A place where couples would pick-nick and others watched their children play. It left the stink and odor from their official positions behind. Fresh air. Sun showering from above. A peaceful site for two soldiers. The war suspended. To share one last friendly discussion.

"Every time I see you, I'm reminded of the bier garten. The young frauline bringing us beer. How festive a time." Alexandr quipped.

"Hope your memories of these contacts will be as pleasant."

"With you, yes!" Alexendr looked away. "With others in your mix, not so much."

"We can agree on that one thing."

"What is that?"

"Your warning about my embassy counterpart." Tom added.

Tom had brought a bottle of German Spatlese. Purchased at the hotel wine shop. Flown in from the Rhine Region of Germany. Pulling it and a cork screw from the shoppers bag he had in hand.

"We hardly have something to celebrate…." Alexandr said.

"What we celebrate today, is our strange friendship. Common interest. The peace we seek being thwarted by evil hearts within our governments." He began to open the bottle.

"What work did Lester Russell perform?" Alexandr asked. His boldness not wasted on Tom McKay.

Tom ignored the question. "Here. Hold this," Tom said, handing him the bottle. Reaching into the bag once more.

"I see you brought your best glassware."

Tom began to unwrap the plastic cups he had lifted from the hotel. Took back the bottle and poured the wine.

"She was not active, you know?" Alexandr said.

"Juanita?"

"Yes. She hadn't been active in the DGI for three years. Even in her last days with the Cuban agency, she did little for them."

"I wouldn't have known." Tom said, handing Alexandr a plastic cup. "She wasn't a subject of my concern." Momentarily, he became silent. "Until our work to save them was overshadowed. What happened to Jaime. Her son?"

Alexandr Dutrov lifted his cup. "DGI protected him. He's alive. Think they sent him back to Jalapa. But, I don't know. Not really."

"To tribes, symbols, ideology and rhetoric trumping actions taken for peace." Tom offered. Cynicism dripping from his words. They both drank.

"We're both pawns, you know." Alexandr offered. "For the greater good."

"Good?" Tom questioned. "I'm about to go back to the only *good* I know."

"Agency work?"

"No, my family. They're the ones who've suffered the greatest. Families suffering for games played at our level."

"Da." Alexandr sensed the somber mood. "It's a shame we can't burn the memorandum."

"Those days of are gone. The last time we did this, it seemed more civilized. We had more control of the operations we ran."

They finished the wine. Tom poured Alexandr Dutrov another cup. Filled his own cup. Recorking the bottle. Placing in back in the bag. He wouldn't waist a $30 bottle of Spatlese, by pouring into the grass.

The conversation spotted the canvas. They had few things in common outside of their respective working positions. They both sensed a need to end this meeting.

"Thank you, Alexandr. Hope your future finally leads you home. Our business here is concluded." He stood, shaking the hand of the Russian. Preparing to walk away.

"The future takes care of itself." Alexandr replied. "We will meet again."

Panama

Hospital

Latitude: 8.915 North

Longitude: 79.519 West

Eastern Standard Time (GMT -5)

3 November 1985

Dr. Wong entered Lester's room. The door clicked when he swiped his badge. The latch securing the door closed once he was inside.

"Good morning Mr. Russell."

"Good morning Doctor."

"How are you feeling. Physically?"

"Better than yesterday. Better every day. The doctor from orthopedics said I might be out here in a couple weeks."

"That is a possibility." Dr. Wong transitioned to a present concern. "What was the thing that upset you yesterday"

"Don't know if I'm allowed to talk about it."

"You're going to have to talk about a lot of things, for me to clear you."

"Feel like they are going to hang me. Like a scapegoat. And, to my recollection I have done nothing wrong."

"You are saying, that they see some unresolved issues. That need to be discussed."

"They think I violated my code. Collaborated with the enemy."

Dr. Wong pulled a chair to his bedside. Placing his back to the window. The parrots punctuated the conversation. Heard squawking at one another.

"My colleague is concerned about the number and frequency of visits with you in a short period of time. Thought there were too many questions. An inquisition."

"There has been a parade of agencies personnel coming through my door."

"That won't happen anymore. We have put a limit on your visitors. Each must be escorted. And, they're only allowed ten minutes per visit." Dr. Wong waited for some type of response. "That is until the psychiatry department has completed your evaluation. You good with that?"

"Let's do what needs doing." The tension eased. It was falling away from the room.

"Our previous sessions helped us determine the need for your ongoing therapy. In coping with your time as a prisoner, you were manipulated. For me to sign your release, we've got some work ahead of us. We'll never undo your memory. But, you need to understand the complex situation you came through. Completely."

"As I told you before doctor, my resistance never wavered. Believe, that I did all I was trained to do. Other than a few sleepless nights after. I am fine mentally."

"Col. Matthews and Mr. McKay want to know your mental status."

"They're people I work for. They'll get what they need."

"Not if you don't release it."

"Let's be real. They'll get it. Claiming National Security."

"Nobody has discussed my preliminary findings. Our department board must review my diagnosis, before it would be official. I wanted to talk with you first. To get some feedback."

They both settled for the words that would come next.

"My preliminary diagnosis was Stockholm syndrome with your attachment to Ms. Perez."

Those words hit Lester with reverberating sound. Seemed to rebound from point to point, within his cranial cavity. Remembering Juanita say, *"Patty Hearst was one of her heroes."*

"Like Patty Hearst?" He tried not to look shocked. "Juanita was a buffer. She prevented my death."

Dr. Wong remained silent.

"I've reviewed this over and over in my head. She was a good woman in a bad circumstance. Yes. I am concerned for her. Have empathy."

"We have a dilemma here. I'm concerned with your state of mind. And that mind must coexist in a society different from that in which Juanita lives. The government will have concerns. I have concerns for you."

"What concern does everybody have for my well-being?" He said with a tinge of sarcasm. "What would Yoda say? I'm apologetic for somethings. But, I not sorry for anything."

"I'm told that you had prior anger issues. Don't you see where that might lead to concern?"

"No. Quite frankly what happened to me as a child is not relevant here."

"Just like your time in captivity should not be relevant here? To the government it is. I want you to be sure, that your thoughts about Juanita can be under control."

"She was a Cuban and a Sandanista. I see that. But, to me she became a contradiction. The woman I was forced to know is not the person our government saw."

Lester began to pull away from the talk. He looked down upon the scene, as one might look at two people conversing. Trying objectivity. He held feelings of desire for her well-being. But, he would have to live with his concern. Pain caused by a broken conscience. Recovery from which this hospital could not help. The conference with Dr. Wong had to continue.

"We all see different sides of people."

"What I saw was a mother concerned for the return of her son. A mature and attractive woman. Wanted by every man in her path. A woman who helped me through. She wanted to marry again. When the right man came, she would seize him. We all know that would not have been me."

"People have been known to marry the wrong person. For them and forever."

"This was not a marriage. She helped me. And, I believe I helped her get her son back."

"You are attached to her. Even though she is an adversary, you still have feelings for her."

"I know. It's perplexing. Confusing. I just need time."

"Let's look at it this way. When I release you from this ward, you will return to a similar job that you did before."

"When the agency gets your diagnosis, there won't be a job I can hold in the government!"

Dr. Wong could not address what might come. His concern was with his patient now.

"We never forget. It's all in there," he said, tapping at his left temple. "We never lose it. It may be tucked away in some region. Inaccessible. Yet, can surface. Though, not to be recalled at will. But, it's all in there."

"Sort of like, 'being the sum, total of the experiences in your life'?"

"Exactly. So, we can work together while your bones heal. Or, you can fight me on this." He shrugged, indicating a decision point. "Which is it?"

Lester thought in quiet. Then spoke, "What do I have to do?"

"Good man." The doctor said, patting Lester on the leg.

Doctor Wong left the session. Feeling establishment of a platform for Lester's recovery.

Panama

Hospital

Latitude: 8.915 North

Longitude: 79.519 West

Eastern Standard Time (GMT -5)

4 November 1985

"Thank you for meeting me, today." Tom told Dr. Wong.

"You said, it was urgent. Involving Lester Russell?"

"Yes, I've been recalled. Leave on a flight out of Howard Air Base this afternoon. I have information that needs to be passed to Lester. He cannot have visitors without a minder. You are the only one I feel should hear this. It's sensitive."

"Sensitive? Will it upset him?"

"Don't know. But, hearing it in your presence may allow him to open to you. It's my way of protecting the information," he breathed. "Him and me. In your presence. Allowing me to sleep."

"Before we go blurting things that may affect the patient, there are things you need to know." Dr. Wong told Tom. He continued.

"Lester may be displaying 'Stockholm syndrome,' laced with 'adult attachment to his female captor." He stopped, then started again "...of all things, add heroin and other drugs. His time in captivity. That worked on his mind. I mean, he was manipulated. Mentally. Through possible sexual exploitation. And, feelings for doing the right thing."

"Sex?" Tom asked, with a surprised gesture.

"Yes, captors have used that tool. In the past. Even though, Lester denies it. There is that possibility."

The psychiatrist gave a brief explanation. What he had gathered through taped interview sessions.

"Can he be de-programmed?"

"Wouldn't put it in those words. But, yes over time," the psychiatrist answered. "That woman holds tremendous power over him."

The doctor paused, then continued. "He may have to be broken before being fixed."

Tom listened. He thought of other manipulations he had observed. And, stories he had heard from returning captured prisoners. It was war. *"All was fair in war!"* In some cases, the Geneva Convention did not apply.

"The information you have, is it important?"

"I believe it's important to him. And, his recovery."

"Can you tell me now?"

"I prefer not." Tom paused. "You know, I don't have an agenda. Other than helping him reintegrate. With his sanity."

"I don't think he's insane. Nor do I think he divulged any secrets. He just may be confused in his feelings."

"Most prisoners have some form of PTSD." Tom replied. "That is an effect experienced by all soldiers. Some deal better than others."

"So, why does this have to be told in my presence?"

"It may give you an insight. A starting point to unravel. Untie the man, so he can move on."

"Let's go."

Dr. Wong led Tom McKay from his first-floor office. Out the building, to the elevator taking them to the third floor. Into the secure ward holding Lester Russell.

"I'm back, with a guest." Dr. Wong addressed his patient.

"Morning," Tom greeted Lester.

"What are you doing here? Thought they'd ship you out by now." Addressing Tom.

Tom nodded. Dr. Wong had to preface his visitation. With what he was about to say.

"Mr. McKay has something to tell you. He says it's sensitive information. He, nor anyone else can visit you without a hospital employee. Being present. We talked about that yesterday."

"That explains Tom's short visit two days ago."

Lester looked at Dr. Wong, as Tom slid a chair next to the bed.

"So, what's up?" Lester asked.

"Lester, I leave this afternoon. Been recalled to Virginia."

"Sorry to see you go. You and Tony are the only friends, I've got here."

"I'm sure Tony will be back to see you." Tom paused. "I'll call him to make sure he knows."

"So, this is your good-bye?"

"Yes. And, something else." Tom was caging what would come next.

"He asked me to come along. Due to the sensitivity of the subject." Dr. Wong added.

Tom jumped right in, "Juanita was assassinated three days ago."

"What?" Lester asked, as if he didn't hear what Tom had said.

"...They left the Cuban Embassy in Managua. According to the report, under heavy security. On their way for a flight to Cuba."

"No!"

"Lester, listen." Tom stopped the shocked patient.

"We can talk about it, after he finishes." Dr. Wong added.

The patient was stunned. Lester Russell waited for the rest of the information.

"She was hit in the terminal. Before they could board the airplane for Havana." He stopped, "Battalion 3 – 16 carried out the hit."

"No!" Shock led Lester to ask questions, in rapid fire. "How'd they know? Who gave them the information? Did she suffer? I asked you to take care of her. What the hell, man!"

"Mr. McKay felt this was important for you to know. It is a shock. For the both of us!"

"There is a reason, I had to tell you."

"What reasons could there be? She was good people. Mixed up in the wrong crowd. There by marriage to that guerilla, son-of-a-bitch! She didn't deserve to die."

"I wanted to be the one to tell you."

"Why? What does it matter now?"

"You are the one left. Only you know what went on behind those closed doors."

"Nothing went on!"

"That's good. But, there is a force which is going to try to implicate you in divulging secrets. To discredit you. They will try to use any piece of information. I know how this works."

"And, who the hell is that?"

"I don't believe I should say." Tom hesitated. "But, trust my gut…trust me."

"For real?"

"…The reason I asked Dr. Wong to be my minder."

What Tom had said would not leave these walls. He wasn't sure if Dr. Wong would be kept from the after-blast. Counter-intelligence spin to the story. Or, if he would be questioned by the same people.

The room became quiet. Lester's emotions had not overtaken his moment of shock.

"There is one more thing," Tom added.

"Be careful," Dr. Wong said, hoping there was not another unexploded bomb.

"I brought you this." Tom said, handing Lester a blue box with gold inlay.

"What is it?"

"Something awarded to me. A long time ago. For shrapnel, I received on one of my tours in Nam. You deserve it."

Lester opened the box. It was a Purple Heart. Numbered and engraved with Tom's name. Date of the order.

"Read you entire file. With all you've done for our country, not once did you get a formal recognition. A medal."

One more silent period fell on the room.

"Thanks, Tom." Lester, looked at the medal. Then looked at Tom. He was brought up from the base of the negative shock. To present acceptance. Sheer gratitude. To the positivity of the moment.

"...The credit belongs to the man who is actually in the arena...," Tom started.

"Teddy Roosevelt." Dr. Wong added. "It's not the critic who counts." He knew the quote. "Not the man who points out how the strong man stumbles." He is interrupted by Tom McKay.

"...or where the doer of deeds could have done them better...Whose face is marred by dust and sweat and blood; who strives valiantly; who errs, who comes short again and again, because there is no effort without shortcoming; but who does actually strive to do the deeds; who knows great enthusiasms, the great devotions; who spends himself in a worthy cause; who at the best knows in the end the triumph of high achievement, and who at the worst, if he fails, at least fails while daring greatly, so that his place shall never...never be with those cold and timid souls who neither know victory nor defeat."

Tom continued, "You have some healing to do." He stepped forward, grasping Lester's left hand for the last time. Squeezing it tight.

"Doctor," he acknowledged his minder on his departure. His steps toward the door were purposeful. It closed behind him.

Dr. Wong sat with Lester for a short period.

"Honest men are hard to find. Sometimes they do things in peril to their own being."

"Yeah, I know. Thanks doc."

"I'll be back tomorrow."

Dr. Wong left the room.

...

The

Stories

Continue

....

Dear Reader,

Thank you for reading Constable Outreach 35.

You have a take-away after reading this book.

Thebes Publishing would like to hear from you. Your comments will be read.

And, we will reply. Your query or comment will be addressed.

If you liked what you read, tell your friends.

If you have a complaint or suggestion, write us.

We want to hear from you. You are part of the communication process.

Your opinion is a valuable part of communicating with our writers.

This small publishing house is a recent startup. Our situation is very fluid.

Our primary means of communication is by internet. Some phone calls will be accommodated – after email communication is established. Postal mail and delivery service packages cannot be received at this time.

Once our business address is established, those following Thebes - or its Writers - will be informed of that physical location.

Our contact information is:

Thebes Publishing, dba

Houston, TX 77058

thebes@thinkwerk.com

Constable Outreach 35 Information

outreach35@thinkwerk.com

Jay Cadmus

jaycadmus@thinkwerk.com

Thinkwerk Business

www.thinkwerk.com

Thank you for this opportunity in being with you.

Sincerely,

Jay Cadmus

for

Thebes Publishing, dba